A BOND WITH THE BLOOD OF ANGELS

BEAUTIFULLY BROKEN SAGA
BOOK TWO

INARA GAGE

APPLE PLAYLIST

HTTPS://MUSIC.APPLE.COM/US/PLAYLIST/A-BOND-WITH-THE-BLOOD-OF-ANGELS-PLAYLIST/PL.U-WABZ69VFED4MYA

A Bond with the Blood of Angels Playlist:

Contaminated BANKS III

Wave of You Surfaces

I'm Not a Vampire Falling In Reverse: The Drug in Me Is You

Voices in My Head Falling In Reverse: Voices in My Head -

All My Life Falling In Reverse & Jelly Roll

Coming Undone Korn See You On the Other Side

Two Weeks FKA twigs LP1

I Love Joyner Lucas ADHD

Feel Better Alana Springsteen

Could've Just Left Me Alone Alexa Cappelli

Hypnotized Big Gemini Hypnotized

COPYCAT Billie Eilish dont smile at me

Oxytocin Billie Eilish Happier Than Ever

Hate the Way (feat. blackbear) G-Eazy

Addiction Yelawolf Trunk

From Austin Zach Bryan American Heartbreak

Love Like This Savannah Dexter & Brabo Gator

MONSTERS Shinedown

Boys Of Faith (feat. Bon Iver) Zach Bryan

Trying To Live Clepto Maniack

Santa Rvssian, Rauw Alejandro & Ayra Starr

Traitor Livingston A Hometown Odyssey

Breakdown (feat. Demi Lovato) G-Eazy

Flames David Guetta & Sia Sunset -

Unbreakable Jamie Scott My Hurricane

Lose Lil Wayne & KSI All Over the Place

Sober (feat. Charlie Puth) G-Eazy The Beautiful & Damned

Still Be Friends (feat. Tory Lanez & Tyga) G-Eazy

Creature (feat. Tech N9ne & Krizz Kaliko) Jelly Roll A Beautiful Disaster

Creature (feat. Tech N9ne & Krizz Kaliko) Jelly Roll A Beautiful Disaster

Already Down Allie Moss

Salt Ava Max Heaven & Hell

45 Minutes (feat. Gmac Cash) KIDJAY

Angel G-Eazy Angel

Sativa (feat. Swae Lee) Jhené Aiko Trip

Love Me Land Zara Larsson Poster Girl

Arcade Duncan Laurence

Fire Fire Flyleaf New Horizons

Famous Last Words My Chemical Romance The Black Parade

Streets Doja Cat Hot Pink

Beautiful Mistakes Maroon 5 & Megan Thee Stallion

Arrow Nilka Year of the Escape

You & Me (feat. G-Eazy) Marc E. Bassy Groovy People

Fall Slowly (feat. Ashanti) Joyner Lucas

Nothing To Fear (feat. Madalen Duke) BURNS & Daughters Of The Deep

Middle of the Night SDM Nation

World on Fire Nate Smith NATE SMITH (DELUXE)
Big Dawgs Hanumankind & Kalmi Big Dawgs
Espresso Sabrina Carpenter
Half Life Livingston A Hometown Odyssey
Ganas de Mí Key-Key Ganas de Mí

A BOND WITH THE BLOOD OF Angels

TRIGGER WARNINGS

<u>*Trigger Warnings:*</u>

This book contains violence, gore, suicidal ideations, and strong sexual scenes. This list is not exhaustive and other triggering circumstances or topics may be present within the work without any further warning beyond this point. You are important and your mental health matters. This story is recommended for mature audiences only.

To everyone who's loved someone so much, you'd dismantle the world to save them.

To the girls who have been the right girl at the wrong time. I see you. I am you. You will be the right girl at the right time . . . for the right person.

To the boys who hurt, and gouge, and break, and shatter women who deserve to be treated like the queens they are . . .

To those boys . . . turn the page.

Your fucking loss.

LOVE TRIGGERS IT

-SAYAH-

"So, you can form into anything? Like air? Or a big cat, like a tiger?" Bash's childlike questions to Laureya ricochet off the surrounding rocks, leading to the cliff's top where we left the car.

"Anything, anything," Laureya answers, her voice tinged with boredom by Bash's questions. We turn our attention to her when she says, "Watch!"

Standing before us, Laureya tilts her head back and closes her eyes, and her red lips mumble words I don't understand. Her skin and clothes tremble and shake, and her very appearance wavers a bit. The image of her folds in on itself and unfolds as a giant owl, flapping its beautiful wings before us.

"Now," Bash says, turning to Dom, "if she bites us as the owl, is it still lethal to us?"

Dom shrugs his shoulders. "Don't wanna find out."

Grasping onto my waist, that familiar shift of air and movement sweeps me up as we ascend the mountainside rapidly; the Earth, rock, and moss becoming a blur of color as we jolt up the hill.

As the movement halts and we arrive at the mountaintop,

Bash's blur of black arrives with the whooshing sound of methodical vampire movements.

The owl lands on the hood of my aunt's car, the one they let us borrow to go for a drive hours ago to clear our heads.

"Laureya, don't, you'll scratch—"

With the same unfolding of energy, she returns to her body, sitting on the hood of the white Subaru.

'—the car," I finish as Laureya grins.

"Relax. It's fine."

"I don't care who you are; that shit's cool," Bash exclaims, his heavy boots clunking on the pavement as he traipses over to the driver's side of the car.

Laureya flashes him a toothy smile, and I bite down on the vomit that crawls up my throat.

It doesn't matter that Laureya is going to help us with getting the marks off Dom and Bash, and help us kill the warlock that spelled them; I don't fucking like my sister, and I sure as hell don't trust her. Her flirting with Bash, even with just her eyes, makes me ill.

I don't exactly know why.

"So," I say, shifting my weight toward the car, Dom and I blocking Laureya a bit to avoid inviting her along, "you'll be at the hotel or?"

"You don't want me to come and see our aunts again?" Laureya asks, slipping off the car's hood, heels clicking as they hit the asphalt.

"You mean my aunts? My mom was not your mom, apparently."

Laureya steps closer to me. "They don't know that."

Dom, in turn, inches closer toward Laureya.

I smile at his *touch her and die* attitude, even though I'm still furious with him, and we both know I can protect myself now.

"Still," I continue, laying my hand on Dom's shoulder to let him know I'm okay. He moves to the left. "I don't think it's wise to come tonight. We've all had a really long weekend. Why don't you give me your number, stay at the hotel tonight, and we'll meet again tomorrow to review plans?"

"I don't know if you heard the bit about how I lit someone on fire with my mind," Laureya spits back at me, "but I can't go back to that hotel."

"So pick a different one," I counter, squaring up to her. Dom moves in front of me again, and Bash advances to the front of the car to stand beside me.

Laureya lends them a devilish grin. "I'll just stay at the Lamplighter Inn. You know, the one our cousin owns."

Although I know Laureya's trying to grate on my feelings—possibly a ploy to get me to agree to her coming with us—there's no *give a fuck* left for my sister. I give no fucks if she goes to the motel.

My cousin Francine and I have never been friends.

But that's a memory for another time.

"Go ahead, Laureya." I turn on my heel to the car. "Text me. I know you know my number."

I clamber into the front seat and shut the door.

The silence of the car greets me softly. Trying to keep my mind from spiraling, I hug my legs to my chest and rest my chin on my knees. My brain has been overwhelmed with so many things in the last few hours, it may explode.

The realizations that my boyfriend killed my mom, that my dad is a supernatural formweaver, and I am the balance of light and dark—part angel, part demon, part witch, part shifter.

How had my dad kept that big secret from me all these years? How had I never known that, in turn, makes me part formweaver as well?

Watching out the windshield, I see Bash say something that causes Laureya to giggle. Of course Bash would say something stupid and witty to her. In the short time I've known him, I know he's inclined to use his dark humor to lighten things.

Laureya looks both ways before she formweaves once more, this time into a raven, and flies away.

Bash enters the driver's seat, and Dom stands outside my window. He raps on the glass with his two knuckles, and I look over at Bash and nod, signaling that he should turn the car on so I can roll down the window.

"Is it alright if I come back with you?"

I hesitate as I exhale a long breath.

I know there are things we have to discuss, and we need the aunts to answer some questions, but I also know they want nothing to do with him right now.

"I have to go in first and make sure they're okay with it," I mutter. It feels like my life has shattered into a million pieces and I'm not sure how I'll ever put it back together again.

Bash leans over me to see Dom better. "I'll vouch for you. See if I can smooth it over with ol' Hildy and Maggie for you."

The annoyance that creases Dom's face is apparent in how the bridge of his nose crinkles. "Thanks," he says dryly.

He climbs in the back, and Bash puts the car in drive and takes off.

"Well, that was unexpected," Bash chides as the car sails back over the pass.

"Very," I second.

"It's been a very insightful weekend, to say the least."

"And it's only Monday night."

"Wow," Dom says from the back, "I didn't even realize it was Monday."

"I know. It's good that I took the week off for 'vacation.'" I make air quotes with my hands.

"Gauge probably needs his mama something fierce," Dom adds.

"Yes. First thing tomorrow, we should grab the earliest flight out of here. But for now, I have some questions I want to ask the aunts."

"What do you intend on asking the old Witches of Anacortes?" Bash asks, maneuvering the car around the twists and turns of Deception Pass.

"Oh, you know, about the fact that my sister is only my half-sister and that I am also part formweaver—small shit."

A chuckle escapes Bash's lips, and a giggle escapes from me in the same wind. Strangely, there's no returned laughter from the back seat, which makes me turn around to look.

As I rotate my neck, the light in the car shifts as though the sun went behind the clouds. The air grows dense, and a chill ravages my skin when I see Dom.

His eyes have gone completely black.

"Dom?" I gasp, blinking as though trying to push the sight back.

Bash spins his head around, causing the car to swerve into oncoming traffic. The loud honk makes him jerk the wheel, correcting the car into the right lane.

"Shit!" Bash scans the roadside for somewhere to pull over.

Dom is gazing out the window, nodding as though listening to something. The pounding in my chest whisks me to the panicky place where my thoughts race, trying and failing to come up with the answer of what to do. Sitting frozen as my chest heaves, it feels like all my bones have shattered and their shards are piercing me everywhere.

"Dom?" I ask timidly, every part of me cautious of what's about to happen.

He turns to look at me. His eyes are a fathomless black when they meet mine. The pallor of his skin intensifies, blue veins prominent in his face, and fangs protrude from his cuspids.

Before I can blink again, he lunges toward me and grabs my head, pulling it toward him as he moves to bite down on my neck. My heart slams against my ribs as I struggle to break free of the hold. I can feel my blood being siphoned out of me; he's too strong, there's nowhere to go.

The fire overcomes us quickly. It starts in my neck this time, burning Dom where he bites me. The red-and-orange-tipped flames emit from me with a fierceness, causing his skin to melt. The smell of charred hair and flesh and cloth seeps through the car. Although the flames come from me, they do not graze me. They merely float around me. But as they engulf him, his body flies to the back of the car with gut-wrenching screams. He flails maddeningly to pat the flames off. Bash catches the same fire in a whoosh of flames that explode outward, causing him to swerve the car into the rocky mountainside.

My eyes fly open, and I gasp.

The car's still moving, and we're passing through the small downtown area of Anacortes.

"Whoa," Bash says as I thrash around, swirling to ensure Dom is still Dom. "You okay?"

Dom's eyes are back to normal, his green eyes graze mine with a questioning, as though he saw the same fate as I did.

"Dom?" I ask, still unsure if what I saw was a vision or a dream.

"I saw," he answers, his voice brutal and indifferent.

"What the hell is going on?" Bash asks.

"We just had a vision," Dom answers quietly, as though he's still trying to comprehend it.

Bash looks at me, his face crinkled in confusion. "What?"

"He bit me. And he burned."

"As did you," Dom finishes cynically, regarding Bash with a tarnished glare.

Dom continues for me, "If I get the urge to bite her, I won't be able to control myself. I'll die."

"Well, the warlock should know that, then, right?" Bash asks, alternating between looking at Dom in the rearview and at me. "And not have her as your mark? I mean, the whole point of having a vampire as a grimspawn is to be able to have you do his bidding forever. You can't do that if you're dead."

His words ease the ragged edges the thoughts of him being bid to kill me caused.

"But why would we both have the same vision if that was not the intention?" I ask.

"Maybe he wants you dead, and he was psychically trying something out," Dom offers.

"It felt pretty real."

"You weren't the one who was on fire. Well, you were, but you weren't burning."

"Do you think I need to give you blood when we get back to the house?" I ask.

"It may be a good idea," he replies. "Just in case that was a sign of something to come."

"Yeah, I could use some, too, just in case." Bash's tone indicates that he's joking, but his face tells me he's serious.

"I'll give you some, just to make sure."

He grins and nods. "So, what will you say to dear Auntie Hildie and Maggie?"

"I haven't really decided yet," I answer, turning back around. We're coming up in the aunts' neighborhood. "I think they should know about Laureya. I just don't know how they're gonna take it."

"Maybe they already know," Dom offers.

"Very true. They seem to have a wealth of knowledge about things I would never imagine they knew."

"Just feel it out," Bash says, "see how they take the Laureya thing first, then bring up that she's a formweaver."

"I gotta make sure that they don't kill that one first," I quip, pointing back at Dom.

"True dat." Despite the words, the heavy sigh from behind me lets me know that Dom is dreading this as much as I am.

CORROSIVE BEAUTY

-SAYAH-

Bash pulls into the driveway and kills the engine.

From where we sit, we have a clear view of the front door. It cracks open a smidge, and Hilda's face appears for a second before closing again and reopening as she undoes the chain lock.

I turn my head to look at Dom. "Okay, you wait here."

He nods solemnly and looks out the window to the neighbor's hydrangeas.

Bash turns off the car, and we both exit the vehicle.

I approach the front door, and as Hilda opens the screen door for us, her eyes narrow at the car where Dom sits in the backseat. "What's he doing with you?"

"Hilda," I murmur. "I know you're upset, as am I. But we still need to help him."

She is about to object when Bash takes her hand in his, and she stops.

"I know you're pissed," he urges in a gentle voice, one that sways even me—seeing Bash being gentle. "You all are. And you have every right to be. But I know my brother. He would never intentionally hurt anyone, especially not someone like your sister. This was all my mother. And she was only doing it to protect our kind. But if you're going to hate anyone, hate her, not him. Believe me, no one will be harder on him than himself. That I can absolutely promise you."

My heart splinters at the thought of how Dom will punish himself, but then I think better of feeling sorry for him by remembering Mama burning in the fire.

Shaking my head to relieve myself of the vision, I focus on my aunts.

Hilda's eyes pierce into Bash's, the objection sitting firmly on her lips, when Maggie slides her arm through the crook of Hilda's. "Let's try to be objective. Bash is right. Dom will punish himself. Let's help them with what we can and get them on their way."

The silence wraps us all in a sincere wind infused with an ancient pain, spiced with a sister's agony and a daughter's suffering, and decanted with the anguish of a ten-year-old who lost his best friend.

Hilda nods and removes her hand from Bash's, retreating inside.

I turn to catch eyes with Dom and nod.

As we all enter the quiet house, Bash's boots are the only loud clunk aside from the ticking of the grandfather clock in the entryway.

"Let's sit, shall we?" Bash suggests, barging between us and sitting at the table in the room full of windows.

Reluctantly, we follow Bash into the dining room and sit at the table.

"So?" Hilda asks, her eyes cautious on the vampires but curious on me.

"Laureya showed up," I blurt out.

"What?" both aunts ask in unison.

"Yes. We were sitting at the pass, talking, and she came."

"I don't understand," Hilda states, incredulous.

"She's a formweaver."

Hilda and Maggie exchange looks, and there's a knowing between them again. Something in their silence, an unspoken word, tells me they knew she was and had known all along.

I can't help the annoyance in my voice when I say, "You knew?"

Anger bites at me, hard. Sometimes I understand my aunts keeping things from me for my safety. And really, I just learned about all these dark things recently. But still, once they had learned of me being the phoenix, they should have told me the rest.

"Sayah," Hilda begins.

"No!" I stand, trying to find the calm that keeps fleeing. The sound of the chair scraping on tile assaults my ears, and I feel Dom's hand on my lower back, but I shake him off and walk toward the windows. Spinning around, I yell, "If you knew this, you should've told me the minute you knew I'd become the phoenix. That would've been the first thing to mention before letting me see my mom, so I could have asked her about it."

"That's why we didn't tell you," Hilda answers. She stands from her chair to walk over to me. "We didn't want you to waste your time with your mom, asking her things that we could answer for you. We wanted that time you had with her to be everything you needed to hear—everything we couldn't tell you."

"We were going to bring it up when you guys got back," Maggie offers, standing too. "We wanted you to go get your air and think about everything, and then when you got back, we were going to tell you because you need a formweaver for your quest."

"Why didn't my mom tell me? Since she said I needed one, why didn't she tell me that Laureya was one?"

Hilda takes my hand. "I don't know the answer to that. Maybe she needed you to figure that out alone, too."

"Come," Maggie says, while grabbing my other hand. "Sit and ask us all the questions you want."

I oblige them and sit down again as Maggie goes to the kitchen to retrieve the tea kettle, which begins to scream.

"So, tell me what you know. Everything."

"Your mom knew your dad was a formweaver from the minute she met him," Hilda begins as Maggie comes in with five cups and sets them down in front of each of us. "He had been suppressing it for a long time but still had moments. Fran could tell things about people, regardless of whether they hid it. It was who she was. She confided in us that he was and had been using a talisman to keep the weave at bay. He used to formweave into things when he was a teen, getting into trouble because he learned to form into anything he wanted. Your dad's family is of the gene, but it is only triggered by something. Something that only your dad triggered."

"What did my dad trigger?" Thoughts are running rampant in my mind as I watch the steam from the kettle fill my delicate china teacup as Maggie pours.

"Falling in love with a demon."

"But you said that he had been formweaving since he was a teen. If he didn't fall in love with a demon until he met Laureya's mom, that would've made him in his twenties."

"It wasn't Laureya's mom who triggered the gene," Maggie answers, filling her cup with the scalding water.

"Then who was it?" Bash asks, leaning forward on his fist, seemingly enthralled by the tale as the steam from his cup warps his beautiful features.

"A woman from his past," Hilda answers. "Not sure of her name. But when he fell in love with her, he began to formweave during the full moons. He hated it and brought it up with your grandma, who told him to suppress it. It was his father, not her, who gave him the gene. As you probably remember, your grandpa was a very hard and cold man. He used to beat your grandma; that's why they divorced. He couldn't turn to him because Larry would have never helped him with something like that. So, he sought out a preacher who gave him a crucifix enchanted by a witch. Your dad didn't believe the witch part of it, or he didn't acknowledge it, but it helped him to suppress it. Sometimes the formweavers can get away with a lifetime of suppressing it if they don't encounter any vampires. Since formweavers were meant to undo the vampires, if there were none to undo, they wouldn't need to become the very thing that kills them."

"Then Laureya must have fallen for a demon?"

"She must have," Maggie says, sitting down again, "if she is formweaving now."

"Your dad met her mom, who was very much part demon. But she hid it with drugs. It wasn't just any drugs, either. It was Ether Dust," Hilda adds.

"What the hell is Ether Dust?" Bash asks.

"A dust made from Feyfire crystals," Maggie continues when we all look at her blankly. "Those are gems infused with the essence of the Luminara Court. To demons and fae, it's like heroin, or so I'm told." She awkwardly looks down and steeps her tea.

More questions mount as to how the flying fuck my aunts know all this shit. Just mind baffling.

Who are these women?

"And what does that have to do with Laureya?" I ask instead, so lost that it feels like my voice is coming out of the wall.

"She got pregnant with Laureya and refused to stop using it," Hilda says, spooning some sugar into her tea. "Your dad had no idea what it was doing to the baby and told her he would take the child from her and raise it on his own when she had it. She also knew he was a formweaver and the baby would be, too. Knowing Laureya would be part demon and part formweaver, her mom didn't want anything to do with her. So, when Laureya was born, your dad was on his own."

Hilda passes me the sugar, and I begin scooping in spoonful after spoonful, catching glances of Dom, whose eyes search mine and then return to Hilda's.

"He was out buying diapers one night with the infant. She was screaming, and he was lost when Fran found him. Her heart went out to him, and she helped him that night and many nights after. She fell in love with Laureya and him. She even helped him with his talisman and made him a stronger one so that he would not have to change. She tattooed it on him."

Hold up. "What? My dad doesn't have any tattoos; he hates them!"

"His is invisible to the untrained eye," Maggie responds, watching as I slide the sugar bowl over to Dom. "Next time you see him, un-glamour his left arm. It's there."

"So the tattoo on his arm makes it possible for him to fight the formweave?" I ask, observing Dom as his hands shake while he stirs in the sugar. "If that's all it takes, why can't we do that for Laureya?"

"'Cause the aunts said the talismans only work if vampires aren't around," Bash adds, then takes a drink of his tea. He winces. "Gah, this shit is gross."

"So why didn't he form when he was around Dom?" I ask, ignoring Bash's tea outburst.

The memory of my dad's absolute uncomforted wince when Dom had shaken his hand at my mother's celebration infiltrates my vision. I figured it was because he didn't like anyone I brought to him for a first meeting.

"It has to be constant for the talisman to ween down with a vampire presence," Maggie explains.

"Why does Laureya not want to be a formweaver anymore?" Hilda queries.

"Because she is in love with a vamp," Bash answers, sarcasm coating his tone. He slams the tea back in two short gulps and shoves the cup away from him. "Neither here nor there. What about the part where Sayah is part formweaver?"

Hilda frowns at Bash, then returns her gaze to me. "When Fran got pregnant with Sayah, she cast a spell on her. She didn't know what kind of world Sayah would be brought into, and because she was a witch, she already knew Sayah would have magick in her bones. So, she put a spell on her that would protect her. But we don't know if it worked because . . ."

"Because I've never fallen in love with a demon?" I ask, rubbing my lips absentmindedly.

"Exactly."

"Well, it's a good thing Domie here isn't part demon like yours truly," Bash chides as he stands.

Dom throws a terrible look at him, and I wonder if the love I felt for Bash in my dreams is just that, something in my dreams.

"I wonder who it was that changed Laureya?" I mumble, more to myself than anyone.

"You said she's been mixed up in the meth world for a time," Dom responds. "Maybe someone in that world was part demon."

"We're not hard to come by these days." Once again, Bash's voice is dressed in cynical humor.

"Was it the fact that my mom was a witch, and he was a formweaver that made them fall out of love with each other?"

"Maybe," Hilda answers. "There were a few times I spoke to Fran on the phone, and she was miserable. I think your dad hated that she was a witch, and a part of him disliked himself for being a supernatural formweaver. When they divorced, he delved into religion, as you have probably been chided for not believing in the same god as him, I am sure. He has been suppressing his formweaver side for so long; maybe there's a part of him that refuses to believe that side of him was ever real."

"And what about the fact that Dom fed him some blood when he had that episode?" I ask, my head swimming with questions. I take a sip of the tea, the warmth soothing my throat and stomach.

"A vampire can feed a formweaver blood," Hilda answers. "If the formweaver bites the vampire, it becomes fatal."

"But Laureya was bitten by a vampire, and he burned. What does that mean?"

"She's part phoenix," Bash answers. "Hence why, when I bit you, you burned."

"But the vampire burned, not her. I'm so confused."

"She's not the actual phoenix," Maggie clarifies, setting her tea down in its saucer. "She's protected by the blood because it's spelled to yours. You're the one who actually had to rise, and because you did, she mirrored what was happening to you."

"And what will happen if she becomes a vampire? I thought phoenix blood and vampire blood could not mix?"

"Guess we will see what happens when we go to make her a vampire." The look in Bash's eyes is something of a corrosive beauty, as though he enjoys the thought of someone dying.

"So, you two knew about the spell my mom put on Laureya to have her receive everything happening to me?"

"We did," Hilda answers softly. The steam from the tea fogs up her glasses. She takes them off and cleans them with her shirt. "From early on, Laureya showed her dark side. She was constantly mean to you and tried to light you on fire when you were a baby; she was only a year older. Fran still loved her, though, and didn't know what to do. She decided to put the mirror spell on her to see if it would stop Laureya from hurting you, if she would learn her lesson and feel the pain she caused you."

"Well, it turned into everything. Laureya was able to feel

every single thing that I went through, with cancer, almost losing Gauge, and the loss of my mom. She said she felt it all."

"I don't think Fran meant for that to happen." Hilda's eyes flitter out the windows to Mount Baker's silhouette.

"She hates me, and now I understand why," I murmur.

"At least you'll leave here with the answers you were seeking," Dom offers.

"So, because Sayah is part formweaver now," Bash inquires, his crystal blue eyes shimmering, twisting his expression from one of confusion to curiosity. "That would make her witch, demon, phoenix, formweaver? So, she's all four?"

"She's all four," Hilda concurs.

"Wow," Bash breathes, his dreamy blue eyes meeting mine, amazed at the power I never knew I had. "That would make you, like, the most powerful being on Earth, then, wouldn't it?"

"She is," answers Maggie. "One of the most powerful beings on Earth."

"I wanna know how you two know so much about this stuff," Bash inquires. When he turns his attention to Maggie, his eyes are still dazed and sparkly.

"Maggie studied about it in school—" Hilda tries to begin.

"You already said she was broken-hearted by a vampire," I cut in, "start there. Spill that tea, Auntie." I grin at Maggie, who shifts uncomfortably in her seat.

"I was nineteen, he was an asshole—that's all there is to it," Maggie spits.

"Mag," Hilda says soothingly, reaching out and stroking her sister's knobby hand, "you loved him dearly. It's okay to let that live."

Maggie's eyes drift off to another place, possibly while she recalls the face of her vampire love. "If I tell mine, you have to tell yours."

"Agreed," Hilda says.

"I was in college," Maggie goes on, toying with the little

handle on her teacup. "I was working nights at the local pub in New Jersey. I was bartending one night and felt his presence before I knew he was there. There was something dark and sinister about him, yet his face was angelic; I immediately found myself drawn to him.

"He sat alone at the bar and looked like the world was ending. I talked to him and felt feelings for him instantly; like I wanted to save him from whatever dark he lingered in. I talked to him and tried to find out why he looked so sad. He had lost someone and all that. His eyes were dark brown, dangerous. I didn't see him for a few nights, and then he came in again, and he looked replenished; his eyes were green. There were a couple of strange attacks around town, people with weird bite marks on their necks and blaming it on kinky sex, but weird things, weird circumstances. This went on for weeks. I would see him, then I wouldn't, then when he returned, he'd be replenished, and more weird things were happening on campus.

"Finally, after a few months of this, he divulged his secret to me. The way that his entire story poured out of him, it seemed as though he had been dying to tell someone—anyone—for a very long time. He thought he was veilweaveling me, so I wouldn't remember what he said. Still, from my studies and stories from my mother's grimoires, I wore this always." She pulls the chain up with the blue stone that I know is the Lapis Lazuli. "It's also coated with a pulverized Nightshade concoction so I could never be veilweaveled. I didn't tell him this; I didn't want him to kill me for knowing his secret. It's dangerous to know a vampire's secret. But I couldn't help myself. I wanted to be in his world.

"One night, I decided to follow him. I don't know why, but I did. He never seemed interested in me more than a barkeep who listened to his tales. We were going down a dark alley; he was walking alone, his head hung, and his hands in his pockets. The sound of my heart must have triggered him because he flashed up to me and pushed me against a wall, baring his fangs. His eyes had gone a white cat-eye shape, rimmed by the green that his eyes used to be. I was terrified, but not. I wanted him to bite me. He told me he could never love someone like me and that I didn't belong in his world. I told him that I knew his secret and didn't care, that I loved, and cared for him beyond measure. He told me it was his power—he drew people in and made them think about him so he could kill them. I urged him that it was more than that for me, that I truly cared, and wanted to be in his world."

Maggie lapses into silence, her eyes glossy, and scintillating, as though remembering her greatest love story. Maggie has never married anyone, never had children, and, as far as I know, never had any boyfriends, love stories, or anything of the sort. This tale is telling me something different. She loved that vampire and loved him with a force beyond anything she'd ever known.

"So, what happened then?" Bash asks, bringing her back from wherever her mind had taken her.

"He bit me. Drained my blood. Left me for dead. I never saw him again."

"Who found you? What happened?" Bash chimed in again.

"I did," Hilda answers with a look at Maggie. "I knew she had been mixing herself up with a vampire—we shared a dorm. I went to check on her, as I knew she was getting increasingly entranced by him. When I got to the bar, one of the waitresses said she had left twenty minutes before, following the strange man she had been crushing on. I followed my instincts and found her lying in the alley, barely clinging to life. I called for help, got her to a hospital, and could not explain to them what had happened; why she had two bites on her neck and needed a blood transfusion because she lost so much blood. I stayed with her that night as she went in and out of consciousness. I was half-asleep, but I'm positive that the same vampire came and fed her some of his blood, veilweaveling the rest of the hospital staff working on her that she had been attacked by a raccoon. When she finally came to, nobody said the real reason she'd been brought in."

"He saved me after he almost killed me," Maggie says solemnly. "I never forgot him."

"She was devastated by that for years and never really got over it. There were a few men in her life after that, but none she loved the way she loved him."

"And what's your story?" I ask Hilda, clasping my hands on the table before me.

"Mine was a sailor. I was actually in a relationship with him. Tim. He was the love of my life. The Navy took him away from me for months at a time, but every time he returned, he would sweep me off my feet and promise me marriage and a life after the Navy. Well, one time, something strange happened to him during one of his deployments. When he returned, he was not himself; he was pale and strange. He said many of his comrades had jumped ship to their deaths after hearing a strange song. He wasn't veilweaveled to jump in, but he said she came aboard and drained nearly all his blood, then fed him some of hers, snapped his neck, and left. When he came to, he was alone on the ship. He was transitioning into a vampire, but I couldn't understand it because he was bitten by a siren. The craving for blood was getting worse, and he knew that if he didn't feed, he would die. I offered my neck to him, and he bit me, but I survived. But after that, he said being near me was too much for him; he always wanted more, to the point that he didn't know if he could ever stop, and he didn't want to kill me. So, he left me with a broken heart."

Bash and Dom share a look between them that signifies they, as well as I, know that Hilda's love had been turned by Jasantha.

"Wow, I am so sorry," I offer, staving off the urge to mention the siren. It's not pertinent and would make no difference now.

"Neither of us ever saw our vampires again," Hilda replies. "But that didn't mean that we ever forgot them."

The noise at the table lulls into silence as thoughts of past vampire loves capture the aunts, sirens dooming beloved sailors encapsulate the vampires, and secrets dwelling within the minds of those aunts haunts me.

THE FIRST DARK

-SAYAH-

"Well," Maggie says, batting a tear away and standing, "I'm going to go to bed. I trust you all won't be far behind?"

"Yes, I'm exhausted," I reply with a yawn.

"I'll show you all to your room if you're ready to go now."

I rise from the table, but Bash's eyebrows furrow a bit as he asks, "Um, where are 'we' all going to be sleeping?"

"There's an extra bedroom downstairs, and the couch folds out to a bed in the living room. You can choose which among you."

"I can sleep on the couch up here," Dom answers, looking up at me like he's expecting me to say no.

"No, it's fine," I answer hesitantly. I honestly don't want him out of my sight. "You can sleep in there with me."

He nods and gets to his feet. "Want me to help clean up?" he asks as Hilda collects the empty teacups.

"No, I'm fine," she says coldly. "Thank you."

I go to her and hug her, squeezing her tight, and kissing her cheek. "Goodnight, my sweet." Then she whispers into my ear, "Are you sure you're okay with him sleeping in there with you?"

"Yes. I don't trust him anywhere else," I say back, kissing her on the cheek.

She pulls away, seemingly staring into my soul to ensure I am confident I know what I'm doing.

I smile and nod again, letting her go.

Bash, Dom, and I silently follow Maggie down to the basement.

Maggie shows Bash to the couch that folds out in the small living room in their apartment, and Dom and I follow her to the little room on the other side of the storage room where we conducted our séance.

Maggie hugs me goodnight and leaves us in our plain room, which has a queen bed, a small nightstand, and an ancient TV.

Dom closes the door then stands with his back against it, eyeing me imploringly. "Sayah," he starts, but I cut him off.

"No. Not tonight. Please," I plead as I slither out of my hoodie and sit on the bed to take off my shoes. "I have no energy left to talk of anything more."

He nods and comes in, sitting down next to me. "Hattie texted me. She thinks she may have found another artifact in London. I think I'll fly to Denver with you and then catch a plane to New York from there."

I slip my socks off and stand to turn down the bed. "I'll have to get you a few vials of my blood to have on hand while you're there. And as soon as I can get out there, too, I will. I have to go back to work at some point."

"Are you sure you want to continue doing this?" he asks, going to the other side to help.

Thinking of seeing his mom again and knowing she is the one who ordered my mother's death makes me cringe. I bite back the bile that threatens to burst from me. I have to face her.

"I have to. I have to focus on getting Gauge safe. Regardless of what your family did to mine, this is about keeping my son out of this. We can't just part ways and forget we ever met."

The agony I feel in his stare causes my heart to stutter. "I didn't mean to hurt you," he says, and I can feel him break.

I can't deal with this right now.

I may shatter.

"Dom . . ."

"Don't say anything." He grabs my hand. "I was thinking, and you can tell me no if you want . . ." His eyes are severe and steady. "I can help with your mortgage and bills for a few months while you take a leave of absence. I think you'll need over a week to settle this."

"I don't know, Dom." I don't like getting help from anyone. I've worked too hard and too long to accept charity.

And this better not be some ploy to get me to forgive him.

"Sayah, I know that you're independent and don't like asking for help. I'm saying that I have the means to help you, and I can." I'm not sure if he'd read my mind or if he knows me that well. "I'll pay your mortgage for a year and whatever bills you need, and—"

"I accept," I blurt out. There's no mistake that I need help. I don't want to lose my job, but I need the time off to get this whole mess sorted out. "I have some insurance money coming soon, so I'll be able to pay you back."

"You don't have to pay me back," he argues, stroking my hand with his thumb. "It's my pleasure."

"Well, thank you." I let go of his hand and get into bed. "But I will pay you back."

He nods, turns off the light, and gets into bed without saying another word.

The air rushing around my face relieves me from the deepest sleep. I open one eye to see a silhouette kneeling right by my face.

Rising with a scathing bolt of energy and backing up to the headboard, I gasp as my eyes open and adjust to the dark, kicking out to the mass next to my bed.

"Ow!" Bash yells as he comes into focus.

"Bash! What the fuck are you doing?"

He's rubbing his forehead from where I had kicked him. "Did you not notice your Prince Charming has gone for a late-night, sleepy walk?"

I turn and see that the spot next to me is empty. The sheets are ruffled and pulled down to the foot of the bed.

"Shit!" I throw the covers off me and swing my legs to the side.

"Whoa!" Bash exclaims, still rubbing the spot where my foot met his face. "You might wanna put on some clothes!"

I'm only dressed in a tank top and some tight-fitting shorts. "Oh, stop. Did you see where he went?"

"No, I heard a noise, and figured it was one of you getting up to get some water."

A scream spears through the silent house. It sounds like Francine's.

My heart drops. Bash's eyes glaze, and suddenly, he's following the screams up the flight of stairs.

I struggle to keep up with him and curse his vampire speed again as I take the stairs two by two all the way to the top and then again to the next staircase that leads to the bedrooms upstairs.

Bash has burst into the master bedroom, and as soon as I enter, I find Dom hovering over George; blood covering him, the sheets, and the walls. Dom's eyes are black. Francine's screaming and blindly looking for her phone. Bash is already working to veilweave Francine, getting her to calm down before he flashes to Dom and pulls him off George.

"Sayah! Phoenix blood, stat!"

Dom is thrashing to get back to George. I blink as my focus turns to the fangs that now live beneath the surface of my gums. I close my eyes and force them to come out, feeling the unfamiliar sting as they elongate and puncture through the tender skin.

Biting into my own arm, the crunch of my skin rattles my stomach, but I push back nausea and run up to Dom, shoving my dripping arm into his mouth. The blood smears across his face as he tries to shake me away, but one sniff of my delicious angel blood and he's hooked. Bash holds him still as he wraps his hands around my arm and drinks, the black of his eyes fading back to green.

As Dom calms down and continues to slurp from me, Bash bites into his own arm and kneels to George to feed him as well. The bite in his neck is profound. Not just two holes, but as though Dom had ripped an entire chunk of skin and consumed it.

I pull my arm away from Dom before he bleeds me dry.

Blood covers his entire chin, dribbling down his shirt, all over his arms, and hands.

"I went dark, then?" he questions, his eyes holding the guilt he feels when he does something that he hates about himself.

"You did," I admit.

"Well," Bash's voice cuts in, "the good news is that, one, Georgie here is going to make a full recovery, and two, either the aunts didn't hear, or they want to stay out of it."

"What are we going to do about all this blood?" I ask, glancing around the room. "The wound in his neck?"

"The neck wound will heal quickly with the blood he drank," Bash states, his white muscle shirt darkened with crimson. "The whole-ass murder scene in here?" he strains his neck, looking up at the blood on the ceiling, "That I'm not sure of . . . unless you have a vanishing spell in your witchy repertoire."

Nothing comes to mind, but something has to be done.

We can't leave it like this.

Francine is sitting on the bed, blankly looking at the floor, and George is about to be veilweaved by Bash. His neck wound is healing before my very eyes. Dom is brooding in the corner, looking from his hands to the scene before him.

I remember the spell I'd done with water when I was learning how to weave the elements together. In that spell, I had gathered water out of the cloth in droplets hovering before me into a ball before guiding it to a glass. This could work the same with this blood.

Closing my eyes, I call to all the power I hold, bending my head back and imagining all the droplets arising from the bed, the sheets, George, Dom, and the walls, coagulating together in the middle of the room and hovering there.

When I open my eyes, the walls shake and the lamp on the bedside table flickers. The drops of blood slowly rise, out of the sheets, off the wall, slithering off Dom's mouth and hands. They arrive together, floating in a ball in the middle of the room.

Bash's watching me, awestruck, and Dom seems to have a slight glimmer in his eye, but he's too upset with himself for hurting my cousin's husband.

"Bash?" I ask. "Dinner?"

"Absolutely." He walks up to the blood hovering in the air and slurps it down like an astronaut would slurp hovering water in space.

"I believe I need to shower," Dom says.

Bash and I follow him out the door and down the stairs. When we arrive back in the bedroom, Bash comes in with us.

"So," he says nonchalantly, "I think you're going to start giving him blood every, like, eight hours or so, I would say. Don't want something like that to happen again."

I nod in agreement.

"I'm so sorry, Sayah," Dom moans, sitting on the bed.

"I know you didn't mean to," I answer, trying to keep all the hurt I feel out of my voice. "It was that wretched mark."

"Speaking of, does Hattie have any news on that?" Bash asks, his shoulder pressing into the wood of the doorway.

"Yes, she thinks she found one in London. I was going to head straight there from Denver."

"You think it's wise to leave *her* that far away?"

"I'm gonna give you guys some vials to take. And then I'll be there after the weekend. I need to see my son and spend some time with him. You guys should be okay with that, right?"

"Should be." Bash eyes Dom dubiously. "You good, brother?"

"Yeah," Dom mutters in reply. He's picking out some clothes from the suitcase the aunts had brought down. "I am going to take a shower."

He moves to leave the room, and Bash slides out of his way. He comes in and sits down on the hope chest at the foot of the bed.

"Will the vials be enough?" I ask quietly, sitting next to him.

"I hope so. If we hadn't gotten there when we did, he would have killed that man. And when he kills someone, he can't handle the high it gives him. He goes off the deep end. It would not have been good."

I don't want that to happen.

For either of them.

My gums tingle as the fangs emerge again and bite into my arm, offering my blood to Bash.

He looks at me curiously. His beautiful features fold in on me in question, maybe questioning himself as to whether he wants to do this or questioning I was sure I did.

"Take it," I say, urging my arm closer to him. "I don't want to risk you going dark, too."

Angels only know what will happen should Bash go back to the darkness.

Eyeing the blood on my arm, his eyes turn white, fold into the vertical slits, and the fangs come out, but he does not bite me.

It's part of the blood, I'm sure. The way it makes fangs come out.

He puts his lips to my arm and opens his mouth over the wound. I feel him sucking my blood—feel it leaving my body and entering him. There's something almost erotic about it; I feel hot and tingly in places that I shouldn't be for my boyfriend's—or ex's?—brother. Maybe it's letting someone drink my blood and how intimate it feels.

Blood sharing.

He continues to suckle my arm until I start to feel faint, then I pull away.

Reluctant at first, he lifts his mouth from my arm and looks at me, wiping away the excess blood that dribbles down his face.

The blue of his eyes returns, and he sits inches from me, not saying anything at all, but something in those eyes spills enough words to fill a mountain range. The beating of my heart becomes very erratic and I feel faint again, probably from the loss of blood, but neither of us moves, and I remember the way I felt for him in my dreams.

Those feelings come flooding back with him so near me, and all I want to do again is run to the ends of the Earth for him; to feel that fire, and burn with him, to find that darkness and dwell in it with him.

When he doesn't speak either, I swear he's going to kiss me, and I back away a bit, not wanting to give in to that temptation I feel, too.

"Your blood," he says finally.

"My blood what?"

"Is the most delicious blood I've ever had."

"Thank you?"

"No, I mean it. There's something about it that tastes unlike any blood I have ever had. There's a fine sweetness to it, almost like honeysuckle. But it also gives me weird feelings in my head, like I drank eight bottles of bourbon."

I rise from the hope chest. "Don't get used to it. You need to share the vials I will give you with Dom, and once we get this mark off you, you won't need it anymore."

But there's something in his eyes; there's more to his observance of what he's saying, a barely tamed fury. It's like watching someone try a drug for the first time. There's an air about him now, telling me he's high off my blood.

And he likes it.

FAKE NICE

-SAYAH-

The following day, when I open my eyes, I turn over to make sure Dom is still here.

He is.

His back is turned, and I admire the lines of the intricate tattoo gracing his back muscles. Black and gray ink covers the entire surface of his back. It looks like a battle scene—a battle between good and evil. A demon-looking character takes up the right side, his bony hand reaching out to grab the angel's light on the other side. There are things of darkness and things of light, and it looks as though it's an equal battle, a battle that Dom probably finds himself fighting daily.

He stirs slightly, rolling over to face me. "Hey," he whispers.

"Hi," I answer back. "What does the tattoo on your back mean?"

"Basically, the demons that live within me are constantly fighting the angels that are trying to save my damned soul."

The sorrow that had lain upon him yesterday and last night coats him this morning. I can feel the weight of his sadness as though it were a heavy blanket that covers him, spilling over the top of him and covering me as well. The need to fight for him, to save him from the mark on his arm, takes hold of me and begins a war with the part of me that hates him for what he did to my parents.

I want more than anything to get up and go find Mederio, to kill that motherfucker, and save my son and figure out my fucking life.

But I know that's impossible.

Gauge's safety is now linked to Mederio's.

The deep creases in his brow cause me to think he's physically in pain from all the angst he has caused me and my family. Granted, he didn't kill my cousin-in-law; but the reality of the fact that he nearly did, mixed with the realization that he took the life of my sweet mama and stepdad, is crushing him. It also tells me that if—or when—he kills someone, it will invariably annihilate his soul, push him to that brink I know exists, and I'm not sure he'll ever recover.

"What do yours mean?" he asks, pulling at my arm and looking at my fairy, the lilies, roses, dragonflies, and butterflies that cover my left arm.

"The fairy is the peace in the aftermath of leukemia. The clock is at 11:11 because of the date I had to send the baby angel back to the heavens and begin chemo. A leukemia ribbon that's been undone and floating away. And the flowers, butterflies, and dragonflies, because I love them."

"That's very deep and moving. It's excellent work."

We're interrupted by a knock on the door.

"Yes?" I say to the closed door.

When it opens, Hilda's there. "Hey, Say, sorry to bother you, but Laureya is here."

"Great." I turn from Dom to look at the ceiling. "I'll be right up."

Hilda nods and closes the door.

"She must've made friends with Francine again."

"Can formweavers veilweave people?"

"Not that I am aware of."

"Must be her natural charm that mirrors Francine's." I inhale deeply and then sit up. "Well, whatever she wants. Let's get this over with so we can get me back to Colorado."

After we both dress and pack and are heading for the stairs, I see that Bash's bed is already folded up, and everything's put away. His suitcase isn't there either, so he must also be upstairs.

"Oh, before I forget . . ." I bite into myself and offer my arm to him.

His sad eyes fall on mine, and he looks hesitant.

"You need to, Dom; it will keep you from going dark."

Reluctantly, he bends his head to my arm and begins to drink my blood. It's the same siphoning feeling as before, but there's no hot rush this time. Maybe it's his energy that's saturating me, flooding into me and making me feel overwhelming remorse, but the sadness that replaces the blood that's leaving me is crushing.

After a long while I pull my arm away, and he lifts his head, licking his lips of the excess blood when he's done.

"Better?"

"A little," he says, brushing the side of his mouth with his thumb.

"Like Bash said last night," I remind him, pulling down my sleeve even though the wound is already sewing itself up, "you should do that every eight hours or so. To keep the darkness at bay."

Nodding, he wipes his mouth again to ensure there is no blood before we head to the main floor.

Bash and Laureya are sitting at the dining room table with Francine and the aunts, and a few of their kids are in the living room, playing a video game on the large television.

"Hi," Francine says, rising from her spot at the table and walking over to greet me. She pulls me into a hug, and all I want to do is bite her.

"Hi." I opt for fake-nice instead.

"How are you doing?" When she lets me go, she holds my hands, and offers me an equally fake smile.

"I'm okay." Her eyes do not indicate what happened last night, and there is no tension in her dark, unplucked eyebrows. Her posture is languid and relaxed, and her straw-dry black hair frames her pale and sunbaked face.

"I didn't know that you and your sister had made up." Her breath is laced with stale coffee and cigarettes.

"Yeah, it wasn't too long ago. Haven't really told anyone," I whisper back, then pull my face away from her as fast as possible.

"Hello, Sayah," George says from the rectangular window into the dining room from the kitchen.

"Hi, George," I reply, letting go of Francine's hands to duck around her head. I glimpse his neck. There's no evidence a vampire ripped out a chunk of his skin last night.

"I've been catching up with the cousins," Laureya says, her lengthy hair cascading in ringlets, highlighted by the red of her lipstick. "They let me stay in the most beautiful room at their lovely hotel last night."

Bash's eyes roll back into his head.

"About ready, hun?" George hollers from the window, slamming his coffee, and setting the cup in the sink.

"Yeah," Francine calls to him and gathers her coat from the back of a chair. "Boys, get ready for school. Now!" The two boys in the living room jump up and shut the TV off, scampering off to their rooms. She looks at me again, slipping on the shit-brown peacoat that matches her eyes. "We have to go to the hotel. I wish I had more time with you, but Laureya said this was a matter of business you four had in the area and were stopping by?"

I glance at Hilda, who nods surreptitiously.

"Uh, yeah. Dom has clients out here, and we came along."

"Sweet brother-sister couples," Francine says, glaring at Bash and Laureya. "I still don't see why Bash didn't stay at the hotel with Laureya last night instead of here with you two."

Great. Looks like Laureya came up with a fabulous little lie about them being a couple.

"We had a fight," Bash lies quickly. "I told her to go on without me."

Francine nods. "Well, we all have lover's quarrels," she says to Laureya and rubs her hand. "You have my number. You call me whenever you need to, okay?"

Laureya smiles and nods. "I will, cousin. Thank you."

"Ready?" George asks, slipping on his hat. "Boys! Now!"

The two boys come charging out of their rooms with their book bags in tow.

"You guys all have a safe trip back," Francine says.

"Thanks," I mutter. Francine and the family disappear through the front door.

"So, what happened last night?" Hilda asks when they're gone, steeping her tea.

Yep. They'd heard it. "Dom's mark," I say timidly. "Were they aware of anything?"

Maggie gives me a stern look. "Not in the slightest."

"And what pretty little lie did you come up with?" I ask Laureya, my voice laced with annoyance.

"Oh, I was in town with you and our boyfriends." She sneers at Bash, who rolls his eyes again. "She didn't really ask too much. I told her I was tired and that you all stayed with the aunts. She kept wondering why I was there alone; I didn't even think to say we were fighting. So nice one, Bashie."

"Thanks," he responds cynically.

"And what do you want?" I ask.

"I wanted to come see our aunts, of course! And to see what the plan was for moving forward."

Hilda and Maggie do not attempt to correct her about not being their niece. They remain quiet, watching.

"We're heading back to Denver today. Then, these two are catching the next flight to New York from there. They're gonna help Hattie with her plan to get the next artifact. I'll try to join them Monday after spending time with Gauge."

"What does your ex think about you being away so much?" Laureya asks me, the edge of her voice heightened so that she sounds more condescending than caring.

"I don't think that's any of your concern."

"I see. So, will I stay with you in Colorado or head with them to New York?"

Shit. I didn't think that part through. There's no fucking way I'm letting her around my kid. He barely even knows I have a sister; it'd be too strange to explain that, let alone why she's suddenly in our lives.

"I can put you up at a hotel in both places," Dom offers after catching my trepidation. The tension between us is so awkward and about as thick as a layer of snow on a mountain peak, but the way he's still trying to boyfriend me is cute.

"I can't stay with my dear sister? Or in the big house in Lake George?" When I shoot her a questioning look, she says, "I had visions of it, remember?"

"I don't think it's wise," I hedge. "You and I have never been close. And Gauge would be so confused as to who you are. And frankly, I don't trust you."

"Understandable. Well, I want a nice, big room, Domie. In both places."

"You'll get what we give ya," Bash snipes at her.

"You can stay with me in my room any time you want," she says with a coy smile.

He makes a face as though he's going to puke. "Thanks, La La." She leans her head on his shoulder, and he shoves her off.

I cannot help the laugh that escapes from my lips.

"We should probably get going soon," Bash says, standing to move away from Laureya. "Wanna make sure we can actually get off this gods-forsaken island."

Hilda slices him with her gaze.

"I mean, you have a lovely home. Thanks so much for having us."

I roll my eyes, shaking my head while Bash tries to slither his way out of my aunt's glare.

HORROR IN THE HALL

-SAYAH-

Flying into Colorado in the middle of a spring storm is one of the most terrifying things I've ever experienced, and it damn near made my fear of flying come back. I nearly kiss the ground when we get off the death trap.

When I think the day can't possibly get any worse, we find out that all flights coming into and leaving Denver have been delayed.

Dom and I barely spoke two words on the plane. The last thing I need is for him to stay at my house and in my bed another night.

I want some space from him.

We catch a shuttle to the parking lot where Dom had left his Mercedes.

The drive home is filled with Laureya annoying Bash the whole time in the backseat. While it makes me chuckle, Bash grips the steering wheel harder and harder.

When we arrive at my house, I disembark from the car and feel a lightness spread through my chest upon seeing my home again. So much has happened since I was last here; I feel like the house should be different, too. I'm a different person, and there's something about the house that doesn't fit me anymore. I grew a little bit—well, actually, a lot—and it seems like the house is part of my old skin, the skin that I'd shed over the last week.

After Dom grabs our suitcases, I open the garage, and he sets them down.

"I'll take Laureya to the hotel," Dom says.

"Do you think you should feed on me a bit really quick? Before you go?"

"I think I'll be okay," he replies tersely.

"You never know when it is coming on, Dom. You can never be too sure."

"I'll be right back. I should be fine. Besides, you fed me less than eight hours ago." The way he repeats himself makes it seem like something is off. I want to trust him, but no one really knows when the warlock will make him murder someone. And Dom doesn't do well with murdering innocent people.

"Okay," I say hesitantly.

"Just let him go, Sayah," Bash urges, setting his suitcase beside mine. "If he gets all murdery in the next twenty minutes, we'll rescue him."

I deliver a threatening gaze to him. "Not funny, Bash."

"He'll be fine, Say," Bash reassures as Dom heads to the car.

"Bye, sis," Laureya calls, wheeling her luggage to the back.

I give her a conniving grin and head up the wheelchair ramp to the garage door that leads inside.

Opening the door, I hold it open for Bash, and when he doesn't follow me in, I look back at him. "Well, aren't you coming in?"

"I can't," he states, looking at me sullenly. "You have to invite me in."

"What?"

The look that befalls his face is slight embarrassment paired with annoyance. He fidgets with the handle of his suitcase. It's adorable. "I cannot enter a mortal's home or dwelling without being invited in," he nearly whispers.

I smile. "That's really a thing, then?"

A big bad villain man has to be asked to be let in. This is fun for me.

"Ask me nicely."

"What?"

"Ask me nicely to come in."

"Sayah . . ." He's teetering on an edge and suddenly I get the urge to push him off it.

"Bash . . ."

He makes a noise in the back of his throat, and I start to let the door close. "Sayah, please. Can I come in?"

"Bash," I say, holding the door wider, "won't you please come in?"

"I would love to," he chides with a playful glare as he enters. "Thank you."

I place a hand on his chest as he stops. "Can I withdraw my invitation at any time?"

"Yes," he answers, right on the shell of my ear.

Chills dance up my spine, and I smile. "Good to know."

He pulls his suitcase into the main room and takes in all the pictures hanging on the walls.

"Very nice home," he says, his eyes darting from here to there at all of mine and Gauge's memories.

"Thanks. I'll show you where you will stay. Up here."

I go to lug the suitcase up a stair, but he grabs it for me, easily lifting mine and his to carry them up the stairs. On the landing, he stops abruptly, and peeks into my room.

"Yep," he says snidely, setting my suitcase inside the door. "That's what I saw."

"Yeah, we never talked about how that happened." I take a step back out of his space. "Especially since I had to invite you in just now. How could you have really been here?"

Bash's dark brows knit together. "I'm not sure. I've only done it once. I also woke up in my room, so I'm pretty sure it was a dream, but it felt real."

"When I woke up, smoke swirled around in the window. It felt so real, but it had to be a dream because I never invited you in before tonight."

His glacial eyes are melting me as he crosses the distance I'd created between us. "Maybe we can dreamwalk to each other."

"Maybe," I breathe, scanning his expression. His breath smells sweet like peppermint. I force myself to move around him to lead him to his room. "Your room's in here. Where do you live, anyway?"

"California," he says, following me into my tiny guest room, which is more suited to be an office.

I snicker, flicking the light on for him.

"What?" Bash asks, wheeling his suitcase to a halt outside the closet.

"I just wouldn't picture a vampire living in California—the sunshine state."

"Technically, Florida is the sunshine state. And I love Cali. It's as lively at night as it is during the day." He does a quick spin to observe the space. "Nice room."

"Sorry it's so tiny."

The charming features of his face dance a bit as he looks at me. I notice the small way his eyebrows cinch together when he's curious; his left dimple curls a bit when he's mischievous, and his blue eyes light up when he's sarcastic. His face is much more animated than Dom's. I'm always hypnotized by how Bash moves his face.

"What?" he asks when I don't move for a few seconds.

"Uh, nothing." I blink, wringing my hands together. "Do you think Dom will really be okay?"

He sits on the bed. "I don't know, Sayah. That warlock has a direct link to his mind. He could snap at any time. We think that the blood you give him will keep things at bay, but we can't know for sure."

"That's what I'm worried about."

"Speaking of blood, I'm starving. Do you know any bars where the local lowlifes like to hang out?"

"Bash, no. You can't go killing off the good people of Wellington."

"Calling them all good is a bit of a stretch, don't you think?"

"Still. No."

"Well, I gotta eat. Any ideas?"

"Here." I bite my arm again before sitting beside him. "Drink from me."

The look in his eyes is devilish, dangerous. The white takes over, and the cat-eye shape forms instantly. He bites back on his fangs. "I don't know if that's such a good idea."

"Why not? You need to eat, and I don't want you killing any of the locals."

"Your blood," he starts, shaking a thought away from his mind.

"My blood what?"

"It's like a drug, Sayah. It does something to me. When I drink your blood, I feel something I've never felt before, and I don't trust myself to stop before I kill you."

The danger he poses to me is supposed to scare me; I feel that I should be terrified of him, and yet, I'm not. I want him to feed from me again. It's like a drug to me, too.

"Please, Bash. Tomorrow, we'll find a local criminal for you to feed on. But for now. Me."

Carefully, he takes my arm and presses it to his lips. The minute he drinks from me, that familiar heat floods me and could have knocked me over. The sound of the slurping, the look in his eyes, and the danger in his tongue floor me. I feel the world spinning beneath my feet. My nipples harden, the tingle in my clit travels to my toes, and the heat in the room might as well be cranked all the way up. It's as if I'm high on the sweetest drug while being tongue-kissed on my pussy. The rush I feel as my life force slips from my marrow and onto his tongue is staggering, and although I should feel drained, I feel alive. Fulfilled. It's as if, while my light seeps out of me and latches onto him, I plunge into his darkness in exchange. I tilt my head back and let him feed for as long as he needs. Too long. I start to feel faint; the heartbeat in my eyes is always a telltale sign that I'm running low on blood and need more.

I hesitatingly pull my arm away, and he reluctantly releases. As the beautiful blood-dripped ivory of his fangs pull out of my flesh, he licks his luscious lips and swallows hard. The guttural sound he makes is almost sexual.

"I feel," he says a bit breathlessly, "that when we do this, we are cheating on Dom."

"Agreed." I watch the wound fade before my eyes.

What is it about Bash feeding from me, leaving me feeling as though we just had sex?

"Um," I say, awkwardly getting to my feet. "So . . ."

"Right," he says, shifting his position to lie across the bed.

My phone vibrates from my back pocket.

> Unknown: You might wanna come get your boyfriend. He's eating the bellhop.

My heart drops. "Shit!"

Bash jolts up. "What?"

"It's Dom," I say, hitting the call button on the new number and flying down the stairs; Bash at my heels.

"Hello?" answers Laureya.

"What the hell happened?" I ask, grabbing my purse, and heading for the garage.

"He went dark. Started attacking the bellhop. I can't stop him."

"Where's he now?"

"Here. Draining the poor bastard." Her voice is calm. I'm not the slightest bit surprised that a vampire murdering an innocent person doesn't shock her.

"Just make sure he doesn't leave." I hang up as I start the car, Bash climbing into the passenger seat.

"Dom gone rogue again?"

"Yes. Shit!" I shout again, reversing out of the driveway as fast as I can before slamming the car into drive. Speeding along the neighborhood roads, I try to call Dom, knowing it isn't going to do any good.

"He's not going to answer if he's gone all the way dark," Bash says as I cruise through a stop sign. "You're gonna get us pulled over if you keep driving like that."

"You can just veilweave the police if that happens." The phone rings five times and goes to voicemail.

"Fuck!" I come to the stop sign and barely stop, screeching the tires as I take a hard left. "What are we gonna do if he's killed someone?"

"He probably has already killed someone by now." Bash is sitting in the passenger seat, calm, and relaxed, with no worry in his voice or demeanor.

I glare at him. "Bash!"

"What? I'm just being honest."

"Try calling Laureya," I snap, throwing him the phone. "See what's happening now."

Bash takes the phone, scrolls to her number, dials, and waits. "La La," he says when she picks up, "what's happening?"

I pull up to the light and go right.

"Another one? All right, try and distract him."

A beat of silence.

I look over at him as he listens to whatever Laureya says.

"All right . . . Okay . . . Yeah, we're almost there."

The hotel is coming up on the left. Bash hangs up the phone.

"What's happening? Where they at?"

"He's onto his third victim," Bash groans. My heart nearly leaves my chest. "Laureya's afraid he's gonna come after her next. She's hiding in her room. She said she could hear him in the hall. Pull around back."

"Fuck!" The tires screech when I pull around to the back. Before I'd fully parked, Bash exits the car and races to enter through the back entrance. It's locked, so he breaks the glass with his body and is out of sight.

My heart's beating so hard it could stop in my chest from a heart attack. I shoot out of the car to follow Bash inside.

All the blood drains from my face.

An old woman—her neck torn open, her eyes wide and lifeless—lies in front of a hotel room door. A middle-aged man lies face down in the middle of the hall, a pool of blood surrounding him, his tweed pants soaked with it. The bellhop down the way is sprawled lifeless over a luggage cart.

Bash is at the end of the hall, kneeling next to what could only be Dom, feeding on his final victim. Bash is trying to pull Dom away from the last one as I race up to them, biting my arm open. The sight of this victim tears at my heart in a way that I'll never recover from.

A little girl.

Bash rips Dom off her and throws him to the other side of the hall. A few pictures fall from the wall as Dom dents the drywall. As Bash tends to the little girl, I rush to Dom and shove my arm in his face.

Then I'm flying through the air, hitting the wall with enough force to knock the wind out of me. Falling hard onto my ass, I watch as Dom flees down the hall and out the door.

"Bash, go after him!" I scream.

He's feeding the little girl blood from his arm.

"Come help her," he yells back before he flashes out of the hall after Dom.

I race up to the little girl, lifting her head, and pushing my bleeding arm to her mouth.

The guy down the hall must've been her dad.

She's only eleven or twelve. Dom had ripped her neck open; scarlet sops her long blonde curls, tangling them.

"Please don't die," I whisper, thinking of Gauge and how I'd feel if this had happened to him. Conjuring whatever magick I can muster, I beg the very moon to inject my blood with whatever elixir she can to help save this little girl. Eventually, the child begins to drink from me.

"Sayah!" I hear Bash's voice call to me. I turn and see him at the end of the hall. "I have him. Come give him your blood. Now!"

Hoping the little girl has consumed enough of my blood, I race to the end of the hall to find that Bash has Dom, who's battered, bloody, and broken at his feet. "I had to get him to stop running."

"What did you do?" Kneeling, I press my bleeding arm to his lips.

"I pushed him into an oncoming car."

Dom grabs my arm and drinks hungrily. He opens his eyes and, to my satisfaction, they have shifted from black to his green.

For what feels like hours, nobody speaks as I let him drink. I let him stay latched to my arm until my knees give out.

Bash pulls my arm away from Dom's mouth before it kills me. "That's enough, buddy. Don't wanna kill her."

I lean against the red brick of the hotel, dizzy from loss of blood. I have no idea how much I have left. Still, Dom remains lying on the sidewalk.

"I have to go veilweave the driver that hit Dom. I'll be right back."

Bash is gone in a flash, leaving me alone with Dom.

He says nothing; the sorrow surrounds him like a shadow,

and I know he's adrift on a raft of misery in his lonely ocean of agony. There are no words for me to speak to him that would suffice as a lifeboat to rescue him from that despair.

Part of me wants to scoop him up and cradle him, tell him that everything will be okay and that we'll find a way to break this mark on him. But he disgusts the other part of me. I know that it wasn't him who had harmed that sweet little girl, but seeing her lifeless and bloody only makes me that much more terrified of him. There is no way in hell he's going anywhere near Gauge now.

Bash is back, and we have not exchanged one word.

"I'm going to check on the little girl," Bash says, stepping over my leg to enter the door.

"I know you probably never want to see me again," Dom finally murmurs.

"It's not that—"

"But you want me nowhere near Gauge. I know."

'I just can't risk it, Dom," I answer. "Seeing that little girl . . ."

'I know," he cuts in. "How do you think I feel? Seeing everything I was doing and not being able to stop. He has a direct line to my thoughts, Sayah. He can see what I see, and when he commands, I have to do what he says. I have no control over it."

Putting myself in his shoes, I feel sorry for him. I know he had no control over his actions.

"She's okay," Bash says when he reappears, sitting next to me. "The other two are deader than doornails. Do you wanna try to work your magick on them, Sayah? Maybe there's some witchy blood in their lines somewhere that will help bring them back."

"I can try." I stand. "Where did you put the little girl? Is that her dad in the hall?"

"She went back to her room. I don't know if that is her dad; I didn't see anyone else in the room with her. I veilweaveled her to think it was a robbery. I wanted to save her from nightmares of ghouls and vampires in the night."

"All right. Talk to him." I motion for him to talk to Dom. Bash nods, and I enter the hall through the glass door.

As I approach the man, I take a deep breath and trigger my phoenix power to the surface. I picture the fire that lives in my bones coming alight and taking over my body. As I feel the warmth of my life, I look at the glow of my arm. Thinking of the innocent young girl, tears seep from my eyes. Kneeling before the man, I turn him over to reveal a gigantic gash in his neck. Biting my hand, I take a tear, and wipe through the blood, then dab it onto the neck wound. I gag at the feeling of the torn flesh beneath my fingers.

Nothing happens.

I sit there, corralling the feeling of vomit creeping up my esophagus as I wait for him to stir for what feels like hours.

Nothing.

I sigh and walk over to the old woman, trying the same thing on her.

Nothing.

The same for the bellhop.

What is the rule for me to be able to bring people back? Is it just immortals? Dark things?

Leaving the bodies where they are, I rejoin the two vampires outside. When Bash looks up at me, I shake my head. "Nothing," I reply. "What kind of story will you come up with for them?"

"Same thing I told the girl. Robbery gone bad, and the bad guy got away."

I nod, leaning against the brick before sliding down to sit again.

Dom has not moved from where he lay, looking up at the dark, starry night sky.

"We should go back to your house," Bash says.

"I'm not going," Dom utters, his voice steeped in sorrow. "I can't risk that happening to anyone else. I need to get to Hattie, and we have to get to London. We must get this mark off me. Or else I'm gonna—"

"Going to what?" I ask, encouraging him to finish.

"End it," he breathes. "I can't live like this."

"Dom, c'mon, man," Bash says, his voice gentle now, not hard like his normal. "Don't say that. We can get this figured out. Don't talk like that."

"I'm serious, Bash. Seeing what I did to that poor girl…and if that is her dad in there, I just took her family away from her. That's going to be hard enough to live with. I can't go on like this."

"Dom, please don't talk like this," I urge, crawling to lie with him. I interlace our fingers, and he grips back slightly. "Let's just head back to my house. I'll get some of my blood in a vial for you, and you can head to New York tomorrow after a good night's rest."

"Say, look what I did in twenty minutes. I killed three innocent people and almost a little girl. What happens if I go dark at your house and kill you? Or end up killing myself in the process? I think I will just head down to DIA and wait for flights to resume."

"Will you at least come back and let me try something with my runes, get you some blood, and then you can go?"

"Hey, guys," Laureya's voice cuts in as she steps through the glass door. "Whatcha doing?"

"What do you want?" Bash asks, sitting on the curb by Dom and me, looking up at the stars.

"Wanted to see what your plan was for the Amityville murder scene in there," she says, lighting a cigarette.

"Bash has it under control," I answer.

"Well, that's good."

"I'll go with you, brother," Bash continues. "Hopefully, Mom can get something done as well."

"I'll give you as much blood as I can. I'll get out there as soon as I can, but I just don't know what's gonna happen."

"Well," Dom says, "whatever happens, it's better if I'm as far away from you and your son as possible. I would never forgive myself if anything happened to either of you."

He squeezes my hand, and I feel the weight of his pain in the gesture. I want to save him from the dark that has claimed him, retrieve him from the depth he's plunging into.

"So, you and I are going out there in a few days?" Laureya asks, puffing her cigarette. The smoke swirls around her red hair in the pale light of the overhead street light above her.

"Yes, we'll leave soon after I see Gauge for a few days."

Bash stands abruptly. "I'm going to go take care of the front desk lady before she sees the horror in the hall and calls the police. Then we need to get the fuck out of here."

Bash leaves through the door again, Laureya sucking on her cigarette as he does.

"I'm so sorry," Dom whispers.

I turn to look at him and see a single tear roll down his face. Seeing a tear on this hardened vampire's face nearly crushes me.

"I'm going to save you," I whisper back.

The uneasiness in his green eyes fractures all the calm in his soul. "I hope so, love."

"All right, Samantha is good and veilweaveled." Bash's voice reverberates through our calm moment. "I made it look like a robbery as much as I could. We shall see how it goes down. We should probably go, though; she's likely to find them soon."

"So, should I stay here or not"? Laureya asks, stubbing her cigarette on the wall.

"Yeah," I say, sitting up. "You can corroborate the story."

Nodding, she says, "All right. Goodnight then." She shoots me one last stale look.

Bash holds out his hand to help me up, then Dom.

"How much blood can a person lose before they die?" I ask as we round the building to the parking lot.

"There's seven–eight pints of blood inside you at all times," Bash says. "If you lose more than that, you die."

"Thanks, doc," I say. "How much is a pint? I don't necessarily have the equipment to take my own blood out and store it. Unless . . ." I pause at my car.

"Unless what?" Dom asks.

"I can use magick like I did that coagulation spell in Washington. I can cut myself and summon just enough to not kill me."

"That could work," Bash replies with a nod, opening the passenger door to the white Mazda.

"I hope that little girl will be alright," Dom says, walking me around to the driver's side to open the door for me. Even in his misery, he's still a gentleman.

"She'll be okay," I reassure him. Although I don't know if that's true, I know he needs to hear it more than anything else right now.

WITCHY VOODOO

-SAYAH-

When we return to my house, I go to the spell cabinet and grab Mama's runes, the rowan wand, and the grimoires.

"What's the wand for, Minerva?" Bash asks, perusing through my cabinet as I grab things.

I slap his hand away. "I don't know, but it makes me feel better when it's near me, like my mother is helping me."

I remember seeing a spell that helps keep demons at bay. Knowing the warlock's power is much stronger than mine, I know it's a long shot. But seeing the toll the death of those innocent people and the near-death of the child is taking on Dom, I have to try something.

Dom is sitting on the couch, mindlessly staring at the blood on his hands.

I go to the altar, light the candles, and thumb through the grimoire until I find what I want.

The spell calls for three black candles, three white candles, thyme, a bowl of salt water, rosemary, and an amethyst.

Walking out to the kitchen, I grab the bowl of salt water and the rest of the ingredients from my cabinet.

"Dom," I say to break him from his trance when I reenter the living room. He looks up at me, eyes still green, and I feel relief that he isn't going dark again. "Sit in the middle of the room, please. You too, Bash."

They oblige me, watching as I place the candles in a circle around them, alternating the colors. Opening the velvet pouch, I spread the runes out and have them face-up between the candles. Then I join them in the circle, sitting with a brother on either side of me.

Pulling the wand up, I flick it around the circle, beckoning all the candles to light. Once flames arise, I set the wand down and close my eyes.

"Sender of the negative energy, with the psychic connection to Dom's mind, we send the energy back to you. This darkness that has encroached upon him rendered him helpless to your pull; we call on the night and the moon with the power as though it were full. With water, we wash it away." I dip my hand in the bowl of water and drip it over Dom's head, and he looks displeased but knows this is important. "With fire, we burn this thyme"—I sprinkle the herb over one of the candles—"to send the energy back to the source and demand that you leave his mind. Wind, we summon you with all your might, and, Earth, we invoke your prayer"—I light the incense with the orange lighter and then hold the amethyst before passing it to Dom—"to cast the darkness out of his mind and return the peace that once lived there. So mote it be."

When I open my eyes, Dom and Bash are watching me. I'm not sure if they're captivated or confused.

"Say it," I demand, knowing they know what I mean.

"So mote it be," they both say in unison.

Once silence falls between us, Bash looks around at the circle. "So, what will this do?"

"I don't know. I just hope it'll keep the darkness at bay until I can get to New York."

"I hope it works," Dom says, looking like he's lost in a storm at sea.

"All right," Bash grumbles, getting up. "I'm done with the witchy voodoo stuff. I gotta piss, and then we should go, yeah?"

Dom nods as Bash steps out of the circle, his black boots clunking on the hardwood floor.

Blowing the candles out, Dom helps me clean up the remnants of the spell.

"I'm not looking forward to leaving you," Dom says, stowing the candles away in the cabinet.

"I know. I'll be worried for you."

"Hopefully, your spell will keep the dark at bay until you can get out there."

"Speaking of..." I grab a knife from one of the drawers of my spell cabinet.

Bash comes back to the living room, gawking at us. "What kind of witchy shit are you gonna do now?"

"I have to do the blood spell," I tell him. "What can we put it in to store in your suitcase?"

"There's a certain amount of liquid you can put in the suitcase, so you can put it in something and glamour it so that it looks like clothes."

"Yeah, that works. I have a pack of water bottles in the garage. We can fill one up. Bash, will you run out, and grab me one, please?"

Bash flashes to the garage. He's back in a flash with an empty water bottle.

While standing over the kitchen sink, I drag the knife along the top part of my arm, careful not to cut enough to not need stitches. I chant to the goddess to not kill me as I fill the bottle. The blood leaves my arm and floats in the air, entering the container that Bash holds. The wound seals up in an instant.

"Dom, grab your suitcase, please."

Dom leaves through the garage and returns with his suitcase, laying it on the floor to open it.

Gripping the bottle, I begin the intricate dance of incantations, each syllable laden with ancient power. The air around me tingles with arcane energy as I chant the sealing spell, my voice resonating with the resonance of hidden realms. Symbols, invisible to the mundane eye, materialize in the air as if inscribed by an unseen hand.

With the final word hanging in the air, I carefully lower the bottle into the suitcase. The suitcase, now containing the glamoured blood, seems to pulsate with a subdued, mystical glow.

Raising my hand above the suitcase, I trace a series of swift, precise gestures through the air. As my fingertips move, a shimmering energy envelops the suitcase. It's as if threads of magick are woven into an intricate tapestry, binding the suitcase, and its enchanted contents. The atmosphere crackles with suppressed energy, and a subtle hum fills the air.

With a final sweeping motion, I will the magick to take effect. The suitcase and its concealed contents respond, vanishing from sight with a subtle ripple in reality. One moment, it's there; the next, nothing but a residual echo lingers in the space it once occupied.

Satisfied, I close my eyes to feel the ebb and flow of the magickal currents around me. Inhaling a steady breath, the weight of the sealed magick is now concealed in the unseen depths of another realm.

"Nice bracelet," Bash says, caressing the glowing band with his finger. "Looks familiar."

"It was Scarlet's," Dom tells him with a sigh.

In all the commotion over the past few days, I'd almost forgotten that Scarlet is still missing, being held captive by the warlock that we're going to kill.

Dom straightens. "We better go."

"Let me just go grab my suitcase," Bash says with a nod.

Dom zips up his bag, and I walk him to the front door.

When Bash returns, the bag thuds as he clunks it down the stairs. He slips by, interrupting the awkward silence, and locks his blue eyes on mine for a split second.

"I'll walk you out," I offer, following Dom out the door.

Bash is throwing his arms around my shoulders next. I nearly jolt at the sudden touch. "See ya, Say. Try not to get in any trouble while we're gone."

"I'll be there as soon as I can. Keep an eye out for him, okay?"

"You got it, boss." He releases me and makes for his side of the car.

"Be careful, please," I urge as Dom stands rigidly beside the driver's door.

"I will. Hurry back to me, okay?" he practically whispers. His words are pleading, and I can feel that he's terrified of what lies ahead without me there to pull him back from the brink of madness.

Even if our relationship is in tatters right now, the jagged rocks pierce our deceptively calm waters. Just because I am furious with him doesn't mean I wish him harm.

"I will try."

He kisses my cheek, and the absence of butterflies leaves a tangled feeling in my gut. So much has changed. Though it wasn't his fault he'd hurt those people, it wasn't his fault that he killed my parents; there seems to be a lot of things he doesn't take responsibility for. Actions he refuses to own. Not to mention seeing the side of him that terrifies me the most—him hurting a child.

I'm a strong ass woman who can handle her own. But when it comes to protecting my child, nothing in the world will harden me faster.

I would watch cities burn to keep my child safe.

He backs away, says, "I love you," and climbs into his car.

I say nothing in return as he closes the door, ignites the engine, and backs down the drive. I reenter the house and collapse on the backside of the door as it closes behind me.

THE CURSE THAT KEEPS US

A few days have passed since Dom and Bash left. Dom texts often to keep me in the loop about what's going on and to assure me he's not gone dark.

The spell seems to be working.

For now.

As I descend the stairs after putting Gauge to bed, my phone rings from the living room. I sprint over to it and see Dom's name on the screen. Pressing the green answer button, I say, "Dom?"

"Hey, Say." His voice sounds despondent, worried.

"Hey, you okay?"

"I don't know. I have a feeling something bad is going to happen tonight. I just wanted to tell you that I love you. Please try to bring me back, okay?"

"Why, Dom? What's the matter?"

"Bash drank all your blood."

I fall back on the couch. "What?" I breathe.

"It's gone, Say. We agreed we'd only take a drink each morning and night until you got here to ration it. And tonight, I went to take my share, and the whole thing was gone."

"Where the hell is he?" I get to my feet again, pacing around the coffee table.

"I don't know. Probably high off your blood somewhere and hiding out."

"Gods-damn him." I kick one of Nox's toys across the room. "Anything your mom can do to help?"

"Not any more than what you've done already. She's still working on a way to get Scarlet back. Working with the fake one to get any information she can to lead us to her."

There's something about Bash's strange addiction to my blood that sets my teeth grinding to the point I want to drop everything, fly down there, and beat his ass for it. But then again, it's kinda my fault he's addicted to it. I knew better after seeing that look in his eyes that first time. And since I have Gauge, there's nothing I can do aside from sit back and wait for Dom to go dark a thousand miles away.

"Can you fly back here? Go to La Guardia and get the next flight. Get to me before you go dark."

"I don't think that's wise, Sayah. The whole point of me coming out here was to help Hattie find the artifact, help me get the mark off, and stay away from you and your child so I don't run the risk of hurting either of you. I can't chance that. I'm sorry. I would rather go dark a million times over than risk hurting Gauge. I cannot ever take that chance. I am sorry."

"Fuck, it pisses me off that he did that!" I yell, and Nox scampers down from his hammock to bolt through the kitty door. "Please text me his number so that I can track him down and kill him myself."

"I don't think it's entirely his fault. Your blood does something to him."

'You drink the same blood, and it doesn't turn you into a moron."

"Yeah, but it affects him differently. My mom thinks it has something to do with how it's partly angel blood on a demon's tongue. It does something like what Ether Dust does to demons. Angel blood to demons is similar to the sweetest drug."

"Damn." I switch the phone to the other ear and sit again. "I shouldn't have given him any at all. I just didn't want him going dark, either. Even though the warlock said his mark would remain inactivated. I knew that."

"It's okay, Sayah, you had no way of knowing. Please don't beat yourself up about it. We have to stay positive about your spell being enough to keep the darkness at bay, and I'll be okay until you arrive in a few days."

I deflate. "Okay."

"I'm going to do everything I can to get this damn mark off me, so I don't go dark again. If you can try your spell from your end, I'll have Mom do hers over here, and I should be good until you get here."

"I'll, uh, do whatever I can."

"I'll keep you posted."

"Please do. I'm going to be worried."

"I will, but I gotta go. Mom is calling me. I love you."

"I love you, too."

"Bye."

When I hang up the phone, a foreboding weight drapes over me enough to feel like a thick quilt, something that's palpable and worrisome.

There's nothing I can do for him now.

To the spell cabinet I go, gathering things I need for another spell, when the doorbell rings. Turning around, I see my sister through the long window that lines the front door.

Setting my things down, I bound over to the door.

"What?" I say as I open it to Laureya.

"Sis," Laureya says breathlessly as she barges in. "I need you to help me."

"Help you with what?" I ask, closing the door behind her.

"It's a full moon tonight," Laureya retorts, sitting on the couch.

"And?" The annoyance I feel drips from my voice.

"And I need you to help keep me in line. I can't prevent the weave. There's been too many vampires around. I will become a wolf, and if you don't help me, I'll run rampant all over the city and kill some of your neighbors."

"Shit. What do you need me to do?"

"I don't know, some sort of witchy shit that keeps a boundary on the house, so I can't leave this area."

This is a good idea. I don't have the slightest inkling as to whether I'll be able to do it, but there must be some sort of boundary spell in the grimoires I can muster up.

But then what?

Once I have the boundary spell up, what will I do? Cage a wolf in my yard for the few hours she must roam as a lupine?

"In the past, how long have you been the wolf for?" I ask as I stand again, moving over to the cabinet to grab the grimoire.

"I think a few hours, from dusk until dawn. I'm not sure; I've never really timed myself."

Pulling a large old book down, I sift through the pages, looking for anything resembling a boundary spell. "Well, yeah, that makes sense. And when was the last time you had to formweave?"

"It's been a while. Like I said, there are ways to control it, to keep it at bay. Drugs are one of them, but I gave those up for Ryan. Mark was the one who taught me to fight the weave, but I just don't think I'll be able to this time. With being around Dom and Bash, I have this feeling in me, this stinging, and that's always how I know I'm going to formweave. The stinging gets more intense until I have to formweave for the pain to stop. But then it's excruciating, so really, it's a lose-lose."

'And it doesn't hurt when you choose to change your form?"

She shakes her head, pulling a pack of cigarettes from her

purse. Her fingers shake as she pulls one out and puts it between her teeth. Then she dives back in for a lighter.

"You can't smoke in here," I tell her.

She glares at me and sets the cigarette on the table. "The only time it hurts beyond fucking measure is when we're forced to form into the wolf, which is during full moons, or if there've been vampires present. It's the most excruciating weave. It's also these formweaves when we aren't aware of what we do. It's almost as though the curse that keeps us is the one in control."

There's a very minuscule part of me that feels bad for Laureya. But only a tiny portion.

Finding the spell I need, I dive into the cabinet's drawers and pull out sea salt, a knife, and my mother's wand.

"All right, come out back. We'll have to bind you back here. I don't know where else I'd put you, and I don't want Gauge to see you like that. It would terrify him."

Laureya stands, grabs her cigarette, and follows me to the backyard.

As she lights her smoke and watches from the deck, I puncture my finger with a needle. Strolling along the perimeter of the fence, I sprinkle salt, and let my blood drip. I have to reopen the wound every few steps, given my rapid healing. Simultaneously, I softly recite the magickal incantations inscribed in the grimoire, creating a sealed circle encompassing my house and yard. Laureya observes my actions, tilting her head at the unfamiliar words. I briefly wonder if she's ever witnessed a witch performing magick before, but I refocus, envisioning an impenetrable force field enveloping the yard—a luminous yellow shield preventing entry or exit. It must be formidable enough to contain a wolf. Imagining the potential sounds of growls and howls emanating from the yard, I introduce a sound barrier to ensure passersby on the greenbelt path remain oblivious to the nocturnal disturbances. Extending extra safeguards to neighbors on the north and west sides, I fortify their fences to prevent untoward sights from breaching the boundary.

When I press the palm of my hands into the air, it feels like there's a glass wall between me and the fence. Although it wavers a bit and seems to bend in with the press of my hand, when I throw a heavy rock at the boundary, it bounces back, and nearly hits me in the shin.

Satisfied, I dust my hands off and lick the tip of my finger.

Laureya glowers. "Gross."

"Shut up and stand over there." There's still a lingering hatred toward my sister, and I don't know if that'll ever go away. "Stay back here until I release the boundary. Do you need water or anything?"

Laureya walks over to the firepit and sits among the chairs, stubbing her cigarette on the pale peach stone. "Can you start this? So I have something to do or look at while being held captive back here?"

"First of all," I rebuke, "you're not being held captive back here; I'm helping you. So. Yeah. Second, what on earth would you do with the fire lit while you're a wolf? Wouldn't that be a bad thing?"

"I don't know. I'm never really me when I go through this. I have no memory of what happens while I'm forced into being the wolf. It's like I go to sleep and wake up in random places. It isn't anything I recommend to people."

"Well, start a fire, do whatever you want. The boundary spell makes it so that no one can see anything out of the ordinary. I just don't want you to set my yard on fire or anything."

Her green eyes turn wistful. "Maybe we'll skip the fire. What about beer? Got any booze or anything I can use to take the edge off?"

"No, I don't drink. You'll have to make do without."

"Great. This should be my most fun weave ever." She huffs

and falls back into the chair, which skids across the flagstone a bit.

"I don't know what to tell you, sis," I say, using the last word with vinegar. "You're lucky I'm even letting you in my yard to do this."

"Whatever."

I walk toward the house. Laureya pulls out her phone and scrolls through whatever she's into. I'm unaware if Laureya has a Facebook account because we're not friends there.

Entering the house, I stow away the remnants of the spell before plopping down on the couch and pulling out my computer to do schoolwork, waiting for her formweave.

I feel guilty at the thought of Laureya alone out there, getting ready to do something incredibly painful I don't know about.

Even though Laureya has hated me our entire lives, and there's a darkness about her because she's half-demon, things out of her control give her every reason to hate me. The fact that my mom had mirrored us together and Laureya had to suffer everything I went through must be so infuriating. Every painful thing I've ever gone through—all my cancer woes and all the pain Laureya did not have to endure—that wasn't her fault at all. She had never asked for this formweaver curse. She has to formweave, and I can only imagine how turning into a wolf would be excruciating on the joints and other things that have to form to become one.

Thinking of all these things, I decide to go outside to at least be with her while she goes through it. Forgiveness is ingrained into me, which often levels me, and reprieves me from the depths other people dig, but I always find my way back to them more than a few times.

I'd forgiven my sister, time and time again, all unrequited. It was as though she never wanted my forgiveness, and now that I know of the mirror spell, I can see why.

It may be different now.

Maybe this time, there'll be a way back to each other now that we're not mirrored together.

Opening the door slowly, Laureya looks up from her phone as I walk back to the firepit to join my sister.

"What are you doing?" Laureya queries.

"I thought I would sit with you, maybe help you through it."

The look in Laureya's eyes is a crude kind of wonder, something that tells me she's suspicious about what I'm really doing out here with her. "Why?"

"I don't know," I shrug sitting across from her. "I figured I would keep you company, is all."

"Okay?" Laureya answers.

"Look," I begin, "I know you and I have never seen eye to eye. We were never close, and quite frankly, you hated me all through our childhood—"

"With good reason," Laureya cuts me off.

I clench my jaw before continuing. "I know that now. You know that now. But I had no idea she placed a spell connecting you to all my shit. I knew you didn't like me; it was clear. But I never knew you were spelled to me to feel all my pain. Had I known, I would have done anything to break the spell. Please believe that."

"I don't see how it would have changed anything. I still don't like you."

"Why? What is it about me that you can't stand?"

"I'm not sure, Sayah. It's not like I choose to hate you. There's something intrinsic in it—something I can't help. Like my DNA is forcing me to dislike you and everything you are about. Maybe it's the demon in me that hates the angel in you. I don't think you and I will ever be close."

The honesty in her words is somehow comforting. I hate liars and when people play nice to keep peace, like my cousin. I like the vicious honesty and wish more people would be brutally honest with one another, regardless of how it stings in the present.

"I get it," I say. "And that's your prerogative. I'll still help you however I can. And now you're not completely spelled to me; I can rest easy knowing my pain won't hurt you. The least I can do for you now is help you through this formweave, and also help to get the lycanthrope curse off you. If I help you with this, I can live out the rest of my days knowing I tried a little to redeem myself for what I put you through."

"I don't think you sitting here watching me writhe in pain will undo all the horrible things your life has brought me, but whatever floats ya boat, sis," Laureya jabs, turning her attention back to her phone.

Explaining what my intentions are to Laureya is a lost cause. From now until the formweave, I intend to be silent and know within my heart why I'm here and what I'm doing.

Pulling out my own phone, I scroll through Facebook.

After around twenty minutes of silence, the moon is high in the sky. A sliver of clouds blankets the middle part of the moon, and as I watch them clear, I hear Laureya's breathing grow a little more ragged.

Laureya starts to shake, dropping her phone. Her green eyes catch mine and they shine a bit, like a deer in headlights. There's a cracking sound, and one of her arms bend at an unnatural angle, causing Laureya to scream. I run back into the house to grab anything that has to do with helping ease pain.

There's a paste my stepdad had given me when I was going through chemo—a CBD called Angel Tears. I grab that and the wand before running back outside. As my sister's body transforms into the wolf, I take the CBD paste, point the wand at it, and command it to go to dust. As the paste turns to powder before my eyes, I pour it into my hands. Walking back out to Laureya, I say, "Pain be gone," and throw it over her head so it lands on her like a snowstorm.

As Laureya's leg cracks and bends forward, she falls onto all fours, glowering at me as her fangs elongate. She doesn't seem to scream as loudly at that crack as before.

Laureya still lunges at me, though, so I flee back into the house and lock the door. I watch from the window as the wolf takes full form. Fur spreads along her body, her ears protrude, and her snout lengthens into a predatory face. Her clothes do not tear off as I thought they would, but merely become part of the dark red fur that covers her.

The wolf shakes as though she'd just been drenched in water and stretches, padding toward the backdoor to stare into the window at me. She doesn't growl or hiss, merely glowers at me menacingly. I know that I'm not a vampire the wolf needs to kill, but not wanting to take any chances, I opt to remain inside.

All that's left to do is wait. Wait for Laureya to be her lupine self and roam the backyard looking for vampires.

Since there is none, it will be an uneventful few hours.

Sometime later, there's a significant bang from outside. I jump up and bound to the backdoor. Looking out the window, I don't see Laureya anywhere within my line of sight. Knowing my spell worked and is particularly strong but still questioning if Laureya got out, I want to avoid going out there to see for myself. Waiting for as long as I can, I stand by the backdoor, hoping that Laureya comes into view. Another loud bang makes me jump out of my skin and now I know I must go outside to investigate.

Turning the knob ever so slowly, I try making no noise as I pull the door open and step outside.

The deck is cold on my bare feet. I take caution walking on the planks toward the end of the railings, hoping I'll get my head far enough over one edge to peek at what the wolf is doing. There's a crack, like a branch beneath my foot has snapped in two. I stop breathing. When no other noise surfaces, I continue padding carefully to the edge of the deck.

Reaching one end, I brace my hands on the railing and lean over to view one of the gates.

There's nothing there; no boards are disturbed, and nothing is out of place.

Satisfied that Laureya isn't on this side, the only problem is now that she must be on the other side of the yard, where there are no lights and no quick access to the house.

I run for the door and shut it behind me, bounding to my car to grab the nine-millimeter pistol I keep in there for self-protection. Cocking one bullet into the chamber—I never keep it chambered because of my child—I go back to the door and brace myself once again to go out into the yard.

This time, I'm extra cautious with my steps, as I have to go right into the darkness and the shadow of the house. Every few steps, I stop, and listen to the silence, to the absence of any movement whatsoever, even the wind.

Carefully, I make my way to the end of the deck and take the stairs cautiously, stopping on the first one before stepping into the grass. Still no movement. I put both feet in the grass and prepare to walk to the end of the house, where there's a dark corner and my second gate.

As soon as I turn the corner into the dark part of the yard, a pair of green eyes are suddenly there, jumping at me from the shadows. Unprepared for the giant wolf's attack, Laureya pounces on me, knocking me to the ground. Feeling the wind leave my lungs, my mind falls dizzy with the blow. I struggle to remain coherent, but Laureya has me pinned to the ground and is viciously nipping at me. I'm dodging just inches from her awful teeth. I pull the gun up between us to get a shot, but Laureya lunges again, narrowly missing my face. As I swerve, flipping myself to the left, the gun becomes dislodged from my hand, a shot firing as my finger slips out of the trigger.

As rage sets in, my skin begins to glow in the dark. A familiar pang spreads through my gums as my fangs protrude. My new defense is to bite my sister, and she will burn.

Having successfully shaken the wolf off, I scope around for the gun. My stomach tightens with the knowledge that the gun will also mean Laureya's death.

Spotting it not far from where I'd fallen, I dive for the gun, the wolf on top of me, the sharp sting of pain reverberating through me as Laureya takes a chunk from the back of my shoulder blade.

Then there's the fire.

The blood that spurts from me and covers the snout of my sister causes Laureya's entire body to burst into flames. The wolf whines and cries as the fire consumes her, and I can only think to jump on top of her to put out the flames.

I pull and push the wolf, willing the moon to let my sister live; I need her to save the two brothers and Gauge.

The flames simmer down, and as they do, Laureya takes on her human form again, the fur fading to the pale skin, her red flowery blouse, and jeans reappearing as her limbs morph back to human form.

Badly burned and crying now, I pull Laureya into my arms and carry her through the yard into the house, laying her on one of the couches

A mixture of feelings rip through me, my heart beating so fast the air drawing into my lungs feels thin and hot. I never wanted this to happen to her. An unfamiliar twist of emotions hits me for my sister, things I've never felt for her spinning a web of softened thoughts for her.

Laureya writhes in pain for a few moments before unconsciousness claims her.

Her clothes are ripped and torn, the black remnants of the flames marking the threads. Her skin is bubbly and black, and half of her hair is singed away. I don't know if Laureya's going to make it through this. Stoking her blackened hair out of her eyes, I swallow the tears looming under my eyes.

Overcome by nausea and guilt-ridden, I quicken to the cabinet to check the grimoires for something—anything—that will help my sister.

I find nothing to help with these kinds of burns.

I pause thrumming through the grimoires.

But wait!

Isn't she the other phoenix? If I heal fast, why wouldn't Laureya, too?

Running back to her, I crouch in front of her to see if Laureya is beginning to heal.

But burns still cover her arms and face, and the holes in her pants show her skin is burned there, too.

Grimoire still in hand, I sift again through it, trying to find a spell that will help with the burns.

Finding one, I hover my hands over Lasayah's badly burned body, chanting words that are written in the book I'm unfamiliar with but find a home on my tongue regardless.

A shimmering light emanates from me, directed toward the angry and melted skin, and as the enchantment weaves its way through the air, the wounds lighten. While not vanishing completely, under the mystical transformation the magick of my words stirs, the severity of them lessening.

The red of Laureya's hair is still singed and black and will not fade. That will take time to grow out and a different kind of style to hide.

After watching Laureya breathe for a few minutes to make

sure she's going to be okay, I decide to leave her be and go to my own room.

I have a lot of explaining to do to Gauge in the morning.

A few times throughout his life, I've mentioned my estranged sister to Gauge, but every time I do, he doesn't understand why the two of us don't talk. It's hard to explain a drug addiction to a kid without getting too deep. After the first few attempts, I finally decided not to bring it up anymore. He knows I have a sister I don't talk to, who he's never met before; but explaining to him why she's suddenly in our lives now, on our couch, will be tricky.

As I undress before getting into bed, I check the bite on my shoulder in the mirror to see if it's still there.

It has all but healed.

Crawling into bed, I lay my head on the pillow, and as I drift off to sleep, the furthest thing from my mind is Dom.

ADDICTED

-SAYAH-

Whatever pulls me out of my dream—strangely about Bash—has my eyes staring straight up at the ceiling, trying to decipher if it was real.

It was hot.

The memory of Laureya slices through my sexy thoughts of Bash, and I throw the covers off, heading for the stairs before I even think about grabbing my phone.

I breathe a sigh of relief, seeing Gauge still asleep in his bed. I wouldn't want him to find the strange, burned lady on our couch.

He normally wouldn't come downstairs without me anyway, as he usually calls me to his room for morning snuggles before either of us heads down, but it wouldn't be a surprise to me if he chose to switch it up on this given morning.

Laureya's still asleep on the couch, her chest rising and falling normally, but the burns have not completely faded. There are angry red marks all over her face, her arms, and hands. Charred pieces of her hair whirl around her as well.

I gently shake her shoulder, trying not to hurt her, but to see if she can be roused awake.

Laureya doesn't stir at first; she winces and opens her eyes.

"W-w-what the—" Laureya tries to sit up. "Ouch!" she yells, looking at her arms while her brows furrow. "What the fuck? What happened to me?"

"Well, you attacked me," I mutter, crouching next to her. "Then you bit me."

"Then you burned me?"

"That's just a side effect of biting me. What's the last thing you remember?"

"You throwing your fairy dust on me—that's the last thing on my mind."

I can't help the small smile pulling at the corners of my mouth. "Well, you formweaved. You banged shit around, I went out to look, and you attacked me. I tried to get you off, but you bit my shoulder and caught fire. I put you out as fast as I could, but as you can see, you're still pretty badly burned."

"Uh, ya think?" she scoffs, pulling up her pant legs to look at the damage. The material sticks to some of the wounds, and she winces again, cussing under her breath.

"What I don't understand," I mention, pulling myself up to sit on the couch next to my sister, "is why you don't heal fast like me. You're the other phoenix. Why wouldn't your wounds heal quickly like mine do?"

"It may have something to do with the fact that it was a burn to a phoenix from a phoenix?"

I nod. "Could be."

"Mama?" comes Gauge's voice from upstairs.

I jump to my feet. "Yeah, baby?"

"Who are you talking to?"

"I have to go talk to him before he comes down here. Stay put," I command, standing.

"Yes, Mom," Laureya chides, falling back against the couch pillow.

I climb the stairs two at a time and crawl into bed with him, being the big spoon as I always am for our traditional morning time snuggles.

"Good morning, Mama," Gauge says as I curl up close to him, lying my head on his back to listen to his heartbeat.

"Good morning, baby," I whisper back.

"Who were you talking to?"

I heave a heavy sigh. "Do you remember me telling you about my sister?"

I can feel him tense up a bit. "No." He turns around to face me. "You have a sister?"

It's been a long time since I've attempted to tell Gauge about Laureya. "Yes. I have a sister. She and I have never been close, as things she's done have prevented her from being a part of our lives. But she's here now, hurt, and needs my help."

I'm cautious about how much I can divulge to him without saying too much. There are things I can't tell him, but ten-year-olds like to ask a lot of questions, and I know the barrage of them is about to come.

"What's the matter with her? How's she hurt?"

"She was burned."

"How was she burned?"

"She was in an accident," I kind of lie.

"What kind of accident?"

"At her job."

"She was burned at her job? What does she do?"

"She's a cook."

"How did she get burned at work?"

"I don't know, love."

"Why did she come here after she got hurt?"

"Because she was in town, and I didn't know. Grandpa David also lives too far away."

"Why are you two not close?"

"Because she was into bad things."

"What kind of things?"

"Things that a ten-year-old doesn't need to know about."

He's quiet for a second, and I hope this is the end of the questioning.

He turns to face me, his brown eyes still curious. "But why's she here now?"

I know this will be hard for him to grasp without my being able to share the real reasons behind my estranged sister being here.

"She needed help, baby," I repeat, stroking his face. "And when there are people in need who need our help, we help them—regardless of what they have done to us in the past."

"What did she do to you?"

"She was just really mean to me growing up. She never liked me, and Grandma and her didn't get along either. When Grandpa David and Grandma divorced, she chose to live with Grandpa and didn't talk to us anymore."

His brown eyes shift and widen in sadness. "Didn't that make Grandma sad?"

"Yes, it made her very sad. That's why she never ever talked about your aunt to you."

"She's my aunt?"

"Yes. She's my sister." Telling Gauge that Mama isn't Laureya's real mother seems irrelevant.

"Can I meet her?"

"Well, you have to. She's downstairs, and we have to get her healed. She has bad burns on her face and arms."

"Should we take her to the doctor?"

"No, we can't take her to the doctor."

"Why not?"

"Because she doesn't have health insurance," I fib again. We probably really do need to take her to the hospital, but something in my heart knows that even if I suggest it, Laureya won't go.

"What's health insurance?"

"Okay," I say, sitting up. "Enough with the questions. I'll get you some clothes so you can get dressed. Come down when you're done, and I'll make you some cereal."

"Okay, Mama."

I swing my legs over the side of the bed, stand, and dive into the drawer underneath for a clean pair of undies and pants for him. Then, in the closet, I grab a shirt, throw it onto the bed, and give him a kiss.

He smiles back at me and starts to dress.

Back downstairs, Laureya's still lying on the couch, scrolling on her phone. She must've gone and retrieved it while I was upstairs.

"I think you should try to take a shower and get those wounds cleaned up."

Laureya says nothing, merely continuing to scroll.

"If I said we should take you to the doctor, what would you say?"

"I'd say no," she snaps without looking up.

I knew that was what she would say, and I really don't know her that well. "Okay, well, please at least go take a shower. I'll get you some clean clothes you can borrow."

"I doubt you'll have anything that fits. I'm clearly much skinnier than you."

"Hey, that's not even necessary, Laureya. I'm taking you in and trying to help you—"

"You burned me!"

"You attacked me!"

"Mama?" Gauge's voice comes from the landing now. I curse myself for talking about what really happened to Laureya so loudly.

"Yeah, baby?"

"I'm ready to come down now."

"All right, honey, come on down." Quieting my voice, I say to

Laureya, "Don't tell him what really happened. I already told him—"

"That I burned myself at work. I know, I heard you. You know, with how your house is built, you can hear everything from those rooms up there. Just letting you know for future reference. In case you and Dom ever—"

"Okay, that's enough," I scold. At the mention of Dom, I want to run upstairs and check my phone. I realize now I'd not been diligent about updating myself on him.

Gauge eases down the stairs and gets into his wheelchair, waiting for him at the bottom. After he's settled in the chair, he wheels toward the living room to meet Laureya.

I know the sight of her burns will make him uneasy, so I say, "Gauge, honey, why don't you eat in here today? I'll get your cereal all set up, and Aunt Laureya will go take a shower, and then you two can formally meet, okay?"

Gauge eyes Laureya curiously before saying, "Okay," and going to the kitchen instead.

I send Laureya a scowl and follow Gauge into the kitchen. "Use the bathroom right there at the end of the hall," I shout to her.

With a grumble, Laureya gets up reluctantly, and directs herself to the stairs.

After getting Gauge situated with his cereal at the table, I go upstairs to make sure Laureya isn't snooping around in my room—since that's what I'm used to her doing—and also to check my phone.

I hear sounds of the shower going behind the shut bathroom door, so I grab my phone.

Pulling it free of the charging cord, there are no new messages.

From anyone.

I try calling Dom, but there's no answer.

Worry plucks at me like a guitar string, reverberating

outward to my very fingers. Something in his voice last night made him worried, and because of the interlude with Laureya, I hadn't been able to think about it much.

Now, because there's no word from him, it could only mean bad things.

I grab a pair of black leggings and a blouse I think is Laureya's style. She really is much skinnier than me, but in my defense, I had a baby and didn't use drugs to keep skinny.

Knocking on the bathroom door, Laureya answers it with a white towel wrapped around her head and nothing else.

Burns cover her—her small breasts, her stomach, her arms, and even her face have angry splotches that are beginning to blister.

"Here," I say, shoving the clothes at her.

Laureya eyes them with disgust. "Is this all you have?"

"I don't know, Laureya. Put a towel on, and I can go with you to look for something else if you don't like what I chose."

"All right," she hisses, closing the door for a few seconds while she wraps a towel around herself.

Opening it again, she waits for me to show her the way into my room.

I have a closet for my dresses at the entry of the bedroom and a walk-in closet in the bathroom portion. I lead Laureya into this and wait while she pursues through my clothes.

After twenty minutes and lots of grumbling from Laureya, she finds something she likes. Laureya returns to the other bathroom while I return downstairs for coffee.

Gauge and I are sitting at the dining room table—him with his bowl of cereal and me with my steaming cup of coffee— when Laureya finally joins us. Her hair is brushed out but looking as though someone who is blind had cut it for her and she's wearing my nice wine-colored blouse I just bought for a job interview. It still has the tags on it and everything.

Brushing it off cause that's the least of my worries right now,

I say, "Gauge, this is my sister Laureya. Laureya, this is my son, Gauge," as I enter the kitchen to grab the scissors.

"Hello, Gabriel, it's nice to finally meet you," Laureya says, feigning niceties, and probably getting his name wrong on purpose.

I pull the blouse hard to cut the tag off for her. You know, so she doesn't look like a moron.

"Nice to meet you, too," he says hesitantly, his spoon frozen mid-air as he takes in her burns.

"Sorry about my boo-boos; I had an awful accident at work."

"That's what my mom said. You should go to the doctor. They look really bad."

"I think I'm okay, sweetie. Thank you, though."

Laureya ambles over to the coffee maker to fix herself a cup of coffee.

I really don't know what to do now. Sensing that Gauge is uncomfortable with Laureya and all her wounds, I consider how I can distract him, but I don't want to leave Laureya alone in my house.

That's when the doorbell rings.

Who the fuck can that be?

I hurry to the front door, feeling just as curious as Laureya and Gauge's stares.

Opening it up, Bash stands before me, looking bedraggled, and pale. His typically blue eyes are brown. The car that brought him here drives off—probably a rideshare.

"Bash!" I shut the storm door behind me so that Gauge can't see. "What the fuck are you doing here?"

"I need your blood, Sayah. I can't help it; it's all I can think about."

Hearing his answer triggers the rage I'd forgotten about from Laureya's incident, and that he'd stolen my blood from Dom infuriates me once again. I smack him across the face as hard as I can.

His head flies sideways, and he stops. The cheek I hit is angry red at first, then fades.

"I deserve that," he acknowledges with a nod, facing me again. "I'm so sorry. I really am. But I can't even function now. It's all I can think about."

"Where's Dom?"

"I'm sure he is all the way dark by now, Sayah."

Worry floods me. "How do you know? You left him after you drank all my blood." I can't help the fury that infuses my voice.

"I know, but my mom texted me right before my plane took off, saying he was dark and it's all my fault."

"It is."

"I'm aware of that, Sayah," he growls. The look in his eyes causes my heart to drop, and I know if I don't voluntarily give him blood soon, he'll try to take it, killing himself in the process. "I need some now. I feel like I'm going to vomit again. I already have, and it ain't pretty. Nothing works. I've tried feeding on a couple of people on the way here, and nothing satisfies the hunger like before. I need your blood to help me feel better. I have the shakes—my whole body aches. And the last person I drank from, I threw up the blood, and it looked like a straight horror flick come to life. Please, I'm begging you." He holds out his hand for me to see that he's trembling.

"All right," I say, my voice quavering.

Taking a quick glance to make sure no neighbors are out walking their dogs, I bite my wrist open with the fangs I can summon easily now, and offer it to him.

He takes it hungrily.

The hot sensation that creeps from my toes to my middle section is not as intense as the first few times, probably because I'm so mad at him. He drinks like his life depends on it, his eyes closing in sheer relief and euphoria as my blood fills him up. I let him drink until I fall dizzy and pull my arm away. Blood spills down his chin, and he smiles at me, his eyes returning to their normal, beautiful blue.

"Thanks," he breathes. Bash has always been beautiful. But to see him unhinged is a stunning sight as well.

"What will we do about this little problem of yours?"

"I don't know, Sayah." His face is slack and euphoric, like he's high. "I've never been addicted to anything before."

I sit in one of the wicker chairs I have on the front porch. Bash wipes the blood off his chin and licks his fingers, sitting down next to me.

"And how are we going to find Dom?"

"I don't know that either. We may have to continue looking for the artifact and try to break the spell ourselves."

"Well, I have a doozy of a story for you," I tell him with a bite. But being mad at him isn't going to change anything. He looks at me with one of his pressing looks, urging me to continue.

I tell him about Laureya, walk him through the previous night's events, and eventually wonder if he's hearing me. His eyes look glossy and drunk.

'No shit?" Bash says when I finish, crossing his legs, and looking enthralled. "What is happening now?"

"She's inside, talking to my child." Sounds of a lawn-mower starting interrupts us and I look skeptically over Bash's shoulder to my neighbor to the west of me. "Shit, we should get inside."

Bash glances over his shoulder at my neighbor, Chris, who's mowing the lawn in pajama bottoms and a gray beanie. "Why? What's he got to do with anything?" Bash's eyes land on me speculatively.

"He's just a dick. Long story. He just owed his lawn yesterday so he's just out here to spy on me." Bash shoots up like he's going to go end Chris and it surprises me how fast I move to grab his shirt. "No. Not now. Right now I need to get back inside."

"What am I supposed to do?"

While talking, I had thrown ideas around in my head. I'd come up with something: "We'll say you're her boyfriend coming to check on her."

"Why am I always her boyfriend?" he asks with an eye roll, swaying a bit as he stands.

"Because it makes sense to little boys and stupid cousins," I retort. "C'mon, let's go."

He follows me inside, the glass screen door slamming into him on the way.

Laureya's at the table with Gauge, looking like they're having an enthralling conversation about elementary school.

Gauge stops talking and blinks at the new stranger in our house.

"Gauge, this is Laureya's boyfriend, Bash. Bash, this is Gauge."

Laureya's face slides to Bash's, and her lips quirk up in a flirtatious smirk.

"Hey, Gauge, nice to meet you," Bash greets, holding his hand for Gauge to shake.

He takes it hesitantly. "Nice to meet you, too."

"All right, you two hang out in the living room while I get him finished with breakfast. Bash, make some calls, would you?"

I don't want to mention Dom is his brother because that would further confuse the situation I'm trying to get away with.

Since it's the weekend and there's nowhere to go, I have to figure out a way to keep Gauge busy while I and the other two flaming hot messes figure out how to do the things we need to do.

"Hey, baby, can Austin come over to play today and keep you company while I figure out what to do with Aunt Laureya?"

"Probably," Gauge says. He lifts the bowl of cereal to his lips to get the lingering milk from the bottom.

"All right, well, text him and ask."

The early afternoon light paints Bash in a glorious golden glow as I sit across from him on the deck a few hours later, Laureya spread out on my tanning chair as she scrolls through her phone.

"Any word on Dom?" I ask Bash, peeking in the window to check on Gauge and Austin, who are playing video games inside.

He flips his phone over, which was sitting on the patio table. "Nope. No new messages from anyone."

"Can you call your mom?"

His black brow perks up. "I guess. But she's gonna yell at me and I don't like when she yells."

Laureya laughs. "Oh, how precious, a vicious vampire who is scared of his mommy."

Bash glowers at her with a look full of venom.

Pushing my laughter down, I say, "Call her."

Bash stands and yanks his phone off the table, walking to the other end of the deck, out of earshot of us. His heavy boots clunk on the boards as he presses call. He glares at me while the line rings and then turns when I hear Adaline answer.

She's mad.

She's big mad.

I can hear some of what he's saying to her, but when he starts to get louder, he goes around the house. When he comes back around, he looks like a little kid who has been scolded by his mother.

"Well?" I inquire.

"He's missing. His phone's in his room," Bash states dryly,

pulling the chair out to sit again. "There's a trail of bodies that leads from Lake George to Schenectady."

"What do you mean, 'a trail of bodies'?" I ask hesitantly. I know what it means, but I want to know how they're pining the body count on Dom.

"There are already reports of deaths with bite marks on the neck. So far, authorities are chalking it up to some sort of rabid animal attack. The reports started happening this morning. Dad works for the hospital; a few came into him this way. He was there with the medical examiner."

I rub my temples. "Where do you think he is heading?"

"Well, *he's* not heading anywhere," Bash snaps, smacking a mosquito on his arm and wiping it off on his pants. "Mederio's the one controlling him. Dom is going wherever Mederio is forcing him to go."

"Poor Dom," I utter. I can only think about the absolute dejectedness in his eyes when he attacked the last round of people. He was on the verge of wanting to end things then; I can't even imagine how things are going to go for him when he comes out of this one.

If he comes out of it.

"How many people has he killed so far?" Laureya asks, setting her phone down on her chest.

"I don't know," Bash answers solemnly, taking out a lighter for the citronella candle in front of him. "The reports are only of the ones who've made it to the hospital. None have hit the news yet. There's no way of telling."

Guilt hits me in a way it never has before. It's my fault for feeding Bash my blood, thinking it was going to save him when, in fact, it made him a crazed addict. Right now, he looks as though he will have to feed on me soon; his eyes are growing browner by the minute, and the pallor of his skin is gaining more and more translucency. Knowing I have to feed him to keep him from getting sick, but every drop of my blood is feeding his addiction, creating more of a frenzy, leaves me not knowing what to do. I have to keep Bash from going over the edge while trying to find a way to bring Dom back from one.

Anger swarms my heart for Bash as well, blaming him for Dom going dark and drinking all the blood that would've kept him from that darkness. But then, I know it's just as much my fault for Bash's addiction. For wanting to feel the pleasure it brings when he drinks from me. Just thinking of that has me near an edge of myself—an edge I didn't know existed until right then. It's my own addictions that have me teetering, as Bash drinking from me is just as much of a high for me as it is for him.

"What are we going to do, then?" Laureya's voice slices through my silent yearnings.

"I have no idea," Bash replies, brushing his black hair back, the veins in his hands bluer than ever.

"Adaline," I offer, and Bash's eye quickens to mine. "Hattie and Adaline. We have to get to the artifact. That's the only way we can save him."

"Then on to New York?"

"Yes, we have to. I just can't leave until this weekend is over. I have to spend time with my son."

"And he can't leave you," Laureya states, inclining her head toward Bash, who's starting to shake.

"What are we going to do about that?" I ask more to myself than the other two. Bash has already stated he doesn't know what to do about an addiction to blood.

"What's there to do about it?" Laureya asks.

I sit back in my chair, crossing my legs. "What about your real mom?"

"What about her?" she scoffs, almost condescendingly.

"The aunts said she was addicted to Ether Dust, which is kind of what Bash is experiencing. Do you have any idea where she is? I mean, how did you find out about her in the first place?"

She crosses her arms defiantly. "My dad told me about her the first time I formweaved. I have always expected that I wasn't really Fran's daughter—never felt a mother-daughter connection to her."

"When he told you about her, did you try to find her?" Bash inquires.

"I did," Laureya sighs, staring at something on the deck, her mind far from where we are.

"And?" I urge her on when she doesn't say anything for a few minutes.

"I first formweaved when I was twenty-five," Laureya finally goes on. "The first time it happened, I was so terrified. I'd fallen in love with a man named Jorge, and to ignite the curse, you must fall in love with a demon, as you know. He did nothing to help me; he watched as all my bones broke to weave into the wolf for the first time. I have no recollection of what happened other than waking up outside of a homeless shelter, covered in blood. When I asked my dad what happened, he told me the truth about what he was. I was so pissed at him for not telling me about myself sooner. He just chalked it up to the fact that he didn't think I would ever fall in love with a demon."

"He should have known better," Bash says, almost in an undertone, but Laureya shoots him a look that says she heard him loud and clear.

"When I calmed down," she resumes, "I demanded he told me everything he hadn't told me before. I threatened to go to the authorities and turn myself in for killing whoever it was I had killed that night. That's when he told me of Carolyn, my real mother. He told me she was a spitfire when he met her at a house party when he was younger. She had the same fiery red hair as me and was ambitious. He pulled out an old box of photos and showed her to me, and we could pass for sisters.

Apparently, she was dabbling with drugs then, but nothing too crazy; just a young twenty-something who drank and did cocaine every once in a while. As their relationship progressed, she started cheating on him with a vampire, and when she learned of Ether Dust, her addiction got out of control. She couldn't quit even when pregnant with me, and no one knew what that does to a baby, as no baby has ever lived through it. As soon as I was born, she was gone and never looked back."

Laureya stops here, and if there's any humanity in her, I can see it seep through. A tiny sliver of sadness creeps through her hardened green eyes. She bats her eyelashes fast and looks away, and it's gone.

"So," she begins again, her voice cracking, "I sought out to find her, and I tracked her to Denver. I drove the nine hours to the city and went to every shelter with one of her pictures, asking if anyone had seen her. From there, I learned of drug dens. I learned of the Neverdusk Dominion from drug dens, demons, vampires, formweavers, not so much sirens in Colorado, but fae for sure. I found her mixed up with a group of fae; they were trading blood for different highs. She recognized me as soon as I walked in. I offered to buy her a coffee and some lunch just to talk to her, and then I would leave her alone forever. She agreed. All the light had gone from her eyes; her hair was browner red, and she was skinny, and awful-looking. She didn't say much; she really didn't eat. I asked her why she never came to see me or asked my dad about me. She just responded that she never wanted to be a mom in the first place. She was drunk and high when she got pregnant and wanted to abort me, but my dad wouldn't let her. He'd told her he would take me and never ask anything of her—that she could disappear and never have to worry about child support or anything else about it. So, she did."

When Laureya stops talking again, it isn't sadness that stops her; it's anger that surfaces and reddens her features, shrouding her burned, and dappled skin with rage.

"What happened from there?" Bash asks in a shaky voice .

"That was it," she says, taking a deep breath and sweeping her burnt hair off her shoulders. "That's all she said. She left right after, asking if she could go. I never heard from her again."

"If she never got sober from it, how would we find a way for you to?" I ask Bash.

"That Neverdusk Dominion she spoke of," he says, his lips now white, as though he's actively dying. "Maybe there's someone there. There has to be someone who has gotten sober from it. They should know of something."

I sit up straight. "Yeah, that could work. Can you guys go now? I have to stay here with Gauge."

Laureya looks less than thrilled to be volunteered to go on a journey.

"They may have something for those burns, too," Bash offers.

"Yeah, maybe," Laureya says.

"We have to help him," I say. "He'll be of no use to us to get the artifact if he's a crazed addict."

He snipes a look at me. "Thanks."

I snigger. "Welcome."

"All right," she scoffs, getting up from the lounge chair. "Let's go see what we can figure out."

"He needs to feed off me first," I say, willing my fangs out.

At the sight of my blood, Bash seems to straighten a bit, similar to a drunk staggering into a bar at eight in the morning. I hand my arm over to him, and the brown in his eyes look at me with sadness, with a silent guilt wrapped around them. His lips curl around my arm, and he drinks from me. Keeping the warmth at bay for the mere fact that Laureya is watching us, it's still hard to fight the euphoria his drinking from me causes.

The dizzy feeling makes me pull my arm away, and I watch as Bash's skin returns to normal, and his eyes resume their blue.

"All right, let's go," he says, rising from his seat.

I walk them to the garage, and as we pass Gauge and Austin, they don't even look up from their game to wave. Grabbing my car key from my purse on the way, I press the button for the garage and let the afternoon light flood in.

Laureya doesn't say anything as she gets into the car's passenger side, clearly stating she won't be the one driving to Denver.

Passing the key to Bash, I say, "Be careful with my car, please."

"Sure, don't worry about us going into the world of blood-suckers, demons from another dimension–not to mention fae, who're pretty much the shadiest fucking beings you can ever encounter–but yes, I'll be careful with your mom minivan."

"It's not a minivan!" I argue. "It's a mini minivan."

"Whatever," Bash says, still with a hint of humor. "Do me a favor; text me now so I have your number. I'll call if anything drastic happens—if you care, that is."

I eye him sardonically, pulling out my phone. "What's your number?"

Plugging the number into my phone, he tells me and I text him.

The phone from his back pocket dings and he pulls it out to check it. "Thanks."

The smile he gives me as he gets into the car is devilishly handsome. I protest against the flutters in my chest as he shuts the door, starts the car, and backs out down the driveway.

His blue eyes are on mine before he drives away, and it almost makes me forget how ridiculous that badass man looks in my silly ass car.

THE NEVERDUSK DOMINION

-BASH-

Something about the way she looks at me levels me. Brings me back from whatever fucked up plain I live my life on. It goes deeper than my addiction to her blood, which is beyond anything I can even try to comprehend. The moment her blood hit my tongue, I was hooked, and I've been chasing that fucking feeling like the thunder chases lightning. It doesn't help that the profoundly deep feelings I felt for her in those dreams are actually real, and contending with the fact my brother found her first is nearly infuriating.

Even though I'm the villain and supposed to cause the chaos.

Ever since I can remember, I've liked causing people pain. I like to bring death and destruction to the world and be the reason people scream. The look of terror in a person's eyes is something that makes my blood run hot. The adrenaline that surges through me makes my dick hard, and I love that part. Feeling a person's life wither underneath my tongue, the phantom stutter of death on my lips, and the vital energy of life transferring from their fading life force to my stolen one are things that feed my darkened soul. Admitting that to myself was the first step toward freedom.

Back in the day, when Ollie changed for the first time, I anticipated joining the ranks. I went looking for danger just to get killed so I could embrace my darkness, own the shadiest parts of myself, and level up infernally. I've always had a nefarious soul, where whispers of madness found solace. The monsters under my bed were my friends, and the skeletons in the closet were my playmates. I owned unhinged and fucked up; it was always my forte.

The night I died, I'd started a fight with some thugs at a local watering hole.

My transition to the dark was the most excruciating thing that I've ever gone through, but I wanted that dark. I craved it.

The bloodlust is something I never deprive myself of. I know how to feed enough to not kill someone, but there's absolutely no fun in that. The victims I choose are often young couples, as they're the most resistant to death. The old don't care if death comes for them; they have already lived their lives and don't find a need to care if it comes for them in the form of a vampire. Old people are also easy targets. I like the chase; I like surprising my victims and having them run from me; only to outrun them, rip their necks open, and drink enough of their blood to feel complete.

I don't drink enough to feel full often, so when those times come, I relish it.

As I drive Laureya and me down the highway to Denver, I can't help but think of Sayah.

Gods, even her name is delicious on my tongue.

Sayah.

Her blood is the sweetest thing I've ever tasted.

When the dreams began about her, I remembered how I'd felt about Sadie. Even though it'd been two hundred years since those dreams, they still returned to me like an old life—a whisper on the wind of a life I once knew. The dreams of Sayah are different, though. They're even more vivid, and the love I feel for her in them is more powerful, like her life is something I need to live.

Never had I imagined falling addicted to her blood.

In the dreams, there's always an urge to bite her, but it isn't to drink from her; it's to pierce into her beautiful skin and be one with her. That's part of my bond with the dark, though, the feeling of my fangs puncturing through the skin, the first taste of the sweet, metallic lusciousness of blood. It's like the universe needs my venom to mix with her blood to save something that's amiss within me, within the world. No matter the cost.

Knowing she's a real person has always been in the forefront of my mind, and having a feeling it would be Dom who'd bring her to me is also something I knew deep within myself. The feud with Dom was more than just Sadie, as we'd spoken since she had died. But there's something about Dom I hate—that I detest more than I have a reason for. Dom is the good one; he's the one who doesn't want to be a vampire; he wants to die with dignity and not have to feed on people to live. That could be part of the reason I hate him. I hate him because she loves him. Because he's the one who found her, even though my mind found her first.

I have never been addicted to anything in my life, so I don't know how to navigate any of it in the slightest. She let me feed on her, and the minute her blood hit my lips, my body filled up with incredible warmth. My head felt fuzzy, and the taste of it was indescribable. Something sweet like honeydew and honeysuckle but wild like summer lightning and spring rain, refreshing like the air after a tropical storm and the mist of a waterfall after a long hike—all mixed together. Like the perfect amount of lightning was combined with a dose of heroin laced into the rain, so much that one bite created a sensation like an orgasm, turning my entire body to mush and making my lungs fill up with hot, squishy matter that spread to my elbows and the tips of my fingers and toes.

It was enough that in New York, the little sip I had to take to ration the blood for Dom wasn't enough; I tipped the bottle and drank it down in one gulp. Knowing I just fucked up, I walked around the city high as a kite for a few hours until I headed to the airport to get more from the source.

When the blood began to wear off, I got sick. I tried to feed on a transient in the subway on the way to the airport, and I threw up the blood almost instantly, making the bathroom look like a scene from the Texas chainsaw massacre. It dawned on me I was not going to be able to feed on anyone other than her until I overcame the addiction. That stirs an uneasiness within me, knowing that revelation could mean leading me to biting her and burning the way Laureya did.

Or killing her if I don't burn.

The plane ride to Colorado had been utter hell, and I know what I must have looked like to the other people on the plane. The lady who had sat next to me in the middle seat, as I was in the aisle seat, smelled of blood. Though instead of flickering the usual bloodlust in me, it made me even more ill. Luckily, I'd fought the urge to throw up the three-hour plane ride until I hailed a rideshare, making him stop at a rest stop halfway to try again. I bit another traveler; this one a lanky man in his thirties, whom I only drank enough to keep me sustained. Before I got back in the rideshare, the blood was back up and all over the floor and walls of that restroom as well.

I barely made it to Sayah's house without vomiting again.

The feeling of Sayah's presence still pulls at me more than her blood seems to at times. When I walked up to her door and saw her face, my heart raced to the moon, and it was the first time in a long time that I felt a bit human.

Talora had settled something inside me for a bit. But nothing compared to the depths that Sayah's eyes had leveled me to, almost reprieving me from my darkness. I'm still the villain and have no desire to change at all, but her soul calms me. The sensation of being a killer lulls to a quiet hum instead of the loud urge that takes me over most times.

My thoughts linger on these thoughts for an hour before I realize something.

It's been decades since I'd last been to Never.

I look over to Laureya, who has said nothing to me, only looking out the window behind her giant sunglasses, her hair mangled from her burns. Still, it whirls from the cracked window.

"Do you think you'll remember how to find the Neverdusk Dominion entrance?" I ask, turning the dial for the volume of the radio down.

"I don't think it should be that hard," she answers, a hint of anger mixed in with boredom in her voice.

"Well, good. I'd hate to spend any more time than I'd have to," I respond, flicking the music back up so we don't feel obligated to fill the silence with awkward conversation.

The demon in me feels like I may be kin to Laureya somehow, considering she's also part demon. But the demon in me also feels at home in me, and I can sense that hers is not at home within her. She makes it so, that's obvious, but it's as though something is fighting her dark, and she's fighting to let it stay.

I'm still pretty high from my last dose of Sayah's blood, and I need to concentrate on keeping this buzz as long as I can. I don't want to fall sick yet, not so far away from the source.

Laureya has strangely nothing to say almost the entire ride there, which makes me wonder where her mind's at, but again, not wanting to exert any energy on it makes me not question it and keep driving.

When we enter Denver, Laureya perks up a bit, looking for exits that may spark her memory.

"You want to get in as close to the big buildings as possible.

The entrance to the Neverdusk Dominion is through one of the fountains on the 16th Street Mall."

I listen and follow the signs that lead to lower downtown Denver.

The buildings are an excellent navigation source; I get as close to them as possible. We park on 16th Street, and the buildings tower over us.

I turn off Sayah's car and pay the meter, then wait for Laureya to join me.

Following her toward the middle of downtown Denver, a fountain rests at the center of all the buildings. The architecture of the founding is modern chic, a group of cubes stacked on each other like Stonehenge. The cascading water spilling from the tops of the cubes is rhythmic against the hustle and bustle of the people coming and going along the mall's streets.

How we will enter this place without people noticing is beyond me. Until Laureya steps under one of the cubes and disappears. I glance around and smile at an old lady passing by me, clutching her purse as though I will steal it from her. I smile and dip my head in that old-fashioned way I haven't quite let go of, sticking my hands in my pockets.

Laureya reaches a hand out from the water and grabs my arm, yanking me into the vortex.

There's a shift in the energy, and suddenly, I feel the glamour around us; I see it using my power. There's a staircase in the center where all the copper fountains meet, leading down to a darkened underground tunnel.

As we descend the stairs, smells of another kind hit my nose, and I wince at the body odor mixed with opium and marijuana. With my hearing superior to any human's, I can hear things hundreds of yards away. Because of all the whispers and voices muffling together, I can't make out anything, only that there are new decibels with which the voices are being spoken.

I'd met my fair share of fae, demons, vampires, and sirens in my two hundred and fifty years on Earth. Fae are my least favorite beings to deal with, constantly having hidden agendas, and double meanings in everything they say. It's easy to spot a fae, as they often have pointy ears, odd-colored eyes, and hair of different colors. Sometimes their skin is a different color, too, but the glamour they use when they're out with people hides it. The only exception is on Halloween, when they can actually be who they are.

As we enter deeper into the tunnel, the stairs spiral up before we reach the bottom. As we go, gravity reverses, putting us upside down. But with the magick, it all just feels right-side up. The entire place opens up as though we're outside. It's because we've entered a different realm, as down here, it's nighttime, but still it's only magick and nothing more.

There's a cobblestone street with shops that line it, high-rise apartment buildings, and all the things a big city would have. It's basically a mirror of Denver above us.

People of all sorts are going about with their business, eating at cafés, and shopping the stores. Horses and buggies are going to and fro on the streets, and traveling through a park with a stream and even the bridge over it.

There are no cars.

As Laureya and I walk down the sidewalk, I'm looking into all the windows. The vampires, formweavers, and demons are more challenging to spot than the fae. There's a bright pink woman with wings waiting on a young-looking couple at one of the cafés, a green man walking his dog, his pointy ears sticking out of his beret. A bright orange woman with purple spots is rollerblading, her black elbow, and knee pads matching her black hair that sparkles like she has tinsel in it.

No one seems to notice Laureya and me, so we seem safe. It must be our blood that helped us through the glamour.

As we walk, a large purple woman with a normal-looking black man passes by, and when they do, I catch that whiff of weed again. I turn to watch them walk and see a cloud of smoke come out of the purple lady's neck.

"My guess would be a weed shop," I say. "It may lead us to the heavier shit."

"Look, there's one." Laureya points to a bright green sign with a marijuana leaf on the front.

When we arrive in front of the shop, the windows are tinted so we can't see in. A yellow man emerges from the shop, holding a bag, and holds the door open for us. As we enter, a magenta lady with translucent wings at a counter stands in front of two brown double doors.

Her eyes are fathomless black, with no pupils or irises within them.

Those black eyes scan me and hold her stare. "IDs please," she says stonily.

I pull my wallet from my back pocket and present it to her. Laureya grabs hers from her purse.

"Who polices Neverdusk Dominion?" I inquire as the fairy studies my ID.

"The NDP. Neverdusk Dominion Police," she answers in an undertone.

Whoever they are, I do not want to get on their bad side.

After the fairy hands Laureya back her ID, she presses a red button, and the click lets us know the doors are unlocked.

As we enter, loud music and the scent of weed hit me all at once.

Around the perimeter of the building, glass counters line the walls, and workers of all colors work behind them. They busily tend to the purchasers, using metal tongs to grab the buds from jars and place them in black pill bottle cases. Once weighed, they're placed in green bags and stapled closed with a receipt.

Exciting pictures of evil enchanted characters hang on the walls, which are painted black. The false-florescent light flickers in places. The menus of all the different strings of Mary Jane decorate the walls. There are no windows.

There are other things on the menus as well. I don't know what half the shit is, but I want all of it.

There's also a list of blood and their types.

My stomach growls.

"What are we going to order when we get to the front?" Laureya asks, shaking me from my grumbling stomach.

"I have no idea," I whisper back, wondering if weed or anything else on the menu would help my cravings.

As we approach the front of the line, I get an idea.

Being honest.

A blue man with long brown dreads is the person who calls on us. When we arrive at his counter, he eyes us suspiciously.

"Whoa, what happened to you?" he asks, glaring at Laureya's burns.

"Burned, obviously," she answers curtly.

"What the hell burned you? They're supernatural burns, that's for sure."

"How can you tell?" I ask, leaning on the glass, and gazing at Laureya. I'm beginning to love torturing her.

"The way the burns glisten, almost as if they have glitter. Look." He sticks his hand out and pulls her chin to the false fluorescent light. Before Laureya wrenches her face back, I catch sight of the glimmer.

"Ah, yes, it does. La La, you sparkle!" I can't help the smile tugging at my mouth.

"Shut up," she spits out. "Do you have anything for them?"

"Is that what you're needing then—dragon burn ointment?"

"They're not from a dragon," Laureya answers, her eyes growing severe.

His bushy brows pinch together curiously. "And what creature did that to you?"

"What helps cravings for phoenix blood?" I assert, offering a bit more information without blatantly saying it.

The blue man's yellow eyes take stock of me, measuring me beyond the comprehension of the words that I'm using.

"Vampire, huh?"

I feel impatience flare up in me, but I bite down on it as hard as possible. What would the blue man's blood taste like?

"Yes. And I am addicted to phoenix blood," I answer with fire in my tone.

His face contorts into suspicious intrigue. "I've never heard of a phoenix blood addiction before. I have heard of Goblin Fire addiction; a cross between siren and vampire venom. The cure for that is detoxing, suffering through the sickness, and feeding on the fae's blood. We sell that in the back. Do you want to try that?"

"Better than nothing, I guess."

"Follow me."

The blue man walks around the counter, and Laureya and I follow. On his way to a swinging wooden door, he opens a cabinet, pulls out a white tube almost resembling a toothpaste container and hands that to Laureya. Then we walk through another glass door. "Take this and rub it on your burns in the morning and night. They should begin to fade after about a week."

Laureya takes it as we follow him down a long hallway to a locked door. He pulls out a key and opens it.

The room we enter is refrigerated and has bags upon bags of blood. They're on pegs on revolving shelves. The blue man leads us in and then shuts the door behind us. Just the sight of all the blood makes that hunger pang in my stomach growl. But then I think of her blood, the high, the rush, and the surge of power that I feel when I ingest it.

I swallow hard and try to focus.

"So, normally, for a newcomer, we recommend Type X,

which is a combination of fairy and elf blood. It's worth it to buy a bag, try a little first, and see if it takes the edge off the cravings before downing the entire bag. You can buy up to ten at a time."

Laureya's expression is pinched. "What's in the blood that helps the cravings?" she asks as she handles a bag to examine the writing.

The blue man flicks her fingers away. "Fae blood has a healing agent similar to vamp blood. It depends on the fae and the mixture of blood. We sometimes mix X and Alpha Zen, which is very potent and potentially fatal to some."

"Potentially fatal?" I ask, cynicism dripping from my voice.

"Well, even to a vampire, too much of this blood will kill you."

My eyebrows cinch together. "You know we are immortal, right?"

"There are things that can kill you," Laureya answers casually.

"I'll take a bag of each," I tell the blue man as I snatch up a bag. Laureya shoots me a look, and I brush it off. I don't care about the risks.

Blue man grabs the bag from me. "You may want to talk to Tallyn before you do that. Just to make sure."

I grab another bag. "And who would Tallyn be?"

"She is the Luminara Queen," he says, taking this bag from me, too. "She knows all there is to know about every blood drop in the bank."

"And where is this Tallyn lady at?"

He stops me from grabbing another bag. "She is here from Feylight Grove—the Fairy Glen in Scotland."

"He's telling us this like we know where that is," I say to Laureya, my patience growing thin.

"That's where the Luminara Court is."

"Ah. Okay, so can we talk to her?"

"I'll text her, tell her to come in here."

The blue man pulls out his phone and punches a quick message to the infamous Tallyn. In minutes, the door opens and she walks in.

She's mystically beautiful; a spill of long black hair graces her back to her waist, pulled back around her face into a crown of flowers, her pointed ears sticking out. Her eyes are the color of an orange sunset over a Caribbean sky. Jewels hang from her ears and neck, and flowers and leaves decorate her body. She's skinny but voluptuous and doesn't wear any clothes, but the leaves and branches fall around her like a dress. Iridescent wings stick out of her back but are folded neatly.

She immediately makes eye contact with me and the moment she does, I feel her inside my head, wandering around in thoughts she doesn't belong in.

There's a ticking inside my brain, and then I think of Dom. The fact that he's gone dark and Mederio and how he's supposed to kill Sayah. The phoenix—the one to save them from the warlocks. My thoughts start spinning out of control— beyond my control.

This woman is pulling these thoughts up from the depths of my mind without my invitation.

"What is it that you need from me, Maverick?" Her voice is cool and commanding.

"Our customers here, a vampire and a formweaver. He's addicted to phoenix blood and needs a remedy. I thought giving him the Type X would be helpful and brought up the Alpha Zen mixture, explaining—"

"Why would you even bring that up, Maverick?" interrupts Tallyn. "The Zen is for our most loyal customers."

"I just—"

"You. Thought. Wrong." Her voice is deep and terrifying. I'm not afraid of her, but I can see how someone would be. "Go back to your counter. I'll deal with you later."

Maverick bows to her and leaves us to the room.

"So, you are addicted to phoenix blood, are you?" Tallyn asks, a deliciously evil smile playing at the corners of her mouth. Her lips are full and painted bright red.

I nod as Tallyn closes in on me. She's not as tall as I am, but something in her gait has her level with me, coming to within inches of my face. "I am."

"I've read your thoughts. I know of the phoenix and her purpose. I know she is the one who burned you." Tallyn narrows her gaze at Laureya. The way she speaks is calm and calculated, as though she carefully selects each word she's going to use and pulls it from the depths of her. "I know of phoenixes; I have heard of them in my thousands of years, yet I have never met one that has ever come to be. They are supposedly mixed with the blood of angels—they have the most potent blood. The fact that you are part demon and survived drinking it is incredible. To survive that, there must be something hazardous and dark about you." Her black pointed fingernail slides down the center of my face. I hear Laureya snort. "It should have killed you. That being said, you will never truly be rid of your craving. Once it has entered your veins, part of you will always crave it, especially when near the source."

"So, there's nothing I can do?" I back up a step to free my face. "I can't even drink normal blood; I puke it up."

"You can use Zen to shake your craving, but you must go through the sickness and drink the Alpha Zen with Type X every time you crave it. Once you get through the sickness, you can keep drinking the Zen X until it eases off you, and you can drink normal blood again. But like I said, part of you will never shake it."

"I can live with that. How much?"

She takes a short stroll around the spinning shelf. "The price is different for everyone. I'd like your blood in return for some of mine."

"What do you want with my blood?" I balk, my eyes tracking her movements.

"As you can see, I have a collection of different beings' blood." She waves her arm around to indicate the dozens of shelves. "I need it for my collection. The fact that you resisted angel blood is something valuable. I want to explore that more."

I hesitate.

Something about the look in her eyes tells a deeper story. The fae can never be fully trusted; there must be a deeper meaning behind her need for my blood. One she will never tell me about.

However, something tells me I'll find out sooner or later, which isn't good.

"All right. How much do you want?"

She stops inches from my face again. Her blood smells citric —like oranges or tangerines. "Drain yourself to the brink of death. Then you can have my blood."

"And just this once, I must drain myself for you?"

"Oh, I didn't say that, Sebastian." The smile she gives me is malicious. I know I'm promising her something much darker than she lets on.

"And how much of your blood do I get for that?"

"Each time you give me yours, I'll give you more of mine."

I hold my hand for her to shake. "Deal."

She looks at my hand and smirks. "You vampires are so humanly; it amuses me. Follow me."

She leads us out the heavy door and down that same hall-way; her dress swooshes in the silence of the seemingly sterile halls. We go into another room with chairs that remind me of something one would see in a cancer ward.

"Sit," she commands.

The way she speaks to me really grates on my nerves, and I wonder what her blood would taste like, dripping—

"It's as sweet as hers," Tallyn answers, sitting next to me in another chair. "Where do you think you're getting the Alpha Zen from?"

"It's literally your blood?" Laureya snaps, also sitting in one of the chairs.

"It literally is my blood," Tallyn responds in a mock tone, making fun of Laureya's voice in mocked Valley Girl from California speak.

My phone vibrates from the back pocket. I pull it out to see who the message is from.

Sayah: How is everything going?

Me: Fine. Text soon. Busy.

A blonde woman comes in dressed in scrubs with a tray full of things to extract blood. She has a collection of plastic bags to put the blood into, as well as a plethora of needles and tubes to do it.

When she sits down in front of me, I can only think of what the sight of my own blood will do to me. Usually, it would make me hungry, but lately, the sight of blood has been causing my addiction to flare and tie knots in my stomach.

"Take your coat off and give me your arm," the nurse demands as she prepares her things.

I'm really getting tired of people commanding things of me. The killer in me wants to thrash her pretty little neck open and drain her to the point of death.

"Now, now, Sebastian, try to keep your thoughts to more subtle things," Tallyn coos as she prepares her arm for the blood draw.

I send her a threatening look, but she just smiles.

The nurse wraps a blue band around my arm and pulls tight, yanking on some of my arm hairs. I wince at that more than when the needle sticks my vein. I watch as the beautiful crimson pools at the bottom of the bag. Hunger prowls deep within me, and all my thoughts drift to drinking Sayah's sweet nectar. Trembles rack my body and I feel woozy as sweat beads along my forehead. By the time she's done, I'm about to be sick.

As the nurse prepares to get the blood from Tallyn, I stand to try to shake the sickness. The faint feeling is from lack of blood, but I'm woozy from my cravings for Sayah's blood. I bite back down on the bile that's creeping up my throat. I hold out my hand and watch as it shakes uncontrollably.

Pulling out the phone, I decide to write Sayah back, but a new message from my mom lights up the screen.

Mom: Call when you can. It's urgent.

I press call and stumble to the corner of the room, where the conversation won't be too much overheard by everyone in it.

"Hello?" Adaline answers.

"Hey, Ma, what's up?"

"Hey, Hattie and I've been working relentlessly to get Scarlet back. We did a spell and saw a vision of where she was. We know how to get her. We need you and the formweaver to get here as soon as possible. She's not going to last much longer."

"All right. We'll try to be there before the weekend is up."

"Try to get here as soon as you can."

"All right, Ma. Love you."

"You too, Bash. Bye."

When I turn back around after ending my call, Tallyn's there with the blood bags.

"Here is your blood. Be on your way. I'll be in touch."

I take the bags. "So, wait, I'm supposed to just drink a few sips at first until I make sure it won't kill me?"

"It won't kill you. If you can withstand angel blood, you can handle mine."

"What do I do when I need more?"

"Once you drink my blood, I'll be connected to you. I'll know when you need more and lead you to me. Just look for the signs."

She turns from us and leaves the room.

Her being connected to me once I drink her blood is not a good sign. None of this is good. The situation is very wrong, but the answers are beyond my grasp.

Sooner or later, I will discover the wickedness within this liaison.

"**Y**ou don't look so hot," Laureya points out as we return to the car.

"Thanks. I'm gonna need you to drive."

"I don't ha—"

"I don't care, La La. I'm sick and need to close my eyes on the way back. You drive."

I climb into the passenger seat and immediately crank my seat back so I'm lying flat. I hear Laureya huff a sigh of utter disappointment as she gets into the driver's seat.

The feeling I have is like the worst hangover that one could ever imagine. My head is pounding, the sun's too bright, which is likely because I'm not used to being out in it yet—thank the gods for the spelled necklace I always wear that Sayah gave me —and the feeling that vomit is lingering close to the back of my throat.

"So that was intense, wasn't it?" Laureya asks as she pulls the car out of the parking spot.

"Yeah, like super," I mock her.

"I felt her snooping around in my thoughts. It was very uneasy."

"Fae are very uneasy creatures," I answer, hoping she'll just shut up so I can try and sleep.

"But I mean, what was the Luminara Queen doing in Denver? That's just so odd."

"I don't know, Laureya. Maybe she likes coming here to bully all her subjects." I shift to face the window, my back to her. I roll the window down a little to get the air to help with my fever.

"Maybe. It would be like the president visiting slums-ville without a press conference. It's just weird."

I say nothing, still wishing she'd shut. The fuck. Up.

"Did she get into your head, too?" she goes on to ask. I feel the car speeding up as we get on the highway, but I don't open my eyes.

"Yeah, she kept pulling up Dom and the fact he's under Mederio's spell. I don't know why."

"Huh. I wonder why that interests her . . ."

"Not sure," I grumble. "You can never be too sure with the fae."

After that, I'm unsure if she says anything else because I fall asleep. The next thing I know, I wake up to us pulling into Sayah's driveway.

All the feelings of sickness are back in an instant, and I feel the vomit coming up fast. I throw the door and heave blood all over the garage floor. There are a few more wretches, and I stay hunched over my puddle of regurgitated blood until I'm just dry-heaving.

Laureya has gone in already, but Sayah steps out.

"Bash!" she utters, running up to me to help. "Are you all right?"

"No," I answer truthfully.

"What did they say? You never wrote back."

"We talked to the Luminara Queen herself," I tell her, getting out of the car.

"What? How?" Her brown eyebrows stitch together in worry, and her dark blue eyes glitter.

"I don't know. But she gave me some blood—told me to

drink it and suffer through the sickness, and then I should be good."

I know I have to tell her that I'll never fully be healed of my addiction to her. I just don't see the need to disclose that information just yet.

"Well, come inside. We'll get you to the extra bedroom, and you can rest."

Even though she should be furious with me, she's still concerned about me. That makes her all the more beautiful.

"My mom had a vision," I share as I follow her.

"What about?"

"Where Scar is. She needs us there soon. I told her we would be there as soon as we could."

"Okay. First thing Monday, we will go."

I follow her upstairs to the extra bedroom. As we enter, she pulls a trashcan to the side of the bed. I set the blood bags on the nightstand.

"You can pull the shades and make the room dark. I got all the bedrooms light-blocking shades. I don't have any clothes that'll fit you, so you can shower, but if you want, I'll wash what you have on until you can get more clothes. I'll run down and get you a pitcher of water. If you need anything else, just text me."

"Thank you, Sayah. You don't have to be this nice to me. I fucked up, and I know that."

"You did. But it's my fault that you did. I shouldn't have fed you my blood."

At the mere mention of her blood, a white-hot flash surges through me. I feel my fangs urging to come out, to sweep her hair from her neck, bite her, drain her, and revel in the high. I turn, putting my focus on taking off my boots. "You didn't know. Neither did I."

"We just have to focus on saving him now. So you get better, let me know if you need anything. When you're undressed, leave your clothes on the other side of the door, and I'll wash them for you. When you feel well enough, the shower is in there. I'll keep Gauge downstairs and explain that you have the flu."

I nod without facing her, waiting until I hear her leave the room.

Taking a deep breath, I undress, leave the clothes on the other side of the door, and climb into bed.

Tremors cause me to toss and turn, violent, and uncontrollable. The hot flashes take over my vision, and the feeling of retching comes again, so I pull the trashcan up to me and dry-heave into it. I have nothing left in me to vomit up, which is so much worse than actually vomiting. At least with throwing up, you get that release. With nausea and gagging, you just always feel on the verge, but never sated.

Pulling one of the Alpha Zen bags and one of the Type X to me, I pop the tops, take a drink of each, and then replace the caps.

The feeling is similar to drinking Sayah's, but not nearly as potent. It does stop the hot flashes, and the tremors seem to ebb, so I lay back, and stare at the ceiling.

This is going to be a long and excruciating process.

The good news is that I don't vomit the blood right back up.

Feeling the hunger ease, I concentrate on her face, knowing I have to make this right by Sayah. I have to get better and help save my brother, no matter how much I don't care to.

It's Dom's turn to belong to the dark for a little while.

WRITTEN IN BLOOD

-SAYAH-

I close the bedroom door and make my way downstairs. I'm thankful I'd sent Gauge to Austin's for a sleepover before Laureya and Bash returned. My focus was on keeping him away from the addicted and sick vampire, and the estranged sister as long as I could. I miss him and haven't gotten to spend much time with him lately, but I need to get Bash better, Dom found, and Laureya un-lycanthroped before I can be assured he's safe.

Even though he returned with a remedy, I would assume that it'll take time for the cravings to wear off, and a section of my soul is still a little terrified of him.

Laureya's downstairs, scrolling through her phone yet again as I enter the living room. There's nothing really to talk to her about and I dread spending time alone with her, so I go to the kitchen to make something for dinner.

I pull a frozen skillet mixture from the freezer drawer and then grab the large skillet from the cabinet by the stove. Ripping the bag, my thoughts linger back to Dom and where he could be. I know he's killing innocent people as I stand here and cook dinner, and the mixture of feelings I have for him are confusing. There is a subtle ache in knowing he's in the dark, slaying those he comes across. He never wanted this life, and each heart he stills as he's under this trance will take him years to recover from.

The fury at him is still present, even though—again—he didn't mean to kill my parents, but there's only so much feeling sorry for him I have in me before it becomes a question of gaslighting.

He blames everyone else on this planet for the woes of his own life. When will he take responsibility for the pain he's caused others? I don't know if he ever will.

Guilt is the next emotion to pry into my mind, wedging between my sorrow for Dom and my worry for Gauge. What the fuck had I been thinking, giving Bash my blood? He hadn't shown signs of that mark coming to life; why did I think feeding him phoenix blood would help him? It's entirely my fault Bash is upstairs, sicker than someone who downed a handle of rum, and I'm the one who caused it. As furious as I want to be at him for sending Dom to the darkness, my anger at myself surpasses the limit of my fury.

There's nothing left to do but wait.

I can't go with Bash to New York to free Scarlet, get the artifact in London, and free Dom until my weekend with Gauge is up. And I can't take Bash anywhere because of how sick he is.

Laureya's just an added annoyance.

If she hadn't attacked me, I wouldn't have had to try and defend myself against a wolf, gotten bitten in the process, and nearly burned my sister to death as a result.

This whole thing is just a whole-ass mess.

As the dinner simmers, I pluck my phone out and wish I'd see a message from Dom on the screen. Knowing it's a false hope, there are no new messages. I wonder what Claire and Anna have been up to.

"Whatcha making?" Laureya's annoying, singsong voice comes from behind me.

"Just some frozen skillet meal," I answer, stirring the contents with my spatula.

"Can I have some?"

"Yeah, there's enough."

Even though I don't particularly like Laureya, I won't let her starve.

"So, what all happened in Denver?" I ask as I grab a glass from the cabinet and fill it with ice from the freezer.

She tells me about their time in Denver as I finish making dinner.

"What does that even mean?" I question, setting the bowls down, and joining her at the island.

"I don't know," she replies, forking some pasta onto the utensil. "The way she made it sound is that he'll never fully kick the addiction to your blood."

The words are clear as they enter my head, but I don't know what to say next. I gulp. Why hadn't he told me that part?

"What do you mean?"

"It means that part of him will always want your blood when he's around you," she tells me. "As long as he's near you, he'll need to drink her blood to shake the craving."

"And if he doesn't have any on him? Like, say, when we go to New York?"

"Then he'll crave your blood."

My mind goes adrift as I consider the meaning behind this. He only had one bag of each of the blood types. If that's to last him all weekend, we'll have to go back down to Denver to get more before our trip to New York. And once in New York, what happens when he runs out? Surely, there's no way to get that particular type of blood out there unless the Luminara Queen plans a trip there—which I find highly unlikely.

"Tallyn said she would know when he needed more,"

Laureya speaks again when I don't return the banter. It's also like she plucked the thoughts from my mind.

"How will she know?" I ask, forking a bite of chicken into my mouth.

"She told him that she would be connected to him once he drank her blood."

"Well, that doesn't sound good. Sounds like a whole new Mederio situation." I get to my feet after shoveling another bite. "I said I'd bring him some water, and I never did. I should do that."

Laureya watches wordlessly, sipping her own water.

I grab my glass of water before heading upstairs.

Once in front of his door, I listen for any signs of movement, then tap lightly on the door. When there's no answer, I open it.

He's standing before me in only his boxer briefs, his abs rippling. The two sexy notches above either of his hips are like seductive signs pointing to that huge bulge that rests between his legs. He's drinking from one of the bags, and his eyes are white with blue rims. His vampire is on full blast.

Once he sees me, he removes the bag from his lips and his fangs glimmer in his mouth.

"Oh, shit, sorry—" I say, turning to leave the room.

"No, it's okay. I just had a craving, so I was trying more blood."

I turn back around. "I brought you some water. I wanted to see how you were and when you didn't answer, I got w—" I stop myself.

His eyes are returning to their standard sapphire blue. "Worried?"

I can't help looking at his chest as he approaches, his muscles, the parts of me that want him screaming at me.

"A little," I utter, gulping down my desire for him. "I brought you some water."

He takes the water from me. "Thank you."

"You're welcome. Are you feeling better?"

He's still so close to me; I can smell his sweat. "A little bit. Not much."

The terror in me knows his desire is for my blood, not that he wants me. But the danger in his eyes is the same as my dreams of him, and it all begins again. The part of me that screams to run and the other part that wants to burn with him. That part—the burning part—is louder, and I want to run my fingers through his hair, fall into the bed with him, and kiss him all over his beautiful muscles, following those notches to the treasure they point to.

"Laureya told me what Tallyn said about my blood." My voice sounds shaky and distant, muffled by my lust.

At this, his eyes dilate. "She did?" He moves away from me and sits on the bed.

"Yes. She did. Why didn't you tell me that part?"

"Because I didn't want you to look at me the way you're looking at me right now. I don't think she's right. I can kick it. She also said I shouldn't have been able to withstand your blood, and I did. So that's saying something."

"What if she's right, though?"

"I'll fight it. I'll always fight it."

"But what if it takes over you one day, and you can't resist? Then you bite me, and you die?"

"Then I'll die," he answers, running his fingers along the condensation on the glass.

"I don't want that," I admit softly.

His gaze collides with mine, and there's a reflection of my feelings for him in his own. The dimple I'm beginning to adore makes its debut on his beautiful face. "You, of all people, should want me dead."

There's that section of me that yells—screams at me that I should be furious with him for making Dom go dark. But again, the all-consuming love I'd felt in my dreams drowns the danger and the terror I feel for him in its wake.

"I know," I say in a whisper. "But I don't."

"Sayah, listen." He's standing again, setting the water on the nightstand. I wish he would've stayed sitting. It's easier to resist him when he isn't standing right in front of me, almost naked. "I'm going to fight this. I'll win. You don't know the dark like I do. I conquered it once. I owned it. I'll own this."

He's inches from my face again, and he's smirking at me. I know that mouth would feel wonderful on mine. Doing things to me that would keep me up all night.

"I bet if I were to kiss you right now, I'd still be able to fight that darkness."

My breath hitches. The beats of my heart increase a thousandfold. He inches closer and cups my face. My hair gets tangled up in his fingers, and my hands fall to his waist, his skin clammy and cool. The danger in his eyes narrows, then strengthens. Terror grips me again, but a different kind of terror. Not a fear of him biting, me burning, us dying. No, it's a dread of loving the wrong man. Whether that means loving Dom when I'm supposed to be loving Bash, or loving Bash when he's to be my demise and me his.

"Bash," I mutter, pulling my face away. "We can't—"

"Oh, c'mon, Sayah. Can't you admit you want to see if the feelings we had in our dreams are real?" He turns from me and walks toward the window, his tight little ass flexing under those briefs.

"Yes, but—"

"But what?" he asks, sitting on the desk.

"It's dangerous. There are too many risks."

"What risks?"

"You wanting to bite me when you get caught up in our kiss, you burning, us dying, Dom and me being together—or at least up until recently—what that'd do to him on top of the fact he's going to hate himself when we bring him back!"

"Sayah," he cuts in. "I already bit you, and you burned. Do you really think it's gonna happen again? You became the phoenix because of my bite; that has to say something."

"And you can withstand my blood." I'm trying to reason with myself more so than with him. "But Dom—"

"Dom is dark. There's nothing—"

"It's our fault that he's dark, Bash!" I yell. "It's 'cause of me you're addicted to my blood, and it's 'cause of you that he didn't have any blood to drink to keep him from going dark. We can't do this!"

I turn to leave the room.

"I get that, Sayah, I do. But at some point, you'll have to come to terms with the fact that something drove us together. Before you ever met him."

I nod and leave the room.

There's truth in his words. Something greater than either of us understands has drawn us together. Whether that has anything to do with me meeting Dom to meet Bash is further than my mind can flex. But there has to be more to it. I feel this incredible pull to him when I'm near him. If it had only been for him to turn me into the phoenix, wouldn't that have made the feelings go away by now?

I return to the kitchen to finish my dinner and leave those thoughts alone.

*A*s I get ready for bed, I hear Bash leave his room. I'm in shorts and tank top, pulling the comforter and sheets down to climb in, when he walks by my bedroom, heading for the bathroom. As he walks by, he looks in and sees me.

"Hey," he says, leaning against the door jamb, still wearing only those briefs.

"Hi," I mutter, climbing into bed. "Feeling okay?"

"I've kept all the blood I've drunk down. The cold sweats and shakes are still there, but the urge is not as bad. I'm not saying I still don't want to drain you of every drop of your blood and sail to the moon, but I'm fighting it."

"Well, that's good."

At least he's being honest.

"I'm sorry I got so upset earlier," he almost whispers. I don't know him too well, but I do know he's not usually the apologizing type.

I'm special to him—that I already knew.

"It's all right. I'm sorry I did, too. But we just can't do things like that with Dom alone in the dark. Regardless of what he did to me, I can't. I can't imagine how I would feel once he gets home, especially if we let it go too far."

"I know," he says, playing with peeling paint on the door jamb. "I just can't help myself when I'm near you, Sayah. It's not my addiction that drives me; it's some force I'm unfamiliar with. Something deep and powerful, unlike anything I've ever felt. Our meeting has a deeper meaning, and I'm willing to wait to find out what that is. But we will find out, Say. Of that, I am absolutely certain."

I know this as well. Until I met him, I was unsure who my end game would be and even had doubts I *had* an end game person. But the moment I learned that Bash was real, it began to change. It was slight at first and diminished a bit when I found out he had a play in Dom going dark, but it still grows daily.

And I'm still determining how long I'll be able to fight it.

"I know, Bash. But right now, we need to focus on getting Dom back."

"We will. I'll help you bring my brother back from the dark. But when we get him back, and everything returns to normal, I just want you to remember how you felt when you were near me."

"I don't think that's something I'll ever forget," I murmur.

He gives me one last wistful smile and continues his journey to the bathroom.

As I curl into bed and find a comfortable position, I hear the shower turn on. Imagining the water running down his muscles in rivulets, I force my mind to think of anything other than Bash naked in my shower.

Why am I having these feelings for this man?

He's the bad guy; there's no good in Bash. And yet when he looks at me, I see a good he doesn't want anyone else to see. He plays the bad guy very well. It makes me wonder why he doesn't want anyone to see there is good in him. What I gather from his family and their interactions with him is that he wants them to believe he is as well.

Dom is in my mind again. It's only been a day since I last spoke to him, yet it feels like it's been months. I never lose sight of the reality of the situation. I had witnessed him go dark at the hotel. He's a rabid vampire on the loose right now, truly becoming the thing of nightmares. Mederio has to keep him under some sort of discrepancy spell. Otherwise, word would get out that vampires are real, and someone somewhere would end up capturing him—or worse, killing him—and yet, we're probably going to be able to trace his steps by the reports of bodies found.

That makes me sick and scared to new ends.

Dom is a monster. Against his will, he's the thing that night-mares are made of. That strikes a string of sorrowful music against my insides, reverberating throughout me as a whole. And there's nothing I wouldn't do to save him.

That's what makes having feelings for his brother so much more complicated than I'd ever bargained for.

My feelings for Bash are hard to ignore. It doesn't help to spend time with him in such close quarters. It's pushing against the force that's pulling me to him. When I'm near him, I don't think of Dom or saving him; I think of Bash and fucking him.

Every time he looks at me, he weakens the force of me fighting it.

He's becoming my weakness.

I grab Mr. Pink from my nightstand and settle my raging sex drive for Bash.

I'm awakened with a start.

Unclear what awoke me, I suddenly feel I should be afraid. The terror that had gripped me earlier is rubbing up my spine, causing a tingling sensation that spreads fast from my chest.

Someone is in the room with me.

I don't move, don't breathe, and only listen to the fan humming in the background. My eyes can only see my antique dresser against the far wall with the exit to the room.

This means someone's behind me, standing beside the window at my back.

There's a sound of someone inhaling, taking a long and forced deep breath. Frozen in fear, I don't know if I should scream for Bash or spurt to the closet to get my gun. All logic is lost on me, as my only thought is to run.

But where?

Whoever is in the room with me is probably faster than I am

and is supernatural because I set the alarm before I went to bed, and it's not going off.

Before thinking too hard, I bolt out of bed, slamming the door behind me and rushing to Bash's room.

Ripping the door open, I flick on the light and jump into the bed with him, causing him to jump-start awake, too.

He jolts up to look at me. "What the—"

"There's someone in my room right now," I say through labored breaths.

"What? How?" His eyes are squinting against the light. "What?"

"Something woke me up. I don't know what it was, but I know someone was in the room with me. I heard them breathing. I didn't know what to do, so I just jumped out of bed and ran here."

He eyes me. "Are you sure?"

"You think I would just make something like this up? What, just to get into bed with you?"

"Why didn't they chase you into my room, then?"

"Bash! Jesus fucking Christ, get up, and go look please! I'm terrified."

"All right," he grumbles, throwing the sheets off him.

I can see the sweat dripping down his back. He's still detoxing.

Rising from the bed, I follow close behind him, wringing my hands together at the thought of what's awaiting us in the dark of my room.

Bash puts his hand on the knob, squares his shoulders, and pushes it open.

Flicking on the light, it's empty of anyone.

My bedsheets are askew—how I'd left them when I fled—but the window is wide open, the wind softly blowing the curtains in the midnight air.

And there, on my pillow, is a note.

Bash walks around the bed to my side, where I always sleep, and pulls the note up to examine it.

Coming up beside him to read it as well, it looks like it's written in blood.

I am lost.
I am his now.
There's no getting me back.
Move on and find another.
I'll always love you,
Dom

"What the fuck?" I cry out through a heavy breath.

"I have no fucking idea," Bash says, his hands shaking the paper in his hands.

"He was in here? He was in my room, behind me? What, to leave me a note?"

"It's his handwriting."

"But how is he even in Colorado? I'm so lost right now," I say, moving around to the foot of the bed where I slide to the floor.

Bash moves to my side and sits down with me.

"I don't think that this is him, Sayah. Truly."

"But you said that it's his handwriting. It was him. He was here."

"But I don't think it's him saying to move on. I don't think that was him."

'How could it not be Bash? If he was all the way dark, he wouldn't have had the right mind to come in here, not try and kill me, and leave me a note in his handwriting. He was only halfway dark, like he was at the hotel when he was coming out of it and laying on the concrete."

Bash says nothing for a few minutes, maybe contemplating what he will say. "Maybe he knows he's about to go full dark and is preparing for it. Maybe this truly is his way of letting you go—move on so you don't try waiting for him."

"But I'm going to save him. We're going to save him. Why would he break up with me in a note like that?"

"Maybe he doesn't want to be saved," Bash mutters, still looking at the paper.

"That could be." Part of me feels like I should be crying. But I'm just so confused; I don't know how to feel. "But I'm not going to stop trying. I can't."

"I know."

There's nothing left to say. Dom had been himself enough to write me a note and let me go, telling me he loved me.

Bash slips his arm around my shoulders, and I lay my head on his, letting a tear slip from my eyes.

Dom is gone, and he doesn't want to be saved.

A loud part of me still wants to go out into the night and find him right now, to question where his mind is, and what's really going on in it. But I know that finding him is impossible.

"We need to get to New York. I'll have Derek come get Gauge tomorrow."

"You sure?"

"Yes. I need to save him."

"Okay. Then we'll head out tomorrow."

It feels good to have Bash here with me. His whole body is tense, and I know it's because I'm close enough to him that he can smell my blood. He's fighting the urge to bite me and drink from me as strongly as he can, and I feel bad. I should just get up and go back to bed. But sitting here with his arms around me is keeping whatever pain I should be in at bay.

After sitting here awhile and staring at the bloody letter, I say, "You better get some rest. I bet you're exhausted from detoxing and then having to comfort me."

His cheek is resting on the top of my head. "I don't mind. It's the least I can do."

"Thanks, Bash. You're making more difference than you know."

"For what it's worth, Sayah, I think he really loved you, and that's why he did this. To make sure you knew he loved you and not to wait for him. You don't know him like I do. He's a selfless martyr. He's looking out for your best interests."

"I get that, Bash. But he was in my room, in Colorado, with enough of a right mind to write me a letter and tell me he loved me. I don't get why he was in here, all creepy and breathing all hard, like a psycho stalker killer. It just doesn't make any sense to me."

"I know it doesn't right now. But once we retrieve him from the dark, I'm sure he'll explain it all to you."

"I hope so," I reply, sitting up and away from his shoulder. "But I really can't think about this anymore tonight. I'm going to climb back into bed and go to sleep. "

"Do you want me to hold you for a while?"

As much as I want to say yes—being held by someone would feel so good right about now—I know what it's doing to his addiction.

"I'm okay. You should go back to your room. But thank you."

I stand and offer him my hand. He takes it and uses it to pull himself up. His hands are still clammy and cold.

"Goodnight then, Sayah." He leans forward and kisses my cheek.

"Goodnight, Bash."

He leaves me in my empty room.

Walking over to the window, I close it, noticing that the undisturbed screen is still on it.

How had Dom even gotten into the house?

The alarm sensors are on all the windows on the lower floors, but I'd not had them installed on the second floor windows because I thought it unlikely anyone could break into the second story.

If he didn't come in through the first floor—as it had not set off any of the sensors down there—and there was no disturbance on the screen of my room, how had he gotten in?

Was it even him who had been in the room with me?

All these questions swarm me as I shut off my light, crawl into bed, and drift to sleep again.

WHISPERING LEAF

-SAYAH-

The sound of retching pulls me awake.

Bash.

The sun is lighting up the cutout stars in my curtains, telling me it's at least past seven in the morning.

I slip on my robe and hurry to the bathroom to check on Bash.

He's on his knees before the toilet, vomiting up the blood he's consumed throughout the night.

"Oh, Bash." I grab a washcloth from the drawer and wet it with cool water. I kneel before him and press it to the back of his neck. "I'm so sorry."

Trying to shoo me away, he heaves another time, and more blood spatters all over the toilet. I stay where I am and keep the cool compress against his neck.

"I thought the blood was going to work," he groans through a stressed breath.

"Me too. I wonder why it isn't . . ."

Flushing the toilet and then sitting upon the closed lid, he says, "I mean, I think it's working. I thought it would help me keep stuff down. I don't feel like such a fiend when thinking of your blood. But I woke up and got queasy."

"Maybe it takes more than an evening to work," I offer, picking the washcloth that fell to press it to his forehead. He pushes back against it and closes his eyes.

"That's probably true."

"So, when should we head down to the airport?"

"Whenever you're ready. I'm ready. I didn't bring anything."

He's still in nothing but his briefs. I let go of the cloth and he keeps it to his forehead, wiping the sweat from it and his neck.

"Go lay back down. I'll wash your clothes if you wanna take those off, so you have clean undies. I'll do that while I call Derek and make up an excuse for him to come get Gauge. He's gonna be so pissed at me."

"Who, your ex? Fuck him!"

"No, Gauge. He's gonna be so mad at me for cutting our weekend short."

Bash's perfect blue eyes meet mine. "I'm so sorry."

"It's not your fault."

"I know, but you being swept up in all this is straining your relationship with your kid. We can take him to Disneyland when this is all over."

"Yeah, I have some serious making-up to do."

Bash stands and towers over me. I'm eye level with the nape of his neck. I look up into the endless pools of sapphire that are his eyes. "I'm gonna go take these off. So you can wash them."

"Okay," I breathe. Being so close to him always has me rushing to another place in my mind—somewhere far away and magical. "Just leave them outside the door with the rest of your clothes, and I'll wash them."

"Thank you, beautiful."

After a few seconds of not moving, I finally peel myself away from him and turn to leave. Entering my room, I gather things for a shower and wait until I hear his door open, close, then open again.

When the sound of it closing once more echoes in the hallway, I grab his clothes, throw them in the wash downstairs, and pull out my phone.

I will tell Derek that I have a family emergency with my sister. Derek knows I have a sister, though he has never met her. He won't ask questions.

> Me: Hey. I have an emergency with Laureya and I have to leave town tonight. Can you take Gauge a couple more days this week until I get this sorted out? I haven't told him yet, but I will make it up to him as soon as I return.

I hit send and start the wash.

When I'm upstairs again, undressing for my shower, he responds.

> Derek: Yeah, that's cool. When do you want me to come and get him?

> Me: As soon as you can. Thanks.

> Derek: No problem. Hope everything is okay.

> Me: It will be. Thanks.

Now I have to break the news to Gauge. The way it makes me feel to break his heart cuts into me in ways that none of this other shit does. I hate cutting my weekend short with him, and I know he will hate it, too. Whenever I'm away from him, he counts down the days and hours, even minutes, until we're together again.

I just want this whole thing over so I can spend quality time with my son.

After Bash's clothes are clean and I'm showered and dressed, I knock on his door to return his clothes to him. He answers, stark naked.

"Oh, fuck, Bash!" I mutter, shielding my eyes, but not before I get a peek at that glorious naked body of his through the cracks in my fingers. And. Oh. My. God. If I thought his brother was glorious. He is just spectacular. He doesn't have the ink swirling around his muscles like Dom, but his body has chiseled lines and curves, perky and tight pecs, and what, are those six abs? No, eight of them. Eight. Of. Them. All beckoning my tongue to glissade down them like a washboard. He has barely any hair on his chest except for a few little tufts I want to swirl my fingers around. And that dick though. My god. It has to be eight inches long when it's soft. He clearly manscapes, as there is hair there but it's trimmed. Like a perfect little black triangle above the thing I want to bow down to and worship.

"I—I just. I was just . . . I was just going to leave these here for you; you didn't have to answer it." Gods, I'm so embarrassed, I feel my cheeks flush.

It's hot in here.

"Don't be shy, Sayah, I'm not," he teases with a sly grin.

Shoving his clothes at him, I turn around and head back down the stairs, trying to calm my racing heart.

"Thanks for the clean clothes, Say!"

As I return to the main floor, Gauge's best friend's mom, Rachel, walks up to the front door with him. I take a deep breath and hope my cheeks have cooled the fuck off.

Opening the door for them, I say, "Hi!'

"Hi, Mama!" Gauge greets, wheeling up the ramp.

"Hi, love. Did you have a good time?"

"Yeah," he says, wheeling right past me and into the house.

"Did they cause any ruckus for you?" I ask Rachel.

"No, they were angels. They stayed up way later than I would've liked, but it's the weekend."

"Well, thanks again for having him. He just loves Austin so much."

"No problem at all. Next time, you should come over, too, and we'll have mommy time."

"I'd love that."

"Well, I have to run. But you guys have a good rest of the weekend."

"You too, Rachel. Bye!"

Rachel wanders back toward her Jeep, and I go in to break the news to Gauge. His dad will be here any minute.

Gauge wheels himself into the kitchen, Laureya still asleep on the couch.

"Hey, love. I have some bad news."

"What?" he asks, frozen in mid-snack grab from the pantry.

"I have to take your aunt to a doctor in New York, so your dad is on his way to get you right now."

"What, no!" he shouts, his hand dropping to his lap without his snack. His little bottom lip pokes out, and tears well up in his eyes. "Mom, no!"

"Baby, I'm so sorry," I say, kneeling to his level to hug him. He throws his arms around my shoulders and cries into my neck. "I know, love. I'm so, so sorry. I'll make it up to you, though, I promise, okay?"

"H-h-how?"

"You and I will take a trip somewhere. Just me and you, okay?"

"Where?"

"I don't know. Harry Potter World."

He pulls back to look at me, his big brown eyes searching, still pooled with tears. "Really?"

I wipe a tear away. "Really." The doorbell rings. "That's your dad."

Gauge finishes wiping his face as I greet Derek at the door. I open the door for him and let him in. Laureya sits up from the couch, her hair a mess, her burns still bright. I hope that Bash stays in his room.

"Thanks so much for this," I mention, wheeling Gauge up to him.

"No problem," Derek replies, eyeing Laureya.

I'm not about to introduce him to my sister, as I know that's what he wants me to do. Our entire relationship, Laureya had been a mystery nuisance that plagued my dad and my conversations, which Derek always overheard.

"All right, baby, be good. Text me lots. I love you."

"I love you, too, Mama," he breathes.

Bending down, I hug him again before walking him to Derek's big red truck.

"I'll let you know when I'm back in town, okay?"

"What happened to her?" he asks after he helps Gauge into the truck.

"Oh, her usual. Some kind of drama with drugs, and now she wants to get clean after she got in an accident at work."

"Jesus," he adds. "That's what the burns on her face are?"

"Yep. Good ol' meth head drama."

"Well, good luck."

"Thanks. See ya later."

"Later," he says as I turn and walk back up to the house.

"So that's the ex-husband?" Laureya coos as I return inside.

"Yep. That's him."

"Very nice. Handsome."

"Yeah? You like that? You'd probably love the way he lies, too."

Laureya snorts and plops back down onto the couch.

I'm not in the mood for her shit. I'm still upset about having to give my son up early and go to New York to face a woman who killed my parents. "Get your shit ready to go and let's go."

"Off to New York then?"

"Yes," I snip at her.

Bounding up the stairs, I pull the suitcase out from the closet and quickly pack it. Once I'm done, I knock on Bash's door once again, hoping this time he's dressed. Seeing him naked like that again would probably make me drop to my knees and lick—

Not now, Sayah! I scream at myself.

He throws the door open. He's dressed, but still looks sweaty and pale. "Ready?"

"Yep. Let's go."

He comes out of the room, grabs my suitcase from me, and carries it down the stairs.

"Do you have any blood left, or do we need to stop and get some?"

"I have some left. But she said once I drink her blood, we'll be connected, and she'll send me signs on how to get to her."

"Yeah, but that's weird. Why can't we just go to the Never-dusk Dominion again and get more?"

"Because it was her blood," Laureya answers, popping up from the couch again.

"Jesus, are you not ready yet?" I grunt at her.

"I'm ready. We need to stop by the hotel to grab my suitcase, though. I cannot spend another day in more of your clothes."

"Bash, can you flash in and get her bags so we don't have to talk to the front desk lady? In case . . . you know."

"In case they think Laureya's the killer? By the way, has any of that hit the news yet?"

"I'm sure," I answer. "I don't have cable, so I don't get the news. But check Facebook—the 'Let's Talk Wellington' page. I'm sure it's all over that."

"I'll check while you drive."

Laureya slowly gets off the couch and we head for the garage.

Bash loads my suitcase in the back for me and gets into the passenger seat, Laureya hobbling into the back.

As we drive to the hotel, Bash checks the page for mention of the murders at the hotel.

"Oh, yeah," he says. "It's a thing. There's a social media movement on it. Apparently, the man Dom killed was that little girl's dad, and her mom died from an overdose after her birth. They were in town for his nephew's graduation. They're calling it a new age Jack the Ripper murder."

"Great. I bet the page is having a heyday with that."

"Yeah, they have threads of people they think it could be—possible suspects. Some of the townspeople have put up neighbor watch lists. It's basically all this page is about right now." As he talks, he scrolls further and further down the page, seeing where talk of the murders stops.

"Who are they saying they think it is?"

"Oh, just meth heads. No offense, La La," he says, turning to her.

She crinkles her nose at him and flips him off, the red-painted nail matching her burns.

"But it doesn't have us anywhere in there, does it?" I ask, maneuvering the car around the roundabout. "I mean, she checked in; her stuff is still in that room."

"Yeah, it says nothing about us. Thank Odin for that one," he says, his voice pinched in concentration.

"So, you never answered me about going to get you more blood," I state as I turn onto the main road. "Can't we stop and get you some?"

"No!" Laureya snorts. "It's her blood. We got it directly from her. Chances are slim that the Luminara Queen will actually be there again."

I bite back an angry retort. "Wouldn't they have a supply for their other customers?"

"We don't have the time to wander down there again," Bash retorts, setting the phone in his lap. "She said when I need more, she'll lead me to it. We have to trust her."

"Trust the Luminara Queen?" I side-eye him. "After how much you told me not to trust the fae?"

"We have to this time. We really need to get to New York. My mom sounded like she wanted us there yesterday. Best to get a move on."

"Shit," I groan as I turn down the road the hotel is on. Police cars swarm the area, and yellow crime scene tape blocks all exits and entrances into the parking lot leading to the building.

"Yeah, I don't think you're getting your shit, La La," Bash points out when I keep driving past the hotel.

Turning around in a Taco Bell parking lot, I return to the main road, passing by the hotel once again.

"Don't you think it'll be weird if I don't come to gather my shit at some point? They could fingerprint off my things and pin me as a suspect."

Bash turns around to scrutinize her. "Why didn't you bring your shit when you came to your sister for help, anyways?"

"I wasn't anticipating being burned half to death."

"My bad," I say as I merge onto the highway. "You'll just have to buy more."

"I'm sure Jasantha will have shit for her," Bash responds. "They look about the same stick figure size, and they're both bitches. They'll get along great."

Again, Laureya flips him off while pulling her sunglasses down over her face and turning her head toward the window to sleep.

*H*ours later, I'm lost in the clouds that blanket the world high above. The sun is still out and bright, making the fluffy clouds seemingly more magical, the way they glow so illuminatingly. It's hard to see inside the plane when I turn my sight to within again. The clouds are mesmerizing, looking like gigantic balls of cotton one could float on, bound from mound to mound, leaving a trail of white mist in your wake. I try to keep my mind from Dom and the letter he left, how I had to leave my son, facing the mother of monsters.

Bash sits beside me in the middle seat and Laureya is in the aisle seat.

Everyone at the airport looked at Laureya like she's an alien, making her all the more unpleasant to be around. She'd finally shouted at a poor old woman walking to our gate when she stared at Laureya's charred face, telling her that she burned herself for pleasure.

The old woman had run from her as fast as her little old legs would carry her.

Bash's cravings were starting to get worse, and I watched him down the rest of both blood bags when we were in the parking lot of the airport. I hope he'll be able to keep the blood down for the duration of the flight.

"How do you think you'll find her when we're in New York?" I ask as I watch his shaking hand put back the magazine he'd been reading.

"I'm not sure." He looks over at me, his gaze trailing down at my neck. My hair is up in a messy bun, and the sight of it causes his eyes to go white. Quickly, he looks away from me.

There's a slight chance we won't make it off the plane without him biting me.

I turn my attention back to the clouds to let that sinister thought fester. If he bites me and I burn, would the plane crash?

A few months ago when I came to New York with Dom for the first time, he had veilweaved my fear of flying away so that I'd no longer be scared to fly. The fear of that veilweaving wearing off creeps up the back of me, but I talk myself out of it.

Bash has his addiction under control.

Still, I see him biting me in the back of my mind, me bursting into flames, and the entire population of the plane going into panic. Then, from the commotion of the people panicking, the plane dropping in elevation, the engine giving out, and the interior of the airbus catching on fire, causing us to plummet to our fiery deaths, everyone on board perishing.

Shaking the thought from my head, I turn back to Bash. "Are you all right?"

"I'm fine," he answers through gritted teeth. He's pale again, and beads of sweat are gathering on the notches of his neck.

"Do you feel anything in your head that may lead you to her once we land?"

"Nothing yet. I'll let you know if I do."

He seems annoyed with me or distracted by something else, but even the delicate fibers of me tell me not to push him, to let him be, and leave him to his own resistance. There's a palpable air between us. Every inch of him is tense and forcing himself not to attack me, not to drain me of every drop of blood right now.

For the next few hours he says nothing to me, only lays his back on the seat and pretends to sleep. I can feel he's not really sleeping.

When we land, Bash pulls out his phone and texts his mom while we wait for my luggage at the carousel.

I anticipate seeing Adaline again. What will it feel like? She knows I know, so will she feign niceties and try to pacify me or just ignore the insidious truth that she had my parents killed? And how will it go with Adaline and my sister?

Bash is right about her being a bitch, and so is Adaline, so it could go one of two ways. Either they'll hit it off and be like two peas in a pod, or they'll hate each other and one will end up killing the other.

My money's on Adaline.

As we watch bags empty onto the carousel, I hear Adaline's voice in the distance. Wondering if my hearing is getting better with my new powers as well, I turn and see her approaching.

"Hi, Bash. Sayah," she says, slightly hugging Bash. It's apparent she's still upset with Bash about her other son's undoing.

"Hi, Mom," Bash says, patting her back. "This is Sayah's sister, Laureya."

Adaline looks Laureya up and down. "What happened to you?"

"She bit Sayah," Bash answers for her.

"Ah," Adaline replies, avoiding eye contact with me.

Laureya says nothing, unimpressed with Adaline—or she's one hell of a pretender.

"There it is," Bash proclaims, running to the purple suitcase and gathering it from the spinning wheel. "Let's get the fuck out of here."

We walk toward the exit of the airport, Adaline leading us, Laureya lagging behind.

"You doing okay, Bash?" Adaline asks from the front of us, not turning around.

"I'm fine," he responds monotonically.

"You don't look so good," she points out as she walks down the long pathway to the exit.

"Does she know about the blood?" I ask under my breath.

"She knows about my addiction," admits Bash, not bothering

to lower his voice. It's not like it matters; Adaline can hear us either way.

"Not about mine," I say through the side of my mouth. There's something weird about Tallyn, and even though I've never met her, I know her name probably precedes her.

"No, I haven't mentioned that yet."

"What about Tallyn?" Laureya blurts out from behind us.

Adaline stops walking.

We do, too.

"What about the Luminara Queen?" she asks, her body still pointed away from us.

"Nothing, Mom, I—"

She faces us then. "What did you do?"

Bash's body language is like that of a small boy in trouble with his mama."I gave her some of my blood, is all."

'What did she give you in return, Bash?" Her green eyes narrow on him, and her face hardens.

"Her blood." His voice is soft, shaky.

At first, she only stares at him, her eyes switching back and forth to each of his. Then she snarls, "Odin's ghost, Bash." Turning again, she resumes walking.

"What? I needed a cure. That was it."

"You have no fucking idea what you've done."

"I know, Mom, but I didn't know what else to do!"

Adaline says nothing, only furthers her distance from us.

Bash shakes his head when I go to speak. When we walk through the glass double doors, Adaline feels miles away. "It's just not good to ever do business with the fae," he explains. And in consuming her blood, I gave her direct access to me, my thoughts, my life."

"And why is that bad?" I ask.

"Because with her having mine, if she drank it herself, it could prove to be her way into our lives, using us for anything she wants. At any time."

"But how?"

"The fae have a way of twisting things to their benefit for as long as they need. She can use my blood to force me to do whatever she wants at her beck and call."

"But what could she possibly want from you? What do you have that she'd need now or ever?"

"That's the thing, Say. It doesn't matter now; but when it does, it will."

Confusion sets my mind in a tizzy as we enter the darkened parking garage.

When we arrive at the car, Adaline's already in the driver's seat, the car running. Her evil glare is cutting Bash apart.

The trunk opens, and he walks around to the back to load up my suitcase. I walk with him and help him lift it in. He seems to be getting weaker.

"Is she going to be alright?"

Bash's gaze pierces into me. His blue eyes are dull, but there is no sign of the white that has been appearing anytime I get too close to him.

As I am searching his eyes for any signs of if I should be worried about his mom being in a mood, a large leaf flutters down from the sky and hovers in front of Bash's face. It had fallen from the concrete ceiling above us, meaning there's no way the leaf naturally fell. And the way it hovers, it's as though it's hanging by an invisible string. Bash plucks it from the air with two fingers.

The giant leaf morphs into a piece of paper lying on the palm of his hand. Unfolding it with a shaky hand, he reads what it says.

I shake my head, not even wanting to try and understand that. "What is that? What's it say?"

"It's a Whispering Leaf—how the fae communicate secret messages. It has directions to someplace in Lake George."

"For?"

He folds the paper up and puts it in his pocket. "To get more blood."

"When?" I query, walking with him back to the car's passenger side.

"Tonight. At midnight. Alone." He opens my door for me and waits for me to get in.

"Is that wise?" I question before getting in.

"I don't have a choice. Get in."

I pause for a second, trying to find something in his eyes that tells me it's going to be okay, but all I find is doubt. His expression grows meaner, and the white begins to spread in his irises. I slump in, him shutting the door behind me and climbing into the front seat.

We don't even make it to the toll of the parking garage before Bash blurts out, "So, Dom was at Sayah's house last night." Adaline looks over at him, her eyes wide and pressing. "Tell her, Say."

I hesitantly share the experience with her.

"What did the note say?" she asks when I conclude my story.

"It basically said, 'I'm lost, you can't save me, move on, and find another, I love you,'" I mutter, and though the words stab me, I'm grateful to finally feel some pain.

"He was in Colorado?" Her tone is full of surprise. Maybe it's that he was even in Colorado, and maybe to that end, was it even him?

"It was his handwriting," Bash concurs. "Have you been trying to track him?"

"I was," she says, again her tone dubious. "The reports that Everett's been gathering had him pinned in New Orleans."

"Which is not too far from New York," Bash states.

"Exactly. There were reports in hospitals from here to there, but none from there to Colorado."

"Do you think this wasn't him?" I ask, hope rising in the back of my throat.

"I don't know who else it could've been, Say," Bash offers, turning around to offer me a smile.

I wince. "My whole thing is that if he is, or was, all the way dark, how would he have half a mind to come into my house—undetected by the alarms, mind you—leave me a note to break up with me while still loving me, and then go back to being dark?"

"The alarm didn't go off?" Adaline questions.

"No. I don't have them on the second floor, but the screen was undisturbed, too. He could not get inside from the second floor, but if he had come through any other floors, the alarm would've gone off."

"Unless he used magick."

"Dom isn't magick," Bash states.

"He has my blood in him, Bash. He is. He just hadn't figured out how to harness it yet. That's how Scarlet is magickal."

"So, you think he magicked into Sayah's house to break up with her? But why?"

"Why what?" Adaline asks.

"What she said. If he had half a mind to write that, to go to her, and not kill her, why wouldn't he just text us? Call? Come to the front door?"

"I don't know, Bash. Why does Dom do any of the things he does? He may have wanted this to go exactly as it is: her here with you and him off in the dark."

"That makes no sense," Bash fumes.

"I can't make it make sense, Sebastian. I can only offer you what I think happened. After all, you two have had periods where you don't talk, and I've always known him. In the time you lost touch with him, I have not."

"And what exactly do you think has happened, Mom?" Bash situates himself in the seat so he's looking at her, arms crossed, ready for whatever she's about to dish out.

"The honorable man in him knew he was about to succumb

to the dark. He knows you have feelings for her and will take care of her. So, he decided to see her in his last fleeting moments of being partially awake. To reason with himself that this was the right thing to do. Then he lost his nerve, and when she ran, he cut himself, wrote the note, and teleported out of there before he saw her, and something he saw talked him out of it. That's what I think."

Listening to her words pierces my heart, and contemplating the potential truth behind them makes them incredibly difficult to absorb.

"Interesting," Bash concludes.

"Yeah, I really like the part about Bash having feelings for his brother's girl," Laureya pipes up from behind. "That part's my jam."

"Shut up, Laureya," I snipe.

"Somebody's jealous," Adaline offers.

Bash laughs, while Laureya snorts and turns her head again to look out the window.

Grinning, I also turn my attention out the window.

If what Adaline says is true, then Dom really had gone to my house to let me go. What's conflicting in my mind is the way he nearly gave up at the hotel, speaking in terms of ending his life to stop himself from going dark. If he knew he was going dark, why did he come to say goodbye and then turn himself over to the darkness? It's not that I want him to end his life—that's the furthest thing from what I want—but why succumb to it?

"And what have you figured out about Scarlet?" Bash asks, changing the subject.

"Hattie and I've been doing everything we can to locate Scarlet," Adaline says, the setting sun casting a fiery glow on the windshield, so much so that Adaline pulls down the car's visor. "We did a locator spell, and that night while tracking her, we both had a vision. It showed she is in a dark part of the Never-dusk Dominion. She's magicked there by Mederio, who has spells around the building to warn him of anyone who enters but has not been invited in. That's how we figured if we get this one grimspawn out of there and have Laureya form into her, using her essence, we should be able to get her through. Since the fake Scarlet has already been invited in, that shouldn't be a problem because we can simply leave her in the real Scarlet's place. Then we'll have Hattie and Jasantha cloak themselves so as not to be detected when entering, all the while having Jasantha spell the fake Scarlet to go along with all of this."

"What about that whole 'vampires can't enter unless being invited in' thing?" I ask.

"With a magick cloak around them, they can trump the old laws of non-entry to dwellings," Adaline answers. "Besides, that's different in the land of the fae. Since all beings are supernatural in the fae realm, that law doesn't work. It's just the magickal barrier that Mederio has over the place. The law of no entry only really pertains to the mortal world, to protect the mortals."

"Ah."

"Well, that sounds easy enough," Bash pipes up.

"As long as the formweaver here doesn't mess it up, it shouldn't be too hard," Adaline says, still laser-focused on the road. "Now, what will you do about selling your soul to the fae?"

"I didn't sell my soul. I'll figure it out, Mom. Don't worry."

"Bash," she drawls in a clipped voice, "you really have no idea what you've done."

"And I'm just supposed to form into some other person?" Laureya interrupts, slicing through the strain Adaline's tone had swept into the car.

"Yeah. You've never formed to another person before?" Adaline asks, her tone unwavering.

"No," she retorts, hiding nothing of her restraint for casual indifference toward an age-old vampire.

"What have you formed into?"

"An owl, a raven, and a wolf. Never another person. And the wolf is usually unwarranted—"

"Unless you're trying to surprise your estranged sister on a cliff in Washington," Bash sprinkles into the conversation.

"—but the owl and raven, I can do whenever I choose," she finishes, gliding right over his jab. "I usually can't help forming into the wolf. I have no control over it at times."

"Then you'll be able to form into this person."

"Uh, I mean, I'll try. I just don't know how to do it as a person."

"Once we summon her out and capture her, you can take her essence and the spells we've prepared for you to make it happen."

'And how are you going to summon her out of there?" Bash questions.

"They're all grimspawns; they're under mind control already. With magick, we should be able to use Jasantha to get into her mind and get her out of there and to us. That shouldn't be too hard with Hattie, myself, Sayah, and Jasantha."

"But who'll be there to help Laureya form into this woman?" I query.

"We'll help however we can. But it's ultimately up to her formweaving to do on her own."

'I think I can manage," Laureya bites out.

"That is, as long as Jasantha and Hattie don't rip you apart first," Bash adds, laughing a bit.

Adaline offers him a scowl, but her eyes never lighten; saying that she, too, worries about Hattie and Jasantha doing what they do best: being monsters.

NAKUPENDA

-SAYAH-

When we arrive at the cabin, Jasantha, Hattie, Everett, and Ollie sit at the dining room table. Laureya hadn't seemed worried about meeting the family of vampires and the half-siren until the very moment she walks through the door and sees them. I feel her body stiffen, and the air changes between me and my sister to a solidifying, agonizing terror. I can feel this on my sister regardless of whether Laureya knows I can feel it.

Jasantha's green eyes pierce into Laureya's and immediately flash purple.

"Jasantha, no," Adaline shoots at her before entering the house.

Laureya lags behind Bash and me as Adaline leads us into a kitchen large enough to host the Kardashian family.

"All right, family," Adaline announces, "this is the formweaver that will help us get Scarlet back. Formweaver, this is the family."

Laureya says nothing, and this is the first time I've seen her cocky, holier-than-thou attitude slither back into a scared little girl, shrinking into the doorjamb by the entrance.

"And that's your name?" Jasantha glowers at her. "Formweaver?"

"It's Laureya, actually," she mutters, squaring her shoulders to appear taller.

I feel bad for not warning Laureya of what she's walking into, but then again, I'm enjoying watching her squirm.

"Laureya," Hattie mimics. "That's sort of like a stripper's name, isn't it?" She laughs, her British accent making the insult sting more for some reason.

"Hattie, enough," Adaline resolves. "Laureya, come in. Let's just head down to the spell room and get started. No time to waste."

Bash lugs the suitcase into a corner and follows us to the basement.

I pull out the chair to the small round table and sit. Bash stomps over to the bar, grabs a bottle of bourbon and three glasses before returning to the table, sitting next to me. Laureya, and Adaline join us. Ollie plops down on the brown leather sofa, Everett hangs by the bar at the back, and Hattie and Jasantha sit in the plush chairs.

"So," Bash starts, pouring himself a bourbon into the small glass tumbler. "Anything on Dom's whereabouts?"

"You mean, aside from the fact he may have been in Colorado last night?" Adaline asks, taking the glass from him.

"What?" Jasantha blurts. The features of her beautiful face contort with confusion.

I know I need to explain the situation again when all eyes fall on me.

After a heavy sigh, I review the previous night's scenario, reiterating that Bash and I believe it was his handwriting.

"I don't see how it could be him," Everett scoffs when I'm done. "The reports we have on attacks matching his signature would put him nowhere near Colorado."

A concerning prick trails down the back of my neck. "What do you mean, his signature?"

Bash and the remaining family members sit in uncomfortable silence for a few seconds, which drags on, making it seem like hours.

Bash pours another bourbon and tips it back, downing the whole thing in one gulp before pouring another glass.

"U-uh," Ollie stutters when no one else offers anything, fidgeting with the fabric of the couch's arm. "He has a thing he does. When he goes off the deep end, he . . ." He stops and looks at Bash, seemingly waiting for him to finish what he started saying.

"*When* he goes off the deep end?" I press when no one says anything. "So, this has happened before?"

"Not this exact thing," Adaline offers, pouring another glass for Laureya and handing it to her. She takes the glass but does not drink.

I feel the weight of the room crushing me and know I don't want to hear the next part. Something tells me what is about to be said will change things forever.

"Dom has known the dark before," Ollie continues. "He leapt off the world once, long ago."

"Eighty years ago, to be exact," Everett says as he opens a bottle of blood from the mini fridge, his eyes narrowing on Bash. "And he didn't so much leap as he was pushed."

I glance at Bash, staring down at his glass, swirling the bourbon around and around. "Bash?"

"I think it's Mom's story to tell, really. She invented the word."

"I didn't invent it," she snipes back. "It was spelled to help you all, and it heightened when you transitioned, and you know this."

Frowning, I say, "I'm confused."

"Mom spelled a word to make us turn off our feelings so we

wouldn't be hurt." Hattie props her feet up on the ottoman. "It just took a different effect when we became vampires."

'It started with a shaman," Adaline begins.

'As it always does," Bash chides, drinking more of his bourbon.

The look Adaline gives him is yet again hostile; she's had enough of his shit for one day. "She gave me a word in Swahili to spell for my children to help calm them when they were overcome with pain or emotions. Before Hattie transitioned, she was going through a tough time with her sexuality and had been hurt pretty badly for being gay. I used the word to help her, and what it did was something different after she changed. Something terrible."

"What did it do?" I ask, almost afraid to hear the answer.

"It turned off her emotions completely. She turned into a monster and went on a murderous spree. We couldn't stop her. She was the definition of a vampire and became the very thing people think of when they think of vampires. A cold-blooded killer."

An imagined chill laps at the nape of my neck.

I look at Hattie, who is wearing a smug smile, as though the killing spree was the highlight of her life. "I did some of my best work over those few weeks."

"How did you get her to come back?" I look at Bash, wondering what this has to do with him.

He looks at me briefly before dropping it back down to his glass. "The person who speaks the word has to say the other part and mean it in order for their feelings to get turned back on. The empathetic side of vampires, which makes them not monsters, is turned off when the Swahili word is spoken. To reverse it, the opposite has to be said and meant by the person who said it in the first place."

"What are the words? Can you say them?" My jaw is clenched with anticipation.

Bash is shaking his head before I even finish. "We can't. Otherwise, we will join Dom in the dark."

"You can say it to Sayah," Adaline corrects him. "One of my children just can't say it to their siblings. It has to be said with meaning anyway, Bash."

"All right, if you want to tell her, be my guest. I will not be responsible for that again."

Adaline sighs and says, "You have to look right at them and say, 'binadamu ganzi,' which means 'human be numb.'"

"And to turn it back on?"

"Nakupenda binadamu. This means, 'I love you, human.' When my children have done this to each other in the past, it has been in anger, and when they tried to reverse it right away, they didn't mean it because they were still mad."

"Wait, more than one of you has done this to each other?" I'm looking at Ollie now. By way of the previous conversation, I kind of figured it was Bash who had done it to Dom in the past.

"Yes," Ollie answers, shifting uncomfortably in his chair. "We've all done it to each other before. It's brutal and instantaneous. We go dark, we flash away, and we kill. It's our nature to kill, so we return to that immediately."

"All but Jasantha have been dark from it before," Adaline continues after drinking the blood, the crimson staining her teeth. "Jasantha didn't have that spell put on her in the womb because she was adopted into the family."

"It hasn't stopped her from using it on us, though," Ollie teases, and Jasantha grins.

She throws a pillow at him. "You deserved it that time, and I only let you stay dark for a day before I rescued you."

"So what does this have to do with Dom and the signature?" I want to know, as the weight of the revelation is sitting heavily on my soul, suffocating me.

"That's Bash's story to tell," Adaline mutters, looking at Bash from under her long lashes.

"It was in the thirties." Bash slams the rest of his drink before pouring yet another. "We'd been talking again for a long time, but things between him and I are always an uneasy alliance. We were at his house: Ollie, me, him, our girlfriends. Everything was fine until he got drunk and said things he shouldn't have."

"Don't blame it all on him, Bash." Ollie turns to face him. "You said things, too."

"Let me guess," I interrupt. "Sadie?"

"How'd you know?" Ollie jokes and winks at me.

I return the smile. "What happened this time?"

"Oh, the woman Dom was with said something about marriage," Ollie answers, taking the blood Everett hands him. "Dom brushed it off. Bash mentioned Dom had been engaged before, but it didn't go anywhere. You can guess what happened then."

"It didn't go quite like that," Bash retorts, peeling off the bourbon bottle label. "She had mentioned being engaged. He said he was once, but I ruined that. I corrected him, mentioned she had feelings for me, too, and had left him. One thing led to another, and we fought. I spoke the words. He went dark, killed my girlfriend, then left."

"Not before you killed his girlfriend in return," Ollie adds, swirling the dark red liquid around in his glass.

Bash winces, then takes another drink. "That's when he turned into a 1930s Jack the Ripper—killed dozens of women, all up and down the East Coast. Ripped them apart."

At the thought of my boyfriend mangling women, I shiver. Chills spread throughout my body.

"Bash let him go on for weeks like that," Everett chimes in, setting his blood on the table and leaning on it to glare at Bash. "He wouldn't go out and find him."

Bash makes a non-committal noise. "I knew I wouldn't mean it if I tried saying the words, and trying to find him would be a waste of time. He left a trail of bodies, though, so we knew where he was."

"He was still in there, though," Hattie adds. "We could tell he was begging to be saved."

"How did you know that?" I ask, wishing I had something to drink.

My mouth has gone dry.

"Because every time he ripped some girl apart," Bash says, rising from the table, "he put her back together and tied her head back on with a scarlet ribbon. Beckoning Scarlet to come to save him."

"Scarlet could have saved him?" I utter, watching as Bash fills his glass with water.

"No, but he wanted Scarlet to convince Bash to." Hattie takes her own glass of blood Everett had given her. "And she did."

"Scarlet helped me find a reason to go out and save him from the dark." Bash walks back over and hands me the water. "So I did. But not before his murders took a toll on him. When I got him back, he was so wrecked. He couldn't even look at me. And that's why we didn't speak for eighty years. Right up until that night I met you."

I nod in thanks and take a drink as he sits again.

"And that's why he hates killing as much as he does," Adaline adds, looking at Bash. "Why it wrecks him. He returns to that lonely place where his brother left him for weeks."

I ignore the way Bash looks at me and get back on track. "And that's what's happening now? If someone says the words, it'll bring him back to the light?"

"Not necessarily," Adaline states, scratching her nose, "He's leaving ribbons on women, so we know where he is. His mind is flipped off, so that's what's similar, but it's because he's marked. It won't be as simple as saying the words and having his mind come back. But his mind is in the same state as when the

Swahili words are spoken. That's likely how he wrote the note and is tying ribbons around his victim's necks."

"And it's because of these ribbons that you've been able to track him?"

"Well, yes and no," Everett says, pulling up a chair to sit beside Adaline.

"Everett has an assistant," Adaline cuts in, holding his hand on the table, "that knows about us and helps keep tabs on other hospitals around the country that have the same systems as we do to try and keep an eye on the other vampires. There are always random incidents with animals and occurrences where people are drained of blood. He was able to somewhat trace him from New York to New Orleans that way. But then came two reports of women being decapitated and a red ribbon used to tie their heads back on. That was in Georgia."

"So it still makes no sense that he was in Colorado last night." I tighten my grip on my glass of water. "Even with vamp power, there's no way he would have been able to do all of this in a matter of days and then end up in Colorado last night."

"You're right; it makes no sense," Adaline says. "But there are no other explanations for it."

"And you guys have tried to do a Locator Spell on Dom already, right?"

"We have," Hattie answers.

"And?"

"The spell did nothing," she says, tying a string around her finger. "It sat still. The pendulum we used didn't even flinch."

I scrunch my nose. "What does that mean?"

"It means he has a glamour on him, so no one can locate him," Bash answers coolly, twirling the bourbon. When no one else speaks for a few minutes, he continues, "Well, let's get this party started then, shall we?" His cheeks are flushed like all the booze has gone to his head.

At least it's keeping his addiction off his mind.

"What should we start with?" Everett asks, shifting his weight in the chair.

"I'd say getting the grim here first so Laureya can do what she needs to do to form into her," Bash offers. There's a slur to his words now. "Then spelling the fake Scarlet, preparing our cloaking spell, and getting Scarlet home. Have you checked in on her recently?" Bash drinks straight from the bottle.

Can vampires get drunk?

"The last time we did, she was barely moving," Adaline answers, taking the bottle from him. "She isn't healing fast, so Mederio is working some magick over her. She had chunks of flesh missing from every limb, and she was emaciated. He's probably feeding her the blood she needs to survive, but just barely."

"What does he even want with her?" I ask, watching Bash try to grab the bottle back. "I mean, he has Dom as his vampire; why does he need Scarlet, too? If he's not using her for his grim purposes."

"To have leverage over us in case you do something to kill one of the warlocks," Ollie clarifies, standing and stretching.

"But he has my son," I retort. "He threatened to do that. I just don't understand the point of keeping Scarlet if she is just sitting in a cell, wasting away."

"If you want to figure out Mederio's mind, why don't you volunteer yourself to be his? You'll have all the time in the world for that," Hattie spits at me.

My heart sinks. That chronic pathological people-pleaser just reduced in height to two inches small. I don't know if I'll ever get the female vampires to entirely like me, and part of me is at war with the other part that shouldn't care so much. They'll always be the murdery villains they are.

"All right." Adaline intervenes again, finally letting go of the bottle, and Bash hugs it to his chest. "Hattie, make yourself useful and prepare the spell we made. Jasantha and Sayah, you can help her with that. We'll prepare Laureya's potion for her as soon as that is done. Boys, just wait for us to need you."

Bash holds up the bottle, saluting, and then drinks again.

Laureya stands, having watched the entire exchange in silence, and scrunches up her nose as she approaches the cauldron. "Oh, what's in that? It stinks!"

Adaline scowls at her. "It's a concoction that'll help me summon the person you need to form into. Now, close your eyes, and concentrate. The lot of you."

With her words, I ask no questions, and try to clear my mind so that I can give Adaline whatever she needs from me.

Adaline chants words in that strange language again, and Hattie and Jasantha say them to her. As their chants grow louder, the liquid in the cauldron absconds its ugly, frothy brown color, and turns a glowing green that bubbles. In true witch fashion, the bubbles and the neon green potion rise to the rim, and at this we all join hands.

At their touch, my mind follows the smoke up through the roof, out into the world, and onto the cool breeze that travels southward toward Manhattan. The buildings and cars whiz by, and within a moment, we're in the city's heart. Continuing its journey, the smoke billows forth, close to the ground, in and around people's legs as they walk the streets.

Through the bustling city, the smoke ripples to the fountains that have been constructed in memorialization of the fallen in the attacks of 9/11. The smoke travels deep into the underground depths through the waterfall and in through a crack. It's a mirror of the city above, except the people down here are much different. The fae are abounding; some with horns, some with hues of pink, purple, and orange. Wings of blue, some with gold, others translucent. Centaurs are among the other horse-drawn carriages that bustle along cobblestone streets.

The smoke waves around the ankles of different fae, among some vampires, goblins, and other dark things, then travels to a dissonant part of the city that would suffice as this city's ghetto. An old, rundown-looking apartment building sits on the corner of two busy streets, and the smoke suddenly shifts upward to shoot up to the second floor through a busted-out window. It passes by Scarlet, who's magicked to a room; the purple-ish shield undulates as the smoke penetrates in and out of it, through the locked door and down the hall to where the culprit who's to inhale the smoke rests.

This woman is frail and sickly looking, her brown hair matted to her head on the mattress she lies on. She's shaking and looks cold. The eyes that are supposed to have color are black, yet she still has a blank stare, as though her mind is nowhere near and hasn't been for a long time. The smoke flits up to her nose and enters her mind, stirring something in the darkness that tells her to get up, grab her black hoodie, and travel to the address where we await her.

Like magick, the woman rises, walks over to the door, slugs on her black hoodie, and leaves the room. The smoke follows her through the rotting hall, down the stairs that are missing boards, and through the front metal door. As this woman makes her way to the street, the smoke dissipates, and my mind returns to the darkened basement and the monsters at my side.

BEYOND DISTURBING

-SAYAH-

"Right then," Adaline says, letting go of Hattie and Jasantha's hands. "She'll be here in a few hours. I'd imagine she'll get on a bus sooner or later."

"What do we need to do to prepare Laureya's potion?" Jasantha asks, wiping her hand where Laureya had touched it.

"It's pretty much ready in the jar up there." She points to the thick, grayish-colored mason jar on the shelf. "We just need to add the grim's hair and then ignite it. Once ignited, Laureya will have to drink it and start her formweave. We need to work on the cloaking spell to prepare for that part of it."

I walk back over to the table. "What do we need to do for that?"

"The crystal Hattie used to make herself invisible when she stole the artifact," Adaline answers, following me to the table. "Once activated again, Hattie and Jasantha can use it to cloak themselves to follow Laureya as the grimspawn in. That's when they can sneak up, get Scarlet, and get out."

"And once this is all good and solved," Bash slurs, "then on to London to get the other artifact?"

Adaline retrieves the crystal before walking over to the drawer. "If we can."

"We have to save Dom," I plead, keeping my voice light and airy, trying to disguise my desperation.

"We will, Sayah," Adaline responds, retaking her place before the fire. It's the first time she's used a gentle tone with me, and I suddenly remember she's why my mama is gone. A fury larger than life takes over me, and I feel my skin threatening to crack open to become the phoenix. Swallowing, I simmer it down to a dull quiet.

It is not the time or the place to solve unrequited murder.

Adaline stands before the fireplace, holding the crystal with her hands cupped over it, looking like she's blowing into it to keep it warm. A shimmering glow lights up the lines of her hands, and before long they glow the way they would if a flashlight were held before them.

The crystal is as bright as the sun when she pulls them apart. "There."

"Now what?" Bash asks, taking another drink of the bourbon.

"Bash, don't you have to drive later?" I remind him, and everyone turns their eyes on him.

"Where do you have to go?" Adaline asks, handing the crystal that's fading in light to Hattie.

"Thanks, Say. Cheers!" he slurs, tipping the bottle toward me and then to his lips.

"Sebastian! Where?" Adaline demands, walking over, and snatching the bottle out of his shaking hands, mid-swig.

"I've got to meet Tallyn for more b-b-blood." He sinks back into his chair with an ungraceful wobble.

"Great. Just great." Adaline scoffs and throws the bourbon bottle into the fire. The flames roar in response. The crashing of the breaking glass makes me jump.

"Tallyn?" Everett asks. "The Luminara Queen?"

"The one and only," Bash answers, slouching off to the left in his seat.

"What the hell, Bash?" Ollie retorts, crossing his arms over his chest.

"Oh, just, please!" Bash yells, standing up with a sway. "Look, I have to get over this addiction for everyone's sake. This is the only way. Should you all find another way, hit me up. I'm going to nap until I have to leave."

And with that, he stumbles out of the room.

"Where does he have to go?" Adaline asks me, regaining her calm.

"I don't know; he didn't say. He got a floating leaf that turned to paper and said he had to meet her somewhere around here at midnight. Alone."

"A Whispering Leaf?" Jasantha asks, a hint of worry in her usually stern tone.

"Yeah, that's what he said it was."

"That's just wonderful," Adaline responds. Everett sits down next to her at the table, placing his hand on her shoulder.

"I'm sorry. Am I missing something?" Laureya asks, her tone starting to re-emerge as her cocky self.

Jasantha's eyes size her up, and purple glimmers like a light on water. "Whispering Leaves are usually just used for the beings of the Luminara and Nightshade courts. When you get one, you're part of it forever."

"And that's not good?" Laureya asks.

"No, it's not good, you twat." Hattie fumes while taking a small step toward her.

"Easy, I was just curious."

"But I thought you were already somewhat part of the Nightshade Courts?" I question.

"We are," Adaline replies. "But not officially. We can go in there, but we don't have any business with them."

"Until now," Everett scoffs.

"Will someone explain this Luminara Court business and the difference between the two?" I ask, walking between Hattie and Laureya to sit at the table.

"The basics are that the Luminara Domain is light, and the Neverdusk Dominion is dark," Adaline explains, playing with the glass in her hands. "But that doesn't really mean much to the fae. The key is the differences in their attitudes, behavior, and how they interact with humans. The primary difference lies in the nature and behavior of the fairy factions, with the Luminara Court being more benevolent, and the Neverdusk Court being more inclined toward mischief and malevolence. The fae in the Luminara Domain are elves and light fairies, unicorns, Pegasus, gnomes, dragons, and anything that belongs to the light. The Neverdusk Court is where we fit in—vampires, sirens, dark fairies, centaurs, giants, trolls, wyverns, and warlocks."

"And so I would just fit between the two realms, then?" I ask with my jaw set tight. "Since I am equal parts light and dark?"

"Yes, I guess you would be." Adaline's eyes reflect recognition in knowing she is responsible for such pain in my own eyes.

"If Tallyn is the Luminara Queen," I continue, breezing past how she makes me feel, "why is she using Bash as one of her pets, or whatever it is she's doing with him? She's of the Luminara Court, not the Nightshade."

"I wouldn't know. I've met her a few times. She's still untrustworthy, but has always kept her word. It's just that whatever you promise in return is completely different from what you bargained for. I can only imagine that something bad has happened between her and Trystan, and she needs Bash for something to do with that." There's a look on Adaline's face, almost a sadness paired with longing. A hint of hatred lingers in the depths of that expression as well, telling me there's more to Adaline's persistence that Tallyn is not a being to fuck with.

I quirk my brows. "And Trystan would be?"

"The King of the Nightshades, or Neverdusk King," she answers, avoiding my eyes. "Her brother."

"And you think something has happened between them that would make her want Bash's blood?"

'As soon as he told me they exchanged blood, I thought of demon blood and what that could mean to the fae." Adaline stops and looks within the glass as though it holds an answer.

'And what could that mean?" I ask, eyeing Laureya in my peripheral view as I walk away from Hattie and sit on one of the cozy chairs.

'With her having his blood, she has access to his mind now. She can see everything he does. As far as I am concerned, that is never good. To have a fae in your mind like that...no good can ever come from it."

There's more to her story she's not divulging, and I know that. I can sense it like one would sense incoming snow.

There's a new darkness hovering over them, and to me, the fog over Bash is just as bad as Mederio's hold over Dom. Tallyn plays a more significant part in their lives, and I'd like to know what that part is.

'If there's a clear-cut difference between the two courts, how can you tell which one is of which court?" Laureya asks from her new spot over on the chair.

'Well, aside from the fact that Nightshades tend to only come out at night," Adaline answers, "there's no real other way to tell. Their antics differ, though. Like I said, the Luminara can be kind; they're usually still after self-gain. But the Nightshades are always unkind unless they have a pet or want you as one."

"Have you had many dealings with the Nightshade Court?" I ask Adaline.

"I have," Ollie answers for her.

"Really?" I ask, turning to face Ollie. "What was your experience with them?"

"Oh, Ayana," Hattie breathes and sits on the couches. "Gods, she was beautiful."

"And deadly," Ollie adds, sitting down on the arm of the chair.

"What happened with Ayana?" Laureya asks.

"Oh, man," Ollie breathes. "What didn't happen with her? She was the most beautiful thing I'd ever seen. I think this was around the time Bash and Dom had met Sadie. I met her riding into town one night. She was off the side of the road; her carriage had broken down. I stopped my horse and jumped down to help. A rock on the road had cracked the wheel. Now, looking back, I'm sure that it was a trap. At first, I couldn't tell she was a fairy; her wings hid beneath her long brown coat." His voice trails off as he recalls the memory. "I helped how I could, but they needed a new wheel. I don't know if she sensed something in me that made her realize I was a vampire, but she was transfixed. Her eyes sparkled. She had short brown hair and wore feathers and beads in it. I didn't realize then, either, that her ears were pointy. I was still so new to the supernatural realm that I didn't know what to look for. I explained she needed a new wheel and asked if she wanted a ride into town. She said yes and climbed onto the back of my horse. We drank at the local watering hole and talked into the night. By the night's end, I was totally in love with her and had forgotten all about the carriage. We got a room in the inn down the street and fucked all night long until the sun came up."

Adaline winces at this and takes another swig of her drink. Blood rushes to my core at the thought of Ollie as a sexual being. I shift in my chair to get it to go away.

Vampire sex is fucking hot.

He goes on, avoiding eye contact with everyone. "The next day, I helped her get her carriage fixed. I then realized it was a very odd carriage for the time; it was black, and the curtains were drawn, but weird noises were coming out of it. Suddenly, she pricked me with her thumb, and I woke up in her lair in the Neverdusk Dominion. She kept me prisoner there for days, maybe weeks. I don't remember. But she had been draining my blood and then feeding me random human blood to keep me alive. She never told me her intentions for draining me, but at the end of my captivity, she drank an entire ladle full of it. The effect of the Nightshade fae drinking a vampire's blood was instantaneous. Her skin turned ash-colored, her eyes went dark, like that of the warlock's grimspawns, and fangs grew out of every place in her mouth to the point where her face ripped open and grew to accommodate the new fangs. She fled the lair and the Neverdusk Dominion, leaving the door open, so I got out. When I returned home, I learned she had murdered an entire village."

"That was when I caught wind of her going into the Luminara Domain and starting an all-out war between the two realms," Adaline mentions, setting her sights on Ollie.

'How did she begin a war between the two realms?" I ask, shifting my legs so my core stops throbbing.

"We aren't too sure. All I know is she went there and began biting the Luminara fairies, turning them into the dark fairy she had become. This pissed Tallyn off and she told Trystan to get a hold of his fae, which in turn pissed him off, and thus the two realms began warring."

"Wow." I glance from Ollie to Adaline. "It doesn't seem like something that would start a war. I mean, it's terrible, yes. But is it worth a war?"

'Honestly?" Adaline answers softly, "I think something happened between the two long ago, and war has been on the brink between them from then on. Still, to this day, even when they've made peace, there's always a chance of war."

"Interesting. I wonder how the two ended up in opposite realms."

"I don't know, but I'm sure it's something that Tallyn won't easily talk about," Ollie says.

"Have you met her before, too?" I ask him.

"No, I've never met her. I've heard of her and seen her in passing. I was in the Neverdusk Dominion, so I saw Trystan."

"So, if it's bad for the fae to drink a vampire's blood, why was there a whole clinic dedicated to it in the Neverdusk Dominion in Denver? Or was that Luminara Domain?" My head is spinning.

"That was Neverdusk Dominion," Adaline answers. "It gets confusing. Tallyn can be in the Neverdusk Dominion, even though she is the Queen of the Luminara Domain, because things are civil between her and her brother. Some fae are right to drink the blood of vampires; it's like a high to them. Hence why you probably found the blood Bash had in a pot shop. It heightens their already sensitive senses. But if the Nightshade fae were to drink the blood, what happened to Ayana could happen again. It all depends on which realms made them. But if Nightshade fae drink, say, Bash's blood, who knows what that would do to them since he is part demon."

"And what if a Luminara fae drank demon blood?"

"That is what I am afraid of. I am not sure of the answer to that. All I know is that it will not be good."

A chill runs up my spine at the thought of how much worse our lives could get. It's already pretty terrible, with Dom on the loose in the dark, ripping people's heads off and tying them back on with scarlet ribbons.

That's my boyfriend.

Now he's the one that's all murdery, and I don't know if anything will ever be the same between us.

All I can picture is Dom, his eyes black while slashing the heads off women in his rage, drinking from them and then putting their heads back on, before tying a neat little bow around their necks to keep them connected. The thought knots my stomach.

It's beyond disturbing.

LUMINARA DOMAIN

-BASH-

Their voices carry up through the hall, and even though they aren't being that loud, my ears pick up bits and traces of what they're talking about.

I'm drunk. I'll be the first to admit that. But it's more so my addiction, her blood, and having to stand so close to her that makes the alcohol call out to me more than usual. It's biting back at the angry whisper for me to bite and drain her.

I close my eyes, try to sleep, and think I do. When I open my eyes again and look at my phone, it's a quarter to midnight.

I roll out of bed, check my reflection in the mirror, and then quietly sneak out the front door.

I don't feel like hearing any more of their shit about what I have to do right now.

The Whispering Leaf told me to meet Tallyn by the fountain in Candlelight Cabin Village on the north end of the lake. I know this because I've seen it every time I visit Mom and Dad.

Using softer footsteps than usual to get to the front door, once I'm outside, I unleash the lock I have on my supernatural movements. After being a vampire for over two hundred years, learning to clench down on those otherworldly powers comes like second nature. It's like a chokehold on a deluge of water, a bandage on a geyser. Sometimes it feels a-fucking-mazing to rip the bandage off and let those powers fly.

Accelerating at top speeds, the rush of it is exhilarating. I use it every chance I get. It's as close as you can get to flying without wings.

It's a clear night. The darkness turns the lamplight coming off the cabins on the lake into pools of gold. The moon is glistening in the night sky, and the stars twinkle softly above me. The wind is cool against my face as I swoosh along the deserted streets, but it feels good against my fever.

The addiction is still ravaging me beneath my skin, and I honestly can't wait until I get more blood from Tallyn to quench my thirst.

The way this hunger consumes me is as if one had been deprived of any sustenance for so long and one bite of even the blandest food tastes like the nectar of the gods. Even though her blood would be like eating filet mignon to a starving person; even the tasteless blood of the fae will suffice this itch.

When I arrive at the village, I find the fountain and wait for her, sitting on one of the surrounding benches.

As I scroll through my phone, looking at news stories and searching for anything about Dom's serial killing—I don't do social media—there's a whooshing sound that doesn't belong to the displacement of water in the fountain. It's two stone blocks separating and moving apart. I turn around to investigate the noise and see Tallyn emerging from a staircase.

"Coming?" she asks nonchalantly.

"Yep," I answer and stow my phone away as I follow her into the depths of the fountain, my heavy boots echoing against the stone of the entryway.

The defiance of gravity as we shift from the floor to the ceiling, spiraling around and being suspended from the tunnel's roof, is mind-fucking. How the energy shifts and solidifies us as though we are still on the ground feels like swimming underwater—but we can still breathe. Gradually, we descend to the depths of the world, and contorted air thickens the darkness, mage lights glimmering from the dirt walls. Broken light distorts the dark, and we emerge from the tunnel into the Luminara Domain.

The tranquil reflection of the city awaits us, shimmering with an otherworldly glow. The mirrored version of Lake George encircles us, the quaint little villages and shops recreated with a supernatural edge. All is quiet here. However, not a being is in sight in the eerie light of the peach-colored sun.

"Any word on your brother's whereabouts?" Tallyn asks as she walks us down a little path along the water's edge.

"You can see inside my mind; you probably already know," I reply with derision.

"Yes," she says as I follow her toward a walkway leading up to a little cabin. "But I just wanted to hear your take on it."

"My take on what?"

"What's really happening with him."

The air in my lungs suddenly feels thin. "What do you mean by that? Do you know something?" Fear of losing my brother completely to the dark skates along my insides like disastrous little spiders, creating sensations I'm not sure I know how to process.

"No more than you do." She stops on one of the steps that lead to the building.

"I don't know much, so any information would be helpful."

"Don't you find it odd that the last body he left a ribbon around was in Georgia, and then he was in Colorado to leave his girlfriend that note?"

I bore down into her eyes, trying to decipher whether she

read that from my mind or if she knew more about it than she led on. "What do you know?" I press.

She smiles and turns, continuing her walk toward the front door.

"Tallyn!" I shout, following her inside.

But she says nothing as she walks down the hall to a room at the end. Whatever it is she knows, she's not going to divulge it to me. Inside the room she leads me to, people are waiting.

There's a chair with an armrest for giving blood, a yellow woman with purple wings that flutter a bit before relaxing on her back, a human-skinned woman in blue scrubs, and a short green man with pointed ears.

"Why the entourage?" I ask as Tallyn leads me in.

'Just people to help prepare you is all," she answers as she shuts, then bolts, the door.

Drawing my eyebrows together, I ask, "Prepare me?"

Dread is a feeling I lack the ability to express, but I think this is definitely a time it should've crept its way up my spine, as this cannot be good. But I'm not afraid of anything, so I shake it off and square my shoulders.

"Sit," Tallyn instructs.

Twigs and leaves speckle throughout her green mesh dress, covering her breasts with their sides on full display. Her hair spills down her bare back, and more leaves and sprigs decorate the long locks.

I'm so drained, exhausted, and still slightly drunk that I don't even feel like entertaining a comeback to her rudeness.

I roll up my sleeve as I sit down and then offer my arm to the yellow lady awaiting me with the needles hooked to the tube.

The human-looking woman tightens a tourniquet around my upper arm, and I wince at the pinch it causes.

Before the needle touches my skin, my addiction flares, forcing me to think of Sayah's blood. That's like the best drug

I've ever done in my entire life. The hot, mushy sensation starts at my heart and creeps through my body, making me want to sink my teeth into her and drain every drop to soar to the moon and never come down. The craving causes my blood to boil, and I can feel beads of sweat collect on my forehead.

FORMWEAVING

-SAYAH-

The sound of the doorbell alerts everyone in the room. Adaline is gone with a blur of colors from the spell room to answer it. When she returns a minute later, she is pulling along the bedraggled looking grimspawn.

"All right," she says, yanking the hooded figure into the room. "Laureya, you're on."

Laureya eyes her, frozen in her seat.

"Well, come on, girl!" Adaline barks, her fierce brows drawn together in consternation. "We haven't got all day."

The grimspawn stands with a vacant gaze while facing the fireplace. Her clothes are filthy and torn, her skin an awful peach color that hasn't been washed in a very long time, and her brown hair is matted to the side of her face. Her black hoodie is severely loose, indicating she hasn't eaten a real meal in a long time.

Laureya walks toward the disgusting being, wincing and scrunching her nose with every step.

'Oh, gross. She smells so bad," she whines, plugging her nose when she reaches the being. She raises her hand, and she yanks a fistful of hair from the being's head.

The grimspawn doesn't move. Although her head sways with the yank, she sits, staring blindly at the wall.

Adaline grabs the jar with the gray matter and holds it before Laureya. "Add it to this."

Once Laureya adds the hairs, Adaline holds her other palm over the top and whispers words. It glows a bit and then sparkles when it's done glowing.

"Now what?" Laureya queries, her large doe eyes wide in questioning.

"Now you drink," Adaline tells her, shoving the jar at her.

"What?" Laureya shrieks, backing away. "No!"

"Do it," Adaline commands, her glare worsening. "Or I will force it down your throat."

I remain quiet. I haven't seen Adaline in full vamp mode yet, and I am curious about what it looks like. Laureya isn't, though. She takes the jar, plugs her nose again, and downs the gray liquid.

Once the liquid is gone, Laureya drops the jar, which shatters when it hits the floor.

Laureya looks as though she's going to be sick. She clutches her stomach and sinks to the floor, her knees falling right on top of one of the broken pieces of the jar. I remain where I am watching, and the other people in the room do the same.

Her image shudders a bit as she keels over even farther, her forehead touching the ground. Her stature grows even skinnier, her hair begins to crimp and clump together, and the skin on her grows pale and dirty. When she finally does vomit, she pulls her head up, and I watch as the features of her face rearrange. Her nose elongates, thinning as it grows the bump where the grimspawn's is, her lips get mousier, and then her eyes go black. When she's done formweaving, she stands, her clothes hanging off her.

"Oh, god, I even smell like her," she cries with her voice coming from grimspawn's lips.

'Perfect," Adaline says. "I'll get the fake Scarlet, and then we'll be off."

'We're gonna drive there, right?" Laureya asks as Hattie begins undressing the real grimspawn and handing the clothes to Laureya.

'Yes, we'll drive," Hattie answers, throwing the black hoodie at her. It smacks her in the face, and Laureya makes a gagging sound as she slips the black hoodie over her head.

"Good. I can't wait for this to be over," she grumbles. "I'm taking an hour-long bath."

"Who's all going then?" I ask as I get to my feet.

"Well, only Hattie and I can be cloaked at once, Laureya as the grimspawn and then the fake Scarlet," Jasantha answers. "But we can all go—just in case something happens."

Adaline returns with the subdued Fake Scarlet. "Ready?" she asks, holding the chain that cusps the prisoner's wrists.

"Ready," Hattie answers, finishing the touches on Laureya.

"Good," she exclaims, leading the way. "Let's go get our girl."

BLACKOUT

-BASH-

As my addiction is hitting full-strength, causing me to feel like I'm going to puke, the human-skinned woman shoves the needle into my arm. As soon as the needle touches my skin, my vision goes bright. Flames scorch me, and a white-hot rage courses through my veins.

I'm no longer sitting in the chair but running through the Luminara Domain in my mind, a part of the realm I haven't been to yet. This area looks as though it was once a grand Mayan city; ruins of pyramids are in the distance, but another modern city is among the ruins. This one is on fire, though. Beings are running every which way. There's chaos in the sky, and the night is alight with flames that engulf the city. The winged creatures fly above, shooting fiery balls of gas at the people running on the ground.

Suddenly, I'm one of the beings running. I don't know what's chasing me, but I know I have to run as fast as I can to get away from the fire. The sun's not up yet, but the fire around me will surely consume me soon if I don't find shelter.

Sayah's running alongside me then, her face bloody and

beaten, with one eye swollen shut. Her lip is busted open, and her long brown hair is disheveled.

"Sayah, what . . ." I try to ask her, but she shakes her head, grabs my hand, and yanks me down an alleyway.

Down the same alley, a gray fairy with no face and rows of razor-sharp teeth jumps out from the dark. It snatches one of the fairies out of the sky, blood splattering on top of Sayah and me. The fairy is ripped apart, and her guts, bones, and part of her wings litter our path to wherever we're running.

HANDS THAT AREN'T MINE

-LAUREYA-

When we pull up to the 9/11 monument, Hattie holds out the stone that will cloak the fake Scarlet, Jasantha, and me.

I'm only able to look at the hands that aren't mine and feel the fear creeping up my insides. I've never been in someone else's skin before, and it's utterly terrifying. At least when I'm the raven or owl, I have wings I can use to fly as far away from a situation as needed. But being in this grimspawn's skin has me so off balance that I'm wobbly when I walk.

Sayah is sitting across from me, trying to grab my hand to tell me she's there, or she cares or some other shit, but I don't care about that. I want this to be over so I can be back in my own skin, out of this car, and hopefully away from this formweaver curse soon altogether.

"Jasantha, do your thing, girl." Hattie leans forward and squeezes Jasantha's knee.

Jasantha's eyes go purple, and she lets out a song that hurts my ears. There's no deciphering what she's singing, but it's such a beautiful and haunting song that it could make time lie down and be still. The pain and sorrow from the octaves bleed into my eardrums, then ebbs and flows away, leaving me feeling changed somehow. I want to take Jasantha's love and heart and fight the world for her. The fake Scarlet cocks her head to the side, and part of her eyes go purple, too. When the song subsides, everyone stills.

"Ready?" Hattie asks me coldly, grabbing the chain from her mom to pull Fake Scarlet closer to her. I shake out of my trance but still feel like I want to run away with Jasantha. I smile at her, and she just winks and blows a kiss my way. My heart flutters.

"Sure," I manage to choke out as I prepare to follow Hattie and Jasantha from the car.

"Be careful," Adaline warns from the driver's seat.

Hattie rubs the stone and goes invisible, holding on to Jasantha as both women turn transparent in front of my eyes.

The door opens, and Fake Scarlet gets out and leads the way.

Following Fake Scarlet, I know from the vision that the fountain will open and let us in.

As soon as we get close, a mirage of stairs appears, and we descend them into the Neverdusk Dominion underneath this large city.

Once below in the under-city of Manhattan, I try not to act like an average person as I meander through the crowd of brightly colored people. I try to act like the mindless grimspawn I am, going through the city to the side where I'd seen the smoke float through.

As Fake Scarlet walks up to the building I'd seen in the vision, I follow her to the broken-down front door and stop as soon as we enter.

Dark beings are all around; sunken into the shadows, creeping in the halls, some standing on the stairs. Scarlet begins to climb the splintered staircase, and I follow, shouldering a few grimspawns as I pass, still trying to walk with their same gait as though I'm a mindless zombie. The beings that linger on the stairs sniff as I pass and my heart races.

Surely, they sense I'm not one of them.

On the second floor, we find our way to the part of the hall where I'd seen the purple force field surrounding it; two grimspawns are stationed in front of it.

Stopping and staring, I don't know if I should just shove my way through or what else there is to do.

"What do I do?" I whisper to the air next to me.

"Just wait here." Hattie's voice comes from thin air. "We'll go get her."

I stand where I am and try to sense when the invisible vampires enter the room.

The hairs on the back of my neck stand as a puff of smoke swirls before me. A Black man in white, with long dreadlocks and black eyes, takes form in the smoke.

SUMMON THE DEMON

-BASH-

As Sayah runs ahead in my vision, which is too real not to be actually happening, she pulls me out of the way in time to see a centaur clobber one of the smaller beings, an elf or a goblin. He's small and green, but as his insides come out of him like a crushed grape—they're all the same color as ordinary beings, dark red, and clumpy.

As we round a corner, a dark fairy flails at Sayah, its webbed wings gray and grotesque, making a harrowing sound as it swooshes in for the kill. With outstretched black-taloned feet resembling an eagle's, it grabs Sayah with them, hoisting her up into the sky.

Sayah shrieks and, as the creature's fangs bury into her neck, her skin cracks open; the lightning that lives beneath her skin lighting up the dark. The creature bursts into flames and combusts from the inside, dropping Sayah hard on her ass.

I rush up to Sayah as sounds reminiscent of a teakettle pierce my ears. The dark fairy melts, her black coal-coated skin cracking to the point she blows up, raining guts and gore onto us.

When I offer my hand to Sayah, she takes it as she squeezes

her eyes shut from the guts. She tries to keep running, but I pull her arm to stop her.

"Sayah, what the hell is happening?"

Her ocean-blue eyes search mine like I'm crazy. "The war, Bash. Did you bump your head or something?"

"What war?"

"This war!" she shouts, flailing her arms around her. "The two realms are warring again, and we're caught in the middle this time."

"What? Why?"

"Because of Dom." She stops and gets in my face, feeling my forehead with the back of her hand. "Where have you been? Are you feeling okay?"

I brush her hand away. "No, Sayah, I'm not feeling okay. I just got here. I have no idea what's happening. I got dropped into the middle of this 'war,' then I found you, and we've been running ever since." I use my fingers to mark the air quotes.

"Bash, there's no time to explain; we must go." Her blue eyes grow wide as she turns to run from something behind me. Before I can even investigate what it is, I wake up in the chair with a needle in my arm, the human-colored lady finishing the gathering of my blood.

The addiction is making me go mad.

It has to be.

Right?

"You all right, Bash?" Tallyn asks from her chair, reading a magazine. "You look as though you've seen a ghost."

"What was that?" I breathe. My head feels heavy and I'm out of breath, as though what I'd just seen was actually happening.

"I don't know. Must be some sort of side effect from the blood loss."

When I narrow my eyes on her, I can see that she's being facetious. "Yeah, I sincerely doubt that. Can I have some of your blood now or what?"

Tallyn stands as though she's about to leave the room. "I don't think so."

"Wait, what?" My vision blurs, and I'm unable to clearly see where she is.

"I have what I need from you. We're done here."

"No, wait! We had a deal!"

"No, we did not have any such thing."

"You said, 'Each time you give me yours, I'll give you more of mine.' I'm pretty sure that was a deal."

"Nothing I say has to have meaning, Bash. Thought you knew that about us."

"What the fuck!" I scream, ripping the needle from my arm and trying to undo the tourniquet.

"It's your fault for trusting the Luminara Queen, Sebastian."

I stagger to the side of the chair, still fumbling with the tourniquet while realizing all my strength has been drained with my blood. They drained me to the point of death. "You . . . fucking . . . bitch! What the fuck are you doing with my blood?"

The human-skinned lady is at my side, the yellow fae at my other side, and the green man with pointed ears is at my feet. I thrash my body, but each movement feels as though I'm moving a ton of bricks. The rope around my arm is causing it to go numb, rendering it useless.

Tallyn's cold stare is hard, unemotional. "That's none of your concern."

'You're a fucking liar!" I scream as the yellow lady ties my left arm to the chair. The human-skinned woman in blue is doing the same to my right while the green man is roping my ankles with twine. "What are they doing to me? Why are they tying me up?"

An evil smile sweeps across Tallyn's face, and the twinkle in her eyes makes them shine yellow. "To play." The laugh that escapes her lips is enough to raise the darkest parts of me, and that white-hot rage seeps into me, devouring all calm.

The rage that surges through the deepest darks of me takes form and commands all of me to bow down in a way that has only occurred a few times in my long life. My soul becomes a guest inside the demon that shares my body.

This is one of those few times.

The last thing I see before I black out is the head of the human-skinned lady flying in a bloody spiral, hitting the wall, and landing on the floor with a sickening thud.

MEDERIO

-LAUREYA-

As I witness the white swirl of smoke emanating from the warlock, I inhale sharply, sensing the evil his appearance exudes.

This can only be Mederio.

Dressed in white amid his dark skin, his long dreadlocks spill down his back, and his dark, lifeless eyes catch me right where I stand.

Before I can even take stock of what's happening or where I am, a blood-curdling scream echoes from somewhere beyond the door.

Forming into a raven is my first thought. I feel the familiar shudder of my limbs and bones and blood folding in on themselves, coming together as a bird. As soon as my wings catch the air, Mederio shoots his hand out, and a murder of crows made of smoke peck into my skin. The attack has me falling back to the ground, hard. When my breath is knocked out of me, I realize I'm forced to turn back into my own form.

The door to the room Scarlet had been held captive in explodes into pieces as Hattie emerges, Scarlet held up between her and Jasantha. Hattie's eyes blow wide and then compound into white as she rushes at Mederio, knocking him into the wall. The rotten drywall collapses easily, causing him to fall through it to the lower floor. The crows dissipate at the break of his concentration.

On the floor below, the grimspawn have become aware of the commotion. They begin their serrated migration, dozens of them lurching, and glitching toward their target. Mederio rights himself, dusting off his white pants, and throws his arms out. Within a blink, he's floated back up to the second floor.

Hattie heaves me up from the ground when one of the grimspawns pounces on her, ripping into her arm. The real Scarlet—who is weak and depleted—hobbles at the creature attacking Hattie and goes to sink her teeth into its leg. The grimspawn kicks Scarlet off him, and she crashes into another wall—dust and debris falling on top of her head.

The ear-piercing sounds of Jasantha's wails cause my ears to ring as I struggle to get up, but Mederio is upon me. Pulling me up, he throws me through the same hole he'd left in the floor.

The moment I land on my back, breathless, dozens of the grimspawns are making their glitched and clunky migration toward me.

RIP HER TO PIECES

-BASH-

The bonds holding me dangle from each wrist when I come to. Standing before the chair that held me, I survey the carnage.

Blood covers me from head to toe.

The human-skinned lady lay at my feet without her head, the likes of which are ten feet in the other direction against the wall. The yellow fae is in pieces all over the room. Although, her wings are still attached to the torso lying before me. The green man, well . . . all that's left of him is a couple of fingers and one of his pointy ears.

There's no telling where the rest of him went.

One clue is the taste of blood in my mouth, which is a little citric.

When the demon takes over, there are times when not much remains of whomever fell prey to that dark. Until recently, I'd always assumed it was just part of the darkness that being a vampire was. Then I found out I'm part demon—now this part of me makes sense.

I wipe my mouth with my sleeve and set off to find Tallyn.

Because I'd just fed, the urge for Sayah's blood shouldn't be as strong as it is. But the need to rip her open bites at me harder than my desire to get to Tallyn and tear her limb from limb.

Fighting against the urge to return to the house and find Sayah, I leave the room of bodies, stopping in the hall to try to sense where Tallyn is in this place.

Since she has a direct line to my mind, I should have a direct line to hers.

Knowing that Luminaras work differently than vampires, this may not work how I want it to, but I'm different.

I'm a tribrid.

Summoning the witch and demon parts of me, I channel the instinct that creeps along the dingy and lonely corners of my being. The witch part of me tingles, while the demon part stings. I think of Tallyn; her gorgeous, evil, nefariously beautiful self, and how she is assuming she can get the best of me.

Dumb fucking bitch.

Letting out an evil cackle, my eyes shift at an essence of crimson in the air.

It wafts in the hallway and out toward the door we came in.

Following it to the scent, I see the door is open, and the crimson floats outward.

Looking around as I step outside, I don't see her anywhere, but the crimson wafts down the walkway and toward a playground in the distance.

Once I arrive at the playground, I feel her. Before she can even appear to me, the tingle of my fangs takes over my mouth, and with a speed that surprises even me, I lunge at her, and feel her appear as I do. I gasp a little at the surprise of it all.

As she comes into view, I pin her down at the wrists and sink my teeth into her neck, sucking the sweet blood into my mouth.

Though unable to fight back against me, she still thrashes with all her might as I swallow.

"Sebastian!" she yells, but I do not care.

I will drain her, and then I will rip her limbs off.

BEING OF FIRE AND FURY

-LAUREYA-

The dark cloud of beings is swarming me, the stench of their presence causing me to gag. I try to scramble backward when one of the giant creatures with melted eyes lunges at me, falls at my feet, and drags his talons down my leg. Another one with matted black hair, beady eyes, and rows of sharp teeth lands at my left arm, while another with jagged features swarms my right. Panic grips me in a chokehold, and as I bat these fuckwads away, the only thing I can do right now is . . .

Formweave.

Something about my darkness beckons the pain to my surface; the awful breaking of bones is swift but excruciating.

As my bones pull and snap and twist and bend, the world swirls to black for a fraction of a second.

Usually, my wolf form takes minutes to occur when it's unbeckoned. For some reason, possibly because I will this formweave, it happens in mere seconds.

I scream as I fold in on myself and come back together as the beast of the forest, immediately ripping apart the grim at my sides.

Most of the other times I am forced to become the wolf, I don't remember what happens afterward.

This time, I remember it all.

I remember ripping apart the grimspawns. I live through the feeling of their rotting flesh underneath my fangs, the way the bones pop as they come out of their sockets, and the sound of the flesh being pulled apart under my jaw.

Some of them bite at me, their teeth like razors slicing my skin open. The blonde fur of my coat is gleaming with crimson. I whip around, thrashing whatever lands in my way. Legs, arms, necks, faces—it all gets slashed to pieces. I howl at the pain, but every part of me knows that if I don't keep biting, keep ripping, snarling, and gouging, then it will be me that'll be left in pieces.

A pile of mangled body parts lies at my feet as I whip around, ready to pounce on whatever comes at me next.

That's when Everett's brutish ass comes barreling through the front door, ripping the door from its hinges with his bare hands. He starts hacking at grimspawns with an ax. Behind him runs Adaline, her eyes white, and fangs barred as she attacks. Ollie and Sayah enter through the broken door behind them; Ollie channeling his earth magick to seduce grimspawns with wind while Sayah starts stabbing at them with the knife she wields.

Sounds of flayed flesh, dripping blood, and creatures emitting sounds that only exist in nightmares fill the rooms. Enough blood is on the floor now that my feet slip with every movement. I go to gnaw at the ankles of one that is thrashing at Sayah, but all four of my paws sprawl.

A male voice shouts, "Laureya, look out!" when suddenly I feel a hundred-pound weight bare down on top of me.

There's a sickening squelching sound, and brown sludge slithers over the back of my neck. The weight of the grimspawn that was on me is gone, and I look up to see Ollie pulling his large blade from its torso.

I nod at him as I get to my feet again. Heart hammering in my chest, I survey what's left of the mangled bodies.

Dozens of grimspawns scatter the floor, and as I search the area for more, Sayah, Ollie, and Everett run up the stairs after Mederio, doing gods know what to the rest of the vampires.

The clattering and banging tell me they're putting up a good fight, and once I clear the ground floor to ensure there are no more surprise attacks, I head up the stairs.

As I reach the landing, I spot Ollie and Everett helping Scarlet from the ground; Hattie and Jasantha are locked in a battle with more grims; Mederio is at the end of the hall, conjuring an angry red ball of power before him.

Sayah, looking battered and beaten, puts her hands out in front of her, conjuring an orange power I've never seen her use before. She thrusts it from her fingertips, and I watch as orange envelopes all the bodies.

I don't know what the power is, but my heart lurches at the thought of becoming the wolf, which is weird because I am already the wolf.

Mederio is treacherously ambling toward Sayah, seemingly unaffected by her power. Death, depravity, and destruction fill his black eyes.

The fire in my bones stirs, and the tingling sensation rapidly spreads until it engulfs me in flames. An adrenaline rush like I've never known fuels me, and I'm running at Mederio, a being of fire and fury while still the vicious animal I am.

He doesn't flinch as I jump onto him, snarling as I sink my teeth into his neck.

A scream worse than death emits from him as fire consumes him. A substance darker than the blackest night solidifies his body, freezing that scream on his lips. The solid black surface smolders, then cracks, lava seeping out from the fissures as I back away. Those fissures burst open, and all the grimspawns around us burst into flames as well.

A STRANGE OCCURRANCE

-BASH-

The moment I've about drained Tallyn, she stops fighting and curls into my mind with her voice.

You can have my blood now. I'll allow it.

Knowing she'll not fight me any longer, for whatever reason, I pull my mouth off her neck.

"You'll allow it, will you?"

Her blood spills from the corners of my mouth, down my chin, and pools in the nape of her neck.

My hands still pin her wrists over her head, and I look deep into her yellow eyes.

Something has happened.

Something has changed.

"Yes," she breathes, her eyes fluttering closed. "I will allow you to take more of my blood. When you need it."

I snarl. "I need it."

"You just took most of it." She still does not try to fight me. Her eyes open again, and in them, I see something I didn't expect from the queen of the fae. "You are a wonder, Sebastian."

I quirk my head sideways. "I did almost drain you. But I will need more. That was our deal."

"It was not our deal. It was your deal."

"I can end you right now," I spit, cinching my hold on her even tighter, bowing my face so near to hers that I can smell the nectar on her breath.

Fear now dangles in her dark orange eyes, where there had only been mischief and mayhem. "I know you can, Bash. That demon in you is stunning. I would love to get to know him more."

"Stop with your games," I snarl through gritted teeth. The demon is lingering on the edge, and it will only take one nudge for it to take over and rip her to shreds.

Tallyn shakes her head, her black hair rolling in the dirt and collecting leaves. "No more games. You may take my blood. I should be fully restored in a few minutes. I heal fast. Like you."

The calm in her voice is replenished, and the fear fades into the depths of the orange wonder her eyes are.

I loosen my grip on her wrists. "What changed?"

She cocks her head to further fall into my eyes with hers. "Nothing," she says in her singsong fairy voice, all mischief and evil gone. The aura about her shifts, and something about her makes me feel she's an innocent creature now, all frolicsomeness gone from her Luminara Queen nature. "Why do you ask?"

Rolling off her to sit in the sand, she remains lying, her breasts heaving in the twilight.

"Come," she says, sitting up. "Let us go back to the house so you may take more blood."

Standing, Tallyn holds out her hand to me, and part of me doesn't want to trust her, but the air about the atmosphere tells me: this time, I can.

SMOLDERING ASH

-LAUREYA-

The room and hallways are smoldering with coals, fire, and ash upon the carnage on the floor.

"What does this mean?" Sayah asks, kicking at a curled-up ash figure of a grim at her feet. It turns to dust, floating on the surrounding air.

I'm in my own form again, blood covering every inch of me.

"It means she killed Mederio," Ollie answers, kicking at some of the soot that used to be Mederio.

Sayah's brow wrinkles. "But does that mean my son is in danger now?" she asks, moving over toward Ollie. "And Dom, is he free?"

"We will soon find out, I'm sure," answers Adaline, who has her arm wrapped around Scarlet's shoulders. "Let's get the fuck out of here, though, and figure it out at home."

"Wait," Scarlet pipes up, wriggling out of Adaline's arms.

"What?" Adaline asks.

Scarlet's face is pale and warped with terror, her hair matted. "We have to get the artifact. I know where it is."

We follow her as she limps down the hall to another stairwell that leads even further up. We climb three more flights of stairs before we reach the old tower that looks as though it used to house a clock.

Up to the very top and into a room that could've been pulled right out of *Dracula*—a room with nothing but skulls, potions, and even a cauldron along with dead things—among these things, the artifact lies on the shelf furthest from the door.

Scarlet runs up to it and snatches it.

Then, faster than my eyes can keep up, Scarlet is gone from the room, fleeing as though the place holds terrible memories. Memories of things that are so awful she doesn't want to spend one second longer than she has to.

SOMETHING WEIRD

-BASH-

As we enter the room in which I'd brutally murdered her subjects, Tallyn makes no mention of it, casually stepping over body parts as she heads to the chair. She presents her arm to me.

"Have at it," she declares.

Scanning the room, I find a kit with needles, tubes, and bags in one corner on a shelf.

As I come back up to her, I wrap the tourniquet around her arm with little delicacy and, as I see the vein pop beneath the surface, the hunger flares.

Not the kind that makes me want blood—any blood—but the kind that makes me want the sweet nectar of blood that is Sayah's.

"Do you have more of the Type X to mix it to make the Zen X?"

"I do. In the fridge."

"So you brought some for me, even though you weren't gonna give it to me?" I snipe as I drive the needle into her arm. My cock twitches at the sight of her flinch.

"I didn't bring it for you," she answers hollowly.

"Who'd you bring it for?"

"That's none of your concern."

As the blood fills the bags, I feel something about her that makes me question her motives again. There's always something underlying what the fae say and do, and this is no exception. There's something weird in the way she has changed, how she's letting me take her blood now—that she had the type of blood I needed but had no intentions of giving it to me.

When all the bags I need are full and her head lulls to the side, I leave the needle in her arm, cap the bags, and turn to leave.

"You will need more again." Her weak voice echoes in the dark room. "That I assure you."

I turn to look at her one last time. She's pale and limp in the chair, her eyes glossy and far away.

"The addiction is getting better," I tell her. Although, I'm absently kneading the blood in the bags. "I don't feel I'll need much more than this."

Her pale lips purse. "You'll always need me, Sebastian. You don't realize it now, but you will."

Stuffing the bags in each of my pockets, I offer her one of my crooked, indifferent smiles. "Maybe that's true, Tallyn, but tonight, we discovered a demon in me that you are growing fond of. So maybe *I'm* the one that *you* will always need."

"The Sangravelli brothers. I like that."

With that, her eyes close, and she says no more.

SOMETHING I WANT TO BOTTLE

-SAYAH-

As we pull back up to the mansion, I cannot help my lingering thoughts as they ponder what the death of Mederio could mean for me, for Gauge . . . for Dom. I wonder how long it'll take for Dom to find a phone and call to tell me he's free of the mark and that he's ready to start the healing process.

A nagging feeling slips under my thoughts—about what he did while he was dark. How much will he remember? There are times he remembers what he does when he goes dark and other times where he remembers nothing.

The car pulling up to the driveway shines its lights on Bash, who's sitting on the steps, seemingly lost in thought. He's holding a bag of blood. He is absolutely drenched in it as well.

When he sees Scarlet, he stands, crossing the distance between them.

The sight of Scarlet is somewhat hard to take in.

Scarlet is normally the most beautiful creature I've ever seen. But her skin has lost its luster. The bruises, bites, gashes, and holes that cover her are unsightly on her normally flawless skin. The clothes she wears are like prison scrubs and they hang off her. Her blonde hair is a mess of tangles. Bruises mar under her eyes, casting shadows from them being so deep their sockets.

The horrors she's endured over the past few weeks are unspeakable, and during her captivity, whatever dark magick Mederio used not only prevented her from healing but also kept her alive on the barest amounts of blood

At the sight of the blood bags, Scarlet's eyes whiten, and her fangs protrude.

Bash backs away, stowing the bag in a pocket of his leather jacket.

"You need to feed," he tells her, though still protecting his bags.

"And you have fresh blood," she points out, inching toward him.

"This is something different, Scar. I need this. We'll find you a nice human. You need to feed straight from the vein."

"He's right, Scarlet," Adaline says. "Ollie, can you go get someone for her to feed on? We'll start a bath and get you into it." She wraps a protective arm around Scarlet to lead her inside.

As Everett, Jasantha, Laureya, and Hattie follow them in, I stop at Bash.

Ollie vanishes into the night.

"Hey," I manage to say, following Bash back to the stairs to sit. "What happened?" I ask, gesturing to the blood covering his body, decorating his face, arms, pants, and boots.

He audibly exhales and gazes up at the dark sky. "What didn't happen?"

"Didn't go as planned?"

"No. They were right. She had every intention of keeping me there and possibly kidnapping me, using me for blood play or whatever the hell that was." There's a venom in his voice and I know that whatever he just experienced is level with me. "What happened with you guys? I see you got my lovely sister back."

"Laureya killed Mederio," I blurt out.

Bash's eyes are on me again, wide with shock. "What?"

I explain what happened in detail and watch his expression barely change.

"I didn't feel anything," he answers when I'm done, touching his neck to feel for the mark.

I think of that suddenly and pull his chin toward me, investigating where the mark used to lie.

"It's gone," I exclaim. I eye the empty patch of skin where his mark used to linger.

"Odin's ghost," he breathes, taking my hand and resting it on his leg. "What happens now?"

"I have no idea. I know that Dom is unmarked now. But I don't know what this means for my son. If the other warlocks will get word of his death and mark him. I have no idea how to find out."

"Well, if Dom is unmarked now, it shouldn't be long until he makes his way home." Bash grows quiet for a second, but he eventually squeezes my hand. "I just thought of something. You weren't the one who killed him. Laureya was. When he put that curse on Gauge, he said it was to make sure you didn't kill him or any other warlock. He never mentioned any other phoenix."

"This is true. I don't want to risk it, though. I need to get back to him and ensure he's safe."

"I know, Sayah." He rubs the back of my hand with his and I eye the dried blood all over it. "But nothing would happen right now. He wouldn't be marked until he was twenty-one."

"Yeah, but I want to look over him to make sure. I want to be sure."

"I understand," he whispers to the moonlight.

It's still baffling to see this softer side of Bash. He still puts off the monster vibe to his family and everyone else. He wants them to believe he's bad.

"What happened with Tallyn?"

"Nothing I want to talk about right now. I need a shower, and everyone else needs to get to bed. It's late."

"Or early," I tease, nudging his shoulder with mine.

I can hear the smile spread across his handsome face.

"C'mon," he urges, pulling me up as he stands. "Let's see what the fam is up to first."

Bash leads me inside, and I let him pull me through the house to Adaline's spell room.

Scarlet is on one of the couches, wrapped in a blanket with Adaline tending to her wounds. Laureya, Everett, and Jasantha are sitting at the table by the roaring fire. Hattie is fidgeting with the artifact.

"Hey!" Bash says as he enters the room.

Only Adaline and Laureya look at him.

"Hey," Scarlet answers, her voice still weary.

"How ya feeling?" he asks as we sit among the brown leather couches.

"I've been better. They just told me about Dom. I'm worried about him."

"I didn't want to tell her yet until she's had time to feed and rest," Adaline retorts, sniping an annoyed glance at Hattie.

"My bad, Mom," Hattie responds, walking up to one of the shelves to get a grimoire.

"What are you up to?" Bash asks, inclining his head toward the artifact. "We don't need that anymore. My mark is gone, and Dom's should be, too."

"That's exactly what brought the whole thing up," Hattie answers, sitting at the table with the artifact and the grimoire. "I want to keep working on this because a different warlock marked Amanda . I'm getting her back."

"And the formweaver wants her lycanthrope curse removed, too. Don't forget," Scarlet adds weakly.

"Your mark is gone?" Adaline asks, rubbing some brown

concoction of an ointment on some of Scarlet's bite marks, causing her to wince in response.

"Yeah," Bash says. "Sayah mentioned that Laureya killed Mederio, and I thought I would have felt something when the mark left. But I didn't."

"Why are you covered in blood?" asks Adaline, just now noticing that he, too, is caked in dried blood.

"Let's just say it didn't go as planned. You were right."

"Bash!" Adaline scolds. "What did she really want?"

"Oh, just me. Long story. I'm gonna go take a shower," Bash retorts before flashing out of the room, leaving only his scent in the air.

I get the feeling there's something he isn't telling us, but I'm too exhausted to press it.

"Did he tell you anything?" Adaline asks, finishing up with the ointment on Scarlet.

"No. Just the same thing he told you. That you were right, is all."

"Well, something happened. See if you can get it out of him tomorrow. But for tonight, I think everyone needs to go to bed."

"I need a shower," Laureya announces, rising from the chair. "Can someone please show me a shower I can use?"

"You need clothes, too," I add, remembering her suitcase was lost at the hotel of horror.

"Don't look at me," Jasantha scoffs when I glance toward her. "I have nothing here."

"Yes, you do, don't be a bitch," Everett scolds.

"Yes, Jasantha," Adaline adds, "Hattie is not her size, and neither is Scarlet. You two are around the same size in clothes, and you have some in the spare room. Go get them and show her to the shower while you're at it."

Jasantha grunts as she stands from the table and storms off, Laureya on her tail.

"Scarlet, honey, you want to take a nice hot bath until Ollie gets here with your food?"

Scarlet nods and lets Adaline pull her up.

"I think I'm gonna do the same," I say.

As I walk up the stairs to the main floor and toward the spiral staircase, I think of Dom again, lost in his darkness. I pull my phone out to check it for messages, but there are none.

The feelings I used to have for him have shifted. They began to morph when I found out he was responsible for my mom's death. But now, it's so warped I know it will never fit back together again. His going dark was not at all his fault, but somehow, the thought of him ripping heads off and tying bows around their necks finalized my evolving feelings for him.

He's different to me now.

He's a monster.

Finding my way to the room I had shared with Dom, I sit on the bed and think for a long time, wondering where he is, or what to do. If I'll be with him after this or let him go. I know Bash is also a monster, but something about him pulls me to him. More so than with Dom. Maybe this is all an excuse to break up with one brother for the other.

Maybe I can have them both?

Shit.

I need to shower.

I undress and let the hot water soothe me once I step in, pooling in my hair, and running down my body in rivulets. I think of nothing as I get clean.

When I step out, I wrap my hair in a towel and slip on the bathrobe hanging from the door.

I realize I need to grab my suitcase with my things, which are still downstairs.

As I'm making my way to the spiral staircase to retrieve the bag, Bash is there at the bottom, bringing it up. Like a flash of lightning, he's at the top, right in front of me, clean and wonderful and only half-dressed, smelling of his danger, cologne, and midnights.

His bare chest ripples in the moonlight that spills in through the windows.

"Hi," he murmurs.

Every time he's before me, I'm left short of breath, feeling my heart thundering while being frozen from top to bottom.

He grips my soul and grazes up against parts of me that feel familiar but have become estranged, like a part of me that existed in another life, not in this one. I feel an ache for somewhere that doesn't exist, a feeling of home that isn't on this plane when he is near me. Bash feels like home.

I manage to find my voice with a simple, "Hi."

"I thought you might need this," he confesses before his eyes align with mine, nodding toward the purple suitcase.

I feel the need to back away, yet my feet are frozen in place. I'm suddenly aware of how naked I am under the robe and my entire core grows hot.

Picturing him in my dreams when he'd come at me with that passion, those luscious kisses, the feeling of his hungry mouth on mine nearly keels me over, and all I can think about is feeling that mouth on mine, just once, in real life.

That magnetic pull of a force that bounds around Bash seems to tug harder at me, and I feel myself lingering longer in his air; his skin beckoning me to run my fingers over his muscles and feel that silk under the tip of my tongue. He must feel the same air because his fingers are suddenly on my face, stroking a wet hair back into the towel that had fallen.

At his touch, a reverberating sensation tingles me, and I feel like I need him to live. That edge is there before me, and I'm ready to jump off it with him into the depths of the unknown wonder that is his darkness.

He inches his face closer, and I'm ready this time. I forget who Dom is and why we're here.

The world disappears; the only two people here are me and Bash. The room melts, the stairs slip away, the walls crumble to the floor, and all that's around us is water and moonlight, the lake, and the stars, the world, and our passion.

His sapphire eyes are a thousand different facets, and they all liquidate my bones to the marrow. The lovely stitches and strings connecting our souls tighten, being sewed back together. It is how it's always supposed to have been. The fabric of his soul melds with mine entirely, as though cut from the same cloth several lifetimes ago and put to the test to find each other in each and every life we live.

"Sayah," he murmurs my name like it's the key to unlocking all the world's treasures. His breath mingles with mine, and I can hear his heartbeat. His hand grazes my hip, and my heart races wildly. "Even before I entered your dreams, I was yours. Every thought I have of you is treason. You're the only one who can bring me to my knees, even though I'm the villain in this story. But you pull me from the darkest depths, and I know I don't belong to any universe that doesn't have you in it."

A glint in his eyes reminds me of something I want to bottle. His darkness is unusual and breathtaking, and I come completely and irrevocably altered by his words.

"Bash." His name on my lips feels like an elixir, a salve for wounds I didn't know I had until they began to heal with his presence. This man. This is the man I've been waiting for my entire life.

I. Need. Him.

"Kiss me."

He puts his lips to mine, and fucking magick is put to shame from the way my body explodes at the mere touch. I crash into him like I've been underwater. He is my air. He is the mountains and ocean and tides and stars and moons and universe. His tongue finds its home next to mine, and I chase it hungrily, pulling him to me in the desperation that clings to me.

His kisses feel like a memory. Like it isn't just a kiss, but as though his lips are trying to remember something they once knew long ago.

We collide with the wall behind me, and I pull my leg up for him to grasp it by the knee. He slides his hands up the sides of my body and pulls my hands above my head, pinning them there.

He presses his body against mine, shirtless, wearing nothing but black pants, and I feel his giant cock get rock hard. It melts my core to a sopping mess. His hands wander down my neck, pulling the towel from my head and stroking my damp hair. I want to find the bedroom. Now. Both of our beasts are hungry.

The sound of someone clearing their throat diminishes the secluded little world we had created, and just like that, the whole house reappears before my eyes.

Bash backs away, his magick and darkness as resistant to leave me as I am about losing his touch.

Ollie stands there with a dazed young woman. She's pretty and thin, her blonde hair bounding around her face in little ringlets.

"Sorry to interrupt," Ollie states. "I just have to get by you to bring Scarlet her dinner."

I'm still pinned to the wall, breathless with flushed cheeks, as Bash moves aside to let Ollie by, fixing his boner by tucking it under the waistline of his pants.

As Ollie walks by me, he smiles and winks, as though saying he's cool with me switching brothers. Yet my heart scolds me all the same.

My senses flood me as I realize how close I got to fucking Bash in the hallway of my boyfriend's parent's house. Even though my head is still spinning from our kiss, and I know how wrong it is, I don't care. I want him all the more.

But. Not here. Not in this hallway. Not in that room.

When Ollie's gone, and before I can think about pulling Bash into my room with me, I turn to go. He tugs my arm and pulls me back to him, not all the way against him but close enough.

"Bash," I start to say.

"Sayah, I know. I know you can't do this with me because of him or blah, blah, blah," he rasps, his cool eyes captivating me in a way that holds me still. I'm against the wall again, and he puts his hands above me, caging me in, looking down at me with his dangerous glacial stare. I'm liquid once again. His mouth holds a neutral line, but I detect a smile trapped behind. I'm undone every time my name is uttered from his lips. "I'll still do all I can to retrieve him from those depths and deliver him back to you. I just want you to remember the way you felt when he was gone." He moves his lips to the shell of my ear. "The way you just felt under the tip of my tongue." Our eyes remain locked for a few seconds more, and then he flashes away, and I mourn the loss of him to the point of pain.

His words hang in the air and clutch me, gripping me so hard I feel I may break from the intensity; chilling me yet heating me like fire.

There's something about Bash that won't let me go. The way he looks at me and kisses conveys he sees me as the woman who hung the moon. I feel trapped beneath the powerful wave that is Dom, threatening to pull me under and wear me down like the ocean would wear down sea glass. Whereas Bash is the air I grasp for after drowning, the rocks on the edge of the world that let me crash into him while being as wild and tumultuous as my soul needs to be.

He is my twistedly wild and chaotic hurricane that's been tempered in fire.

And I want him more than I want my next breath.

UN-LYCANTHROPED

-SAYAH-

The following day, I open my eyes, and immediately pull my phone from the cord plugged into it.

There are no new messages or calls.

Dread creeps up my sides and slithers down my arms to my fingertips.

He should've found a phone by now.

I choke back the emotions that threaten to break apart my eyes.

It may also be guilt.

After the kiss with Bash last night, it was all I could think about for hours. I think I got out of bed four times and had my hand on the knob before talking myself out of it.

Regardless of what happened between Dom and me—the animosity that is curdling my insides about my parents and the horrendous things he's done while being dark—I still need to make one hundred percent sure we're done before going all the way with Bash.

I'm usually not the cheating type.

Rising out of bed, I quickly dress and head to the kitchen for coffee. The only person stirring around this part of the house is Ollie.

I'm kind of dreading what he's gonna say to me, catching Bash and me in that lust-filled lip-lock, nearly tearing each other's clothes—what little we had on—off.

He had to have seen Bash's boner, too; it was hard to miss.

"Good morning," he says, filling a teapot with water.

"Morning," I offer shyly, grabbing a cup from the cabinet and walking over near him to the coffee maker.

"Sleep well?" he asks as I set up everything for my cup. I can tell he's just being nice; there's no venom or ill will toward me in his voice at all.

"I did, thank you. Did Scarlet enjoy her dinner?"

"She did," he replies as he sets the kettle on the burner. The clicks of the burner fires as he turns the knob all the way up to ten. "She got her fill, and we sent the human on her way. No murder."

Not surprised that this is the topic of conversation— whether or not there was a murder—I brush right past it. "That's good. I bet she's just glad to be home."

"Absolutely. We're happy she is, too."

"Of course," I answer, spooning some sugar into the mug. "What's the plan for the day?"

He laughs as he sits on the barstool at the island. "Oh, you know. Breaking curses and making vampires."

There's something more that Ollie wants to say to me; I can feel it. But I brush it off, smiling at him as I turn to go to the spell room.

"Sayah," he calls after me, and I know now he will mention something about it.

"Yes?"

His eyes are soft and comforting. "I know both of my brothers better than anyone. I don't know you that well, but I can tell you're a good person who's been through some tough times." His voice is as soft as his eyes, and I know he isn't going to belittle me about my midnight rendezvous with Bash. I listen intently, gripping my hot coffee as though it will protect me. "Dom needs someone like you to keep him sane, save him from the dark he detests, and keep his soul serene. Dom has a pure heart, and his intentions, and soul belong in the light. But Bash . . ." At this, he looks toward the windows and out at the lake, his mind gently caressing the thoughts of his brother. "Bash needs you for entirely different reasons. Bash has always yearned for the dark, as though he was always meant to be a part of it. Be that as it may, it might have always been the demon in him leading him to that dark. He needs someone like you to show him the part that belongs in the light. He has good in him, too; it's just buried deep, so deep not even *he* knows it's there. He believes himself to be a monster, so he needs someone like you to show him that side of himself. I think that person is you."

I grasp his every word and let them surround me like heat from a lamp on a cold Colorado morning. I was scared that Ollie would have told me horror stories of Bash or list reasons why I shouldn't have been kissing him. Instead, he decided to tell me lovely little stories about how Bash has a side of him not even he knows exists. It warms the cold that had sunk into my bones at the thought of betraying one brother for the other. Strangely, Ollie's words warm me, soothing the regret I know I should feel more of.

Words escape me, though, and I don't know what to say.

"I know you love Dom," he continues when I say nothing. "I know you probably will have a choice to make at some point—one that will nearly kill you to choose. I just want you to know I will support whichever brother you choose. But when that time comes, just know you will lose the other one. Bash loves you, and it's easy for me to see, but I don't even think he knows it yet. I have never seen him so unlike himself to anyone before, except toward me. Not even toward his sisters. He's gentle with you.

You bring out the human in him that I haven't seen in over two hundred years."

Catching his gentle green eyes again, I feel at ease. Although I've never gotten to talk to Ollie like this one-on-one, it isn't awkward or uncomfortable. That's one of the traits of vampires—having the power to make you feel calm, collected, and at ease right before they bite or kill you. But this isn't at all what's happening here. The empath in me knows it's genuine.

"Thanks, Ollie. I don't know what to do with that right now. But I will remember it."

"No problem, Sayah. Now"—he stands as the tea kettle starts to whistle—"go help them cure your sister of her formweaver curse."

Giving him a gentle smile, I turn and walk away.

Hearing Ollie say that Bash loves me is incomprehensible. I never put that word to what I feel for him in my waking life, though I know that's what I feel in my dreams. But that's where the feelings remain for him—in my dreams. In real life, yes, I'm drawn to him. That's also part of his power; every time I'm near him, I can't move or breathe, and I know that's something in his magick that causes me to feel that way. But saying I love Bash is hard to wrap my mind around.

He's also addicted to my blood, which could also play a massive part in why he's drawn to me. But does he love me? I can't answer that, fathom it, or even think more about it because it hurts my brain.

Entering the spell room, I find Adaline, Hattie, Jasantha, and Scarlet sitting together.

Scarlet looks a bit better than she did last night. Her skin is beginning to take on its standard apricot hues, the tangles in her hair are gone, and the bruises and bites are almost vanished. But she still looks too skinny and doesn't carry herself with that proud 'I will strike you dead where you stand' gait.

Laureya looks better today as well. The ointment she'd

gotten from the Neverdusk Dominion looks like it's working wonders. The burns on her face look like a nasty rash now, and she's free of all the blood she had been covered in last night. She's sitting in one of the cozy chairs, legs tucked under her, reading one of the grimoires.

Adaline, Scarlet, and Hattie are at the table with the artifact and more books open in front of them. They are studying hard to break the curse. Meanwhile, Jasantha is sitting on the couch, scrolling through her phone.

There's no sign of Bash or Everett.

Or Dom.

"Good morning," I say as I enter the room.

"Morning," mumbles Adaline, who looks deep in concentration. "Okay, so I think we have it. We just need a way to know whether the curse is broken without having the full moon."

"You really think it'll work, Mom?" Hattie asks, leaning over her mom's shoulder to see what she's looking at.

"Yes, we just need all of these things here," Adaline points to something in the book, "a few things in this other book I've found, and then a moonstone."

"I have this," I offer, dangling my bracelet before them.

At this, Scarlet strains her eyes to see it better. "Hey, that's mine!" She immediately gets up and flashes over to me.

I back away, seeing the determined look resting on Scarlet's face. "Dom gave it to me."

"Yes, I gave it to Dom to keep him safe."

"It has brought her great power, Scarlet," Adaline says, not looking up from the books. "Let her be. Besides, she's had it on this entire time, and you've never noticed it."

Scarlet glances back at the bracelet and then glares at me. Somewhat defeated, she returns to the table.

"You really think it'll work?" Hattie asks again.

"Why are you so interested in me being cured of the Full Moon Curse?" Laureya asks a little shortly.

"It's not you I care about, wench; it's my girlfriend," Hattie spits at Laureya. "If this works on you, I will use it to find Amanda and free her from her warlock mark."

Laureya returns the glare and resumes looking through the book on her lap.

"What do we need, then?" Hattie asks, preparing to grab the items listed to do the spell that will break Laureya's curse with the moon.

"Seven white candles in a circle," Adaline answers, rising from the table with the grimoire. "A bay leaf to burn. The moonstone. And blood."

"Who's blood?"

"Well, with your curse for Amanda, Hattie, you will need the blood of the person who put the curse on her. For Laureya here, since her curse has been passed down for generations, we will need her and her sister's blood."

"My blood?" I ask.

"You would be her sister," Adaline retorts.

I gulp at the thought, but don't argue.

Hattie sets the candles out in a circle, putting the bay leaves in the center in a small cauldron the size of a salsa dish.

Adaline sets the grimoire down and waves her hand to bring the candles to light.

"What I still don't know," she resumes, "is how we will tell if the curse is broken without the full moon."

"I can probably figure something out," I mention timidly.

I don't like stepping on Adaline's toes, but she asks, "What are you thinking of?"

"I don't know, summoning the full moon's power. I mean, it's still up there. It's always full. It just doesn't have the sun shining on it entirely at all times."

"What?" Scarlet scoffs.

"No, that's good," Adaline interrupts. "We can summon the sun's power with you, who is half dark and half light and summon the moon's power through us, who belong to the dark, and command the moon to show itself on a night that isn't supposed to be a full moon. That should work. Good job, Sayah."

"Thanks," I respond again.

"What are you witches up to?" Bash asks upon entering the room.

I didn't hear him enter.

"Breaking the Full Moon Curse on Laureya," Jasantha answers, almost sounding bored.

"Ooh, sounds so intriguing." His eyebrows raise an inch with false excitement. "If you need me, I'll be at the bar."

"Bash," Adaline scolds. "It is eight in the morning. I don't think that's wise."

"Well, what you think and what I think are two totally different things," he points out as he makes his way to the bar and pours himself a bourbon.

"Just ignore him," Adaline mentions to the group.

Bash snorts his derision. "The bourbon helps the cravings, believe it or not."

Shaking her head, Adaline walks up to Laureya. "All right. Get in the middle of the circle. Hattie, prepare the knife."

"With pleasure," Hattie resounds and fetches the knife from one of the drawers.

"Sayah, your hand, please."

I offer my hand to Adaline, who takes the knife from Hattie and slices my palm open. Taking my wrist, she lets the blood drip into a chalice. After she reasons she has enough, she goes to Laureya and does the same thing.

"Let me see your bracelet? Please?" she asks me once there's enough blood in the chalice.

I reluctantly take the bracelet off and hand it to Adaline, eyeing Scarlet at the same time to see that she has her eyes on the bracelet.

As the candles flicker in the darkness, Adaline stands before Laureya with the moonstone and chalice, reading the words she'd memorized for the spell. Hattie has the artifact, and together they chant, the candles intensifying as the words they recite grow louder.

When the wind is blowing bits of paper around and off the table, Adaline takes the moonstone and pours blood over it, spilling it onto the floor, and then retrieves the artifact from Hattie.

Reading the ancient words from the artifact, the hieroglyphs on it glow blue.

Laureya remains still, her hair blowing in the wind as Adaline chants to her. Then Adaline takes the knife once again and slices open Laureya's other hand. At this blood, she lets it fall over the artifact itself, igniting the bay leaf with a flick of her wrist.

The smoke from the bay leaf encircles Laureya in a strategic dance, wistfully pirouetting around her from her head to her toes. It then enters her body, causing her to stiffen as though it's an entity; her arms are thrown outward, and her chest lurches forward.

When the smoke returns from her mouth, Adaline catches it in a solid wood wand.

Her chanting dies down as the wind simmers, and light seeps back in as though her spell had shaded the entire house. As everything returns to normal, Adaline breaks the solid wand over her knee. A shockwave emits from it, a thunder with no sound and the ripple effect of noise issues outward and forth into the world.

Laureya falls to her knees at this, breathing heavily, her entire body seemingly going weak in the absence of what had been with her for her entire life.

"All right. That should be it," Adaline says, walking the wand to the fireplace and throwing it in. With a wave of her hand, the fire devours the wand. "Later tonight, we can do your moon spell, Sayah, and see if it has worked."

"I'm pretty sure it worked," Laureya answers, her voice heavy as though this is a loss for her. She shifts her weight to sit on her bottom, legs crossed before her.

"Why do you say that?" Bash asks from the bar.

"I can feel it. Before, there was always this weight that lingered in me. It buzzed here and there like an electric current, and the buzzing intensified as the moon got closer to being full. I don't feel that at all now."

"You should still be able to formweave," Adaline responds. "You just won't be a slave to the full moon anymore. Your forms will be your choice, when, and what you want to."

"Really?" Laureya asks, her eyes wistful.

"Yes. The spell we broke was just the curse you had with the moon, not the part of you that makes you form. That is intrinsic."

"And when are we gonna do this vampire business?" Bash asks.

"Don't you think we should wait to see if the curse is broken?" I move to the couches to sit. "To make sure it doesn't kill her?"

"She just said she could feel it's gone. I say we do it." His eyes flash white as he stands, and the fangs emerge.

"Wait!" I say, stepping closer to Bash. "What about her phoenix blood? Didn't you say that vampire blood couldn't be mixed with it? I mean, look what happened to Sadie."

"No," Bash answers, his fangs still out. "It can't. But she was not born the phoenix; she only inherited that from you by being mirrored to you. Her blood is not part angel blood."

Adaline steps in. "Bash is right. The angel blood is what prevents the phoenix from becoming a vampire. She doesn't have that. You, on the other hand, would never be able to be a vampire."

"I don't think I would want that, anyway. No offense," I say. "All right. If that's what she wants."

"I do," Laureya answers. "It's what I have wanted for a very long time."

Laureya pushes herself off the ground and steps out of the circle, making her way to Bash. Once she's standing before him, she tilts her neck and brushes her hair to the other shoulder.

With a rapid and fierce movement, Bash grabs her hair with his right hand and pulls to make her extend her neck, the tendons becoming more defined as he does so. With an awful crunch, he sinks his teeth into her neck, and the sound that emits is gruesome. Laureya's eyes close, and her eyebrows cinch together as Bash drinks feverishly.

The more he drinks, the more her body seems to relax. Her knees give out, and they fall to the floor together, Bash still drinking hungrily.

When she's as pale as a sheet, Bash lets her go. He rips into his own arm to force her to drink.

She grasps his arm with both hands and drinks weakly. His face squints in the pleasure it seems to bring him. He pets the back of her head as she drinks, her blood dribbling down his face.

He still has hold of her hair. He glances up at me with his white eyes rimmed with blue and snaps her neck in one swift movement.

Her pale body falls limp to the floor, and a gasp escapes my lips.

"Bash! What the hell?" I say, running over to Laureya, and cradling her head to look at her face.Her face is slack and pale, the features of it softened by death. Her bright pink lips are agape, hung open as she meets her end swiftly and without warning. The dark red lashes of her eyes rest softly on her cheeks, her ivory cheeks looking more like porcelain in death.

"What?" He stands, wiping his mouth with the back of his hand. "That's the quick way to make a vampire."

I look over to Adaline, who's sitting at the table. She nods imperceptibly.

"What happens now?"

"When she wakes up, she'll be thirsty," Bash answers, returning to his bourbon. "And strong. We should probably go out and get her someone to feed on."

"We can send Ollie again," Scarlet replies. "He's good at that."

"She'll probably kill them, though," Adaline says.

I imagine the young girl that Ollie had brought to Scarlet and her dying for the simple thirst of a vampire. I can't let that happen.

"Let me do some research," I say, laying Laureya's head on the floor, and standing.

"What kind of research?" Hattie asks, retrieving the artifact from the ground.

"Just this thing I do to find people who don't deserve to live. Rather than killing someone innocent."

"How do you deem someone more deserving of life than another?"

"People with criminal records with bad crimes tied to them. I did it for . . ." I trail off at the memory of what happened the last time I did this for someone.

"Yeah, and that ended brilliantly," Hattie hisses.

"Hattie," Adaline scolds. "Do what you need to do, Sayah. Hattie, where are you going?"

"I'm going to go find Amanda. Now that I know this thing works."

"You need a witch to do the spell, you wanker!" Scarlet barks.

"I know, you twat," she retaliates, grabbing a brown satchel from a hook by the door. "I'm taking this with me for safekeeping. I don't trust you a lot with it anymore."

"Just let her go," Adaline says. "We don't need it anymore. If

Bash's mark was broken when Mederio died, Dom's mark is gone, too."

"Where is he then?" I ask, finally giving life to words that have been on my mind all morning.

Adaline's eyes are complex and unreadable. "Hard to say."

"Okay, well, I'll be in touch." Hattie tucks the artifact into the satchel. "I have an idea of where she is, so I'm gonna head there and see if I can track her down."

Bash tips his glass at her. "Good luck."

She leaves without another word.

"What should we do with her?" I ask, inclining my head toward Laureya.

"I'll put her on the couch," Bash says, slamming his bourbon and walking to Laureya.

I return my attention to Adaline once Bash lies Laureya down. "If you have a computer I can use, I'll get started on the research."

"Yeah, there's one in my office, down the hall," Adaline answers, picking up the remnants of the spell.

"I'll help," Bash pipes up, following me before I have the chance to leave the room.

"Don't you need to wait for her to wake up?"

"Oh, it'll be a few hours before she does," Bash says, grabbing his bourbon on the way and leading me out by the small of my back.

"How are the cravings?" I ask as we amble down the hall.

"Eh," he answers with a simple wave of his glass. "This actually does help. That and Tallyn's blood mixture, along with my little snack. The good news is that it isn't coming back up."

"That's good."

Bash pushes open the heavy wooden door to Adaline's study.

A beautiful room full of ordinary books, an enormous mahogany desk, and a delicate reading lamp greet me, with a plush leather chair and ottoman tucked in the corner, and another sliding door leading out to a quaint little reading room filled with plants.

Her computer is resting on the desk, and it has the largest screen I've seen.

"Wow, they really do have tons of money, don't they?" I ask, pulling out the black desk chair and flicking on the Mac.

"Yeah, well, they've had a few centuries to save up," Bash answers, sitting in the brown leather chair opposite the desk. "So, what do you look for when doing this?"

"Oh, I just pull up the most wanted list for the area, get a name, and then pull his or her criminal record. At least, that's what I did the one time." I laugh awkwardly, nervously. Dom is on my mind, again.

Where is he? And why isn't he calling me?

Focusing on my search instead of what's happening with Dom, I pull up New York's most wanted list.

When the page is up, I click on the Top Ten Most Wanted Fugitives. The page's filled with mainly men, and below their pictures are their crimes. A lot of them have counterintelligence under them and some drug trafficking, but it's the ones listed "Crimes Against Children" that I take interest in.

The first one is an ugly-looking white man who's balding. He's convicted of molesting a young girl who he was in the care of from ages ten to fourteen. When he failed to appear for sentencing, he became a fugitive.

I jot down his name and birthdate and then click on the next name.

By the time I'm done with my search, I have eleven names on my list, all convicted of crimes against children.

They all can die for all I care.

Bash is quietly scrolling through his phone, sipping his bourbon this time instead of slamming it like last night.

"All right, I have some names."

"Yeah?" he asks, setting his phone down, and scratching his nose. "Who're the lucky death-by-rabid-vampire winners?"

"Erik, Elby, Frantz, a couple Jose's, Bruce, Gerard, Roger, Kent, William, and Curtis. All convicted child molesters."

"Word," Bash whistles. Strangely enough, the slang sounds right on his lips. "Let's go get these fuckers." This time, he downs the remaining bourbon in the glass.

"I'll have your mom help me with the locator spells. Hopefully, at least two of them will still be in New York. A lot of the information on them said they may have fled to other countries."

"You would think that at least two of the stupid fucks stayed in New York."

"You would think."

A NEW VAMPIRE

-SAYAH-

The list of names sits on the edge of the table beside a map of New York Adaline laid out for me. As I whisper each name to the charcoal dust in a pile at the center, the dust dobs shake and shudder, then shoot off the map, indicating the said fugitive has fled this part of the country. For each name whispered, the dust acts like those magnet games I used to play as a kid, following my hand around until I lift it, commanding it to show me where the villains dwell. The dust falls off the table with each name. All except one.

I whisper the last name. The dust shivers, lifts, shimmies to the side, and rests in a circle over a neighboring town of Whitehall.

"All right," Bash says, both hands straddling the map as he looks down at where the perpetrator is. "I'll go get him."

"Take your dad and brother," Adaline tells him. Bash's anguish over being alone with Everett is apparent.

"That's okay." He licks his lips, biting the bottom one. "I think I can handle it."

"Bash," Adaline scoffs. "You have no idea what kind of person you're dealing with."

"And look what happened to Dom when he went to do this alone," I add, placing a hand on his shoulder. "You should really take someone."

He looks at my hand, and I timidly remove it. "How about Ollie and me go?" he offers, standing up straight. "Let dear old Dad stay here."

"Fine," Adaline concedes, then rolls the map back up. "As long as you take someone."

"I'll go," Everett answers, suddenly in the room with us.

The look on Bash's face is a cross between annoyance and shock. "Y-you really don't have to." Bash moves away from the table to look at Everett standing in the doorway.

Everett crosses his arms over his chest. "I want to. I think it's better if I go than Ollie. He's had enough hunting for the week."

"I don't mind going either," Ollie says from behind him.

Everett faces him. "You sure you don't want to sit this one out, son?"

"Yeah, I don't mind."

Bash rolls his eyes. "Awesome. It'll be a Sangravelli men family affair."

"Get your shit, and let's go then," Everett directs the two boys. "She'll awaken soon; she'll need to feed."

"Yeah, don't want her to feed on one of you," Bash adds, heading to the door.

"She wouldn't dare," Jasantha resolves, her eyes cascading into that beautiful, deadly purple.

Scarlet chuckles. Meanwhile, I cringe.

"All right, boys. Be safe." Adaline flashes to Everett to kiss him, whispering to him, "Keep me posted."

Everett takes her in his arms and kisses her lovingly on the mouth. "I will, dear."

Bash, in turn, flashes up to me. "Do I get one of those well-wishes for my treacherous journey ahead?"

I shove him back. "Get out of here with that." Even though I love the idea and giggle lightly, I look over to Scarlet, who looks anything but amused.

"Oh, so now you have your eye on another one of Dom's girls when he's away?" she deadpans.

"Ease up, you harlot. I was only playing," Bash shoots back, turning to leave.

Scarlet's a whoosh of light and color as she speeds to stand in his way. "You always do this, Bash. You play innocent or joking when you know you're not! My brother is missing; Odin only knows where on Earth he is, and you're over here trying to play house with his girlfriend." Her voice shakes with anger.

Bash gives her his crooked smile, one side of his mouth tilting upward, and goes to move around her.

That's when she smacks him hard on the face. "I hope something terrible happens to you out there. You'll deserve at least that."

His face doesn't even move. The half smile stays painted on his face as he moves past her and walks out the door. Scarlet stands there for a second longer, then retreats to somewhere else in the house.

"Her and Dom are very close," Adaline offers.

"I didn't mean to hurt anyone." Feeling my cheeks flush, I sit next to Laureya's lifeless body on the couch.

"She's just worried about Dom and is taking it out on Bash. Those two have been at odds since the day she was born. He's never been good to her like a big brother should be."

"It's 'cause he's a monster," Jasantha offers, filing her nail with an emory board.

"I had him first," Adaline interrupts as Jasantha scoffs. "He grew jealous when I had the twins. Bash was never gentle or caring. When Scarlet was young, he always took her toys, pushed her down, and made her cry. As they got older, he would tease her, and call her names—never protective like a big brother should be. It just kept growing as they grew. I think he was also jealous about Dom and her being close, as Dom always protected her. When they became vampires, it just heightened—their dislike for each other."

"We all dislike him," Jasantha voices.

"You have your own different reasons, but the kids all had theirs, too." Adaline sits at the table again. "The darkness in him always tugs him to that end rather than the lighter shades of him. It's who Bash is. Regardless of what you see, my kids all have palpable and valid reasons to hate him. And up until very recently, it seemed as though he enjoyed their hatred."

"Why do you think that changed?"

"Something changed in him that I don't think even he sees."

Adaline is the second person to mention something has changed in Bash that he does not realize. I don't know him well enough to see the change they're talking about, but I know more than anything else it has to do with me.

He's changing something in me, too.

Then there's a sharp pain in my leg, and I realize Laureya's coming to because her legs kicked straight out and hit me in the thigh.

"Shit, she's waking up," I say, moving away from my sister.

Adaline and Jasantha are beside me in the flash of light, bracing themselves for whatever's about to happen.

Laureya's outstretched legs tremble as though she has a bad cramp and is trying to elongate her limbs to stretch it away. Her back twists at an unnatural angle, her head contorts to the side, her eyes still closed. Her brow is soaked with beads of sweat, and her long red hair—although still singed in places—is stuck to the side of her face where she'd been lying on it. When her eyes finally open, they're white with green rims, slit like a cat's, but the black of her pupils are so tiny that they look almost white. She arches her back and neck and opens her mouth, letting out a horrific scream as fangs pierce through her gums for the first time.

Jasantha moves to the couch's arm and catches her arms as they fly up. Adaline holds her shoulders as she shoots straight up and hisses.

Her eyes are on me, and as she lunges, Adaline and Jasantha use all the strength they have to hold her back. Laureya's on her feet in an instant, arms outstretched, pulling with all her might to get to me.

Before I know it, Laureya breaks free and is about to crash against me when Jasantha lets out her wail. I have to cover my ears against the ringing.

Laureya falls to the ground, dazed, still staring at me, and breathing rapidly.

"All right, let's get her down to the basement," Adaline instructs. "We'll need to lock her up until they get back."

Jasantha hooks her arm through one elbow and Adaline the other, hoisting Laureya up to heave her toward the stairs.

"How long will the siren power work on her?" I ask as I follow them to the dungeon.

"As long as Jasantha allows," Adaline answers.

"Well, that or a few days," Jasantha adds, her voice echoing in the tunnel to the dungeon. "I once had this man in my room for—"

"That's quite enough!"

"Sorry, Mom," Jasantha mutters with a smirk as we reach the bottom of the stairs.

Once we arrive at the cell on the right, Adaline opens the door, and they walk her in and set her down on the cot inside.

When they let her go, they leave her in the cell and close the door, locking it behind them.

As we retreat to the larger part of the dungeon, I ask, "Do you think she'll be able to formweave while under the power?"

"The power makes it so that their only thought is what I make them think. For her, I told her to remain calm and collective."

"So, there are actually words in the wail?"

"Yes, there are words there," Jasantha snipes at me as though she's insulted that I couldn't distinguish them. "You only hear the words when I want to sedate you. You weren't my target, so you couldn't hear them."

"It's fascinating, is all," I defend. We sit around the room again. Jasantha will probably never like me, as with the rest of the Sangravelli women. But the mystery about her makes me want to know all about her. Since no one says anything, I ask, "Can you tell me how you came to be part of this family?"

Jasantha eyes me and sits back, crossing her legs. "My family and I lived in our colony called Thalassara. Everything was wonderful for a time; we had a home above and below the island. My mother and father, two sisters, and three brothers were part of a community of sirens, but we still maintained our life above water; only going out to sea to feed off the pirates and other enemies of the sea." She pauses to take the glass of blood Adaline hands her. "My sister, Aaralyn, met a sailor and fell in love with him, trusting him with our secret. That proved to be a fateful mistake. His captain overheard them talking one night, and only gold came into his eyes. He arranged to have my entire family captured and waited out by our island to begin taking us hostage. They got one of my brothers, Caspar; my sister, Aaralyn; my other sister, Ianthe; my mother, Galen, and a few others from our community. My brothers, Ronin and Seagar, and my father, Cephas, were murdered while trying to protect us. I was the only survivor of my family from this mayhem."

Her voice shakes as tears well in her eyes. Adaline rubs her back. Jasantha lays her head on Adeline's shoulder and collects herself.

I sit awkwardly on the other couch, my heart panging at how I brought up such a painful memory for her.

Cleaning her throat and wiping her tears, she continues, "They cut out their vocal cords to prevent them from singing their siren song and pulled them aboard the ship. I followed them as far as I could, but I could only swim so fast, even with my tail. A few months later, I subdued another pirate who'd told me how the captain of the ship had taken my family and sold them to a man who ran a freak show circus. My mother, Caspar, and Ianthe had died in captivity, but my sister Aaralyn was in Naples, heading for Rome for the next show.

"When I went to Naples, I was at the docks one night trying to find word on where this so-called circus was, and that's when I ran into Bash. He was beside himself with rage, getting ready to take his own life, when he spotted me. I just wanted companionship, but also information. I knew he was a vampire, so I figured he would have some sort of knowledge. I subdued him, as I was still able to then before he turned me. We spent a few hours together, at the end of which something had set him completely off. I didn't know what it was, but he went mad. I triggered the demon in him, and he ended up coming out of his trance of mine to beat me senseless, drained my blood, and fed me his own. He stabbed me eight times and left me for dead. I don't know if he knew that was how to turn non-spelled people into vampires. I honestly have no idea. All I know is that the transition was brutal. I died on the docks, woke up in excruciating pain and starving, a hunger so ravaging it actually hurt. After murdering five people of my own at random, I made my way into Naples. Bash had divulged his life story to me, and I knew it wouldn't be hard to find the Sangravelli family. I totally forgot about finding my sister and just wanted to find him, to find his family, and murder them all. When I found Adaline, well, she can tell you the rest."

Adaline, who's intently watching Jasantha, leans back and inhales. "One night, I was tending to the horses when I saw her coming onto our land. Even in the moonlight, I could see she was covered in blood; her dress was stained and darkened with the multiple stab wounds that Bash had left. I figured it had to have been Bash, as that was what he was known for. Well, bashing heads in more so than stab wounds, but nonetheless, violence. I called out to her, and she opened her mouth to wail at me when I countered her siren call with my own magick. When she fell to her knees and sobbed, my heart immediately went out to her. I pulled her up and brought her inside, and that's when she told me about her horrific last few days. She was only a girl, seventeen years old. Sirens age a lot slower than humans, so she really was around forty, but to me, she was still just a girl. I took her in and comforted her, helping her with the rest of her transition by feeding her the blood Everett and I had stored away. When she was finished transitioning into a new vampire-siren hybrid, I didn't want her to leave. I felt she needed me, us—our family—she was so devastated over losing hers."

I wipe my own tears away. "Whatever happened to your sister? Did you ever find her?"

"Yes, we found her," Adaline resumes, sipping her blood, and wiping her mouth. "We tracked down the circus and killed the ringleader. We freed the beings we could, but some saw the ringleader and the circus as the only place they ever truly belonged, so they stayed with the remaining folks who ran it. Aaralyn was in a tank in the back; her tail was withering, and the scales were coming off; her vocal cords had been shredded, and her skin was beginning to deteriorate from being in fake salt water for so long. We managed to get her out of the tank and took her back home, where we nursed her back to health. We, of course, couldn't repair her voice. All that, and she failed to recover from the death of their parents and siblings. She just wanted to go back to the sea to try and make a new life."

Jasantha's eyes are staring into the distance, and I can see more tears. My heart bleeds for Jasantha. So much loss with her whole family and then Bash killing her fiancé during the tragic battle with Matrasia. This woman has known sadness, yet she still seems so strong.

"We brought her back to Thalassara and let her go," Adaline goes on, setting her glass on the table. "We watched her walk into the ocean and disappear."

"Did you ever see her again?"

Jasantha's eyes are on me at the question, the lonely tear falling swiftly down her face.

"I saw her a few times after that. I would go to the island on her birthday and Yule, and she'd resurface to see me. She found a man she loved below the sea and was going to start a family. But once we left Naples, I didn't make it down to the island as much, and once we left Italy, there was no way to go there in the hopes she would come up."

"How long were you guys in Naples?"

"We lived in Naples for ten years," Adaline continues. "Then moved on to Rome and other parts of Italy. Once we were all transitioned, we couldn't stay anywhere for too long. We lived in England for a long time, which was my favorite, and we all adopted the accent from there. Then, we moved to Scotland, Ireland, and Spain for a stretch. We moved to the States around the early 1900s and have been here ever since. Everett and I have been in this house for ten years and figure we have another ten before we move on again."

"Before people start noticing that we don't age," Jasantha adds with a vindictive smile.

"And what happened after you transitioned?" I ask as I draw my knees to my chest. "Before you left Naples?"

"When Bash showed up a few months later, she almost killed him," Adaline confirms. "But I convinced her it was just a part of his grief for Sadie and his brother, and believing he had something to do with Sadie's death. I knew that his demon side was getting stronger, and something she had said triggered it and brought it to life. Having not been there, I didn't know exactly what was said, but I didn't divulge it was that part of him that murdered her. Somewhere in her, she found the strength to forgive him enough to not kill him, but there still is that hatred that lives inside of her that will never go away. However, she thrived as a hybrid, learning from Ollie, Dom, and her new sisters. She could go out in the daylight, which we weren't until we met you. So, she would always do the things we needed done in town and was our normal-ish daughter. Everyone in the family accepted her as our new daughter and sibling, and from then on, she was one of us."

"Do you ever think about trying to find your sister again? Like going there and seeing if she's still around?"

"She would be long gone by now," Jasantha murmurs, wiping the tears from her face. "Sirens live longer than humans, but they are not immortal. She probably died of old age a hundred and fifty years ago or so."

"I see," I whisper. I'm happy Jasantha let me into her life as much as she had.

None of us speak for a few minutes and are only brought back to the here and now when Laureya's screams come bellowing from her cell.

BURN FROM THE INSIDE

-SAYAH-

The look on Jasantha's face is a cross between shock and worry.

She jumps up, and runs to the cell. Adaline and I follow close behind.

When we arrive, we witness Laureya crouched in a corner of her cell, her arms outstretched, her skin burning her from the inside out. Her charred flesh is breaking apart in what appears to be fissures of tar. Her insides, instead of blood, are bright red like lava. Laureya's screaming, watching her skin burst apart.

"What the hell?" I shriek, my voice echoing the panic I feel in my heart. "Why is this happening to her?"

"I don't know!" Adaline yells back, unlocking the door.

"Do you think the phoenix in her is rejecting the vampire blood?" Jasantha asks, closely on her mom's tail.

"It shouldn't be," Adaline says, kneeling and pulling her to her feet.

"It hurts!" Laureya screams, holding her arms out. "Make it stop!"

Adaline rushes to Laureya, shooting a glance at Jasantha. "Why isn't your calming power not working anymore, either?"

"I have no idea!" Jasantha shouts back.

"Where are you taking her?" I ask as they pull her from the cell toward the dungeon stairs. The fissures climb up her arms, and a black spiderweb of veins crawls outward from the cracks.

"Upstairs to the spell room," Adaline answers, suddenly out of sight with her vampire speed.

As I climb up the stairs by myself, I move as fast as I can get my legs to go, but I'm only part human—well, half human, and half phoenix—or a third human? A fourth? Odin's ghost. The truth is I don't know what the fuck I am. The pressure of what is happening to Laureya weighs heavily on me, paired with the fact that I still haven't heard from Dom and the fact that I can't call Mama about any of this anymore, has me feeling like at any moment, the pressure will surely break me.

Laureya's screams echo down the long hallway, and when I arrive at the spell room, Laureya's sitting by the cauldron on her knees.

"Make it stop!" she yells, holding her arm above the elbow to try and stop the spreading burn.

Adaline is frantically sifting through her grimoires, searching for anything to help. "I don't know how!" Adaline screams back at her.

Before I even think this through, I bite my arm, and run up to Laureya, shoving my bleeding limb into Laureya's face.

Laureya turns her head away at first, "What the fuck are you—"

"Just drink it, gods-damn it!" I shove my arm back in her face.

As Laureya drinks from me, I feel the familiar pull of my blood from my body I've grown used to from letting Bash drink from me, but it's not the same. There's no pleasure in it.

Laureya drinks feverously, and it isn't just because she's a new vampire who needs my blood; it's also because it's helping.

Whatever's causing Laureya to burn from the inside out, as

my blood coagulates with hers, the new angel blood in her veins starts to mend the fissures, forcing the red lava-looking matter back into her flesh. The black spiderweb veins are seeping back into her skin, beginning to look normal again.

"It's working," Adaline says, pushing the book back onto the shelf and dropping to her knees before me.

"Don't let her get too much," Jasantha warns, "she'll easily drain you and kill you."

As if on cue, Bash and the boys are back, dragging behind them a scraggly-looking fellow who's about six-two, and very bloody and beaten.

"What the hell is going on?" Bash asks, pulling the ropes that bind the criminal by his wrists.

The bloody man is yanked and falls to his knees, looking dazed and in a trance.

Laureya's still drinking from me, even as I start to feel woozy and lightheaded.

Bash flashes up to me and wrenches Laureya's head from my arm. "What the hell are you doing?" he yells as Laureya tries to get back to me, but Bash holds her by the forehead, and Adaline, Everett, and Ollie are there as she struggles to force her way free.

"She began to burn from the inside out," Jasantha offers as the others drag Laureya back to the dungeon.

"So, let her burn!" Bash shouts.

"I couldn't do that," I say weakly, holding my bitten arm. "I couldn't let her burn."

"So now she's just gonna be addicted to you, too. Great." His voice is edging more on exasperation than anger.

"She may not," I chide him. "Dom didn't get addicted to my blood."

"Dom isn't part demon."

I've got nothing to say back to that.

He's right.

I probably just put myself in more danger by getting yet another vampire—and a new one at that—addicted to my blood.

"Fuck. We'll get to that later. First, we gotta finish feeding her." He scowls, helping me up, and yanking the hostage back to his feet. "On your feet now. That's a good boy. Time to die, here we go," he coos as if he's talking to a pet dog that's about to get a bath.

I follow Bash and the criminal down the stairs and watch as Bash takes the rope off his wrists and shoves him into the cell.

Laureya's eyes go whiter somehow as she pounces on the man like a rabid dog, his screams now filling up the dungeon with his pain. Blood splatters everywhere as she devours his neck, and the sounds of her drinking from him become louder as he dies.

For what he's guilty of, I'm not at all saddened by his death.

When Laureya has had her fill, she makes her way back up to the bars, covered in blood and looking at Bash like he's some sort of god to her.

"I want more," she whispers, her fangs still present in her mouth.

"You don't get more tonight," Bash states, turning away from her.

"Don't leave me!" Laureya shouts as he heads back up the stairs, leaving her alone in the dungeon.

"Shut up and lay down!" he yells back to her, not looking over his shoulder while he climbs the stairs.

I do, however, and what I see makes me question things.

Laureya does exactly what Bash told her to do: she leaves the bars and lies down on the cot.

I knit my brows firmly together as I reenter the spell room behind Bash, taking a seat on the couches as he heads over to the bar.

"What do you think happened to her?" Jasantha questions him as he walks by, seated at the table with Adaline.

"It must have something to do with the part of her that is phoenix," Adaline concurs, fighting with one of her crystals.

"What exactly happened?" Bash asks, pouring himself more bourbon.

"She just started screaming," Jasantha answers. "We ran to see what was happening, and her skin was coming apart, all black and veiny, and this red lava-looking stuff was coming out of the cracks. It was fucking odd."

"Is that like what happened to Sadie?" I ask Bash.

When he catches my eyes, I can see the hurt behind the question as it sparks his memory back to life. "No," he answers after a very long pause. "Sadie was only convinced in her mind that she was burning from the inside, so much so that it made her feverish. But she did not actually burn from the inside."

Adaline nods. "It has to be because Sadie was a chosen phoenix, and Laureya was only one by default."

"But why was she burning from the inside out?" Ollie asks, taking the bottle from Bash.

"It has to have something to do with angel blood in Sayah and the demon blood in her, mixed with the vampire blood that was turning her," Bash says, sipping on his bourbon when he's done talking.

"What are you guys doing?" Scarlet asks, back again from wherever it is she'd gone.

"Oh, you know, making vampires and killing child molesters," Bash answers casually.

Scarlet rolls her eyes at him and takes a seat on one of the couches.

"Where did you go?" Adaline asks her.

"Just for a walk," she replies. "Has anyone tried a locator spell on Dominic yet? Since his mark has been broken?"

"No, we haven't tried it recently," Adaline answers.

"Can we try? I'm worried about him."

"Sure," Adaline replies as Scarlet walks up to the table. Adaline unrolls a map of the US.

With a flicker of hope flaring through me, I walk up to the map as well.

"Let me see your finger," Adaline asks of Scarlet.

Scarlet gives her finger to Adaline, and Adaline pricks it with the knife on the table. She squeezes her finger with the blood to make it drop on the map. Taking her pendulum, she holds it above the map, whispering words with her eyes closed.

Neither the map nor the pendulum moves.

Nobody says a word while we watch the map and the droplet of blood lying on the surface. When the blood shivers a bit and then moves an inch, I gasp. The blood divides into four different droplets, all different sizes. The small drop stays where it is in New York. The medium droplet moves to Colorado. Another moves to California. And the largest one drifts across the ocean and falls off the table, plummeting to the floor.

"What the hell does that mean?" Scarlet asks.

"I have no idea," Adaline answers, observing the blood drops on the map.

"It went off the map of the US and then fell to the floor," Bash says as he looks over Scarlet's shoulder.

"Yeah, we know we saw," Scarlet retorts with annoyance.

"But it went off the US; that doesn't mean he's off the map," Bash offers.

"But the other drops went to Colorado, and California, and one stayed in New York. What is that?" she asks, turning to look at him.

"I don't know that. I just want to see where the other drop would have gone."

"Here." Adaline turns the pages of the atlas to the world map. "Give me your finger again."

Scarlet presents her other index finger.

Again, Adaline pokes it, and squeezes it above the map.

Repeating the same steps, the four drops of blood move to California and New York. One stays still, and the largest one moves across the sea and lands in Scotland.

"Scotland?" I ask dubiously. "What's in Scotland?"

"What's in Colorado and California?" Bash adds.

"They're all places he has been before," Everett answers.

"None of this makes any sense," Adaline says, leaning over the table to look closely at the blood droplets. "It should just move to one spot. There is no rhyme or reason why it would move to four different spots."

There's a loud commotion coming from the house beyond the spell room.

All the vampires look at each other and then clear the room in a whoosh of air, leaving me alone. Sighing to myself and annoyed that I can only move at human speed, I follow the banging to the living room.

I find Laureya banging on one of the doors to get out, tripping over an extension cord hooked to a lamp that's now broken on the floor.

"Let me out!" she screams, banging on the glass, and futilely turning the knob to no avail.

"How did you get out?" Bash asks, walking up to her.

"Let me out!" she yells again, hissing at Bash.

"You can't get out," Adaline says. "I put a boundary spell on the house to keep you in when I undid your moon curse."

"I knew I understood some of that voodoo you were chanting," Bash says, ignoring Laureya momentarily.

"I need more!" Laureya continues her ranting.

"Not until you tell me how you got out," Bash answers, calm and collected, before telling us, "She's high as fuck from killing that dude."

"I'm a formweaver, you fucktard," she hisses.

"What about the siren power?" I ask Jasantha.

"It must have gotten snubbed out when she began to burn," Jasantha says. "Sometimes trauma can override the power."

Laureya turns around and screams at the top of her lungs, not words, just an ear-rattling screech. Then she ends the screech with, "I NEED MORE BLOOD!"

"All right," Bash appeases, calmly putting his hand on the small of her back. "I'll get you some more. Just come down to the spell room and drink with me, okay? I promise it'll take the edge off while I find you more blood."

Like something of a spell that's spoken from his lips, she calms down, and nods, allowing him to lead her from the living room. "Just promise not to lock me in that cell again, okay? I don't like it in there."

"As long as you promise to behave, I'll let you stay out."

"I'll behave. Promise."

We follow them down the stairs and back to the spell room, where Bash guides her to sit down on the couch, makes her a drink, and hands her the glass for himself.

She takes the short glass with shaky hands and slams the bourbon down in one gulp.

"Easy there, tiger. Don't wanna drink too much of it too fast after a full sitting of human blood. You'll just puke it right back up."

Pouring her some more, she looks up at him with her doe eyes, the white still very adamant and vivid.

"Pour me one, too," Ollie says, sitting beside Laureya. "Fuck it, let's get day drunk." He nudges her with his shoulder, and she smiles at him.

I shake my head and move to sit at the table, contemplating the droplets of blood and why they moved the way they did across the map.

"What are we going to do about getting her more blood?" Scarlet asks Bash, who's pouring a drink for Ollie.

"There were more criminals on that list," I answer for him. "They don't have to be the most wanted, or child molesters even. Anyone who has committed a violent crime will do it for me."

"Being that it's still daylight outside," Everett says, "I can just run to work and grab some blood bags. It'll suffice for now until you start to collect more criminals."

"That's a good idea, darling," Adaline says.

"All right." Everette moves toward Adaline once more to kiss her goodbye. "I'll be back."

Once Everett's gone, the drinking continues between Bash, Laureya, and Ollie. Scarlet and Jasantha eventually join in. The only two who aren't drinking are Adaline and me. When Adaline finally caves and begins drinking with them, I just hang out in the background like I do when my friends drink around me.

The time is used for quiet reflection on how absolutely worried I am about Dom. The four drops of blood are moving in different directions, and one of them is in Scotland.

What in the world can that possibly mean?

And why doesn't anyone seem to care like I do?

I understand Bash does not care as much, but Scarlet does. And his own mother?

I hover at the table, looking at the four drops on the map, and am quite unaware of the time that passes when Everett shows up again with the blood. The droplets have even dried a little on the map, and the people drinking over on the couches are getting louder with each round.

"Here," Everett says gruffly, handing Laureya a bag. She's still in full vamp mode, with her white eyes and her fangs. She takes the bag and bites the top off, beginning to down the blood as quickly as one would water.

"That's all you get for now, so slow down," Everett orders and Laureya listens, slowing her gulp to a stop and holding the bag like a drink.

"I know you feel as though you are starving and could keep eating and eating and not get full," Adaline tells her, "but it's important to not drink too much for your first day. If you feed the way you want to and kill another person, you could turn into the monster that vampires are destined to be."

"I don't understand," Laureya replies, her white eyes questioning.

"If we give in to our urges," Adaline says in almost a motherly tone, "kill indiscriminately, feed unyieldingly, the darkness will take over, and you'll become that forever. What you are right now, at this moment. That part of you that lingers as a human will disappear, and all your love, and humanness will get shut off and never return."

"Never?" She resembles a little girl in the 1800s who was told about what happens to women when they go out at night unchaperoned.

"Well, almost always never. Bash came back from it."

"Not really," Scarlet scoffs.

Bash sniggers at her and rises to fill his drink. "I'm not as bad as I used to be."

"This is true," Ollie confirmed. "We call him Bash for a reason, remember?"

I'm not sure I ever want to hear that story.

"Exactly. I haven't bashed anyone's head in for a really long time."

"I wouldn't call a year a really long time, Bash," Ollie teases.

"That was different! He threatened me!"

"All right, enough," Everett interrupts. "This is serious, Laureya. We can't have any rabid vampires out terrorizing the city we live in. We have made a home here. We want to remain here as long as possible, and that involves not drawing attention to ourselves. Had it not been for my wife's boundary spell, you would be out right now, terrorizing the good people of Lake George. I don't care who you are or whose sister you happen to be; I'll end you if you threaten mine and my family's place here again. Do you understand me?"

This is the most I've ever heard Everett say.

"Yes, sir," Laureya replies sheepishly.

"Good." Everett nods before walking her over to the chairs by the fireplace. "Now, make that bag last as long as you can. I will not give you more for the rest of the day. As a new vampire, you must learn to control yourself, your hunger, and your cravings. We allowed you to kill a person on your first feeding, but if you want to make it in the world as a vampire, you'll have to learn to stop before their heart stops. If you drain someone each time and kill them, you end up drinking blood that died with them, which releases a substance that is like a chemical to vampires. It's what Bash is experiencing with Sayah's blood. You will become addicted to the stuff and kill a person every time. You probably won't be able to notice it this time because everything is new to you. Your heightened hearing, your speed, your agility—it's all a chemical rush to you right now, so it's nearly impossible to distinguish between the blood rush and the new vampire rush. Take it from me; you're better off not knowing about that altogether, so you are never tempted when you drink from humans directly."

Laureya remains quiet, nodding, eyes locked with his.

"Now, try to get yourself to calm down so that your eyes go back to normal, and your teeth go back in."

Taking a deep breath, she focuses on Everett, and squints her eyes shut. A few seconds later, when she opens them, her eyes are back to their normal green, and her fangs retreat back into her gums.

"Good." He nods approvingly. "Go take a shower to get the blood off you."

Everett walks away from her and up to the bar, where he pours himself a bourbon. Laureya takes the bag with her and leaves the room.

"Bash," Everett says, "Go with her. Make sure she doesn't go nuts."

Bash grimaces and shakes his head, downing the rest of his drink before leaving the room, too.

"She's actually doing really well for a newly transitioned vampire," Adaline offers to Everett, who joins them again on the couches with his drink.

"She is," he confirms. "I still don't trust her yet, though."

"Why do you think she's transitioning so well?" I ask. "The way Dom and Bash made it seem was that it's a long and excruciating process."

"I think it has something to do with the fact that she's a formweaver; she was under siren control, and she's part phoenix," Adaline responds. "That's the only thing that makes sense to me."

"Sayah's blood probably numbed a part of it, too," Jasantha says.

"When she would form into the wolf, she said that was the most pain she has ever felt. Maybe that's why she doesn't seem in much pain."

"That's very true," Adaline confirms. "Her pain tolerance is higher than a human who would transition to a vampire from just being human, like we all did."

"Yes, she will make a fine vampire," Jasantha says mockingly with an eyeroll.

BROKEN BONDS

-SAYAH-

I linger at the table, still trying to piece the puzzle together the entire time Laureya is showering. When she and Bash emerge again, they join the others on the couches and continue drinking until the sun sets.

I suddenly feel my stomach rumble with hunger, and realize I haven't eaten all day. I also realize I'm the only human in the house who needs to eat real food.

"Adaline?" I say, interrupting their talk of stories when Everett and she first met.

"Yes?" she asks after finishing her giggle.

"Is it alright if I make myself something to eat?"

"Sure. Help yourself."

"I'd ask if anyone wanted anything, but . . . " They all stare at me with blank expressions. "Right," I answer and leave through the door.

Bash shoots out of one of the cozy chairs and follows me into the kitchen.

"I'm not the one who needs a supervisor," I state coolly, not particularly sure why I'm upset with him.

Maybe it's him spending time with Laureya. What had he done up there while she showered?

"I just thought you might want some company, is all."

"Thanks."

When I arrive at the kitchen, I look in the fridge, pulling the double French doors open. The light comes on and offers his handsome face a stunning glow.

Other than some milk, beer, and other condiments, there's little to choose from.

"Also, to help you forage for some food." He shuts the left door while I close the right. "I figured it would look like this. The good stuff is in here."

Walking to the right of the fridge, there's a long door that looks like it would simply open on some shelves. But when he opens it, it exposes a long hallway lined with copious amounts of dry storage food. The hallway leads back to a larger area, where there are kegs, shelves of wine, bags of rice, jars of pickles, cans of every vegetable, and chips of every kind, among many other products. It resembles a small aisle in a grocery store.

"Whoa, why do they have all this?" I ask as I take in the food.

"Honestly, I'm not sure," Bash answers, pulling down a bottle of wine to examine the date. "They've always had a storage of dry food. Maybe it was all the plagues and disasters they've lived through. We can eat real food, you know."

"I know, I know, it just doesn't sustain you like blood does. So why don't they have a storage like this for blood?"

"You have to keep blood cool; otherwise, it will go bad. And it still goes bad after a few months or so, even in refrigeration. Here's a better question: why aren't you drinking with us? Or why is it I never see you drink?"

"I don't drink."

"Oh?" Bash sidles up to me with a drunken sway. "And why is that?"

I move away from him and grab some salted chips and a jar of French onion dip from one of the shelves. Then I grab a container of hummus and a jar of green olives. "Because I got tired of not feeling anything."

"Nice dinner," he adds, following me out of the dry storage area. "Why were you not feeling anything?"

"Long story," I say, setting the food on the counter and sitting on one of the stools.

Bash rummages in a drawer for a corkscrew. "I got time."

As I open both jars and the chips, I dip one into the hummus and pop a green olive in, chewing it before I share my story.

Bash undoes the wrapper from the top of the wine bottle and screws in the corkscrew.

"I survived cancer," I utter through chews. His sapphire eyes are on me instantly. "I had insomnia from chemo. I was in a miserable marriage. When I got divorced, he had a new family right away. I got so used to drinking the pain away that I began to drink just 'cause it was Tuesday. Or when I had a good day. And then it was just everyday. I got the shakes, I lost weight, and then I really began to do stupid shit. I screwed over one of my best friends. And then I drove home drunk from Denver one day, and when I got home, I realized that if I didn't fix my shit, I'd lose the rest of what I had. My son, my house, my license, my job. So, I quit. And haven't drank since."

"Wow," Bash answers, his blue eyes locked on mine, holding my world still. He pops the cork out, and the noise echoes through the house. "That was very strong of you to do that."

"Thanks," I say, dipping a chip into the dip to take a bite. "I also wanted to break generational curses. I had to break the cycle for Gauge."

"And your mom and stepdad's death? You didn't drink at all?" he asks, pulling a wine glass from one of the cabinets.

Fury nips at the back of my neck. The woman responsible

for the death of my parents is in this house, and I have not confronted her yet. I know I need to. I just don't know how.

Swallowing my chip in a loud gulp, I say, "Not a drop."

The sound of the red wine glugging into the glass is the only sound for a few seconds. He picks it up and swirls it around, examining the legs on the sides. "Do you ever miss it?"

"Sometimes. Certain aspects."

He sips the wine, his calm eyes holding mine as I pop another chip into my mouth. "Like?"

"Like having wine with dinner. Drinking for a celebration. Not having a filter while hanging out with my girls. I always feel as though I am the boring one out. They get to a point where they're all giggly and saying or doing stupid shit, and I'm just sitting there like a square. I miss it then."

"I can see that." He pulls out the chair next to me, and sits down. "You're very brave, you know."

Dipping a chip in the hummus, I pull out another green olive and mix it in. I like the flavor of the hummus with the green olives. "People keep telling me that."

Looking over at him, his nose is crinkled. "Is that good?"

"It's delicious," I say through my mouthful. "You should try it."

"I'm good." He leans on the counter and props the side of his head up with his hand. "So, what else?"

"What else what?" I ask, stirring a chip in the hummus.

"What else about you can you tell me?"

I don't know if he holds that power over me, but I feel completely at ease and would divulge anything he asks.

But at that moment, Ollie walks in.

"Hey," he says, opening the fridge, and grabbing a beer. "What're you two doing?"

"Just talking while she eats her disgusting dinner."

"It's not disgusting, it's good!" I quip, putting another chip, and olive in my mouth.

"Looks good to me," Ollie says, sitting on my other side. "Let me try."

He leans over me, grabs a chip, and swirls it around in the hummus. I hand him the jar of olives, and he takes one out and adds it to his mouth. "Mmmm. You're right, that is good."

"You're both gross," Bash says, shaking his head. "What's everyone doing in there?"

"Dad's just talking about his boat days."

"Oh, no," Bash answers, laying his head on the counter. "Not the boat days."

"What?" I ask.

"You don't wanna know," Ollie answers, grabbing another chip.

"What's up?" comes Laureya's voice now, joining us in the kitchen. "What's happening in here?" She stumbles up to Ollie and puts her arm around him. "Yuck, what the hell are you guys eating?"

"Hummus," Ollie tells her. "C'mon, let's get you over to the couches." He stands, and she stumbles; he catches her before she falls.

I look at Bash as he lifts his head, and his blue eyes and disheveled black hair catch me sideways once again. The world stands still, and nothing in it exists anymore, again.

Is that part of his power, too? Making the world disappear?

Gods, I want those lips on mine again.

"Ollie!" Laureya whines, and the world returns. "Make me another drink!"

I look over and see Laureya sitting sideways on a couch.

"I really don't think you need any more," he mentions, returning to the counter and sitting again.

"Ollie!" she whines, staggering to get back up again.

"I think we need shots," Bash says, jumping up, and heading for the pantry.

"Yes, shots!" Laureya squeals, sloppily getting up and stumbling toward the kitchen again.

Ollie shakes his head and takes a swig of his beer. Then Bash emerges from the pantry with a giant bottle of Jack Daniels.

"Oh, no, not Jack," Ollie protests.

"Yes, Jack. Gentleman Jack," Bash utters, pulling three shot glasses from another cabinet and setting them on the table.

"We need music!" Laureya shouts, leaning on Ollie again. Ollie just ignores her and takes another long drink.

"Hey, Siri, play T-Pain," Bash commands as he pours the shots. The pod from the living room plays "Bartender" as Bash passes the other two their shots. "Sayah, can I get you something? Water? Soda?"

A moment after asking for water, Bash fills a glass of water with ice and sets it before me, lending me a wink.

I smile back and take a drink.

"Cheers!" Bash shouts, holding up his shot glass. "To new vampires."

"Salud!" They chink their glasses together and shoot the whiskey back.

"I don't miss that," I say as they all hiss at the sting of the whiskey.

"Nah, it's great," Ollie says, his eyes squinted. "It's a wonderful sting on the roof of the mouth and the back of the throat."

"You guys have fun with that."

The back of the chair is uncomfortable, mirroring my discomfort of being around people taking shots. It's not that the alcohol itself bugs me, it's that I feel out of place being the only one not drinking.

I stand to take my food to the living room.

"Wait, wait, wait, where are you going?" Bash asks me, coming back around to sit by me again.

"I thought I would leave you all to your drinking and go watch something on TV."

"I'll come with you," he says, grabbing his wine and my chips for me.

We go into the living room and sit on the couches. I set the hummus and olives down next to the bag of chips, and Bash sits on the coffee table.

The music is still playing, so Bash scoots up as close to me as he can. Part of me thinks of scooting away, and the other part begs me to stay.

"So," Bash asks, leaning close to me, "where were we?"

"I don't know," I say, tucking my legs underneath me and grabbing a pillow to cuddle on my lap. It's something I've done since I can remember. "You wanted to know more about me."

"Ah, right. So? What can you tell me about the beautiful and mysterious Sayah I don't already know?"

The way my name lives on his tongue makes it sound like some magickal floating city in the sky. "There are lots of things you don't know about me."

He drinks his wine, and the red liquid spreads across his lips almost seductively. "I know. I want to know it all."

His blue eyes are earnest about wanting to know me. All the parts. Especially the parts of me I'm proud of.

But it's my darkness he yearns to know.

"What do you really want to know? Just say it."

"What did you do to your friend that led you to quit drinking?"

"Uh-huh. There it is. You want to know the bad parts of me."

"I want to know all the parts of you," he replies, leaning further into me, and twirling a bit of my hair around his index finger.

His breath on my neck sends tingles down my wrists, and again I fight the urge to face him, to catch his lips in mine again, and lose myself in his kiss.

"I just did some terrible things when I was drunk," I blurt out, and Bash's finger pauses around my hair.

"Tell me about that," he whispers. Though I sense he doesn't want to know the details, he wants to know the facts behind the incident.

His fingers resume the twirling.

I tell him all the dirty things about my past—the things alcohol made me do and the people I hurt. He listens intently and doesn't judge me for what I confess to him.

"So, I just let her go," I conclude.

"Sometimes letting go of people we once loved is best for us. I know I have done that with Dom a million times over."

"Yeah, what's that about? Besides the Sadie thing, why is there such bad blood between you two?"

"It's just one of those things where he's never really liked me, and I've never really liked him. He's always had this attitude, like he's better than me, and I've always had this 'I don't give a fuck' attitude, and that's where we clashed."

"And he was bothered that you didn't care what he thought of you?"

"Pretty much." Bash lets my hair loose. His focus turns to tipping his wine glass for the last drop. "I need more wine. Want your water?"

"Yes, please."

"Be right back."

Since the living room and kitchen are attached, I can see that Laureya and Ollie are talking about something in Ollie's life. She's leaned in close, enthralled by whatever tale he's telling. Bash pours himself more wine and three more shots, tipping one back before returning to me with my water.

"M'lady," he coos upon return, handing me the water.

"Thank you."

"My pleasure." He sits down next to me and sips his wine. "My bet is on those two hooking up tonight."

"I was thinking the same thing," I quip, letting a little giggle escape. "Can I ask you something?"

"Anything," he responds, looking deep into my eyes.

"Where do you think Dom really is?"

"That's an interesting question you pose."

"Why?"

"Because it imposes the notion, first, that you think I know where he is and am not saying anything, and second, that he's not under a spell anymore and choosing not to come home."

"Well . . ." I say, situating myself to face him, "Yeah. That's exactly what I think."

"Why do you think I would keep it from you if I knew where he was?"

"I don't think you know where he is, and you're keeping it from me—sorry, I should have worded that better. Or corrected you. Or whatever. You may know why he's not back yet, and why we can't do a locator spell on him."

"Well, I don't," he replies, staring into his wine. I get the impression he isn't telling me something and won't budge on it.

"Okay, fine." I turn back around, but he grabs my legs, and forces me to face him.

"Sayah, I'd tell you if I knew where he was. I promise you that."

"Okay," I say again.

"You are so amazing," he purrs, eyes locked with mine, smiling simply.

"Why?"

"Because. You just take all the shit that life hands you and turn it into diamonds. Some of the stuff that I've heard about your life—cancer, losing your mom and stepdad, divorce, what you go through with your son. Anyone else, and they would be a big ball of mush on the floor. But you look at life with this light that could make anyone want to bask in it. They gave a woman the pressures of hell and instead of becoming a diamond, she became a phoenix."

The sound of the door opening draws both of our attention.

Hattie walks in with a woman whose arm is draped around her shoulder.

"Hattie!" Ollie beams, meeting her at the door to help her with her human.

Bash stands and waits for them to bring the bedraggled human to the living room. "And who might this be?" he asks as they lay her on the other couch.

"This would be Amanda," Ollie answers. "Although she looked a lot better last time I saw her."

"The warlock had her in his clutches," Hattie answers.

"Mederio?" Bash asks as Hattie sits down next to her, stroking her hair.

"No, another one. I went to her apartment to try and get a sense of where she might be, and she just showed up. She told me the warlock who had her just burst into ashes last night, and she managed to escape."

"Interesting," Bash states, his eyes diving into mine with curiosity. I shrug.

Amanda's eyes are closed, and she seems to be in some sort of stupor. I've never met her, but she looks the same way Scarlet had when we rescued her. Malnourished, dirty, sunken in cheeks, and eye sockets. Basically, like a meth addict.

"What's interesting?" Hattie asks, covering Amanda with a blanket that had been hanging over the couch.

"The warlock that had her burned up around the same time that Mederio was killed."

"What do you think that's about?" I ask.

"It would seem that all the warlocks Mederio made may have burned up when he did."

"And if that's so . . ." I continue.

"Then that should mean Gauge is safe," Bash finishes.

A relief I didn't know I needed washes over me, and I feel a little lighter. This overwhelming worry I always carry for Gauge lessens just a few notches.

"Do you really think that's what happened?" I ask.

"I don't see what else it could mean. Why would a warlock just up and burst into ash?"

"That's true."

"I need a drink," Hattie says, rising from the couch, and heading to the kitchen.

Bash follows her, exclaiming, "Yes, sister, I like where your head's at."

My heavy eyes and intermittent yawns tell me it's time to lie down.

After rolling the top of the chip bag closed, I bring the hummus, and dip back to the kitchen to put away.

Bash is pouring shots for everyone, and by the time I'm back from putting the chips back in the pantry, they're all shooting them back.

Deciding to leave them to their drinking, I sneak away.

When I arrive at the room I'm staying in, I use the restroom and change into my nightclothes, flicking out the light, and getting into bed.

It isn't long before I hear a soft knock on the door, and even before I say come in, I know it's Bash.

"Yes?" I call to the door.

It opens, and his silhouette fills the space between the door jamb and the door. "Sayah?" he whispers. Soft moonlight pours into my room just enough to light it with an austere glow, although most of the room is pooled in darkness as he enters, drink in hand.

"Yes?" I say again.

"What are you doing?" he asks, sitting on my bed, swaying too much to the left and almost falling off the edge.

"Going to bed."

"Why? I thought we were having a good talk."

"We were. But I'm tired, and you're all drinking, and I'm just getting to that place where I'm not on your level."

He scoots closer to my head on the pillow. "I don't like downstairs without you."

"Bash, you're drunk. I'm tired. Just go have fun. We'll talk more tomorrow."

He doesn't say anything for a few minutes, and although I can't see his face, I know he's looking at me longingly.

"All right," he says after a long pause.

He gets up and moves toward the door. When he arrives at it, he turns to look at me again and stands there as though he has something to say. Then he simply says, "Goodnight, beautiful."

"Goodnight, Bash."

And he shuts the door.

TRAIL OF BLOOD

-SAYAH-

The infancy of morning paints the world in a dusky blue that sneaks in from under the navy-blue curtains. This is the type of light that shines when the sun is just starting to wake up and the sky is that perfect shade of rinsed blue with freckles of pinkish-orange clouds dusted by sunrise.

I pull the covers off and grasp my phone, checking it for new messages.

> Gauge: Mama. I miss you. Please come home soon.

Seeing Gauge's message confirms I need to get home, and soon. There's no point in me staying here anymore. We'd broken the mark on Bash and Dom, Gauge is no longer in danger, and Laureya's now a vampire.

We've got exactly what we came here for.

And then some.

After a quick shower and throwing my hair up into a messy bun, I brush on some makeup and am about to make my way downstairs when I notice blood on the floor in the hallway.

It isn't just drops of blood; it's a trail that leads from the spiral staircase, all along the wood floor, down the hall, and into a bedroom in the back. It's a thick streak, as though someone had drug a bleeding body along the hallway.

In a house full of vampires, this usually wouldn't phase me, but since Laureya is new and is supposed to behave herself, I need to follow the trail of blood to check on her.

Careful not to step on the blood, I follow it to a room at the end of the hall, where I know Laureya's staying.

The door is ajar, so when I push it open, I'm not expecting to see what I see.

The giant four-poster bed is in the middle of the room. Everything's flung off the bed except for the sheets, in which Laureya's wrapped up, her left leg exposed, and draped over the legs of Bash. He's naked too, the other half of the sheet just covering his middle region while she covers his bare chest. Laureya lies with the sheet wrapped around her breasts, her left arm encircling Bash.

Something similar to rage hits me first. The sight of my sister with Bash grates over me in a way I hadn't expected. I want to scream, rip the sheets off him, and beat him with them. But no words or sounds come to me. I simply stand here, staring at their naked bodies, imagining what happened and how it led to where they are now.

And where's the source of the blood?

My eyes haven't even scanned the rest of the room yet; they are stuck on the two naked people in the bed before me.

I clear my throat.

Bash stirs slightly, barely cracking one eye to notice my figure in the doorway. As he lifts his right arm to rub his face, Laureya shifts and groans. He blinks again, focusing on me. His other eye snaps open, both of them widening in surprise. He glances down at Laureya asleep on his chest, and before I can witness anything else, I turn and get the hell out of the room as fast as I can.

Bash is in front of me in the hall within a heartbeat, a sheet wrapped around his middle. "Sayah, wait, it's not what it looks like—"

"Really? Because it looks like you fucked my sister," I spit, my voice venom. I try to move around him, but he flashes in front of me so I can't get by.

"Wait! I know that, and I'm sorry; I was really drunk, and she hit on me, and it didn't mean anything to me, I swear—"

"Get out of my way, Bash!"

"Nothing to you? Ha!" comes Laureya's voice from the room. "Not what you said last night!"

A sound similar to a growl emits from my mouth, and I shove past Bash, unable to articulate why I'm so mad at him. I'm with his brother or used to be with him; I've had sex with Dom, so why am I so upset that Bash had sex with Laureya? It's almost the same. It's pretty much the same thing.

"Sayah, wait!" Bash flashes in front of me yet again. "Please wait. I'm so sorry." His black hair is a tattered mess on top of his head, and the black circles under his eyes reveal that he's hungover; the aroma of whiskey on his breath tells me he's still a little drunk. "I didn't mean for this to happen. I honestly don't remember how we got there. The last thing I remember is us being downstairs playing a card game and taking shots."

I glower at him, and still, no words come to me.

"Sayah, please, I'm so sorry. Please don't be mad at me."

"Get out of my way, Sebastian. I need to think."

Bash's eyes reflect a careful wonder, and a pleading is tucked beneath the depths of the blue. I'm mad at him because I have feelings for him that I don't want to acknowledge yet or can't, and the only way to get past this is to go cry for a minute and move on.

After a long pause, Bash moves out of my way to let me pass.

The weight of my crushing emotions is almost too much to bear. It isn't just that I'm upset about Bash and my sister hooking up; I'm upset about Dom and being away from my child and that my mom isn't here to help me through any of it. It's really starting to get to me.

I've heard it takes time for the death of someone close to you to really hit home, but I hadn't expected it to start hitting me until six or seven months after the actual passing of my mom.

I thought it would have happened the day of, or the next.

But up until this point, I'd been pretty numb to it. I miss my mom every day, but really, I thought the world would've stopped moving when I lost her.

It didn't.

Until now.

I felt the crushing ache of it a few days ago, and it literally felt like it's taking all I have to stay together. Even the slightest movement of an inch threatens to break apart the fault lines that are living across my existence. It creeps up on me increasingly with the happening of things that I can't call Mama about. But now, I feel the cracking of those fault lines; the thread I've been hanging on by breaks, and everything I know falls to pieces around me.

Collapsing on the bed, I bury my head in the pillow and fall apart.

DRUNKEN, BLOODY MISTAKE

-BASH-

What the flying fuck was I thinking? How could I have let this happen?

I curse myself as I return to her room to get my clothes.

There's nothing in this world that could calm me at this moment; I'm so utterly pissed at myself and at Laureya for letting this happen.

As I make my way back to the room, I see the trail of blood. A flash of memories cross my mind.

Me and Laureya giggling during our card game and her telling me she was hungry again. Going outside alone since she couldn't leave to get food. Hunting on the bike path that lines the lake for some poor, unsuspecting runner. Knocking one out with a rock. Bringing him back to the house, dragging him through the hallway and back to the bedroom so the others wouldn't say anything. Then feeding on him together before veilweaveling him and letting him go free once he awoke.

Laureya kissing me and me fighting it at first, but then, us both being drunk from blood and booze, licking the blood off each other and then going from there.

When I enter the room again, Laureya's stark naked, throwing things around while looking for her clothes.

"Oh, hi," she says, her voice bordering anger. "How was your chat?" She throws a pillow at me with the last word.

Catching it, I toss the pillow, and scan the floor for my clothes.

"What's the matter, Bash? Cat got your tongue?" she seethes, pulling on her pink bra and securing it in the back.

I say nothing.

I spot my boxers in the corner by the window and move in for them when she throws my pants at me.

"Say something!"

I slide my boxers underneath the sheet still wrapped around me, only dropping the sheet when the boxers are secure. "What do you want me to say, Laureya?"

"I don't know," she murmurs, sitting on the bed, and pulling her pants up. "Say it wasn't just a drunken, bloody mistake."

I don't know what to say as I scour the room for my shirt. I really don't care if I hurt her; I'm in no mood to pacify her.

"Bash!" She stands up again and retrieves her shirt from the other end of the room. "Say something!"

"Why the fuck do you care, La La? Huh? You have a vamp back in Kansas who you wanted to be relieved of your lycanthrope curse. Go get him."

As she slides her shirt over her head, she eyes me venomously, as though that's not the thing she wanted me to say.

I. Don't. Care.

"What?" I ask, seeing my shirt in the other corner and gathering it up. "What did you think this was?"

She sits on the bed again and just looks out the window.

No part of me entertains the slightest notion of caring for this woman's feelings.

I see my boots strewn haphazardly at the end of the bed,

scoop them up, and start for the door. Laureya throws one of her heels at my head.

The heel digs into the back of my skull, and the sting of it makes me want to turn around and snap her neck again. Instead, I stand still to let her fear me and then turn around to look at her.

Her eyes are a cross between anger and sadness.

I pull the heel out of my head and toss it her way, landing a few inches from her bare feet.

"I'm leaving. Today! I want a ride to the airport, and I'm getting the fuck out of this horrible city!" she screams.

"Call a rideshare," I tell her, but then point to the blood trail. "Clean this shit up first."

Again, I don't care.

I hear her shouting something about helping her with the blood cleanup as I walk away, leaving her alone to her sadness or anger or whatever the fuck it is she's feeling toward me. I head to my room to take a shower and wash her stink off me.

BLOODLINK BOND

-SAYAH-

After a long, hard cry, I return downstairs for coffee. I need to get to the airport and get back home to my child as soon as possible.

As I wait for the coffee maker to warm up, Laureya comes storming down the stairs. I have nothing to say to her, but I don't have any real reason to be upset with my sister.

Bash is not mine to get jealous over.

Laureya stomps all the way past me and to the front door.

When it still won't open, she screams, "Somebody let me the fuck out of this place!" She yanks the handle over and over again, thinking the harder she pulls, it will have to open, eventually. "Sayah! Let me out! You're a witch; counter her boundary spell and let me out!"

"I can't. It's not my spell."

"Goddamn it!" She stomps off toward the spell room.

Shaking my head to myself, I put the coffee pod in the hole and push the power button.

A few minutes later, Laureya returns without anyone trailing her.

Sobbing quietly, she sits at the counter and pulls out her phone, opening the app to summon a rideshare.

"My ride will be here in twenty minutes," she says. "That boundary spell better be lifted by then."

"Did you find Adaline?"

"No, but Jasantha was passed out in the spell room, and I woke her to either get Adaline or Scarlet to let me the fuck out."

"Where are you going to go?" I ask, pouring creamer in the coffee.

"Back to Kansas. You guys don't need me anymore, and I can't wait to get back to Ryan."

"Oh, right. Ryan." I snigger at the notion that Laureya has a boyfriend whom she loves and wants to change for, and yet still had sex with another man last night.

"What are you laughing at?" Laureya asks, tapping something on her phone before setting it down.

"Nothing," I reply and direct myself toward the back porch.

"Morning!" Ollie declares as he comes down the spiral staircase.

I glance at him and give him a half smile, continuing on my path to the porch.

Ollie must sense something from me because instead of joining Laureya in the kitchen, he follows me to the porch. Either that, or he just doesn't want to be alone with Laureya.

"You okay?" Ollie asks, sliding the door closed.

I take one of the chairs surrounding a table on the deck overlooking the lake—the same deck I'd had those dreams about Bash on.

"I don't know," I answer truthfully, cupping my mug.

"I think you probably walked in on something you didn't want to see," he says as he takes a seat across from me.

Ollie has the kindest eyes one could imagine, even for a vampire. His soft blond hair is a little longer since it isn't slicked back, giving him more of a biker vibe. He is wearing a plain white T-shirt, dark jeans, and white shoes to match the shirt.

"You could say that, yeah."

"Well, before you let it affect you too much, I have to tell you about the bloodlink bond that happens when one vampire sires another."

I look at him blankly, waiting for him to continue.

Ollie's face scrunches up, the morning sun lighting the features of his face. "When a man turns a woman into a vampire"—he pulls a white lighter from his pocket—"the exchanging of blood is seductive. Not only does his blood make her a vampire, but her body is drained of life, and the life force that enters the vampire creates this sort of high. He is feeling high and then feeds her his blood, which has the same effect on her. When her body dies with his blood in her system, she is actually revived back to life by the vampire's blood. Thus creates a dancing of blood." He grabs the half cigar sitting in the ashtray on the railing, flicking the lighter to the end of it. "Usually, after the female transitions, that bloodlink bond fades. Only every so often does it carry on and become something. But if they have sex and exchange more intimate fluids, it is intensified. Not so much for the male sire, but for the female subject. Yes, he feels a pull toward her that's almost impossible to resist at the time, but afterward, it's take it or leave it for him. But for her, she feels she's in love with him, would do anything for him; but if he doesn't return those feelings, it hurts worse than a breakup."

I watch as the smoke butterflies around his head when he puffs. "And if the roles were reversed, and the female made the male?"

"Same thing."

"What about same-sex?"

"Same if there is an attraction from one to the other."

"So you're saying that Bash fucked her because he felt he had to, and now she's in love with him and angry with him because he doesn't feel the same?"

He taps the ash off the cigar. "Essentially, yes."

"That still doesn't make me feel any better."

"I had hoped it sort of would."

"Why?"

"Because he didn't fuck her 'cause he wanted to or 'cause he was attracted to her. It was the combination of the blood exchange and the booze they drank."

"Have you experienced this before?"

"I have, yes."

"Who did you make into a vampire?"

"Her name was Katie. Or is Katie, I should say. She's still around. I see her from time to time."

I take a long drink of my coffee. "Tell me about it." I bat my eyelashes at him, so he feels veilweaveled to tell me.

"Your veilweaving doesn't work like mine," he chortles, taking a few pulls from the cigar. "She was just some woman I hung out with when I was younger. She liked me, but I was never attracted to her that way. I liked her as a person, but nothing more. She was like my best friend; she knew my secret and loved my sisters, and they loved her back—"

"What?" Now I'm shook. "Jasantha, Hattie, and Scarlet liked another girl?"

He laughs again, and his straight white teeth shine. "Yes, they did. There was a time when she finally convinced us to make her a vampire. She loved our family and wanted to be a part of it. We agreed to it because she had lost her family to the plague; she was the only survivor. We had done this the old-fashioned way. Draining her for three nights and then feeding her my blood and letting her die. I was the one who did it, and maybe because it was a process back then, I began to feel something for her. When she was fully transitioned, we drank to celebrate. The more I drank, the more drawn to her I was, to the point where I had to have her. I couldn't resist her anymore. We fucked like rabbits all night that night."

I blush at the mention of Ollie's sex life.

"I didn't feel anything," he continues after stubbing the cigar out, "but she was obsessed. She followed me around and wouldn't leave me alone, trying to do anything to make me happy. Finally I had to ask her to leave, and that caused a huge fight. The girls got involved and had to threaten her, and she finally left for fifty years or so and found her own way. The last time I ran into her, she still acted like there were some residual feelings for me, so I just kept it casual and let her be."

"You don't think there's a way to break the bloodlink bond?" I ask, taking another sip of my coffee.

"Not one that I am aware of. But you, being a witch, can research it."

"I can, yeah. But she's leaving right now. She wants to go back to Kansas."

"Good," Ollie says, leaning back in the chair, and crossing his legs. "Let her go. Still, figure out how to break that bond because it'll never go away for her. And if you ever see her again, which I am sure you will, it'll probably be hard for you and Bash, especially if you're together."

"But we're not together."

Ollie gives me a wistful smile. "Not yet."

The dance my stomach does at the notion is hard to ignore.

DANCING BLOOD

-BASH-

After my long, hot shower, I scour the closet and drawers for something fresh to wear. Typically, this is not my room, but Mom keeps the closet and drawers stocked with things all her children are likely to wear in case of an impromptu visit.

Deciding on dark jeans and a black button-down shirt, I dress, put on my boots, and head to the kitchen.

Laureya's sitting at the counter with her purse slung over her shoulder and her phone in hand, barely looking up at me when I enter.

I grab a cup from the cupboard, and instead of pouring coffee, I go to the spell room to get bourbon. The alcohol seems to take the edge off the addiction I feel rear up. But that's when I see Sayah and Ollie outside talking on the back deck.

This bothers me more than I'd like to admit, and I flash down the hall to grab the bourbon and return to the main room in a second.

Ignoring Laureya, I zip toward the deck where they are sitting.

I open the sliding glass door that leads out to them, and they immediately stop talking.

"Hey," I say, sliding the door closed behind me.

Ollie nods at me, and Sayah glances at me, then away again, cupping her mug to her chest.

She looks beautiful today, as always. I noticed how pretty she was in the hallway earlier, with her hair up in a messy bun when usually it's down and wavy. I like how she looks with her hair up; I can see more of her face. Her ears are showing, too; she has petite ears that are small and cute, but she adorns them with a multitude of tiny diamonds. Not just the double-pierced lobes girls typically have, but she has four tiny diamonds crawling up her right ear, and a heart decorates the middle. On the other side, she has three opals in the middle section of her upper ear, a hoop through her conch, and another diamond sitting on the inside middle of her ear.

It makes her sparkle.

I pull out a chair at the end of the table and unscrew the cap on the bourbon, pouring a healthy portion into the coffee mug.

"What are you two talking about?" I ask when no one speaks.

"Oh, just how Laureya is blood linked to you," Sayah says, catching my eyes then looking over to Ollie.

I spit the bourbon back into the cup. "What?" I ask, looking at Ollie, too.

"Oh, c'mon, man," Ollie groans, his green eyes staring into mine in earnest. "Don't tell me you didn't know about the bloodlink bond."

I've heard of it happening from time to time from other vampires, but have never truly experienced it for myself. I thought it happened when you make a vampire the old-fashioned way.

"What?" I say again.

"Laureya," Ollie confirms, recrossing his legs the other way.

"She is bloodlinked to you. That's why you felt like you had to . . . you know."

I take a drink of my bourbon and then look at Sayah.

Is that what that was? Because before last night, I'd not been attracted to Laureya. Even today, nothing about her makes me want to do that again. Ever. I even fully regret it; it makes me sick to think about it.

"Is that what that was?" I ask, leaning back in the chair.

The sun's still low in the sky from its morning ascent, painting the lake a dazzling color of orange. But the way it's backlit against Sayah makes her all the more magickal, her dark brown hair sticking up in spots from the messy bun it's pulled into. A slight breeze picks up, and I catch a whiff of her blood—that beautiful, glorious scent of Sayah blood. I feel the fangs yearn to be set free and plunge into the depths of her jugular. To taste that pungent, sweet nectar of life that fuels her and catapults me to the moon.

Thinking to myself where my Alpha Zen is, I take another drink of bourbon and concur that I need to go get some soon.

Willing the fangs back into my gums and taking a deep breath, I look again at Sayah, who's looking to the right of her, away from me.

"Yes," Ollie resumes, as though we hadn't skipped a beat. "The exchange of your blood, the booze, the death of her at your hands, and also her revival. It's a very seductive dance of blood."

I stir the bourbon around by swirling my wrist. "So that's why she's all coo-coo?"

Ollie smiles a bit. Sayah still hasn't turned. "Yes."

"Will it ever go away?"

"Not to my knowledge. I was telling Sayah about Katie. You remember her, don't you?"

"Oh, yeah, crazy Katie. Gods, I haven't thought about her in ages. That's what made her all psycho for you?"

"Yes. That's why she went nuts and had to go."

"And it never got better?"

"No. That's what I was telling Sayah: Maybe she could help you break it. There's got to be a way to break a bloodlink bond."

"I have to get back today," Sayah says suddenly, as if the talk of breaking curses makes her think of something.

"I'll come with you," I state, although I'm not sure she wants me anywhere near her anymore.

"Do whatever you want," she snaps with a hint of annoyance.

"I was thinking," Ollie mentions, "I could come, too. Maybe help you guys try and find Dom."

"I don't mind you coming," I say, asking Sayah for approval.

"You can come, too. I don't mind."

Laureya's at the glass door, banging on it.

Ollie stands up and slides it open.

"Will one of you please go get your mom and tell her to let me out? My ride's here."

Ollie sighs and goes in, shutting the door behind him.

Sayah doesn't look at me, returning her gaze to the lake and the scenery to the right of her.

"Sayah," I say, leaning forward. "Sayah, please talk to me."

"There's nothing to say, Bash. I have no right to be angry with you for sleeping with her."

"Yes, you do. I know if you'd hooked up with Ollie, I'd be pretty fucking pissed at you."

"But that's just it, Bash. I didn't hook up with Ollie, but I have hooked up with Dom. And I'm still with Dom. I mean, I think I am. The point is, I can't assume his letter to me was actually him. And if it wasn't, or just a fragment of him, and he still wants to be with me, I owe it to him to not . . . fall . . . for one of his brothers. What kind of shitty person would that make me? I guess this whole thing was a wake-up call for me. To . . ."

She trails off here, and I cling to every last word she says. "To?" I press her.

"To let go of whatever it is I've been feeling for you and focus on finding him and getting him home."

The words sting, for the meaning behind them, is that she had been falling for me, and I fucked it all up by sleeping with her sister.

I don't give a shit about Dom and my relationship, or Dom's feelings. Sayah's a person I'm drawn to for more reasons than just her blood singing to me. She's the reason I want to be a better man. She's the whole entire reason I exist.

No other person on Earth makes me want to be a better human.

"Sayah, I'm so sorry," is all I can say.

Here, she looks at me, and her dark blue eyes catch me. That summer storm I feel brewing inside me when I look at her powers on and turns the insides of my body to mush, quieting the monster that rages on internally.

When that monster met her storm, all became right within the world beneath the surface of my soul. The encounter with the hurricane that lives in her bones quiets the demon, and even though it's like saying there's a hushed calm in the storm, I feel like that's what the eye of the hurricane would feel like. Chaotic winds and torrential rain rage all around me, yet I feel safe clinging to this one little palm tree in the middle of a tiny island in the center of this furious storm.

"There's really nothing to be sorry for, Bash. Honestly, let's just keep being friends, move past this, and keep trying to find Dom. Okay?"

Nodding at her, I put my hand out on the table for her to take. Surprisingly, she takes it, and I caress her hand with my thumb.

While I tell her with my eyes and the gesture that I will be her friend and help her find Dom, only one is true.

I will help her find Dom, but I will never be her friend. I will have her as mine, with no other exceptions.

She's my person.

Ollie appears again, shutting the door behind him.

"Did Mom get the boundary spell down for her?"

He nods his head. "Yep. She's gone."

"Thank gods," I say, letting go of Sayah's hand and leaning back, as Ollie eyes our touching hands while sitting down again.

"So, when are we leaving?" Ollie asks.

SMITTEN KITTEN

-SAYAH-

The morning sun bathes the deck in the soft light, cascading through the planks on the side and dappling the wood with star shapes from the trees. I try to focus on the sunlight, the water, the wind—anything that will lend me strength to breathe truth into the words I just spoke to Bash.

His blue eyes hold a sinister softness; like he agrees with what I just said with words, but I know he'll never accept being only my friend.

I'm still upset with Bash and the fact that he had sex with my sister. There's no denying that. But after letting myself fall apart and then also hearing what Ollie had to say, I know it wasn't lust that drew Bash to Laureya. It'd been the bloodlink bond.

It makes me feel a bit better, but knowing I have to let him go to find Dom also counters my raging hormones for Bash.

"We should probably get going soon," I tell the group.

My phone vibrates from my back pocket. I pull it out and see Claire video calling me.

Getting up, I walk to the edge of the porch with the boys behind me and answer it.

"Hey," I say as Claire's pretty face appears on the screen.

"Hey, girl! What are you doing? I haven't heard from you in a while."

Where do I even begin to tell Claire what I've been doing?

"Oh, boy, where to start," I answer. There isn't a way to tell her about the whole ordeal, but maybe just mentioning that my sister's back will satisfy Claire. She always knows when there's something wrong with me. "So, I can't really get too much into it right now, but let's just say my sister made an appearance in my life, and I had to come to New York to sort some things out."

Claire's eyes blow wide with shock. "Holy shit, Laureya hit you up?"

"Yeah," I say, holding the phone up by resting my elbow on the balcony. "Super long story. But I'm coming back tonight, I think. Stop by later if you want I'll catch you up."

"Yeah, I will, for sure." Her eyes light up as she looks beyond my shoulder. "Hey, who's that behind you?"

In the little square with me, I can clearly see Ollie. As well as Bash.

"Oh, those are Dom's brothers."

"Brothers, huh? Wow," she says, and I can see she's interested from the way her eyes light up.

"Yeah. Dom isn't here right now. He, uh, went to the store." I glance behind me and see both boys are looking in my direction. Bash tips his mug to her and takes a drink.

Claire's eyes narrow in on Ollie, her perfectly sculpted brows drawing together mischievously. "Who's the one in the white? Is he coming, too?"

I smile at my best friend. "That's Ollie. And yes, he's coming back with me and his other brother Bash."

Her face folds with worry and confusion. "Bash?"

"Yes." I smirk, looking at Bash surreptitiously through the picture on the phone. "It's short for Sebastian. You'll meet them both tonight, and I can explain things better in person."

"Sounds good. What time should I come by?"

"I'll text you when I land. That'll give you an idea of when to head over."

"All right, girlie, I'll see you soon."

"Okay, hon. Bye-bye."

I hit the red "X" to end the call and turn around. Ollie's leaning back with his hand cupping his chin, and Bash has a shit-eating grin.

"What?" I ask, returning to my seat.

"Who's your friend?" Ollie inquires, his dark brown brows arching.

"That was Claire. My best friend."

He scratches the stubble on his face. "Wow."

"What?"

His cheeks are flushed bright pink. "She's beautiful."

"Oh, yes, yes, she is. You should see her in person. Even more so then."

"She's coming by tonight?" Ollie asks, leaning back in his chair.

"Yes. I'm gonna have to come up with something about where Dom is and why I am returning to Colorado with his two brothers and not him."

"We'll come up with something on the plane," Bash says, tipping back his mug to chug the rest of the bourbon. "Let's get going, shall we?"

KALEIDOSCOPE OF NIGHTMARES

-SAYAH-

While on the plane, Bash and I had devised the story to tell Claire. Dom had an emergency work trip to London and sent his two brothers to Colorado with me to not only look after me when he cannot, but also to take care of his house while he's away.

That sounds like a good enough story for me.

The other stuff? Well, I will have to tell her sooner or later. I just don't know how.

When we arrive at my house, Bash and Ollie unload the car, and I go inside to check on Nox. Even though I'd had the neighbor watching him for me while I was away, Nox meows madly as I enter, letting me know how upset he is with my being gone.

As I scoop him up and snuggle him close, Bash thunders in.

"Where am I going with these?" Bash asks as he enters the house from the garage door.

I set my purse down on the end table by the TV and say, "You and Ollie will have to pick who gets the guest room. The other one of you will get the couch. Or Gauge's room until he gets home tomorrow."

"I'll take the couch," Bash offers. "Ollie can have the room."

"Um, can someone let me in?" Ollie yells from the garage door.

I'd forgotten I have to invite them in.

"Ollie, please come in!" I shout, smiling at this silly little perk.

Dangerous killers having to be asked to come in. It's utter nonsense.

"Thanks," Ollie says, entering the house with the other suitcase. "We can always go stay at Dom's house, too."

"That's okay," I say, letting Nox bound to the ground. He's had enough snuggling. "I don't mind the company."

"I'm gonna put this upstairs then and then run to grab some bourbon," Bash announces, wheeling both bags to the stairs and then flashing up to the top.

"The room is up there," I say, nodding in the direction Bash flashed off to.

"I figured," he replies with a wry smile.

Bash's back in the blink of an eye. "All right, I'm gonna run up to the liquor store."

"I'll come, too," Ollie states. "I want some beer."

"You cool with us drinking here?" Bash's jaw is clenched from biting down his addiction, from being so close to me.

"It doesn't bother me," I state, slipping out of my shoes.

"Cool," he adds, winking. "Be right back."

When Bash and Ollie are gone, I climb into the oversized, comfy chair and prop my legs on the ottoman, grabbing my computer to see how behind in homework I've gotten.

A knock on the door interrupts my concentration.

I make my way to the door, seeing it's Claire through the long window lining the side.

"Hi," I greet her when I open the door, giving her a hug.

"Hi," Claire says, entering with two plastic grocery bags. "I brought stuff to make s'mores. I figured we could hang out by the fire. It's almost summer."

"Great idea!" The Colorado nights are growing warmer. Night chills the bones with remnants of winter, so being outdoors without a hoodie is ill-advised. However, outside fires are good to have in the spring. "Let's go back there and get it going. The boys will be back soon."

"Yes, the boys. I want to know about this statement," Claire says as we slip out to the back. "That man in white . . . Oh. My. God."

"He's a really great guy."

"Ollie? That's his name? And the other one's Bash?"

"Yes. They're both . . . interesting," I say, pulling the lid off the firepit.

"Where are they?"

"They went to go get beer and bourbon."

As I grab wood from the pile I'd made by the fence, Claire's there to help, setting the bags down by the pit. "So, is your man with them?"

"No," I answer, putting a few logs on the top of the pit. "He had a crazy emergency happen with work and had to go to London." I hate lying to her, but saying he's in the States also feels like a lie.

I don't know why.

"So," she continues, her Caribbean green eyes sparkling, "why are his brothers here with you?"

"He wanted them to keep me company since he couldn't, and to also go by his house to water his plants and take care of the trash and lawn. He doesn't know how long he'll be away for."

"So what's Ollie's story?" Claire questions, laying another log on the pile.

I grab the newspaper under the stones and crumple pages for kindling.

With how loaded a question it is, I wish the boys would

hurry up so that Ollie can tell her himself. I'm not sure what his human story is.

"Um, I'm not too sure about that. I just met him a few weeks ago and haven't spent much time alone with him."

Almost on cue, Bash comes out of the back glass door with a bottle of bourbon in hand, and Ollie's behind with a twelve-pack and some tequila.

"What's going on out here?" he asks, walking off the deck, and joining us by the firepit.

"Oh, we thought we'd start a fire and make some s'mores," I say. "Bash, Ollie, this is Claire, Claire, Bash, Ollie."

"Pleased to meet you," Bash says, shaking her hand.

"You as well," Claire says back.

"Claire?" Ollie says, situating the beer under his left arm so he can hold out his right hand to her. Claire gives him her hand, and he kisses the top of it. "Enchanté."

Claire blushes a little. "Nice to meet you, Ollie."

"Would you like a beer?" Ollie asks her, stepping onto the flagstone and setting the beer beside a chair.

"I would love one," Claire answers, sitting in one of the chairs, and Ollie sits beside her.

As they begin chatting, Bash approaches me, and I resume crumpling paper to put in the firepit.

"Need any help?" Bash asks, unscrewing the top of the bottle and taking a swig.

"Sure. Do you want a glass for that?" I ask, handing him some of the pile of paper.

"Nah, I'm good with just the bottle." He sits on the edge of the firepit and sets his bottle on the ground, scrunching up paper, and sticking it into spaces between the logs.

"We need music," I say, leaving Bash to do the kindling while I fetch the speaker from inside. While at it, I grab the orange lighter from the spell cabinet and return to them outside.

I turn the speaker on and set it on the firepit. "What does everyone wanna listen to?"

"Girl, you know I'm good with whatever you play," Claire answers.

"I'm not picky either," Ollie says, taking a sip of his beer.

"Tupac it is." I laugh and pull out my phone to press play on the playlist.

Tupac isn't what comes on, but he'll make an appearance at some point.

After the music plays, I take the lighter, and light all the pieces of paper sticking out from between the logs. To get them to catch fire, I lean forward and blow into the flames, causing the different paper particles to alight and set the logs on fire. As the fires all dwindle, I take the lighter, and try to get the fire going again, all of which go out before the logs catch.

Bash leans in ever so slightly and blows, every paper catching flame so much that the logs ignite after.

He winks at me.

"How'd you do that?" I ask, sitting down in one of the chairs.

"Magick," he answers, still sitting on the firepit.

Claire and Ollie are too into each other to notice what Bash has done with the flames.

"You better move," I say giggling, and he moves into the chair next to me, scooting in closer. "But really, how did you do that?"

"You know how vampires all have a secret power that's individual to them?" he says quietly so that Claire can't hear him.

Ollie definitely can, though.

"Well, I remember Dom telling me about veilweaving and memory erosion. That's really all he said about it."

"Yes, his weirdo power is changing people's memories," Bash says mockingly. "One of mine is fire and air. I can control fire. Along with using vibrations of the earth. It's weird, too."

"What? That's not weird—that's cool as hell. And also, a little coincidental about my whole burning alive and coming back from ash thing."

"I'd never thought of that as being a connection to why what happened happened," he says, picking up the bottle of bourbon.

"What are some of your siblings' powers? I mean, besides Jasantha. I know hers."

I've asked Dom before, but want to see what Bash says about them.

The way his black eyebrows and lashes compliment his eyes always has me in a trance just looking at him. The way the brows bob and weave with inflections of his voice is captivating. "Scarlet can subdue people with her voice—not too much unlike Jasantha, but Scar can manipulate emotions. Jasantha can't do that. Scar can make them calm, or feel drunk, or maybe even love someone. My mom can give powers to people, as she has an abundance of them since she's a witch. One of them is seeing their worst fear, as you know. She also has visions sometimes. My dad's is mimicry. He can mimic sounds and even faces with enough power. Hattie can spell people to see what she wants them to see. This is how she spelled us to always see this face in the mirror that you get the pleasure of looking at right now." At this, he smirks, and takes a drink from the bottle. "And Ollie is an elemental vampire. He can manipulate water, fire, earth, and air. He also has visions sometimes. Subjective futures."

"Ollie can see subjective futures?"

"Yes. He can see a future where someone's path is placed at the time if it aligns with his own path. It's subject to change with a person's choices, with his choices. It doesn't always come true, but sometimes it does."

This makes me think back to what he said to me this morning. At the time, it had seemed that he'd known more about what he was saying than he was letting on.

"Is that why he was being all weird when I was talking to Claire earlier?"

Bash gives me his sideways smile. "Yeah, you could say that."

"What did he see?"

Looking over at the two of them, Bash says, "He saw some things."

I glance over the fire at them as well, the fire that's now raging, and it seems that every time I look over at them, Ollie's chair is an inch or two closer to Claire's.

The look on Claire's face is serene. I can tell she's drawn to Ollie, but I'm not sure if he's using any powers or if she just finds him that interesting.

"So, these visions," I continue, "they're subjective? Also, how does he have them? Can he control them?"

"It's a finicky power," Bash answers, directing his attention back to me. "He can only have them if they're related directly to him, meaning if he's in them. He can't tell you your future—only the parts he's in."

"Oh," I say, my mind drifting back to Dom and wondering where he is. "Well, if Dom is in Ollie's future, can he see that?"

"Can Ollie tell if Dom is dead or not?"

The way Bash says it so casually rips at a seam I didn't know had come undone. "Well, yeah, I guess."

"I honestly didn't think to ask him that. I don't know how his visions work. I know he doesn't always have them, but when he does, they're unexpected flashes. I don't know what triggers them."

"Do you think when he saw Claire, he saw a flash of something for the two of them?"

"I do. Because he just decided to come with us when he saw Claire on your screen, he may have seen this scene right here."

"And if he hadn't made the decision to come here . . ."

"He wouldn't have seen it."

"Okay, I kind of get it. So if he makes a decision in the next few days that affects his path and puts him on one that leads to Dom, he may see a vision of him?"

"Exactly. He may have already made a choice that will affect a vision. He came here to help us find him."

"I still don't know how all of us being here will help find him, more so than being in New York."

"The map showed one dot here. May as well start here," Bash says, tipping the bottle to his lips again.

"And the other three were not here. One in New York, California, and Scotland. I just have no idea where to even start."

"Well, we would have known if he had been in New York. My mom would have seen a vision, or something would have told us. But for all of us to think he was elsewhere, that's like seven vamp powers telling us he is somewhere else."

I cringe at the thought of his mom again. It's something that's bubbling inside me and will boil over soon if I don't confront it. Or fester and rot. "Can I ask you something?" I ask timidly.

His sapphire eyes hold me captive. They make me feel safe asking this question. "Anything," he replies, and the way the word rolls off his tongue sparkles.

"Did you know your mom killed my mom?"

His face falls. "What?" he says on an exhale, inching back to see my eyes clearly.

"So you didn't know," I murmur, picking at one of my cuticles.

"Sayah," he says, pulling my chin up to look at me. "Tell me what happened. Please."

Swallowing my hardened feelings for his mother, I tell him the story about how I found out his mother had my parents killed. His expressions change with my story, and the depth of sorrow in his eyes is evident.

"Oh, Sayah, I am so sorry. I had no idea," he offers when I finish.

"And I know she didn't just have my mom killed for shits and giggles. I know her intentions were pure, trying to capitalize on the prophecy. But it doesn't change what happened. Or bring my best friend back. I just . . . I don't even know what to do about it. Do I confront her? Do I let it go?"

Bash says nothing, only looking into my eyes, seemingly searching for the answers I haven't found. "No. You don't do anything."

My brows draw together. "What do you mean?"

"Nothing for you to worry about. I'll handle it."

"Bash," I snap, grabbing his hand. "Don't do anything rash. I know she was just trying to protect her children. You guys. I—"

"Sayah. Please don't worry about it. I will handle it."

"Sebastian—"

"Oh, using my full name." He smiles wickedly. "Next thing you know, you'll be middle-naming me."

"What is your middle name?" I ask with a grin.

He shakes his head. "Uh-uh. Nope. Not telling you."

"Ollie!" I shout over to the snuggly couple, but then Bash wraps his arms around my shoulders and cups his hand over my mouth.

"Yes?" Ollie says, smirking.

"Nothing, brother, she just wanted to say hello."

"Whmgasg himgsgj midsgljsg snagmdge," I try to shout through his hand. When Bash tickles me, I squirm and scream, getting up from the chair and running into the lawn.

He chases me, and without using his supernatural speed, he still tackles me and lands on top of me, breathing hard.

All desperate looks and smoldering dreams wrap up into a moment sealed by stars and stamped by fate, causing the world to disappear again.

Our breathing hitches us to each other, and those eyes become a kaleidoscope of nightmares and daydreams. My world triumphantly comes to a halt before my own life and up becomes down, left is now right, and the Earth stops and starts rotating in the opposite direction. The magnetic pull of Bash to my heart is similar to when you slam that last puzzle piece home, when the magnet finds the perfect metal, when the waves taste the sand of the beaches, or when a seed nestles in fertile soil. He is home.

I found home.

Our souls begin their secret exchange of something more than words. His lips inch closer to mine. I lick my bottom lip again, anticipating catching those hungry lips on mine—

"Ahem," Ollie's phlegmy cough slices through our near-kiss and the world stitches itself back together again.

I look over, and Claire is staring at us. Ollie is standing above us, clearly stopping us from doing what we were about to do.

"Yessss?" Bash asks, still not getting off me.

"I gotta piss," Ollie says nonchalantly.

"So go piss," Bash says, and I scramble out from under him.

"Bathrooms are . . ." Ollie asks as I get to my feet and dust the yellow grass off.

"Right inside. One on the main floor and two upstairs."

"You're a man; just pee on the tree right there," Claire calls to him from her chair.

"I'm a gentleman above all else," Ollie says, bowing his head before walking toward the house.

"I gotta go, too," Bash says, leaving just us girls outside alone.

Claire gets up and joins me in the empty chair next to me.

"Oh, my god," Claire breathes, leaning close to me. "Where the hell have you been hiding that man?"

"That good, eh?" I ask, smiling.

"He's something else. Like completely. I can't even tell you what kind of connection I feel to him, but it's intense. So intense. Like hypnotic."

I'm pretty sure that's part of the power they all have. I can only nod and stay quiet, as no words come to me that would make any sense to Claire.

Claire stares into the fire as she drinks her beer. "What is it about him? I mean, there's something off. I can sense it. What's up with them?"

I shrug and grab one of the s'mores sticks from the side of the firepit. "They are all like that. They're just very . . . chivalrous. Old school. Even Bash."

"Bash seems like he's into you. Like mad into you. Do you feel that, too?"

Oh, Claire, how I wish I could tell you the whole story.

"There's some connection, yes. But he knows I'm with Dom, and I think that's what causes the tension. You know, forbidden fruit and all."

"Yeah, that's true. But damn! He's hot, too! They both are. Well, they all are—I just don't look at Dom like that."

I touch my lips where he almost kissed me. "Yes, they are."

"Do you think I should hook up with him tonight?" Claire takes another gulp of her beer.

"Fuck, yes, you should, girl. Get yours." I laugh. I also want to know the tea about how Ollie is in bed. Vamp sex is hot, and I want Claire to experience it. I also wonder how Bash is in bed. Fuck Laureya for finding out first.

"Hand me that bag, will you?" I ask before my libido spills over into my heart and causes me to find out. Tonight.

Claire hands me the bag with the marshmallows, graham crackers, and chocolate. "Can I stay here tonight if I have another few beers?"

"Of course, love. Ollie's staying in the extra bedroom anyway, so it'll give you the room alone."

Claire grins ear to ear and downs her beer as the boys return. She stands and moves to the chair next to Ollie, who sits back down again and hands her another drink.

Bash takes his seat next to me once again.

"How was your chat with your brother?" I ask snidely,

opening the graham crackers, and putting two on the edge of the firepit.

"You're confusing us with two teenage girls. Men don't gossip about things."

"Right. So, no talk about the two hot girls by the fire?" I grin, pausing putting together my s'more to look back at him over my shoulder.

"Well, that wasn't a chat. That was facts."

"Mm-hmm." I giggle, opening the bag of marshmallows.

As I put a marshmallow on the end of the poker, it slides down faster than I'd expected and slices the tip of my finger open. Blood seeps from the wound and drips onto the flagstone. The breeze drifts the scent of my blood toward Bash. I look at him, finding his eyes deadly white, right before he lunges at me.

RELAPSE

-SAYAH-

iving to the side before he can pounce on me, I quiver as the crest of nightmares fully abounds. He catches himself somehow and stops inches from my face, his jaw clenched tight. The hard lines of it expand as he bites down on his hunger. The blue of his irises tries to seep back in and he looks away, clenching his eyes shut as his fangs slowly retract. Quickly, I put my finger in my mouth to get the smell of blood out of the air, but it's too late.

Bash speeds over to the fence in a blink, away from me and my cut finger. Claire sees what happens, and her eyes blow wide at the sight of Bash moving at inhuman speeds. Ollie grabs her head by the chin and begins whispering to her, veilweaveling her to think nothing of what's happening.

As I look at Bash by the fence, his mystic demeanor blends in with the murky shadows of the night, the somber sky covering the world in a blanket of darkness. He's leaning against the fence with his back to me, one arm propped up against it and head down as though trying to catch his breath.

I have to get inside to wash the blood away, to get it to stop bleeding, to cover it with a bandage so he can't smell it anymore.

Fuck, why aren't my healing powers working right now?

Ollie's still whispering to Claire. She's in a trance, frozen in time, her arms crossed across her chest, her beer dangling in her left hand.

I stand and cautiously back up to the door of the house to ensure that Bash doesn't follow me. But before I'm even at the sink, he's there, creeping into my space.

I watch as he walks into the dining room attached to the kitchen, eyes white, fangs bared, and my heart plummets. His beautiful face is vacant, and I know that he wouldn't hear me if I tried to reason with him.

The familiar feeling I'd had in the dreams washes over me again. He is my death, and I'm okay with it. The beautiful dark creature before me is to be my undoing. I feel perfectly okay to be undone by him.

My hand's hovering over the sink, blood dripping into it, and Bash is in front of me with one slick movement.

"Bash," I warn calmly, putting up my bleeding hand to keep him from getting closer. "Bash, snap out of it. You know you can't bite me; we'll burn. It's happened before."

He doesn't seem to hear me; he just keeps inching closer to me.

I back up to the counter, and he's pushing all his weight against me.

Terror grips me and I know I should run, but something holds me frozen in my tracks.

His arms straddle both sides of me and grasp the counter. His breath is hot on my neck, but instead of moving away from him, I tilt my head further to make it easier for him to bite me.

Instead of going for my neck, Bash's lips seal around my finger, and it burns with the most exquisite sort of pain as he sucks the blood dripping from the wound. The urge to scream is overwhelming, but not from fear. It's from the pleasure and pain mixing together until it's impossible to decipher one from the other.

The wonderful, euphoric feeling hits me as my blood leaves me. I'm immediately aroused, my clit tingling as he sucks my life force from me. I don't want him to stop, don't care that all the hard work he's done to rid himself of the addiction is now gone, and it's back and overwhelming.

I bite my arm and then feed it to him; his hungry mouth moving from my fingertip, his breath growing erratic and heated. With every drop of my blood Bash pulls from my body, he gives me something back in return. Something I've been grasping at since the moment he entered my dreams, my life. The exquisite pain of it intermingles with the pleasure and melts together so much that I can't tell where one ends and the other begins. The pain flares up inside of me, tormenting me until it reaches a new height, and I don't think I can take anymore, when suddenly it shifts. Buttery creamy warmth fills up every inch of me, coating my insides until even my eyelashes feel heavy. The world disappears, and all that's left is me and Bash. The sweet torture of him feasting on me while replacing the bits of me he takes with himself, strands me in the ether, and I become unhinged, wanting him to bite me everywhere and drain all my blood.

What would happen if he bit my neck?

I already burned once. I almost don't care if I did again, as long as it is with him.

Something snaps into place between us, something I cannot quite grasp onto, but it isn't just physical. It's as though every fiber of who we are is screaming at the world for keeping us apart so long. Everyone before us who had made us feel like shells of who we were before this moment welds us back together stronger than before. The conjoining of our blood unites us, making us feel more alive and more of who we've always meant to be than we ever have before.

As he's feeding on my arm, I hear the door open and hurried footfalls on the hardwood, but I have my head tipped back and my eyes are closed, and I just don't care.

"BASH!" That's Ollie's voice, but it sounds far away like they're crashing against my skin in waves. Even though I think he's in the same room as us, he sounds muffled, as though he's a world away. Everything is too much and not enough all at the same time.

I feel Bash leave me, stopping his feeding from me, and when I open my eyes, Ollie stands between us, holding Bash at arm's-length.

"Really, Sayah?" Ollie scolds me as I blink back to reality. "I didn't think that much about Bash being able to control himself, but I definitely thought more of you." The look in his green eyes is haunting and stern, as though I'd just pissed off my favorite teacher.

"I'm sorry," I murmur sullenly, although I'm really not sorry at the moment.

"No, you don't understand. Now, he's just going to have to start over with his detox. Way to go, guys. And your friend is out there dazed as all hell because I had to veilweave her to not notice the vampire debauchery happening around her!"

I look over Ollie's shoulder at Bash, who looks like he'd just shot up the biggest and best dose of heroin. His dark blue eyes are filled with white hot power and lust; I feel it thrumming from him like it were a tangible thing.

Not only is he high off my blood, but something happened between us just now that will never leave us.

We will never be the same.

"I'm sorry, Ollie. I don't know why it draws me in, too. It's like he's my drug."

"Well, you both need to stop." Ollie lets go of Bash and turns to look at him. "Go out there and drink some bourbon. Wait for your high to come down. Then, drink some of the Alpha Zen to taper the craving. You're gonna have to start from scratch."

I don't know if he's veilweaveling Bash, but Bash says nothing as he walks out of the house to the backyard.

I feel my heartbeat thundering in my chest and ears when I turn to Ollie. "Did you just veilweave him?"

"No. We can only use veilweaving on each other if we use that word. But he's so high right now that he'll do whatever anyone tells him."

The further Bash gets from me, the more I realize what happened. The intensity and severity of the situation increase tenfold.

"Shit. What did I just do?"

"You didn't mean to, Sayah. It's all right. Now we just have to get him through his detox again."

Going into the cabinet for a glass, I walk to the fridge to fill it with ice. "Yeah, that's just what we need right now. Fix sick Bash while we're still trying to figure out where the hell Dom is. Fuck, I'm such an idiot!" I throw the ice into the glass, ready to shatter everything in sight.

"Hey," Ollie says, kneeling in front of me to pick up some of the cubes that had bounced out of the glass and onto the floor. "Sayah, he's like your drug, too. The two of you together, you can't help it. It's whatever is drawing you together."

I slam the freezer drawer shut and stand, walking over to the sink to get some water. "I just . . . I knew better. But it's like all sensors and filters were shut off. And when he drinks from me, it's so fucking euphoric. I feel high while he's doing it, and when he's done, I feel drunk. What is that?"

When the cup is full, I turn the sink off and spin to face Ollie.

He picks up the last two cubes from the floor and walks them over to the sink, where he drops them. "I don't know,

Sayah. I've never known a human to enjoy being drained of blood."

His words form in my brain but don't make any sense.

Surely there must be another instance where a human feels what I feel when a vampire drank from them?

But then again, I'm not fully human.

"Do you think it has to do with my angel blood, and him being part demon?"

"Probably," he says with a nod. "You two just have to be careful around each other. With you loving the way it feels when he drinks from you and his addiction to your blood, it can only end badly."

Badly?

But blood isn't like heroin, where too much will kill you. If he drank from me forever, and we both got something out of it, what harm could it do? Like, not all of me at once, that would kill me; but just a bit every day.

"It could do a lot of harm, Sayah," he warns, reading my thoughts.

I tilt my head to ask if he just peered into my mind.

"We all can reach into someone's mind if they let us," he says simply. "And no, I don't read your thoughts all the time. That one just popped out at me. Listen"—he clasps my free hand to his chest—"you letting him drink from you and you getting high off it can end badly. There'll be a time when neither of you will know when to stop, and he will drain you. He'll be too high to care. And you'll be too drunk. And there's also the question of if you get too drunk and want him to bite your jugular, and then you burn again. What happens if Dom isn't there to raise you from the ashes this time?"

"But who's to say I'll burn again?"

"Sayah, who's to say you won't? Just be careful. If you're not, you'll both end up dying." His last words dangle between us, and his eyes are an arresting shade of green. After a few seconds, he lets go of my hand. "I'm going back out there to make sure your friend is okay. You'll have to babysit Bash. That's your punishment." He smiles at me, and I smile back at him.

"Okay," I say. "Hey, have your visions shown Dom at all?"

His eyes turn cooler. "No. I haven't. I keep trying. But I can't control them. They just happen."

"What did you see between Bash and I?"

Ollie backs away from me and shifts all his weight to the foot farthest from me. "It changed, Sayah. It always changes. But let's not talk about that right now. Let's make sure Claire is okay, and Bash is behaving."

Ollie saw something with Bash and me the other morning, and it's changed now because of what just happened. My stomach is in knots over what it might be.

Ollie's smile fades, and he turns away from me to step out the door to the backyard.

I call after him, and he spins to face me.

I gulp. "You'd tell me if there was something I absolutely needed to know, right?"

He nods slightly and walks out the door.

I stand still for a moment, contemplating what Ollie had seen. Then I head to join them at the firepit.

Bash is talking to Claire, bourbon in hand, and they both seem happy, as though nothing has changed. Bash appears drunk. His jubilation is on high, and his voice is turned all the way up.

"Sayah!" he coos, holding his arm out for me to hug him, or to sit next to him, or whatever the drunken gesture means.

"Bash!" I call back mockingly, imitating his drunk demeanor.

I lean in and hug him, and he tips over a little too far, almost falling out of his chair. "Oh, Sayah, I just adore you so."

Uncomfortable, I let him go and sit down next to him.

"I adore you, too, Bash," I reply.

"Bash was just telling me about his life in California," Claire says from across the firepit.

"I was," he concurs. "About my fun and exciting life as a boat captain."

"A boat captain?" I wonder if this is his truth or his made-up human story.

"Yeah, I have a houseboat," Bash sort of whispers to me. "Mmm, you smell good."

"Bash, will you come inside with me for a second? I need to talk to you about something."

"Sure," he answers, tipping the bottle to his mouth and letting some of the bourbon spill down the sides of his lips.

Ollie gives me a nod, like I'm doing the right thing, and opens another beer.

Bash tipsily makes his way up the deck's steps, tripping on the last one and almost falling. I catch him and hold him up as we walk inside.

"Bash, I need you to drink some of that Alpha Zen. It may help with the disaster you are right now."

"But I like being this way, Say. I feel great!" he whines, emphasizing the "r," reminding me of Tony the Tiger.

"I get that, Bash, but another person here is human and can't have you making up random stories about being a boat captain. Do you understand?"

"But I am a boat captain," he slurs, tipping further into me.

"Whatever, Bash, just get the blood, and drink some of it. Please?"

The blue of his eyes sweeps me to another realm, and I relive how his lips make me feel. Shaking the thought away, I pull him into the living room to his things.

He stumbles in behind me and clumsily sits on the ground by his suitcase. Kneeling, I unzip the bag and wave my hands over the contents to reveal the blood bags I'd glamoured for him earlier. Picking up one, I hand it to the intoxicated Bash, and he sets the bottle down and grabs it from me.

"I meant what I said out there, Sayah. I just adore you."

I sit quietly, contemplating the depth of his eyes. He's just so beautiful; it almost hurts to look at him at times. That prominent jawline clenches when he's thinking about something, the little dimple that comes out occasionally when he's mischievous, the way his eyebrows dance when he's talking about something he's passionate about. There are so many things I adore about him, too.

"You know," he goes on, "you have five different smiles that I adore." He uncaps the blood and takes a swig. "One where you are pleased and in love with the world. I've seen this smile of yours when you talk of your son. Then, there's the one where you're nervous about a situation and trying to fit in; like you want to smile, but you're only doing it when you know you have to. I saw this one a lot when you were around my family. Believe me, I do it, too."

I can't help but grin a little at this.

"Ah, then there's that one. That's the smile you give when you know someone is complimenting you, but feel you aren't good enough for the compliment, so you don't offer the person giving it your full smile."

At this, which I know is true, I look away and down at the suitcase.

"Then there's the gentle one, when you're remembering something about someone you love or lost. You smile this way about your mom. It's a soft, quiet smile, and it plays gracefully at the corners of your lips. Your eyes light in a way that is like candlelight. Soft. Gentle. Then there's the one that's like Christmas morning. This one is my favorite because it's when you get excited about something or something you're passionate about. It makes your dimples come out of hiding. It brings about a crisp, fresh breath of air from the depths of someone who hasn't had a nice deep breath in a long time. Pure. Like Christmas morning."

Bash.

The stone-cold killer, Sebastian, is sitting across from me, telling me the loveliest story about myself. The fact he knows I have five distinct smiles and that he's noticed my face enough to study them is something out of a storybook.

At this moment, the world grows small. This time, as everything disappears, it isn't his power that does it; it's the human in him that comes forth, only for me.

If ever there was a time I wanted to kiss him more than I do right now, I can't recall; but all my senses and sensibility and loyalty to Dom come crashing around me, and I want nothing more than to kiss Bash, to feel his darkness fill me up.

But I don't.

His blue eyes leave mine, and he takes another drink of blood.

"But alas," he sighs, turning to lean on the back of the couch, "you belong not to me but to my brother. My brother's girl." He sighs at this and takes another drink, chasing blood with the bourbon. "Will you hand me that other bag? I have to mix them."

I rummage through the suitcase for the other blood bag and hand it to him.

"Maybe in another life," he adds, taking the bag and biting off the top, to which he downs the entire contents of the bag.

"Bash!" I grab for the container, but it's too late. It's gone in a flash. "Now you're going to have to get a hold of that psycho fairy for more."

Bash shrugs. "That bitch doesn't scare me."

He drinks more of the other bag when his face goes white, and not with vamp fury. This is the look of someone about to be sick. Before another word is uttered, he flashes to the bathroom, where the resounding echoes of hurls fill the room.

Sighing, I get up, and go to the kitchen to get water and to wet a dishrag.

Bash is kneeling before the toilet, blood everywhere, throwing up everything he had just put into his stomach.

"Oh, Bash," I groan as I place the cold cloth against his neck. "We are so stupid."

"I know." His deep voice reverberates off the porcelain. "I just can't resist you, Sayah."

Remembering what Ollie had said to me moments earlier, I say, "Bash. Maybe it's better if you stay at Dom's place and are far away from me. We're no good for each other. We're toxic to one another."

"No," he insists, still with his head hanging over the toilet. "No, I won't leave you."

"Bash," I say, rubbing his back. "I'm not good for you. And you're not good for me. If we let something like this happen again, we may end up killing each other. I just think—"

"Sayah," he snaps, flushing the toilet before facing me. "I've never felt more alive than when I'm with you. Granted, I'm addicted to your blood. But I refuse to walk away from something I've been yearning to feel my entire existence. Whatever the consequences, I'll take them. As long as I get to be near you."

"I just—"

"Shh," he says, and I feel all my senses turn to mush. Maybe he's using his power on me, or maybe it's just him that I don't want to be done with either. But I stop talking. "I will do better. I'll get through this damn detox again, and I'll resist you. I'll do better. I promise."

I nod. "But you can still be around me and not be here all the time. Besides, Gauge will be home tomorrow, and it would be better if you and Ollie weren't here. We don't have to stay apart. We shouldn't be together as much while you're getting through this.

"If you think that is best, I will go to Dom's tomorrow."

I resist a sigh. "Thank you."

"All right. Let's go back out there and hang out with your friend and her new boyfriend."

I laugh and help Bash off the floor. He grabs the bourbon from the floor and collects the bags of blood. Before heading to the backyard, we toss the empty bags into the trash and shove a full one into his pocket.

We don't make it halfway before spotting Ollie and Claire making out in the firelight.

Grinning, Bash turns back around, and pulls me inside by my hand. "Let's just leave them to themselves."

"What do you want to do?" I ask him.

"Well, I want to lie down. But my bed is in here so . . ."

"You can lay with me. Only if you promise to behave."

"Scout's honor," he says, crossing his heart with his fingertips.

"I just need to be held."

"Sayah, I would hold you forever if you let me."

I give him a soft smile in the dim light of the dining room ceiling fan and lead him upstairs.

MISS SEX HAIR

-SAYAH-

When I open my eyes the following day, I feel his arms around me. In between all the bouts of him getting up to get sick, he held me close the entire night. But the number of times he had to flash out of bed to the bathroom to puke caused me to not get very much sleep.

Stirring slightly, he rolls onto his back and zips into the bathroom to be sick again.

It's going to be a long detox for him, again.

I rise from the bed and grab my phone from the charger.

When Bash emerges, he looks wretched.

His black hair is tousled and sticky with sweat. "Fuck me. This sucks."

"See, you going to stay at Dom's is a good idea. You won't be so close to the source of the problem."

"Maybe." He sounds uncomfortable. "I'm gonna take a shower. What time is your boy going to be here?"

"After school, I'll go pick him up. There is only a week left of fourth grade for him. I can't even believe I will have a middle schooler soon."

"Yeah, life goes by fast," says the vampire who never ages. "I'll hang with you for a bit. Then I'll head to Dom's to try and see if I can get some clues as to where he's at."

"And you really have no ideas?"

"None," he says, slipping out of his black shirt.

The way his body ripples fucking stops me in my tracks, but before I let my mind carry me away to the shower with him, I head to exit the room. "Have fun in the shower."

"It'd be a lot more fun if you were in it with me!"

Grinning to myself—'cause, duh—I close my bedroom door.

Claire's coming out of the extra bedroom, wearing nothing but Ollie's white T-shirt.

I give her a wide smile. "Morning, sunshine!"

"Morning," Claire answers, a hint of embarrassment in her voice, closing the door behind her.

"So, how was last night?" I ask, leaning against the railing.

"So good," Claire whispers. "Come downstairs with me? I need coffee."

I nod and descend the stairs with Claire on my tail. Out of the corner of my eye, I notice Claire has a slight limp in her walk, as if she'd been horseback riding. When we make it to the kitchen, I turn on the coffee maker and listen to it purr to warm up.

"That good, huh?" I ask, flicking the tangles in Claire's usually straight and perfect hair.

"Oh. My. God." She breathes, leaning against the counter. "Something is up with him for sure."

I open my mouth to ask what she means when we hear the bedroom door open. Footfalls follow, and then the other bathroom door shuts.

"What do you mean?" I ask, trying to feign wonderment.

"It's like he could read my mind, girl. Every time I wanted him to slow down, go deeper, go harder, to stop, or tease, kiss me, flip me, what have you—he did it. It was the strangest thing."

"Strangest and most wonderful?" I laugh.

"Fuck yes. Like ten times wonderful. I have never climaxed that many times in one night in my life. I'm weak in the knees, sore, and completely exhausted. That dick, though? Goddamn."

"Big?"

"Fucking huge. Just my type."

Not gonna lie: Thinking about Ollie being good in the sack and having a big dick has me clenching my thighs.

No, Sayah! Two brothers are more than enough!

"So, are you two going to see each other again?" I ask, pulling two mugs down from the cabinet and switching my thought process lest Ollie come down and read my lascivious thoughts.

"Absolutely. I think we may go out to dinner tonight. He wants to take me on a proper date."

I smile. "They're old school like that. Dom is the same way."

"Speaking of Dom. What does he think of his brother having the hots for you?"

I about choke. "What?"

"Oh, come on, woman, you know he digs the shit out of. He basically looks at you like you hung the moon."

When the coffee is done brewing, I take the cup out and hand it to Claire. "Cream in the fridge, sugar over there."

"Oh, my god, you like him, too!"

"Shh!" I scold. "I don't know what I feel."

"Sayah. You have to do what is right in your heart. If you want Bash, break up with Dom. We're too old to mess around with things that don't set our souls on fire."

Bash does more than set my soul on fire. He sets my world on fire. And then some.

"I know, but it's just complicated."

Claire, adding sugar to her coffee, turns to look at me. "Life is complicated, love. I know you. I can sense you're not sure you're with the right brother."

"Yeah, but what kind of person does that make me? I meet

Dom, hook up with him, meet his brother, then break up with him for his brother? That's awful."

"Who cares what it looks like, Sayah? Dom is a big boy. I'm sure he'll get over it. You guys haven't been together that long. It's not like you two were married, and then you ended up with his brother."

I stare into my mug. "I know. It's just—gods, I just feel so awful for having these feelings for his brother."

"What is it you feel? Just like you wanna fuck and be done with it? Or is it deeper?"

"That's just it. It's so much deeper than I ever felt for Dom. When I'm around Bash, my world clicks into place. Like all the dark in me, flaws and faults, shine just as bright as the rest of me. Like all of me matters. He told me last night that I have five different smiles he adores. And then proceeded to tell me about each one. I mean, who does that? No one has ever told me about my smiles."

Claire's eyes sparkle like mine probably did while he told me my personal fairy tale. "Oh, my god, how sweet," she coos, sipping her coffee, and cupping it to her chest.

"I know, right? And the thing is, Bash is not really a good guy. It's hard to explain, but I bring out the good in him. His mom, sisters, and even Ollie tell me that I do something to Bash that not even he realizes is happening to him."

"What do you mean, he isn't a good guy?"

I wish I could tell my best friend everything there is to tell about the Sangravelli boys, but there's nothing I can divulge at this moment.

"He just has a past," is all I can think to say.

"Sayah, I know something is up with those two. I feel it. You can tell me, honestly. I won't say anything."

Looking at my friend in her oversized white T-shirt and nothing else on, her hair disheveled, and her hazel eyes, my heart yearns to tell Claire everything, all that has surrounded my life in the last few months.

Something tells me that Claire will soon find out our secret.

Soon, she will know the tale.

Footfalls on the steps announce Bash before his heavy boots even land on the hardwood.

Bash finds it difficult to move at normal speeds when he knows he has to, and also the fact that he's tired, hungover, and fighting the addiction.

"Morning, ladies," Bash greets as he enters the room.

"Morning," Claire says as she moves out of the kitchen. "I'm gonna go see if Ollie wants some coffee."

"Yeah, okay, miss sex hair," Bash teases as he flicks her hair when she passes.

Claire grins, flips him off, and leaves the room.

"What were you two birds tweeting about?" Bash asks, coming to stand beside me to make some coffee.

"Oh, you know, girl talk."

He pulls a cup down from the cabinet. "Well, they definitely got it on; that much is obvi."

"I just love it when you use millennial slang," I say, bumping my hip into his.

"Totes adorbs," he says, turning to me, and smiling. "So, are the two lovebirds going to see each other again?"

"Yeah, I guess they're going to hang out tonight," I mention, moving over to the barstools.

"Oh, good. Well, I'm going to have to rent a car to go down to Denver. See the crazy bitch."

"Why don't you just drive Dom's car?"

"We left it at the airport when we left to go to New York. I've no idea where the keys are."

"He's probably got a spare at his house."

"I'll call a rideshare to his house then and see if I can find the key. Then get a ride to DIA to get the car."

"Sounds like a full day."

"Yeah, so much fun," he chides, taking a drink of his black coffee.

"I'd offer to come, but—"

"But I may murder you on the way there?" He laughs, and his laughter has a hint of realism.

"Funny," I state, sipping on my coffee as well.

"No, but really. We should do this. You're right. I need to get to Tallyn for more blood and just chill at Dom's and throw up violently all over his bathroom. Not yours."

"And try to find out anything about where he is."

"I mean, I'll try. But I honestly have nowhere to start."

"Why don't you start with the last place a murder was reported, where there was a red ribbon found tying a head back on. Go from there."

"Good call," he chides, taking another drink of his coffee. "They're coming down, shh."

"Morning," Ollie's voice comes behind me a few seconds later.

"Good morning, Ollie," I say, turning to see Claire, who has dressed back in her own clothes, and Ollie in his.

"Hey, Ollie, I have to leave pretty soon. Gotta run by Dom's and get the keys to the car and then to Denver to get the car. I'm gonna order a rideshare to take us to Windsor. You gonna be ready soon?"

"I can take you guys," Claire offers. "My mom has my daughter for the next few days since her school has already got out for summer. I don't have to work today."

"You sure, doll?" Ollie asks.

She smiles cheekily at him. "Sure. I don't mind."

"I'll put some gas in your car," Ollie says, scooping her up in his arms and kissing her on the neck.

"You don't have to do that," she tells him, but closes her eyes, loving being swept up into him.

Claire is totally smitten with him, and I definitely don't blame her.

If I hadn't met Dom first and had dreams of Ollie instead of Bash, I could see how any girl would be intensely smitten by him.

"I don't mind," Ollie insists, letting her go. "Besides, if Bash takes our only car out for too long, you'll probably have to come pick me up for our date tonight."

Claire laughs. "No worries. I don't mind. I like driving my new car."

"Okay, let's head out then," Bash interjects. "I need to get to Denver soon. Sayah, I'll be in touch later, okay?"

"Okay," I answer, getting up from the barstool.

Bash slams the rest of his coffee, puts the cup in the sink, and moves over to me.

I give him an awkward hug that's only half of what I want to give, and he snuggles my neck, his whiskers rubbing harshly on my skin.

He pulls away sharply. "Gotta go grab the bags."

Once he's back down and Ollie and he both have their suitcases, I follow them out to the car.

Claire hugs me on the porch. "Thanks for letting me chill, Say."

"Thanks for coming over," I return, hugging her back.

"Bye, Say," Ollie says, next in line to hug me.

I give him a quick squeeze and watch them head toward the white Cadillac.

Before Bash gets into the back, he looks at me, and gives me his own Christmas morning smile.

BLOOD IS THE CAUSE

-BASH-

All the way to Windsor, I can't help but think of Sayah. She's become all I ever think about.

Isn't there some psychologist who said if you're unable to get someone out of your mind, it indicates that you are also on that person's mind? I love how she moves with a grace that keeps her still but is as wild as the winds of a hurricane, yet as graceful as a ballet dancer's pirouette. The scars she's earned throughout her life would cause anyone else to fall and die, but she rose up with each thing that happened to her and faced her demons, wearing her troubles like war paint. She's the most beautiful woman I've ever seen, and yet she has absolutely no idea how beautiful she is; she's modest in that nature, carrying herself with quiet humility instead of an arrogant stride. The beauty of her soul decorates her aura and dresses her up like a shining ball gown, her heart as pure gold delicately interlaced as the ribbons on that gown. Her ex hurt her beyond comprehension, yet she wants nothing but the best for him, to be happy and find his soulmate, knowing it isn't her. Then she stood by and watched him create a happy life without her and swallowed that pain, thinking nothing of it while focusing on her child and the life she's creating for him.

Everything about her changes everything about me.

She vexed the demon that lives in me, calling out to my dark and pulling me toward light, surrendering its hold on the darkest parts of me that are being saturated by her light.

My only problem now is that her blood also calls out to me. It is the best high I've ever felt in my life, and I know I have to find a way to fight the demon in me that wants her blood.

I'll bring it up again since I have to go to Tallyn, anyway. Last time, she'd said there's nothing I could ever do and that part of me will always crave her blood, but there must be something she isn't telling me.

Or something she wants that I could offer her in exchange for the cure.

Ollie and Claire talk of things all the way there, and when we pull up to the mansion that is Dom's rental house, I really have no idea how we'd gotten here so fast; I'd been so lost in thought.

"Thanks for the ride," I say, getting out of the car to grab the bags from the trunk and leave them to their steamy kiss goodbye.

I'm waiting at the front door for Ollie to join me. When he does, he's very obviously smitten and relaxed.

"So you had a hell of a night, huh?" I tease as Ollie hovers his hand over the keypad, magickally learning the code to open it.

"I did." He smiles as the garage opens up.

Inside, there's a red Porsche in the third bay.

"Oooh," I say, rolling both suitcases to a stop to go over and admire it.

"You're not taking that one," Ollie orders, heading toward the door.

"Why not? I'll be careful. I'm a good driver."

"That car belongs to the owners he's renting this place from. If anything happens to it . . ."

"Nothing's going to happen to it. I just have to drive to Denver to see Tallyn, and then I'll be back."

"I'll drive you in it to get the Mercedes from the parking lot in Denver. We gotta get that one out of there before it racks up a fortune in parking fees, and who knows how long he rented it for. I'll search his email to see if I can extend the rental time."

"Let me drive it to Denver, then. I'll be careful, and you'll be with me, so you'll dampen all the fun."

Ollie's looking at me sternly when a Whispering Leaf flutters into the garage and lands at my feet. My heart sinks a bit as I pick it up and watch it morph into paper so I can read it.

"What's it say?" Ollie asks, taking a step toward me.

"Well, I don't have to go to Denver to see Tallyn."

Ollie comes over and grabs the message from me.

> *There is an island in Windsor called Pelican Lakes. Meet me at the bridge at midnight tonight.*
> *Come alone.*
> *T*

I crumple up the paper and stuff it in my back pocket. "There appears to be an entrance to the Luminara Domain in Windsor, Colorado."

"There's probably one in every city. It's just a portal to one giant city called Luminara Domain. Same for Neverdusk Dominion."

"Either way. I don't have to go to Denver."

"Wrong. We still have to go get that car."

"Why?" I whine, moving over to the suitcases again.

"Because," Ollie counters, grabbing hold of his bag, "he's our brother, and he's lost right now, and we have to take care of things."

"Right," I drone, following Ollie into the house. Upon entry, he quickly makes for the alarm to disarm it.

"How do you do that?" I ask, meandering over to the liquor cabinet right away.

"Visions show the people who've pressed codes in before," Ollie supplies, rolling his suitcase toward the hallway. "He video-chatted me when he was looking at renting this place. There are two guest bedrooms upstairs and one on this floor; the master suite is in the basement."

"Say no more, my brother. I will be occupying the master suite."

"Just don't get blood all over everything down there. There's a lot of white."

"Oh. Well, maybe not then. What about where Dom stayed?"

"That's where I'm staying. I'm his favorite brother, after all."

I smile and nod. "This is true. Maybe I'll just redecorate."

"Down the hall, there are stairs. The room's down there. You'll find it to your liking."

Ollie walks away in the opposite direction, toward the vast living room and double staircase I can see from the kitchen.

Sighing, I pull a bottle of bourbon from the cabinet and head down the dark hall.

When I arrive at the bottom of the staircase, Ollie was right. There's an ocean of white. It looks like I'd stepped into a suite in the Ritz-Carlton.

White carpet blankets the wide room, and although I'm in the basement, the house is on a slope, and the back patio opens to the private lake. The giant bed is somewhat in the middle of the room but cornered at an angle, with large white dressers on either side of the bed. Floor-to-ceiling windows take up the walls, and on the far side, a wide-open bathroom with a giant jacuzzi tub in the corner and a large walk-in four-person shower.

A hunger pang hits me the moment I walk in, followed by a hideous bout of nausea. Pulling out my phone to look at the time, it's going to be a very long day waiting for the meeting with Tallyn.

Even picking up a random stranger to eat would give my body the wrong blood, and I'd throw it up anyway, so I park my suitcase by the dresser and unscrew the lid to the bourbon.

Tipping the bottle to my lips and savoring the sweet burn as it slides down my throat, warming my insides, I head back upstairs to meet Ollie.

"Ready?" Ollie asks while rummaging through one of the drawers in the kitchen.

"Yep."

"Do you mind if we stop at a bar at some point? I need to get a snack."

"Sure," I say, taking another drink of bourbon.

"Do you think you can stomach something?" he asks, finding the spare key to the Mercedes and shutting the drawer.

"Don't wanna chance it. I'll wait until tonight. This should tide me over until then."

"Yeah, what the fuck were you thinking, anyway?" Ollie asks, but he's already trudging toward the door to the garage.

"I couldn't help myself. As soon as I smelled her blood, the demon took over, and it was all I could think about. Well, there was no thinking involved at all."

Ollie hands me the key as we enter the garage and presses the button to open the third bay door. "Be careful," he orders, getting into the passenger seat.

I grin, and slide into the driver's seat.

"But it's not just her blood that you're into, right?" Ollie asks, pulling his seatbelt on as I hit the button to put the top down.

Finding some aviators in the visor, I slip them on, and reverse out of the garage. "No. And you know that. Because you've seen some shit, haven't you?"

"I may have seen a thing or two," Ollie says, slipping on his sunglasses.

"And you're not going to tell me what you've seen?"

Ollie doesn't say anything for a minute. I know my brother, and he doesn't like sharing his visions, especially since they change frequently.

"Can you at least tell me if Dom is alive and coming back into the picture?"

"From what I've seen, yes. He's alive. But he's not the same. And from what I can tell, neither you, nor is she. As far as I can tell, you all are about to enter a future that would hardly be recognizable right now."

"Damn it, Ollie, just tell me what you've seen. And plug in where to go; I have no idea how to get to Denver from here."

Ollie pulls out his phone, searches DIA's address, and plugs it into the GPS on the large screen in the dashboard. "Bash, it's blurry. It's just bits and starts of things I can't really make out. I would have told you and Sayah if it was anything of significance. She seems genuinely worried about him. I can tell you are worried just because she is. You care for her. And I don't judge you for that, Bash, I really don't. I'm glad you finally found someone who makes the human in you come out more than I have ever seen it. But there's a storm brewing that you started by making deals with the fae. It isn't going to end well for any of us. Especially Dom, from what I can tell."

"Then what, Ollie? What have you seen?"

"A war, Bash!" Ollie shouts, his voice reaching a tension I never like to hear in the soulful Ollie. "I've seen a war."

I remember the very real vision I'd been having when Tallyn almost drained me to death during our last encounter. Not realizing it was of any significance at the time, I didn't say anything to anyone about it. But now that Ollie has seen it, too, it must mean something.

"What war?"

"A war between the realms. And blood is the cause of it. Your blood."

"Between the Luminara Domain and Neverdusk Dominion?"

"Yes. From what I can tell, we're all pulled into it, and Dom is on the wrong side. Or under some sort of mind control from Tallyn—"

"Wait, what?"

"Yeah. Like I said, it's all blurry, and it happens in fits. But she has him somehow—"

"She said the strangest thing to me when I saw her last."

"What did she say?"

"I met her the night you guys went to get Scarlet. And Mom was right; she tricked me. She was going to drain all my blood and keep me there for whatever she needed my blood for. I blacked out, and during that time, I had a vision of war; of fire and running, wolves ripping apart fae, and Sayah was there, running from something. When I came to, I had ripped apart the fae who were draining me. I left to find Tallyn and nearly killed her, and at first, she was fighting back. Then, like a switch, she stopped fighting at a particular moment and said, 'The Sangravelli brothers, I like that.' Then she spoke no more."

"What the hell, Bash?"

"What?" I ask, turning onto the freeway as the wind whips our hair around.

"Why didn't you say anything about this?"

"I didn't feel it was that important."

"No, you just didn't want Mom to know that she was right and that you shouldn't have mixed yourself up with them."

"No, that's not—"

"Yes, it is! You know it is! You hate when she's right and you didn't want to say anything because you knew you were wrong. Odin's ghost, Bash."

"It's fine."

"It is not fine, Sebastian. It is far from fucking fine. This is a fucking mess."

"Why? What could what I saw and what she said possibly mean?"

"It means that she's doing something with your blood, Bash. And she has Dom somehow."

"How could she have Dom?"

"How could she not? The bond was broken when Laureya killed Mederio; your mark disappeared, and so did his. And the moment that it did, Tallyn knew it, and quit fighting. By the Goddess, Bash, how could you not put that shit together?"

"What do you think she did?"

"Who knows? She must've learned of him when you went to see her the first time, and put a spell on him to be hers when the mark was broken from Mederio. That must be how he was able to write the letter to Sayah and how he was able to travel so far, so fast. How he was able to tie those scarlet knots again. It all makes sense now."

"No, it doesn't. How could he have been in two places at once?"

"She is the Luminara Queen, Bash; anything is possible."

"Earlier, when you said that the Luminara Domain is just one giant city, would the entrances we go into be portals to that city? Could you enter one in Colorado and simultaneously come out in New York?" I look over to Ollie and can tell that his eyes went wide, even under the sunglasses.

"That's it! Why didn't we ever think of that?" Ollie pulls his phone out and starts typing.

"Wait, who are you texting?"

"Mom. We have to tell her."

"Wait." I push the phone into Ollie's lap. "Just wait."

"Why?"

"Because. I have to meet up with her later. Let me see if there's anything else I can glean from her first."

"I don't know, Bash. That might not be—"

"Ollie, just trust me, okay? I have everything under control."

SWEET ROT OF CORRUPTION

-BASH-

The yellow lights of the Mercedes reflect on the gravel along the deserted parking lot of Pelican Lakes, and the giant American Elms cast eerie shadows from the half-full moon along the bridge that leads to the island.

Killing the engine, I stuff the keys into my pocket, thinking of Sayah as I walk toward the bridge. Somewhere in the deepened recesses of my darkness, it comforts me that she and I are under the same moon, scattering soothing layers of comfort over what I am about to do.

The last encounter with Tallyn was not the greatest; truthfully, I'm dreading what's about to go down.

From what Ollie and I had discussed, the only thing that makes sense is that Tallyn has Dom. It's the only thing that works for where Dom is leaving bodies and how he ended up in Colorado the same night that one of the bodies had been found.

Approaching the bridge, there's a viable shift in the air as I reach the middle, and slowly, the rocks on the lake's beach shift sideways. The water in the lake parts, revealing a staircase underneath.

I sigh as I go down the rocks, descending the stairs into the world beneath the lake.

Gravity betrays me once more. The tunnel swivels around to the ceiling, and the air grows denser. Mage lights line the stone walls and gleam a faint purple glow. As the mouth of the tunnel appears, what it opens up to is far different from how I'd ever seen it.

It's not a mirror of Pelican Lakes.

This part of the realm is in ruins.

Reminiscent of the ruins of Greece, decaying pillars of something once grand haunt the field the tunnel spills out into. Large stone blocks lay fractured everywhere I look, speckling the haunted wheat that stretches on forever. Blue stars dot the velvet sky; the moons here decadently paint the destruction in a silver light. Fragments of an entire metropolis, complete with crumbling roads and aqueducts lay in tattered ruins. Pyramids even dot the horizon, shedding light on the vision I had when I last saw Tallyn.

What was this part of the city used for?

As I walk along the path around large blocks that resemble sandstone, I catch a glimpse of Tallyn in the distance.

In the dark, the white gown she has on gives off a luminescence.

She moves around a pillar, and I can no longer see her.

Moving closer to the spot where I'd seen her, when I came around the bend, I find her sitting on the foot of a giant ruined statue of a goddess.

Tallyn's eyes hint at something terrible and terrifying. "Hello, Sebastian."

"Tallyn," I say curtly.

"I told you that you would be needing me again." Her lips curl up in a wicked grin, and she crosses her legs, her bare and shiny skin gleaming from under the slit of the white gown.

"What have you done with my brother, Tallyn?" I ask,

keeping my distance, and become aware of another fairy watching us. My vampire hearing causes me to hear every breath, every rustle, every pebble displaced beneath bare feet.

"He's safe," she says, shifting her weight so her gown causes her voluptuous breasts to flex slightly. Jewels decorate her entire body. She adorns long black hair, twisted into braids, which are decorated with gold rings, bright jewels, and flowers. A diadem of black jewels and pearls sits atop her head, and the same jewels cover her face and pointed ears.

"Where is he?" I demand, moving so my back is against a crumbling pillar.

"He's in Feylight Grove, where my kingdom is. He's safe," she says again.

"Scotland? He's in Scotland?"

"That would be where Feylight Grove is."

I cross my arms over my chest. "What do you want with him? How did you get to him? And what are you doing with my blood?"

"So many questions." Her voice is like a cursed remnant of a storm passed, arising from the foot of the statue. "You know my deal: I give you what you want, you give me what I want."

"No. I do not want your blood this time; I want the cure I know you have. And I will only give you my blood if you give me answers."

Behind more of the broken pillars surrounding the area, fae resembling children begin to seep out, dressed in white, wings fluttering on their backs.

"You want the cure for what, exactly?" she asks, moving to an open area where the little fae gather. A light wind sweeps up, and I can smell her immortality—the sheer lifespan this being has lived—and the sweet rot of corruption lingers in every pore of her.

Fae smell different from humans. Humans are usually blood, sweat, and other perfumes—things they wear on their skin and use to wash their hair. But Tallyn. She's a mixture of chaos and corruption, of earth smells and magic; the mystery and mischief lay heavily on her heartbeat.

I feel my shoulders tense. "A cure for the addiction to angel blood. I know you know how to get rid of it. You only gave me enough of your blood to satisfy me enough until you could get mine. Now tell me the reason you want my blood, the cure, and how to get Dom back! Sayah is the phoenix. If you don't give him willingly, you know she will stop at nothing to get him back. You cannot defeat her. She is the undoing of all the world's dark things."

There's a palpable shift in the air to this information, as though Tallyn had never thought of that before. One of the tiny fae moves toward me, baring its fangs, and Tallyn holds her back before she can get any closer to me.

"All right," she returns, stepping to the side, and the little fae moves out of her way. "I will tell you how to get Dom back and how to get rid of your addiction. But you know my rules. I will need something in return."

I step closer to her. "What do you want?"

Her orange eyes brighten. "You in exchange for Dom."

"What? No. Absolutely not."

"Sebastian," she groans, her bare feet on the soft ground making no sound as she inches closer to me. "Listen to me. I don't need you forever. I just need you long enough to get what I need. And your blood is better than Dom's, anyway. Everybody wins." I can hear her smile, her red lips parting with a sweetened sting. "Well, almost. Since you are in love with his girl and she wants him back, I suppose you lose that way. But for the most part, everybody wins."

The way that bristles over my every nerve breathes an insult my bones have not yet known.

If I agree to her terms, go to her side, and do whatever she needs to be done, it will all be over as soon as she gets what she wants.

But what is that?

"What is it that you need done?"

She moves closer, the fae behind her fluttering close. Her long, pointed fingernail grazes the side of my cheek and curls around, jabbing me in the bottom of my chin as she forces my head up. "In due time, will I divulge that to you. Just know for now it's a little tryst between my brother and I." She lets go of my face and walks away. "The sooner you come to Feylight Grove with me and we get this done, the sooner you can be back and continue pining after your brother's girl."

I follow behind her. "Does this 'little tryst' you have with your brother have anything to do with the influx of warlocks and grimspawns taking over the mortal world like a plague?"

She glances at me over her shoulder and gives a slight nod.

The fuck?

"And if I agree to this," I continue, trailing her to a building reminiscent of a crumbling church, "you will release Dom and then tell me how to get rid of my addiction?"

She climbs up a few of the steps. "Yes."

Stopping before the steps, I kick a rock out of my path. "And how long will this little mission of yours take?"

"That's hard to say, Bash. I cannot give you an accurate answer, as I don't know how long this undertaking will take."

Once Sayah has Dom back, she won't want me around anymore.

What's the worst that could happen?

"All right," I say, eyeing her speculatively.

"Good," she smirks, approaching me again while holding her arm back for the fae to stay where they are. "Give me your hand."

I hesitantly hold out my hand to her.

She pulls a crystal wand from her hair and marks my arm

with a golden rune. This is like the mark I had from Mederio, but it's glittering within my skin. It stings like I imagine a tattoo would feel, but I don't flinch.

I like pain.

"What is that?" I ask when she's done.

The glow of the golden rune lends her face a serene look, stealing the murderous vixen appearance from her a bit. "My insurance that you'll keep your word." She stows the crystal back in her hair and walks toward another fractured pillar. "Go back to your little world and wait until the next new moon. I'll send a Whispering Leaf showing where to find the portal to the Luminara Domain to Feylight Grove. You will find a pack of unicorns in the field surrounding my castle there. You'll need to steal the horn from the largest one when you get there. They grow back, so do not fret over that—not that you, Basher of Heads, would—but take the horn. Have Sayah feed you her blood, then pierce yourself with the horn. Into the open wound from this horn have Sayah drop her angel blood into it. The magic of unicorn horn and the angel blood will devour your addiction. Then I will exchange Dom for you, and then we will begin the next phase of the plan."

"Steal the horn of the unicorn? Right. Easy enough."

"They are more dangerous than you would believe, Sebastian. You will need strong magic to make them come to you and lull the male enough to take his horn."

I hold out my arm and admire my new tattoo. "What does this rune do if I don't do what you ask?"

"The rune makes you mine, regardless of what you want. I will own your mind. Like the Mark of the Warlock."

"Cool," I say sarcastically. "And what do I do about my addiction until then?"

"Take this." She holds out her hand to one of the little fae, and a small boy with brown clothing resembling loincloth approaches with a satchel made of animal skin and hands it to her. She walks over and hands it to me. "This mixture of blood will help take the edge off, but will not cure you. You need the horn of the unicorn yourself to be cured of it completely. Take that blood and put a few drops in the blood you drink already. Only a few drops; it's very powerful."

I take the satchel and she starts walking me back the way we came. "How did you get my brother, anyway?"

"Let's just say he fell in with my brother Trystan, who was in an alliance with Mederio. That's all you need to know."

"Does he have anything to do with the tryst you spoke of?"

"No more questions. I have answered all the important ones you need to know. Now go; be on your way, and I will be in touch."

We arrive at the stairs.

I pause, hesitation flooding my veins. "Something about this doesn't seem right, Tallyn. Like there is more to this than you are telling me, and I am getting into something deeper than you have let on."

"Instincts are a bitch, aren't they?" She smiles. "Good day, Sebastian. I'll see you soon."

With a wave of her hand, the water begins to close in on the staircase, and if I don't exit now, it will drown me. I hurry down the stairs.

When I arrive back at Pelican Lakes, it's within seconds of being drowned beneath that water.

*B*ack at Dom's, Ollie's sitting in the living room watching something on TV. He turns it off and gets up from the couch when he hears me enter.

"So?" he asks, approaching me as I go right for the liquor cabinet again.

"Well. I've got bad news and then really bad news," I answer, twisting the cap off and taking a long drink.

The sting of the bourbon on my throat feels wonderful. It warms me up and takes the edge off my hunger and this horrible thing I just agreed to.

"What?" Ollie says, taking the bottle, and drinking himself.

"She has Dom. She said he's in Scotland, and we can have him back . . ." I trail off because I know Ollie isn't going to like the next part.

"In exchange for?" Ollie presses.

"Me," I say, offering him my sideways, apathetic smile.

His brows draw together, his mouth a firm line. "You didn't agree to this, did you?"

I take the bottle back and take a swig, heading into the living room to sit in the recliner.

"Bash!"

I hold out my arm and show him the new rune tattoo.

"Fucking A, Bash. What the fuck?"

"Look," I offer as I sit on a black leather recliner, "she said she doesn't need me forever. She just needs me long enough to help her with a situation with her brother. She said after the next new moon, she'll send me a Whispering Leaf, and I'll go with you guys to get Dom. There, in Feylight Grove, I have to take the horn from a large unicorn to be free of my addiction, then she'll give us Dom, and I'll take his place."

Ollie exhausts a loud exhale and sits on the couch. "Oh, Bash, what did you do?"

I lean back, admiring the bottle in my hand. "What? It'll be fine. Besides, we have Sayah. We can just have her kill Tallyn and be rid of the bitch for good."

"You know it doesn't work like that. The entire Luminara

Domain would come after you—us—if anything happens to her."

"We'll figure something out. We have what, a few days?"

He leans forward to rest his elbows on his knees. "Maybe a week. What does she want with you? I mean, why does she want you in exchange for Dom?"

"I don't know. She didn't say much. She just said my blood is a better fit for what she needs it for and said it's a little tryst between her and her brother. That's how she found Dom. Her brother is allied with Mederio."

"A little tryst? Bash, did you not even think of what I said to you about the war I saw, what you saw firsthand in your vision?"

"You think that's what's brewing?"

"It has to be. Trystan is the King of the Nightshades, pissed about Tallyn getting Feylight Grove when their mother died. He wanted that land for himself, and when she got it, their fragile alliance ended."

"So that's what happened between them to begin with?"

"All I know is that when their mother died, she left the entire realm to Tallyn. This made Trystan mad, and he warred with Tallyn until she gave him parts of the Luminara Domain, which he renamed Neverdusk Dominion before naming himself the Neverdusk King. So ever since then, he has used any excuse to go to war with her, to conquer more of the Luminara Domain as his own Neverdusk Dominion."

"Ugh. This shit makes my head hurt." I massage my temples to relieve some of the pressure I feel trying to understand this. "So, now, you think that they're using Dom's blood somehow to start a war with each other, and why she wants my blood?"

"Well, remember what happened with me and Ayana?"

"Yes," I answer, pulling up the memory.

"Trystan used that knowledge to infiltrate the Luminara Domain with dark fairies infected with vampire blood. Tallyn could be doing the same thing with your blood since you're part demon. Who knows what the fae turn into when they drink demon blood?"

"Well, I think I'm about to find out, come the next new moon."

I remember something my mom had told me about the Neverdusk Dominion and how I'd never seen parts of the Luminara Domain. The place I just met Tallyn in had been in ruins and all those little fae, hiding behind the ruined pillars of once grand buildings.

"The place that I just went to...I think it was the Luminara Domain."

His face turns contemplative. "Why do you say that?"

"The place was in shambles. It reminded me of a ruined city in Italy or Greece. Once giant and grand buildings in ruins. Do you think that's what's left of the Luminara Domain?"

He leans back, crossing his legs. "Quite possibly. The fae are very illustrious and inexplicable. It's hard to know what they are really up to."

The hunger pang inside me rumbles, and I feel lightheaded as a roll of nausea rumbles through my stomach. The satchel in my pocket Tallyn gave me beckons me, and I wonder what kind of nightmare I'm about to enter when I consume whatever's in this pouch.

But what do I really have to lose?

THE FIRST WEAVE

-SAYAH-

I've been feeling like something is off all week. It isn't a feeling about the boys in trouble or something wrong with Gauge. Rather, it's something buzzing inside of me that doesn't feel right, like something is shifting—something out of place and is working to shift back into place. I try to ignore it as much as possible, but it worsens every night.

It's Friday night, and as I'm putting Gauge to bed, there's a sharp pain in my ribs to the point where breathing is nearly impossible. I put pressure on my ribs to temper the pain while I tuck him in, but stressed breath is causing my ribs to feel like they are exploding. And it only seems to get worse.

I kiss him before Gauge can see the anguish and say, "Goodnight, baby. I love you. Sweet dreams."

"Night-night, Mama. Love you," he says as I walk to the door and turn out the light.

As I head downstairs, the pain quickens to my stomach, but I ignore it, and push it down to not think about it. Going through cancer and those awful bone marrow biopsies, I would always put myself on a beach in the Caribbean. I picture that beach now, but the pain is too unbearable.

Climbing into my chair, I lean forward to grab my laptop to do some homework, but white-hot anguish floors me. I fall from the chair to my knees. I'm about to throw up when I watch my arm break at the wrist and bend back into another position, hair beginning to sprout from all my pores. I stifle my scream, biting my other fist to stop me from bawling.

As the transition hits me, I realize what's happening.

I'm formweaving into a wolf.

The moon is full and high in the sky, as I can see from my large bay window over the tall door archway.

For a formweaver to turn for the first time, they must fall in love with a demon.

I'm part formweaver.

And I've fallen in love with Bash.

Pulling my phone out with my unbroken arm, I find his number.

I need someone to watch me, so I don't kill my child while I'm the wolf.

I nearly yell out when my leg breaks in two, but Bash answers on the first ring.

"Hel—"

"Bash, get here now," I say in a near scream, holding in the anguish that's ripping my skin apart as I form.

"Sayah, wha—"

"Just get here," I repeat, and my voice is harsh, broken, and stressed. I hang up and crawl to the backyard, shutting the door behind me.

My phone buzzes from my back pocket where I'd stowed it, but there's no chance I can answer it now.

The form takes twenty minutes of complete anguish. I watch and feel every bone break in my body and rearrange. The feeling in my face as it elongates is horrendous, and my head explodes as my skull grows. My back arches as the bones crack and realign until I'm on all fours, and I watch as blonde fur fills in where my peach skin used to be.

Then there is darkness.

SOOTHE THE TURMOIL

-BASH-

When I pull up to her house, the lights are on, and the front door is wide open. I slam the car into park once I'm in the driveway and exit in a flash.

"Sayah?" I call, looking up the stairs to where I know Gauge is.

I use my vamp speed to ascend the stairs and find nothing but the sleeping child in his bedroom. My heart's pounding as I check her room and bathroom, but she's not there.

Then I hear something jumping on the back door and flash down the stairs.

Nox is cowering in his cat tower, hissing in terror as I pass. It sounds like a large dog is trying to get in.

That's when it hits me.

As I approach the backdoor and see the large, blonde wolf with dark blue eyes looking at me, mouth salivating, and teeth barred, I know it's Sayah.

She has fallen in love with me.

Now, I have no idea what to do.

No idea what to do with the wolf at my door.

No idea what to do with the knowledge that she loves me back.

No idea what to do about the sleeping child upstairs.

No idea what to do about Dom and his deal with Tallyn.

With a gulp, I pull out my phone.

"Hello, Bash?"

"Mom, hey. I need your help."

I explain what's happened over the last week and what's going on with Sayah.

"You're part witch, too, Bash; you can do this," she says through the phone as I head for Sayah's spell cabinet. "You just have to put the boundary up so she doesn't leave the yard, and then when the moon is done peaking, she'll turn back, and you can talk to her then."

"All right," I reply as I rummage through the cabinet.

"Just take the things I told you, go around the perimeter outside—not inside, or she'll eat you—and make sure to chant the words. Don't half-ass it, Bash. You have to mean it."

"And if it doesn't work?"

"Then you'll have an angry fucking wolf on the loose tonight and an even angrier girlfriend in the morning."

"She's not my girlfriend."

"Yet," says my mom. "I know you love her, too, Bash. I worry about what this will do to Dom, but I've seen what she's done to you. Dom is good for her because he has a pure heart. But she is good for *you* because she calms the darkness in you—your violence. In return, you quiet the darkness in her. She's equal parts light and dark; you call to her darkness and beckon the danger. You surprise her and challenge her, making her question her life. She's good for you, Bash, because she soothes your turmoil and brings your humanity to the surface. I've never seen you more human than when you're around her, and for that, I can get over how this will hurt Dom. Because she makes you a better man—a man I always saw in you, but you could never see."

I know exactly what she's talking about.

There has never been a time in my entire existence that I've felt more human than when I'm with Sayah.

Not even when I was just a human.

"Thanks, Mom. I gotta let you go now so I can do this."

"Good luck, son. And call me if you need anything else."

"Will do, Mom. Love you."

"I love you too, Sebastian."

I hang up, grab the salt, the wand, and the wolfsbane, and head out to the front yard.

As I spread the salt around the perimeter, I chant the words my mom told me to say, and Sayah soon hears me and is at the fence, jumping on it and yowling.

I take the wand and whisk it around. I honestly feel like a complete fool doing it, but I close my eyes and speak the words and truly mean them, as I know it will keep my love safe.

The boundary is up; I can see it with my unique vision. Even pressing on it with my hands, I can feel a substance almost like a bubble, but more solid at the touch.

I do this around the entire perimeter, even jumping the fences of the neighbors' houses to cover all sides of the yard.

When I'm done, I go inside to wait.

LIFE-THREATENING LOVE

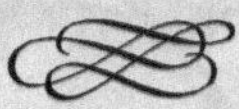

-SAYAH-

When the fog finally lifts, I'm lying in the yard by the gate, fully dressed, a little bedraggled and very, very sore. An overwhelming fear pulls me upright and I struggle to find the balance on my feet again.

The dusky infancy of morning is in that hushed, quiet space where the dew is accumulating and the whispers of night are fading into the promises of tomorrow, but that does nothing to quell the racing blood beneath my veins. The rising sun leaves room for nothing but darkness, and I find myself falling over the sky like a curse.

What did I do?

The backyard is wrecked; chairs in tatters, claw marks down the fence, tree branches strewn all over the yard as though a tornado had plummeted through my yard alone.

The moon has ended its peak, but I can barely focus on that, with worry about Gauge and if he's okay soaking into my every thought.

Panicked, I frantically look around for my phone to see if Bash ever made it.

It's almost four in the morning.

He must have, or I'm just a natural at controlling myself as the wolf. There's no blood on me; I examine my arms, legs, and stomach, making sure that there is no evidence that I ate him. I'm dirty and bloody; my hands are shaking and I cannot control the convulsions, like waking up from surgery and trying to get warm even though you're not cold.

Entering the house, the back door shutting must have roused Bash awake because he's lying on the couch inside, slightly stirring, and rubbing his eyes.

"Hey," I say as I enter the living room in a heated rush. "You came for me?"

"Yes. I came."

"I have to check on Gauge," I say, making my way to the stairs.

"Hey, he's okay," Bash insists, sitting up and grabbing my wrist as I pass by. "I kept checking on him throughout the night while you wreaked absolute havoc back there. He's still sleeping peacefully, not an inkling about the wolf that was his mom in the backyard."

Thank the gods his window faces the street and not the rear of the house.

"How did you keep me back there?" I ask as I sit next to him, trying to calm my breath and racing heart.

"I had my mom help me put up the boundary spell, so you didn't escape and go eat the neighbors."

I find solace in his eyes, trying to use them as my anchor to the here and now. "You did witchy voodoo stuff. . . for me?"

"I did," he answers, his fathomless blue eyes sharpened with a protective edge.

I swallow, as his face becomes the most peaceful remnant of home I've ever known. Something deep inside me has changed. Something clicks with finality into place and pulls my spinning world back to reality, to the here and now. My heart is beating wildly in my chest, threatening to tear my ribcage apart and escape, bound around the world and come back twice as large as it was or perfectly whole. Nothing makes sense but everything is perfectly clear.

I'm unerringly in love with him. The storm in my bones explodes within me, shattering my foundation and wrecking any calm I'd been trying to find.

I can hardly catch my breath. I look toward the fireplace to try to calm the tumultuous hurricane within me. I can hear his breath catch and feel his heat next to me. I cannot wrangle any wind into my lungs, it feels like I ran a mile in the rain trying to find shelter from a tornado and I try breathing in for a count of two and out for ten but I cannot catch my breath. Dizziness takes over my vision and his beautiful face swirls in front of me. Before I can say or do anything else, I run for the front door, running out into the yard to look up at the early morning sky.

What do you do when you realize everything you've ever wanted is sitting right before you, wanting you back; offering you a love you've only dreamed about in the deepest recesses of your mind? This vicious killer who has proven time and time again he shatters his monster before your feet and wants to become something he's scared of more than anything else in the world?

I hear him come out behind me and I don't know what to say or do. I can only breathe and look up, begging the last bit of twinkling stars for an answer about what I'm supposed to do now.

"Sayah," he says, his voice deep and dark and taunting. That danger I want to be in with him, that wild I want to roam in with him, that world I want to jump off with him, that fire I want to burn in with him, all come rushing back to me. Every dream I've ever had where he was my world and that all-consuming, maddening, life-threatening love floors me, plunges me down to the deepest depths with him, and the world begins to fade again.

This time, when I turn around and catch those midnight blue life-piercing eyes, his smile shatters what's left of my resistance. He takes a step closer to me, eliminating any bit of space I'd been trying to gain. I fucking dive into his world head first, with the world dropping away around me; I run to him, throw my arms around him, and crash into his lips with my own.

He catches me and wraps his strong arms around my waist, pulling me into him, melting into me, his tongue colliding with mine in the most passionate kiss I've ever felt in my entire life. The way he brings his mouth up to meet mine and kisses me roughly; it's as if it's taking every bit of control he has not to consume me. Every part of me is a live wire that hits the hurricane in my bones and causes the storm to electrify, my heart thundering in my chest as he moves, my lips opening and closing as his do.

We kiss each other as if we're one another's last bit of air on a sinking ship, alone together on a little island during a hurricane, fire spreading all around us, yet living inside our bones. His hands search my body, his fingers twisting in my long hair, mine tangling up in his dark tresses. Somehow, we move to lean against the house; him slamming me against the brick and me exhaling with ecstasy.

His lips wander down my jaw until they reach my neck, then jump back up to my lips. He feeds off me again, but not biting me nor yearning for my blood, but my soul, my heart, the very essence of me.

"Sayah," he growls through his kisses. The way he says my name undoes something within me, wrestling free a knot constricting my airways. "It has taken all I have to not fall to my knees before you and worship you like the goddess you are."

"Bash," I breathe back, kissing him and feeling as though I'm being given something that belonged to me forever ago, a bit of me I've missed without knowing I was missing it. Every word he speaks is like a stroke along my starving skin.

The crazy butterflies of fire swell and flutter on those edges of me that I only just discovered when I realized who Bash really was.

He is my person.

He is my endgame.

It's always been him.

"I love you," he whispers between bouts of passionate kisses. "You have fucking ruined me. To the deepest . . . depths . . . of my forsaken soul." The way he bows his head to touch his forehead to mine makes me wonder what such a powerful predator would look like on his knees before me.

"Bash." I return the fevered kisses, that one glimpse of his desire makes me feel like I'm starving. "I love you to the ends of me. The way I feel for you, it's so intense; an emotion so foreign, I can't even name it. All I know is that it's you. It's always been you."

He stops kissing me but holds my face and looks into my eyes with an urgent grace. "It doesn't matter that he found you first when every part of you belongs to me." He takes a stuttered breath, swiping his thumb along my lips. His touch is like a whipster, a promise of what is to happen between us. "My brother's girl. I think we both know that I could do things to you that he could never even dream of." He arches his brow and his dark eyes feel like they're holding back a thousand years' worth of things unsaid, a million questions he's been dying to ask. "When did you know?"

The look in his eyes could quiet the thunder. It's pure awe— like I'm the most beautiful thing he's ever seen. Like I'm a fucking goddess, and he wants to worship me until the end of time.

Holding his gaze, I admit, "I've known I was falling for you for a while. But when I actually fell was when you told me about my smiles."

He grins at me and kisses my lips again, causing me to smile so big that he says, "I get a Christmas morning smile."

The way he takes my lips within his, soft and slow; the feelings of him consuming me, setting every molecule within me to freeze with the most delicious set of chills. It's not a heated rush like before—no, this time, this is deliberate. Soothing. Soul quenching. I chase his tongue with my own while wrapping my arms around his neck, gripping his caress like a lifeline as he leans into me; the sensuous feel of that mouth on mine is the only thought in the world I have right now. Until I feel him harden against my leg and my core heats up, chasing the freeze, sending tingles dancing along my spine. The world disappears, leaving only the two of us in the vast universe. I kiss him as though he is my salvation; like kissing him will retrieve my soul from the depths of hell, even if I had wandered in there after him.

He makes the most delicious sound as he tousles my hair, drunkenly sipping and savoring my essence with his mouth, and when I run my hand along his giant cock, that moan becomes a plea that begs me for something I now know how to answer.

I don't know what magick he uses on me, but before I know it, we are inside, in my room; his lips are still on mine as he lays me down on the bed, climbing on top of me, his muscular body like a cage I never want to be freed from. He feathers kisses from my mouth to my ear, down the column of my neck, and finds his way to my shoulder blade, where he slips my shirt down just a touch to pepper kisses there.

I let a withering moan escape my lips as he reaches my breasts, and it sparks a determination in him to set more moans free. For in a wisp of air and magick and wind, I'm topless and sitting on top of him, his back against my headboard. His fucking glorious mouth is on the peak of my breast, pebbling my nipple. I look down to watch him take it in between his teeth and bite down just enough to cause my clit to quiver.

"Harder," I utter, and his eyes turn icy white; his fangs emerge, and for a split second, I worry if that was a wise choice, but he doesn't use the fangs to bite me. He uses his two front teeth and looks up at me as he grabs both of my breasts and pulls them together in front of his face, biting one nipple and then the other. I rock my head back, basking in the warm summer sin it creates in my insides as he brings me to ruin.

"I love watching you writhe for me, darling," he murmurs in a calm and dangerous cadence. "I will leave not one inch of your body undiscovered. You are mine to worship, my fire queen. And I will worship you til the sun falls from the sky."

Bash. The man who bows to no one. So willing to bow down to me.

I cannot take much more of this. His hard cock is rubbing on my clit, the fabric of my pants blocking us from connecting on the only level I've been dying to meet him on since that first night he visited my dreams.

I slide his shirt up and my tongue sets out on its own expedition; licking his abs and biting his nipples, teasing him with the tip of my tongue, taunting the demon to come meet my angel and take the scenic route with me to Hell. I want to touch him everywhere and commit all of him to memory.

Slowly I make my way down to his navel and pull at the button of his pants, undoing his zipper, looking up at him as his massive erection is revealed layer by layer, inch by glorious inch until all eight or nine of them are staring me in the face. I salivate at the sheer size of him and cannot help my tongue from licking down the entirety of its shaft, cupping his balls as I lick back up and tease the tip of him with the tip of my tongue. I kiss the head of his cock like it is an ice cream cone on a hot summer day, and when I hear him say, "Oh, fuck," I take him—all of him —into my mouth. When he hits the back of my throat, I see stars and tears water my eyes, but the desperation in his moans causes me to go deeper. I want him inside of me.

This vicious killer is putty at my fingertips, and I have the power to turn him to mush, to melt him from the inside out, but I kind of want the demon to come out and play. I stroke his cock with both of my hands as I fuck him with my mouth, sliding up and down while sucking, kissing, gagging, twisting, feeling myself drench as he writhes beneath me.

"Fuck, Sayah, I love what you do to me."

I look up at him while taking his cock to the hilt, swallowing back the sensation of gagging as I do it again and again until he can't take any more of it.

In a motion so fast, I'm flipped onto my back and his pants come off. He peels off my own as he gazes at me as though I am the only woman he sees, the only woman he'll ever see.

"Bash," I moan his name hungrily, desperate to taste his name on my tongue as he takes my clit into his mouth. He's teasing my sensitive spot with urgency, a need wound so deeply within him that only my release will set him free. His tongue grazes my clit, rocking it back and forth, causing that live wire of exquisite torture to electrify me down to the tips of my toes. He slides his mouth down the slick center of me, and when he puts a finger inside I arch my back, grasping at a pillow to muffle my cries. When he adds another finger, I let out a whimper that sets my body on a collision course with an orgasm which skyrockets me out of my body, feeling as though the fire that lives in my bones is consuming me. I ride the wave of the euphoria and calm the fire as much as I can, but he slides on top of me and enters me with one rough push, and the orgasm metastasizes, setting us both aflame in its wake.

"Sayah," he snarls into the shell of my ear as he stretches me to fit him in slow motion until he's buried to the hilt. He's so far in me that his hips are flush with the inside of mine, and he takes my legs up over his shoulders, rocking back and forth as the head of his cock presses right into my G-spot. Scattered stars shatter my sanity as I temper the flames threatening to engulf me, my orgasm lingering, spreading as wide as the vastness of space. "I fucking love you, my fire queen. I'd bring the world to ruin for you."

"Oh, fuck, Bash," I moan as he removes himself little by little until just the tip is kissing my clit, then drives into me again, swirling his hips as he does so. My orgasm flits across my existence and trudges me through another realm.

"Cum for me, my queen." He rocks back and forth across the spot that causes me to see gods, and I whimper. He steals the sounds of it with his lips. I drag my nails down his back and pull him to me, using him as my anchor; I'm losing myself to madness, and he is piloting me there.

"I've been cumming since you put it in," I exclaim into his mouth as he claims it with his own once again. Bash rocks again and growls, his hunger igniting the darkness in me to combust into light. "I fucking love you, Sebastian," I exclaim as he pulls out and shoves himself into me once again, banging my headboard against the wall.

"You're so fucking wet for me. Gods. Damn. Sayah. Holy. Fuck." He's still kissing me as he drives into me over and over again, the crescendo of the orgasm nearing its peak.

I can't help the fire that I feel is about to explode, and as his thrusts get hungrier and heavier and harder and fiercer, his kisses get deeper and my moans get louder. He cups my breast with his hands as he launches into his own orgasm. My eruption engulfs us in flames as I'm overtaken by mine, the flames burning me from head to toe as we finish together, dangling us into another world. A combustion of old paths and new lives, a shattering of ancient oaths, and an utterance of new promises intertwine as our souls leave our bodies and braid together in the ether while we climax. His shadowy soul bows to my fiery one, and they bring us to ruin on another plane. When they land back into our bodies, his shadow enters me and my fire enters him, coming to rest as we collect our madness and sanity in labored breaths and hungry pleas.

He kisses me some more as the world reemerges and his new pieces within me flit through me eagerly, as though trying to get to know me. The early morning light paints the room in sharp angles and delicate colors, setting angelic features alive on his face. His eyes meet mine, and we stare longingly into each other's eyes.

"It's always been you," Bash murmurs, stroking my hair. "In every life. In every realm. In any form. You level me. My demon bows to you as you are both our savior and demise, my fire queen. Until the end of time and the last star falls out of the sky." Kissing me again, he says, "My queen who'll ruin every part of my darkness."

Never in my life have I felt more beautiful than at this moment.

DEMON MELTS AWAY

-SAYAH-

We fall asleep together for a while after we steeped into comfortable silence. When I open my eyes again, the light paints the room in sharp angles and delicate colors, spreading over Bash's sleeping naked body next to me and painting him as a god. He's so fucking beautiful. When he stirs and looks up at me, he immediately kisses me, the light of the morning setting angelic features alive on his face. When he releases my lips again, I look into his eyes and there's danger in them. Trepidation. Something he needs to tell me but doesn't want to.

"What's wrong?" I ask.

"I found Dom," Bash supplies, and my stomach hollows out.

I sit up slightly to better look at his face. "What?"

"Yeah. I had to go see Tallyn the other day. And when I did, Ollie and I put some things together."

The beautiful morning we just had is now tainted with emotions I can't quite rein in. Some of them linger from anger over how he's just now telling me, sprinkled with guilt from how far we let things go, to—well, part of me doesn't even want to mention the next part.

Part of me doesn't want Dom to be found.

What an awful thing to think. There's an undercurrent of guilt, yet conflicting emotions rage war in my head, battling for dominance.

It isn't that I don't want him to be found; I take that back. That isn't true. I just don't want to be with him anymore. If the letter had been from him, it would have been easy because he had broken it off already. If it hadn't, explaining how I'm now in love with his brother would still be a sticky situation.

Bash detangles himself from my limbs and sits up beside me, his face dented with a sadness that stills him. The air in the room is coaxing, undulating like a soft wind came in through the curtains and sucked the air out of them.

His blue eyes search mine. "There's something I didn't tell you guys the night you went to rescue Scarlet. As you know, I went to see Tallyn, and she tricked me. She was going to drain my blood and then keep me for something. I blacked out and woke up in a vision where there was this war going on. And you were there, and we were running, but I didn't know from what. Then the dream ended. My demon had come out and ripped some of her fae to pieces. I found her and was going to kill her; she was resisting me right up until the moment when Mederio died. When that happened, she stopped fighting. It was like a switch had gone off in her. She said something about the Sangravelli brothers, but then stopped talking. Well, while driving to Denver, I asked Ollie what he sees in the visions he gets, and he said that he sees war and that Dom is under Tallyn's mind control somehow. Then it dawned on us that when I went into the Neverdusk Dominion. It was always through a portal to the same city, although it was in different parts of it. So if she were to have Dom under her control . . ."

"He could've gone into the portal in Georgia and come out in Colorado on the same night?"

"Exactly."

"So where is he now?"

"She said he's in Scotland."

"So, the map was right!"

"Well, sort of. We still don't know why the other drops were in other places. Tallyn is not the most trustworthy, so she only told me what she needed to, and nothing more."

"So, what now?"

"She told me how to break the addiction to your blood and also how to get Dom back."

"That's great!" I'm ready for whatever it takes to break the blood addiction.

"Well . . ."

The air between us at what he's about to say is thick.

"I have to take his place."

"What?" I exclaim, sitting back to examine him better.

"Sayah, listen. Before you get upset, I only agreed to this before I knew how you felt about me. Also, we can find a way around this."

Then I notice the golden rune on his arm that was not there before. I pull up his arm to examine the rune. "What is this?"

"It's her way to ensure I stick to my bargain."

"Jesus, Bash," I shout, throwing his arm back down. "Your mom warned you not to make deals with her. So, what, we have to go there, and you get exchanged for him, and then what?"

"I'm not entirely sure," he admits, interlacing our fingers. "I just know it isn't forever. It's just until whatever she needs done is done."

"And what is it that she needs done?"

"I don't know that either. I know it has something to do with her brother and my blood. Sayah, listen," Bash pleads when I angrily turn away. "We are smarter than her, okay? This can't be that hard to avoid. We'll go to Feylight Grove, I'll get my cure, and then you can kill her or something."

"Kill her? Bash!" I get up from the bed and walk over to the window. I'm so mad at him that I can't think straight now. "Why did you ever go and do something like that?"

"Because, Sayah, it was the only way I could think to get him back for you."

In that instant, the fire of mad that had engulfed me is extinguished, and I fall a little harder for him still. "Oh, Bash," I murmur.

"I didn't know you had fallen for me. I mean, I could sense you were feeling something. But even if I had known, I still would have agreed to it. He's my brother, and he may hate me, but I have something she wants. If I just oblige her and give it to her, then we can get him back. And I can be cured of the addiction. It's a win-win."

"Yes, but we have no idea what she's doing with your blood, Bash. And what of the war that Ollie and you both saw?"

"Whatever it is, we'll get through it, okay?" he says, rising from the bed, and coming to me, taking my hands. "She's not stronger than me; she's definitely not stronger than you. We'll do this: go to Scotland, go to Feylight Grove and get Dom, get my cure, I'll go with her for a bit and give her what she wants, and then I'll come back to you, okay?"

His hands are on my face again, stroking my cheeks with his thumbs.

"When do we go?" I ask.

"The new moon. She'll send a Whispering Leaf to portal me there."

"Okay. So, a week. What happens to us? Now that I am a formweaver, what do we tell Dom?"

"Well, we should go to New York and get the curse off you. So, you don't have to form on full moons. My mom will probably have something to help you figure out how to form into other things, even though I'm sure you'll be able to figure that out on your own. But as far as Dom is concerned, I think it's best to be upfront and honest with him."

"How are we gonna do that, Bash? Get him back and then say, 'Welcome back! Oh, and by the way, Bash and I are together now, so you'll just have to suck that right up.' Yeah, I don't know, Bash. I really don't."

"We're together now?" Bash's smile spreads from ear to ear as he slides his arms around me and pulls me closer.

I can't help the smile that takes over my face as well. "Well, let's cross that bridge when we get to it. We have to figure out what to tell Dom first."

The smile on Bash's face fades fast. "You aren't going to be with him again, are you?"

"No," I vow, pulling him closer to me. "No, Bash. I don't love him the way I love you. I never have. Even when I used to have those dreams of you and felt those feelings, I wished so much that I would feel that way about him. But I never did."

"Really?"

"Yes. Really. I yearned for a love like I felt in those dreams, and now that I'm truly starting to feel them, I can't imagine going back to mediocre. I want a love that consumes me. You consume me, Bash. I think a part of you has always lived under my bones. Every time you touch me, the flames within me feel like they recognize you, like they knew you before I even ever got the chance to. I don't ever want anything else, and my fire would never allow it."

He pulls me into him and kisses me so soft and serene that I can feel the demon in him melting away.

SECRETS REVEALED

-SAYAH-

Jamming to This is America by Rodney Atkins is my tradition on the Fourth of July. The badass ballad to America blares as I come in from starting the grill.

I'm preparing for my Fourth of July barbecue, for which I've invited a few friends, including the newly official couple Ollie and Claire.

They had declared themselves a couple after their third date.

The only downside is that Gauge is at his dad's this holiday since I had him last year.

There's a knock at the door as I'm sprinkling seasoning onto the burgers. Peeking my head around the corner, I see that it's Bash, Ollie, and Claire.

It's been a week since Bash and I declared our love for each other, and since then, we've not been able to keep our hands off each other—even though every time we see each other, I tell him we need to behave until we see Dom and make sure things are really over between him and me.

I signal them to come in and continue setting things out on the counter.

Bash enters with a giant box of fireworks, trailed by Ollie and Claire.

"We have brought the festivities," Bash announces, setting his box on the kitchen table. He walks up to me and pulls me into him, hugging me close. "Hello, beautiful."

"Hello, handsome man." His black shirt is hot from the sun, and the smell of him is summer and wind.

As hard as it is for me to not give in to temptation—and even though I lose every time—he's completely understanding and in agreement that it would be unfair to Dom, or us, to continue our relationship without closing the door on Dom and me first.

It almost makes it hotter; like the forbidden fruit you aren't supposed to eat or that drug you shouldn't do, but know how wonderful you will feel when you do it.

He flirts with me, which is wonderful, but he tries his hardest to keep his distance, which I hate.

Every second of being away from him now is like torture.

We have figured out how to dreamwalk to each other, though, and so we get to fuck in our dreams, which is almost just as good. It's like old times—in that field in the mountains where we make out under the stars, or the time at the lake house on the deck with the moon painting the water, where he fucks me against the banister of the deck.

Fucking. Hot.

It's almost better for us this way for now, since the addiction is still a low growl within him.

Bash quickly lets me go before the fervent rush sets in and the world melts away. He returns to his box of goodies, pulling out a bottle of bourbon.

I open a cabinet and take down two glasses, handing them to him over the island. He winks at me as he takes them, filling one up, and handing it to Ollie.

Ollie holds Claire's hand until he has to let go to take the glass.

"Need help with anything, Say?" Claire asks, hanging her purse over the back of a chair.

"Yes, please," I answer, trying to figure out where I'd left off before Bash consumed my thoughts. "There are side dishes in the fridge if you wanna start pulling them out and putting spoons in. I gotta get the burgers on the grill. The others will be here soon, too, I think."

"Who's all coming to this shindig?" Bash asks, getting the speaker off the shelf of plants and turning it on.

"Um," I reply, grabbing the plate of burgers, "my neighbors, Katheryn and Travis, and a few friends from work."

His dark brows quirk up. "Who are the few friends from work?"

I haven't returned to work basically since my mom died. I'd come into some money after her death and haven't had the will or want to go back to normal yet. My job is waiting for me at any time, but I plan on finishing my degree first and returning with purpose when the time is right.

Bash and Ollie have also been helping me with bills, which is nice.

"Oh, just Kaylee, Michael, and Jill."

"Okay. I'll throw these on the grill," he offers, taking the plate from me and brushing my fingers with his.

"I'll help," Ollie says. He walks up to Claire and kisses her lips before following Bash out to the backyard.

She watches him go and touches her lips, turning to me and practically glowing.

I smirk at her. "How are things with you two?"

"Just wonderful," Claire states as she gathers spoons from the silverware drawer, "but I gotta tell ya, sis, there's still something off about him I can't quite grasp."

"Like?" I ask hesitantly, trying to distract myself by opening a jar of mayo.

"Like, he just knows things," she replies, pulling a lid off the potato salad and putting a spoon in. "He seems to have this extremely old soul, and sometimes he talks of things like he's been around for hundreds of years." She gets lost in thought as she sets the sides on the table. "He gets weird occasionally, looks pale and sick, and his eyes change color. Then, when he returns, he looks pinker and fresh. It's like he's some sort of animal."

I busy myself with opening more condiments. "That is odd," I say, trying to sound surprised.

I know we're getting closer to having to tell her our secret, especially since they're a couple now.

"Have you guys said 'I love you' yet?"

"Oh, yeah." Claire smiles, looking at him from the window to the backyard. "He told me he was falling for me on our second date. On our third, when he asked me to be his girlfriend, he told me he loved me."

"Did you say it back?"

"Not right away," she answers, walking back to me to get the chips to lay out with the sides. "I mean, I knew I was falling for him, but I'm being careful with my heart. But a few nights ago, we were drinking and dancing, and he made me laugh so hard, it just came out." She stops and meets my eyes. "I love him, Sayah, I really do. He's so wonderful with Sarah, and my parents met him, and he's just so gentlemanly and genuine with everyone. Like I said, it's like he's from another time."

As much as I want to tell her right then and there what Bash and Ollie—and I—are, it isn't my secret to tell. Ollie should be the one to rip the bandage off since they've made things official.

I offer her a genuine smile. "That's great, Claire. I'm so happy for you two."

She smiles back and walks the chips over to the table. "What about you and Bash? I can sense something has changed between you two."

"Yes," I admit, fidgeting with the towel on the counter. "I'm in love with him. I told him that, and he said it back. But we have to wait until we get Dom back to tell him before things go any further. It's not fair to Dom."

"Get Dom back?" Claire questions, her brows drawn together into a tight line.

My heart plummets.

I slipped.

"Um, yeah, well . . . Claire, there are some things we need to tell you . . ." I begin just as Ollie and Bash walk back in.

"Burgers are on. What else can we help with?" Bash states.

"Shit, I left my phone in the car," Claire says, walking over to her purse to grab her keys. "I'll be right back." She looks at me, concerned, and nods for me to follow her to the car.

I hold up a finger to tell her one second. When she's gone, I turn to Ollie and Bash. "When are you going to tell her?"

"I've wanted to," Ollie says, taking a beer out from the box they'd brought. "There just hasn't been a right time, and I don't even know how to."

"Well, you have to soon; she knows something is up. And I just slipped that we have to go get Dom back. We need to tell her today."

"I don't know, Sayah—" Bash starts to say.

"It'll be okay, I promise. I've been best friends with her since the ninth grade, and she's the most loyal person you'll ever meet. She won't run away screaming, I promise." I say the last part to Ollie, then start to make my way out of the kitchen. "I'll start it, you finish. Okay?"

Ollie's green eyes are hesitant as he nods.

I round the kitchen through the archway, into the living room, and out the front door. Claire's coming back up the walk with her phone. I'd thought it was only a ploy to get me to come outside.

Claire watches me take a seat in one of the chairs on the porch. "What's up?" she asks hesitantly.

"You may wanna sit for this," I tell her, patting the chair beside me.

Brows drawn together, Claire sits down. "Oh, no, what is it?"

I take a deep breath, silently asking the goddess to guide me. "There are some things about the Sangravellis you may have noticed aren't exactly normal." I hold her stare. "That is because they aren't normal. They are very different. But what I am about to tell you, you mustn't let it cloud your judgment on Ollie, okay? He's the best one of them. He has a heart of gold."

Her face withers. "Sayah, you're freaking me out. What is it?"

"Ollie is a vampire, Claire. Bash and Dom and their sisters and parents are, too."

Her face rearranges into confusion, and her brows cinch together so tight she looks mad. She gazes at me as though she doesn't recognize who I am. The information paints her expression in a distracted daze, and her head tilts like she's trying to process the words that just came out of my mouth.

"I know it's a lot to take in," I continue when she says nothing. "But they didn't ask for this life. Have Ollie tell you his story. If anything at all, it's a fascinating tale. He means well. And they don't kill people unless they're bad, they—"

"What?" Claire exclaims, anger coating her voice.

"They don't kill people unless they are bad. It's—"

"Are you fucking kidding me with this, Sayah?" She launches to her feet. "A vampire? Stop playing right now. What's really going on with him?"

"That's the truth, Claire. I swear."

The expression on her face would have scared anyone who didn't know her the way I do.

Then, before I can say anything more, my aunt's Subaru pulls up to the front of the house.

"Who is that?" Claire asks, following my gaze to the white car.

"My aunts," I say, standing up, and walking by Claire.

"Wait, Sayah! You have to tell me what the hell is going on!"

"Go talk to Ollie, Claire. He'll tell you. I told him to."

I leave Claire on the porch, focused on finding out what the hell the aunts are doing here.

Hilda hobbles out of the driver's side as Maggie struggles to get out of the passenger side.

"Hey," I say, approaching Hilda and hugging her. "What are you doing here?"

"Oh, we thought we'd surprise you," Hilda replies, letting me go and wobbling over to the passenger side to help Maggie out. "We had some business in Denver with George and the hotel, and since it was the Fourth of July, we thought we'd come up here and crash your party."

"You guys are always welcome here." When Maggie is out, I hug her, too, before leading them up the driveway. "I have some more people coming over, and there is plenty of food. The boys got fireworks and all that, so it should be a pretty fun time."

"The boys, as in Bash and Dom?" Hilda asks as she hobbles behind me.

I haven't spoken to them since Bash, Dom, and I left them in Washington.

"No, Dom isn't here," I explain, looking over my shoulder at them. "But Ollie and Bash are, as well as Claire. Some more people will be over in time, too."

I open the door and let the aunts in.

"If you guys wanna hang and make yourselves at home, I just have to find Claire really quick and then I'll be right back."

"Okay, sweetie," Hilda says as she and Maggie make their way to the couches.

As I enter the kitchen, I can see Bash outside manning the grill, and Claire and Ollie are having what looks like a deep discussion by the far fence.

Claire looks mad and terrified at the same time.

Exiting the backdoor, I approach the railing to talk to Bash.

"Hey, what's going on?" I incline my head in the direction that Ollie and Claire are in.

"Well, Ollie has been telling her his secret since you started to but then left her hanging," Bash says cynically, flipping the last burger and closing the lid.

"My aunts showed up."

Bash's blue eyes catch mine as he sips his bourbon. "Good old Hildie and Maggie are here? Wonderful, I'll throw on some more meat." Bash opens the grill and adds a few more patties. "What are they up to?"

"They were in Denver on business and thought they'd come up here to crash my Fourth of July barbecue. How do you think she's taking it?"

"Well, I don't think she knows how to take it, Say." Closing the grill again, Bash walks toward the opposite side of the lawn, me following him on the deck. "She's one of those people that are too street-smart to honestly believe in the boogie man. She'll have to see proof, and when she does, she's not gonna like it."

I step down from the deck and join him on the lawn. "She'll accept it after a while. I know she will. She loves Ollie. I can see that."

"Let's hope so. We always worry about telling people like this because it could go one of two ways. One: they freak out, walk away for a bit, then come to terms with it and be part of the secret. Or two: they freak out, threaten to tell the church elders, and we have to veilweave them to forget us altogether, which would hurt Ollie."

I scrunch my nose at him. "The church elders?"

Bash lets out a whimsical laugh. "Yeah. The church. The police, the world, the neighbors, the journalists—all have varied over the decades. People confronted with something they've been led to believe were old wives' tales and suddenly find out the monsters that live in the fairytales are real and don't know what to do with that information. They react differently. I'm interested to see how your girl handles it."

"I think she'll handle it just fine," I insist, stealing a glance over at Claire and Ollie.

He grabs both my hands. "Just why, pray tell, did you decide that now, right before our Fourth of July festivities, was a good time to tell your bestie that her man's a monster?"

"I slipped and she already knows something is up with him and I hate keeping secrets from her." I lend him a wry smile. "It's just who I am."

"Well, I love ya kid, but your timing sucks."

I chuckle. "I'm gonna go check on the aunts."

"Wait," he says, vamp flashing me over to the side of the house where no one can see us.

Bash pushes me against the side of the house, his hands leaning against the wall above me, caging me in, and kisses me. I let him because I'd been yearning to feel him against me since the last time.

He touches me like it's his new form of breathing; like my blood and life and limb call to him like a fucking prayer.

When he's done, he lets me go and keeps his nose touching mine as he says, "Sorry. I just couldn't live without your lips for another second. I should be good for a while now."

The way he's looking at me, it's like he would pull me through falling cities and crumbling worlds. He would burn with me if it were on fire, if only just to hold me two seconds longer.

Minutes might have passed. We're so lost in each other's eyes, him holding me like I'm a promise he intends on keeping.

"Shit! The burgers!" he suddenly shouts, kissing my neck before flashing away. I blink at the loss of him, like a saddened glimpse of wonder that's left me all alone. As I round the house, he's already back at the grill, looking all hot and sexy in a domesticated vampire sort of way.

Ollie and Claire are still talking by the fence.

I climb the deck stairs and enter the backdoor, seeing Maggie and Hilda in the kitchen helping themselves to some of the snacks I had set out.

"So, where's Dom again, Sayah?" Maggie asks, getting herself some ice in a glass.

Claire comes in and scowls at me, storming past and making for the front door.

As Ollie comes in behind her, Maggie drops the glass of ice on the kitchen floor. The glass breaks apart, and ice goes flying everywhere.

"Jesus, Maggie," Hilda says from the barstool. "Are you all right?"

"Oliver?" Maggie whispers; her face is as white as a ghost.

Hilda turns around and sees Ollie and gasps.

"Oh, my god," she manages to squeak out, her voice trembling.

Ollie's face is confused and stoic, with a timid smile as he glances between Maggie and Hilda. "Do I know you two?"

My heart sinks to my knees.

Ollie is Maggie's vampire.

MAGGIE'S VAMPIRE

-SAYAH-

Maggie remains unmoving, and Bash comes in behind Ollie.

"You," Maggie seethes, taking a step closer.

Ollie's the vampire that Maggie had fallen in love with as a girl.

"What's going on?" Bash asks as he comes up behind us.

Claire had heard the noise and returned from wherever she had been going.

"You!" Maggie shouts again, taking another step toward him.

"I—I—I'm confused," Ollie's features fall into utter confusion. "Sayah?"

"All right, everyone, calm down," I say, stepping between Ollie and Maggie. "Ollie, I think my aunts knew you when they were girls. Maggie had been in love with you, and you nearly killed her one night in a dark alley. Hilda found her and took her to the hospital where you showed up and tried to veilweave everyone, but they always wear Nightshade around their necks so they couldn't be veilweaveled."

"Oh, my gods," Ollie says, moving to the table to sit down. "Margarite Cartwright?"

Maggie doesn't let up her scowl; it only intensifies on him.

"Margarite—Maggie, I'm sorry I didn't recognize you. It's been a long time."

"You nearly killed her!" Hilda deadpans, rising from her chair.

I move to stand between Hilda and Ollie.

"Ladies, ladies, please," Bash interjects, the tone of his voice in mock concern. "There has to be some explanation; Ollie is not like that. Ollie? Do you remember what happened?"

"I do," Ollie says solemnly, glancing at Maggie. "I was awful to you, and I am truly sorry for that. Maggie, I know you have no reason to trust or believe me. But I was in a really dark time in my life, and I was lost. It was you who made me feel better, who brought me back to life. I only meant to scare you away from me; I never meant to almost kill you. I just let my grief and anger get the best of me."

"So, it's true then?" Claire asks, her eyes a strange picture like she's trying to decipher fantasy from reality. When Maggie dropped the glass, Claire froze in place with the rest of us. "You two knew him when you were young girls, and you recognize him now because he hasn't aged?"

"Oh, Claire, honey," Hilda says, "we're so sorry you are finding out this way."

"This is too much. I need air," Claire snaps, and Bash opens the back door for her.

"So why, if she helped you, did you almost kill her?" Hilda hedges as Claire moves closer to the door.

Ollie shifts in his seat, grabbing another beer from the box on the floor and popping the top. "I had just lost my love, Silva, in a car accident. I was going to propose to her the next day, and when she died, I didn't know how to go on." He stops here, and the whole house falls silent. The loss he'd felt then slathers over him, and he looks at the bottle in his hands. "As vampires, Bash and I and our family have learned to deal with loss, as we have lost so many people in the two hundred-some-odd years we've been alive. But that doesn't make it any easier when it happens unexpectedly." His eyes find Maggie as she steps closer to the table, enthralled by him. It's painted into her ancient eyes. "I came to that bar one night looking to drown my sorrows, and I came across a beautiful woman who was drawn to me."

Maggie approaches the table and sits across from him, clasping her hands in front of her.

"I was trying really hard to turn off my power," Ollie continues, holding her stare, "but knowing now that you were wearing Nightshade, you were insusceptible to any power of mine, repelling included. You listened to me and let me spill my story, so I came back, night after night, for months, not even thinking I was making you fall for me."

Bash shifts his weight, taking a loud sip of his drink.

"The night you followed me, Maggie, I only meant to scare you." He slides his arms across the table to cover her clasped hands with his. "I had reached a point in my life where I didn't want to be with any woman or ever love again. When I bit you, my grief hit me, and I blacked out, only to come to a few hours later and be flooded with guilt. So I went to the hospital not only to make sure my tracks were covered but to make sure you were okay. I even fed you some of my blood. Hilda was there, sleeping. But I know this is not an excuse for what I did, and no words will ever express how truly sorry I am."

"She never loved anyone again because of you," Hilda snaps at him. "She loved you beyond measure, and you almost drained her and left her, never to be seen or heard from again."

"I know," Ollie says, taking his hands away from Maggie's. "Sometimes our powers hit people differently. I am truly sorry it hit you the way it did. I was really trying to turn it off. You never saw me come back because I chose to stay unseen. I returned to check on you for months before my family left the area. I kept tabs on you until you graduated from college and moved to Philadelphia when you got that job with the Philly Tribune. I read your articles every time I was there."

"You did?" Maggie breathes, and a palpable snap within the room tells us all has forgiven at this moment.

Ollie's soft green eyes graze hers, and I can almost see the thread Maggie laid bare for him being unraveled. "I did, Maggie. I loved you, too. I'll admit, not in the same way as you loved me. But you and I became extremely close for our short time as bartender and patron."

"See, vampire senses are heightened," Bash offers, walking over to Maggie, and squeezing her shoulder. "Everything you all feel, we feel, like, ten times more intensely. So when Ollie was mourning Silva, it was the most intense grief you could imagine. Life-consuming. And when Maggie was there for him, even as a bartender, he had strong feelings for her, too, just not in the way that Maggie did for him."

"I cared for you like a best friend," Ollie adds. "I was worried about you, and after I hurt you, it made my grief worse. I was not normal again for about ten years."

"It's true, I was there," Bash agrees. "He was even more insufferable than Dom."

"I can't believe any of this is true," Claire whispers, pressing her head into the door jamb behind Ollie. Ollie stands and goes to her. She smacks him across the cheek and runs in the opposite direction.

"She'll be fine," I tell him. "Just give her a minute."

Ollie goes after her.

"Poor girl," Hilda tuts, her face still red with fury.

"It's hard to discover that the person you love is a vampire," I add, looking at Bash.

"Yeah, where is Dom, exactly?" Hilda asks, changing the subject. "I know there is something you aren't telling us."

Bash looks at me as he sits in the chair Ollie just vacated. "Dom's mark went dark when we got back here. He and I went to New York to try and find another artifact, and that's when I fucked everything up."

"What did you do?" Maggie asks, wiping her glasses off with her shirt.

"I got addicted to her blood," he says, making a gesture toward me with his bourbon glass. "And I drank the substance that was keeping him from the darkness."

"Oh, my god," Hilda gasps, looking at Bash. "So what happened to him?"

"He went all the way dark," I explain. "We haven't seen or heard from him since."

"Well, kinda," Bash says, sipping his drink. "He did leave us the scarlet ribbons. And the letter to you."

"What?" Maggie asks, closing the freezer drawer.

"Long story," Bash answers sternly. "People are starting to show up, though. We'll have to get more into detail about it later."

I nod and walk around the corner to see my friends Kaylee, Michael, and Jill walking up the drive.

Greeting them at the door, I let them in.

"Help yourselves to anything in the kitchen," I offer as they mingle around the food. "I just have to check on something."

Going past my friends, I look around for where Claire and Ollie had gone. I spot them walking in the middle of the green-belt across the street, seemingly calm and collected. When I reach them, Claire still looks extremely upset.

"Hey, guys, how's it going?"

Claire's hair is blowing wildly in the breeze. "Oh, just great. Found out I'm dating a killer. You know, no biggie," she spits.

"Can you give us a minute?" I ask Ollie, who obliges and walks back to the house.

"Hey, I know this is a lot. But—"

"But nothing, Sayah. He should have told me. *You* should have told me!"

"Now, stop. That isn't fair, hon. It wasn't my secret to tell."

"Well, he should've told me then," she snaps, crossing her arms and walking away.

"Claire, listen," I plead, catching her shoulder, and turning her to face me. "Think about that. Think of the kind of secret that he had to keep from you. Can you even imagine being a vampire in this day and age and having to live with that? And then meeting someone you truly love and having this dark secret that could potentially end the relationship because of the false belief about vampires? You know how I am, being a witch and all. I don't tell just anybody what I am because there is this old school belief that witches are bad. So, I carefully pick who I tell and at the right time. Ollie is a good man; he's a good soul and wanted to tell you–he just didn't know how."

"Yeah, but, Sayah, yours is that you practice magick; his is that he eats people."

I stifle the giggle. "He doesn't eat people. See, there is that belief that vampires are bad."

"Aren't they, though?" Claire shouts. "Do they not drink human blood?"

"Well, yes, but—"

"But nothing, Sayah! That's not good. That's not a quality I want in a man. 'Hi, I'm Claire. I like long romantic walks on the beach and a man who can eat my ex for dinner.' Yeah, not something I put on my dating profile."

"Claire, I know you're upset. But they didn't choose this life and most of them hate what they are, Ollie included. He was the first to turn, and he has the kindest soul despite it. He only kills if he has to, and when that happens, it's someone who deserves to die. Believe me, I struggled with this when I found out about Dom. But I could feel in my heart that he had a good soul, even if it was damned. Ollie is even better than Dom. Give him a chance, Claire, you won't regret it."

"He told me that you are something supernatural, too, now. A phoenix?"

"Yes. I am. I was chosen to balance all the world's dark things."

"What the hell does that mean?"

"It's a long story that I will tell you some other time. Right now, I have an aunt who just discovered her long-lost love, a Bash who can't be trusted with anything, and friends showing up to a house full of vampires. Please come back? Have some drinks and just listen to his stories. Please, Claire?"

"It doesn't change the fact that I am still mad."

"You can be mad. You have every right to be. But don't let go of him because of this. He truly is one of the best people I've ever met. And he knows things, so ask him about his visions. It's a trip."

"So, who is the bad one, then?" she asks as she reluctantly follows me to the house. "Bash?"

"Yes, but I think I'm changing him. Everyone does. But wait until you meet the sisters. They're even worse.

"Scarlet and Hadley?"

"Hattie. Yes. They fucking terrify me. Jasantha, too. And his mom is scary A.F. too."

"Great. This sounds like just the kind of family I want to be in," Claire says sarcastically as we walk across the street.

"I think you, of all people, will fit right in."

"Why do you say that?"

"Because you are one of the scariest humans I know. You will definitely give those bitches a run for their money."

Claire laughs at this, and I know her anger has come down at least two notches.

Once we're back inside, Kaylee, Michael, and Jill are in the kitchen talking to my aunts while drinking wine coolers. Bash and Ollie are at the grill, flipping the burgers and discussing something. I smile at my friends and walk back with Claire on my tail.

When Ollie sees Claire with me, he immediately stops what he is doing and walks up to her. He wraps his arms around her and pulls her close, and she lets him in, still stiff to show him she's still angry.

I glide up to the railing to see Bash.

"How's the food coming?"

"Just fine. About done. Have a good chat?"

"I think I got her to reason with him. That's about all I can do."

"Well, this is almost done. Got a clean plate?"

"Yes. I'll go grab it and figure out music."

"Good call," he says, turning the burners down before closing the propane.

THE NEIGHBOR FROM HELL

-SAYAH-

little while later, we're outside on the patio, eating, mingling, and having a grand time. I notice that my neighbor—the creepy one who lives west of me and shares a fence with me—is standing on the back patio watching us. I wave, but he just scowls.

"What's up with him?" Bash asks around a bite of his burger.

"Oh, he's a grumpy war vet who hates anything I do. He even put a camera in his window to spy on me."

I feel him tighten with tension. "What?"

"Yeah. When I first moved in with my ex, he was friendly. We exchanged recipes and helped each other with weeds and things. He has a live-in girlfriend I've never seen. She uses the garage to get in and out, never setting foot outside. I've actually wondered whether she was a vampire."

Bash chuckles.

"Anyway, when I kicked the ex out, the neighbor, Chris, stopped talking to me, and just started treating me badly. I never knew what it was that happened. But he started calling the cops on me during the day for playing my music too loud, throwing shit on my lawn, purposely watering me while I was out doing yard work. Once he even sprayed me with weed killer. He just went fucking weird. Starting coming out at night and taking pictures of little girls on bicycles and sitting on his porch asking little boys to come mow his lawn for candy. Just fucking snapped."

Bash's face stops mid-chew, the burger bite bulging his cheek. "What the fuck?"

"I know. I have no idea what happened."

"Did you do something about it?"

"Played my music louder." I laugh. "Not much I can do. He just worries me. He has that air about him like he may just one day snap."

"Odin's ghost, Sayah. Why didn't you let Dom kill him?"

"Because. He just has PTSD, and he's weird. He doesn't deserve to die."

Bash's chewing loudly, deadlocked in a stare with Chris. "Spraying you with weed killer? Yes, he does. I'll kill him."

Bash moves to get up, so I grab his shoulder. "No, Bash. If he does anything else, I'll let you kill him."

"Promise?"

"Promise."

The sun sinks below the mountains, setting the sky to a decadent pink while signaling to prepare for the fireworks show. We move to the front yard to continue listening to music, carrying on, drinking, and talking. Meanwhile, the boys and I start lighting off fireworks.

Claire's a little more relaxed and continues to be so with every beer she finishes.

Ollie's right by her side.

Bash and I are by the curb, lighting Black Cats. They whistle into the sky above the greenbelt so as not to hit any houses. Other people around the neighborhood respond with glowing bands and colorful mortars in the sky.

I stand hip to hip with Bash as we watch the colorful displays, and his fingers graze mine again, igniting those wild butterflies.

When Bash bends down to grab another Black Cat, a rock comes out of nowhere and hits him in the head.

He straightens up and rubs the place it hit, looking around for the culprit. I spin around to see Chris standing in his drive-way, holding a handful of rocks. "Light another one of those things, and I'll call the cops."

"What the fuck?" Bash shouts, taking a step toward him.

I pull him by the shirt to stop him. "No, Bash, don't."

Bash shrugs me off and flashes up to Chris faster than I can help, and Chris drops the pile of rocks. I quickly run up to them and step in between them.

Bash stares at Chris, inches from his face, eyes white, fangs bared. "You got a problem, perv-boy?"

Chris is shaking, and wetness spreads from his crotch to his knees.

Bash sniffs and looks down. "Ha! A war vet, you said?" he growls, looking at me. "You think this guy has valor, Sayah?"

Chris doesn't move. The greasy black hair under his beanie frames his face, which is coated in shock.

"Nothing to say, freak show?" Bash seethes.

"Bash," I mutter. "C'mon, let's just go back to the party."

I look over at my guests; everyone is standing in the driveway watching Bash.

Luckily, his back is to them, so they can't see his vampire on full blast.

"BASH!" I repeat sternly. "Stop it, they're watching."

Bash backs up, his blue eyes returning, fangs retreating. "Go somewhere else for the fourth, ya dipshit. You should know by now there's fireworks."

Bash walks away, and I follow. I look behind me now to see Chris staring after him, a quiet fury reddening his face.

This is not good.

Bash and I return to our fireworks. But as I'm lighting a bottle rocket, I look over to see Chris has left the driveway.

$\mathcal{A}$s the night grows darker, we're sitting in the driveway watching the fireworks show that Bash and Ollie are putting on. Every house in the neighborhood is competing with each other until the town fireworks show starts.

Ollie and Bash had brought the works, including flashers, screamers, sparklers, and smoke bombs, and they would set off the mortars between every small show.

I'm loving all the laughter, the bright lights, the joy that's filled in all my friends.

Bash seems like he's happy, too.

But that changes in an instant.

I hear something that sounds like fireworks, but has that familiar sound of my hunting days with my dad and time spent on the shooting range. There is also the indistinct sound of an automatic shotgun spraying bullets into the crowd directly in front of my house.

Everything slows.

I turn and see Travis fall to the ground, clutching his chest, Katheryn screaming as he does. We all become acutely aware of what's happening—the people closest to the garage are safe as they run in and take cover, but those of us out in the open are in danger.

A barrage of bullets come slamming through the crowd of people. I swallow a scream as some hit Bash and Ollie. I duck down and dodge, running for the garage, and as I do, I watch Jill get shot through the head, blood and brains scattering all over me and the driveway. I try to remain calm as I watch Kaylee and Michael try to run for cover as well, Michael getting hit in the stomach and falling while Kaylee ducks, screaming, and trying to pull him to cover.

The only thing I can think to do is run to the house to get my assault rifle out of the upstairs closet, and as I run for it, I see my best friend Claire get shot four or five times in the chest.

"CLAIRE!" I scream, my voice trembling in a wild panic.

Ollie had been on his way to her and scoops her up before any more bullets can hit her. I suddenly feel the world whip by as Bash grabs me and takes me into the house, where Ollie's carrying the limp and bleeding Claire.

Panicked, all I can think is to get the gun. I need that gun.

What stops bad guys with guns?

Good guys with guns.

Bounding up the stairs, Bash is there with me in seconds.

"What are you doing?" he asks as I go into the closet to grab my AR. He's bleeding from a gunshot wound to the shoulder.

"Gonna kill that fucking bastard," I seethe through my tears, grabbing the loaded clip, and slamming it into the gun.

"Sayah," he says, pulling the gun away. "You don't need those anymore."

I feel the tears streaming down my face as I contemplate what he's saying. "My phoenix power?" It had not even crossed my mind.

He nods quickly and pulls me up.

"But I thought it's only for killing grims?" I state as we fly back down the stairs.

"Sayah. You're a supernatural badass. Your powers are for anyone deserving of the mayhem," Bash shouts when we land on the ground floor again.

Ollie is leaning over Claire, whispering to her. He has bitten his arm and is holding it to her mouth.

Gunshots still echo outside as I go to the back porch.

"Where's he shooting from?" Bash asks as we make our way to the back deck.

"I think his upstairs window." I point to his roof. "Can you get us over there?"

"Absolutely," Bash says as he swoops me up, and we fly over the fence. Landing on Chris's roof, Bash creeps around to the side, and I follow, listening to the bouts of gunfire echoing in the night.

My heart slams so hard against my ribcage that I think it may burst wide open.

Thinking of my anger, letting it fester, rot, and consume me, the tingles in my bones light me up and crack me open. I emit a glow as the cracks on my skin light up, the wings of fire breaking my skin open on my back. My power drenches me as we reach the front of the house. I have no fear as I stand tall.

Following Bash to the open window, a cylindrical metallic barrel of a gun protrudes from the opening, glinting off the bright light of the moon.

Bash's there in the blink of an eye, ripping the gun from Chris's hands. My body begins to stretch to fit my phoenix form, my spine elongates and the wings tingle as they emerge from my back. Grabbing hold of both sides of the window as Bash holds Chris from behind, his beady black eyes blow wide as he stares death in the face.

The tousles of Bash's black hair drape over his forehead as

he leans into Chris's ear, holding his hands behind his back as he whispers, "Time to die," as I step in.

"Please," Chris pleads while I take my predator's gait toward him.

I catch my reflection in a dresser mirror. My eyes are glowing gold, the fissures and cracks of my skin casting a foreboding shine into his disgusting pigsty of a room. I shake my head, approaching him. "You are begging for your life?"

"Please don't kill me." Tears and snot are falling down his face, causing a gross film in the corners of his mouth.

Bash is over his shoulder, pulling his head to the side. "We don't concede to the requests of cowards and psychopaths," he snarls into his ear.

Chris sobs. "I have a wife and a . . . a . . ."

"Shut up!" I yell and bound up to him, sinking my fangs into his neck.

Bash does the same on his other side, but whereas Bash's bites only puncture, mine sizzle and burst, causing Chris's body to turn black like burnt toast. The blackness spreads from his neck to his knees, his stupid face locked in terror as his skin breaks apart and bursts into flames.

His screams fill the air where the bullets once did.

There's a blistering scream from behind us and Bash is immediately on Chris's girlfriend—the one and only time I see her face, and it's in the moment she's dying.

Bash cuts her screams short as he snaps her neck.

The thud of her lifeless body mingles with the flames of Chris's; he collapses at the knees and sets flame to the carpet.

"We gotta get out of here," Bash states through the wavering dance of fire, grabbing my hand, and flashing us out the window.

We land on the ground noiselessly.

Fireworks boom in the background, shooting over the trees to the east.

The finale has begun.

All that's left of the massacre in front of my house is panicked voices and muffled cries. I can barely hear anything else over the thundering of my heart.

"You okay?" I think I hear him ask, putting his arm around me as we hurry back to my house.

"No," I answer honestly, not knowing who had lost their lives during the last ten minutes.

Rushing up to the front door, blood is everywhere.

Jill is dead.

She's lying face down in the driveway, parts of her skull missing from her head and scattered on the driveway.

Travis is also dead; Kathryn is slumped over him, sobbing.

Kaylee's crouched in front of Michael, who's clutching his stomach, blood seeping through his shirt and pooling on the ground. My aunts are both okay; they're helping Kaylee apply pressure to his wound.

Bash bites into his arm and holds it up to Michael, veil-weaveling Kaylee and him simultaneously to let him drink.

As Bash feeds Michael his blood, I hurry into the house, dreading to see what I may find inside.

Ollie's kneeling beside Claire, stroking her face. She is unmoving. Her beautiful Caribbean eyes are wide open and gone, staring at the ceiling.

"Oh, no! No, no, no, no, no," I say, the very heart that beats in my chest stilling. "Did you get her the blood on time?"

Ollie's eyes are rheumy and wet. "I think so. We can only wait and see."

As much as I don't like the idea of my best friend becoming a vampire, I know it was Ollie's only chance at keeping her alive.

She'd been shot four times in the chest. There's no way she would have made it out of that.

Kneeling next to Ollie, I smudge a tear over one of the

gunshot wounds in her chest. Taking her hand in mine, I caress it, willing her to live through this transition.

"Please come back, Claire-bear. Please."

The sound of Bash's heavy boots on the hardwood makes me look up at him. Hilda and Maggie are behind him.

"I think that Michael guy will make a full recovery," he tells me, holding the back of the couch. His eyes scan over Claire, then track to me. "I had to veilweave them so they would not remember the part about me. But as for the two dead people on the driveway and the two dead over there, I think you have to call the cops, Sayah. This is too messy for me to clean up."

"What are we going to say about me killing them, though?" I ask, sniffling. "And what about the fact that now his house is burning down?"

"We'll say we don't know what happened. He just started shooting everyone, and then his house was on fire. We think his girlfriend tried to stop him," Bash says, his face hardened with concern. "We'll all corroborate and veilweave as needed. Neither one of us will go down for murder, okay?"

"Okay," I reply, still clutching my dead best friend's hand. "We should get Claire upstairs, though. Did you veilweave my neighbor, Katheryn?"

"I think she may be dead, too."

I shoot him an insolent glare. "What?"

"She wasn't moving last time I checked. She was hovering over her man."

"Go check, please," I order. "Ollie, take Claire to the extra bedroom and I'll call the police. They're gonna wonder why we took so long to call them."

"Tell them you were panicked and were trying to figure out what to do," Maggie offers.

"Yeah, I think we just need to skip this whole thing about calling the cops," Ollie says stiffly.

"What? Why?" Bash asks.

"When they find the neighbors dead, they're gonna come knocking over here to find out if we know anything."

"We can veilweave them, then," Bash replies. "Chalk it up to murder-suicide."

I rock back onto my heels. "And what of the three dead people in the driveway?"

Bash sits on the arm of the couch. "We'll just get rid of the bodies."

"Get rid of the bodies, Bash? Fuck, what, are you new at being a killer?" Ollie snorts, the anger in his voice clearly because he's worried about Claire.

"We can't 'get rid of the bodies'!" I shout. "Guys, these are my friends. Katheryn and Travis have kids. Grown kids, but kids nonetheless. And Jill is my friend from work. You can't just throw her body away; she has grown kids, too."

Bash tilts his head at me. "What do you suggest we do, Sayah?"

"We have to call the cops. You two veilweave them to whatever suspicions they have. We have to do this. For their kids to have closure. We'll just tell it like it is, a crazed neighbor who flew off the handle because of the sound of fireworks."

"All right," Bash agrees. "Call them, then. I'm gonna go check on the Katheryn lady."

"Is she going to be okay?" Hilda asks, stepping closer and seeing Claire dead on the couch.

"Ollie fed her his blood before she died," I answer. "She'll be okay; she's just going to be a new vampire."

"Oh, good," Hilda says, and I can't tell if that's a sarcastic tone or an interested one.

I rise from the ground by my dead friend and pull out my phone to call 911.

A TRAGIC MELODY

-SAYAH-

Because of the gory details of the scene, the cops were here for hours. Luckily, with the two vampires veil-weaveling them, there was no murder investigation opened, and it was chalked up to be precisely what it was: a crazy person who committed murder/suicide after unleashing fury on a party.

They removed the bodies and the blood was cleaned up; all who remained from the party are now sitting in the living room, exhausted and not speaking much.

Michael has made a full recovery; he and Kaylee were left with thoughts that he had injured himself with a firework, and Kaylee was to take him home to rest.

Ollie is upstairs with Claire, waiting for her to wake up.

I'm sitting on the big chair with my feet on the ottoman. Hilda is perched on the loveseat, and Maggie is on the oversized couch, everyone quietly processing what happened.

Bash had been upstairs with Ollie and when he flashes down the stairs, he makes me scoot over so he can sit beside me. He pulls me in close.

I'm devastated about losing my friends, feeling guilty for

them being gone, mad at myself for killing my neighbor—I should've let Bash kill him. Now, the weight of my guilt sinks me beneath dark water, suffocating with emotions I know not how to feel.

"You okay?" he asks me in a hushed voice.

"No," I answer honestly. "I can't believe this happened. I've never killed anyone that wasn't a warlock before. I don't regret it— he killed my friends—but . . . it's hard. And my friends are dead."

"I know, love." Bash kisses the top of my forehead.

"Are you two a thing now?" Hilda asks bluntly.

"No," Bash answers quickly.

"Well, you have yet to finish the tale of what's been going on." There's almost a ferality to Hilda.

Shoveling my feet under me and grabbing a pillow for comfort, I finish the story for the aunts.

"So," I conclude with an exhale, "when the new moon hits, Bash and I and the others will travel to Feylight Grove to meet Tallyn, get his addiction under control, and get Dom back."

"None of this is good, you guys," Maggie sighs, her eyes hardening, and her gaze on us is cool and collected. "This sounds like she's preparing for something huge."

Hilda's wide eyes are concerned beneath her glasses. "We need to ask Freya."

Bash shifts next to me, leaning his leg on mine. "You have a direct line to talk to her or . . ."

Hilda scratches her nose. "We can summon her."

"Well, by all means," Bash says, scooting to the edge of our oversized chair.

Hilda goes toward the spell cabinet and grabs one of the old tomes she had given me that belonged to my grandma. "We need a summoning spell."

Finding the spell she needs, she takes a deep breath. Closing her eyes, the room immediately feels charged with anticipation.

"All right, everyone, gather 'round," Hilda instructs, her eyes glinting with determination.

Bash raises a skeptical eyebrow but joins the circle, standing beside her. I follow suit, taking my place beside Bash as Hilda recites an incantation in a language that seems to echo with ages of forgotten power. The room hums with otherworldly energy, and the air thickens with a sense of connection to something beyond our Earthly realm.

As Hilda continues her incantation, symbols and sigils appear on the floor, glowing with an ethereal light. The room's temperature drops, and a soft breeze rustles through space, carrying the scent of distant flowers.

Bash shoots me a sidelong glance, a mix of awe and skepticism in his eyes. The air seems to shimmer as if responding to Hilda's words, and the room feels like a bridge to realms beyond.

A flickering image materializes in the center of the conjured symbols—the form of Freya herself, the ancient goddess. She appears regal and composed, her eyes holding timeless wisdom.

"Freya"—Hilda speaks with reverence and urgency—"we seek your guidance and assistance. A grave threat looms, and we need your insight."

Freya regards us with a calm expression before finally nodding, her voice resonating in the room like a tragic melody. "Speak, children of the night. I am here to listen."

Maggie and Hilda spin the tale for her, and the conversation unfolds between Freya and our group. The room remains charged with mystical energy, and I can't shake the feeling that the fate of our lives is hanging in the balance.

"What you are speaking of is part of the Arcane Nexus War," Freya explains, her voice that strange mixture of magick and water rushing down a cliffside, "which will ultimately lead to the Riftstorm Conflict."

She says this so matter-of-factly that I have to blink to wrap my mind around the meaning.

"The Arcane Nexus War would be..." Bash says for me.

"The Arcane Nexus War is the conflict between Tallyn and Trystan that has been raging for thousands of years," Freya continues. Her ghostlike form is iridescent, see through, and her white gown billows in an invisible breeze. "It revolves around a central powerful point, Feylight Grove, that serves as a nexus between realms. Factions vie for control of this nexus, knowing that dominance over it grants immense power over multiple worlds."

"A-and the Riftstorm Conflict?" I ask.

"The Riftstorm Conflict is the catastrophic event that will cause breaches in reality, resulting in violent clashes between entities from various realms drawn into the fray by the instability of the fabric of existence."

"Is she speaking English?" Bash asks Hilda, and she shoots him a disgusted glare.

Freya claps her hands in front of her in a very human way. She walks to the circle's edge and looks Bash in the eyes. "Tallyn and Trystan—Luminara and Neverdusk Courts—have been at war since the beginning of our time. While there are periods of reconciliation and alliances, they are always on the brink of war. Tallyn was given the entire realm because she was the elder of the two, and this infuriated Trystan."

As she walks the circle, she looks at each of us. "The wars began early on, and Trystan is a much darker being than Tallyn —more prone to violence and mayhem. The entire fae realm used to be the Luminara Domain. But with the wars he waged, the parts of the realm he won, he began calling the Neverdusk Dominion. It eats the sunlight and devours light, so all realms under the Neverdusk are in perpetual nighttime. Fae in the Neverdusk Dominion are like witches who aren't Wiccan. They don't have the same laws, practices, or even magick. Their magick is dark, and therefore, they tend to win every war."

She moves over to Hilda. "With each passing century, Trystan wanted more and more of Tallyn's realm, especially Feylight Grove. So, he created the Eclipse Wars. These conflicts he wages involve the convergence of different realms during a celestial event, such as a rare solar or lunar eclipse. As the worlds align, it triggers a massive war between realms fighting for dominance or survival."

Silence is deafening in her pauses, and the entire world stops breathing to hear her speak.

Then she stops in front of me. "Trystan is the ruler of the warlocks that create the grimspawns. He creates *them*. So he had them open portals for him at certain times of year to take hostages in other realms and bring them back to the Neverdusk Dominion to fight in his army. Tallyn has lost so much; the only remaining part of the Luminara Domain is Feylight Grove. The rest of them are owned by Trystan or in ruins."

"Oh. My. Gods," I gasp. "Trystan is the one who created the warlocks?"

"He is," Freya replies, moving back to the center of her circle.

"Makes sense to what I saw then," Bash mutters.

"So what is this Eclipse War?" I ask, brushing over Bash's realization.

"There are certain moons and celestial events that open up certain realms," she answers, her bright green eyes turning grim, hollowing out all my calm. "Dread Harvest Eclipse opens every realm. So, in preparation for this, starting at the new moon of the last full moon before a Dread Harvest Eclipse, the fae of the Luminara Domain prepare for war. This is when they call on Odin and give him offerings, preparing for battle, and asking for gifts of strength and agility. The gods are said to give them supernatural powers or heighten the ones they already have. It is known in the mortal realm as the Wild Hunt."

"But I still don't get what Tallyn would be preparing for?" I say quietly.

"If the Dread Harvest Eclipse opens every portal, and the Shadow Hunt Moon just happened, Trystan could be using the Dread Harvest Eclipse and Wild Hunt to recruit every soldier he can to invade Feylight Grove with the next full moon," Freya answers. "She is preparing for the greatest battle of her existence."

Bash scratches the stubble on his face. "Which would make sense as to why she has been stealing my blood."

"Making those dark fairies that Ollie saw?" I ask.

"Well, worse than dark fairies, Say," he answers, and his blue eyes are the only calm I cling to. "With my blood, who knows what they are becoming."

"Oh, no, what have you agreed to, Bash?" I glare at him with a deep concern even I can't lasso.

"I have no idea." I can hear the detriment dripping out of his voice. "And if Trystan had a direct line to Mederio, that's probably how Tallyn came across Dom. Who knows what she has been making him do?"

"So what do we do?" I ask Freya, who is beginning to waiver.

"If she already has the blood of a demon, there's no stopping what will happen now. A war is coming. Just make sure that you are on the right side."

"Thank you, Freya," Hilda says.

Freya's eyes me one last time. She nods and fades back into the night.

"Bash!" comes a yell from upstairs, injecting our séance with a new sort of panic.

Ollie.

Bash is gone with a streak of black.

Hope swells in my chest. Luckily, before the cops came, the two vampires and I had stashed some of the blood from the victims to feed Claire when she awoke.

"Sayah!" Bash yells from upstairs. "She's asking for you."

"Be right back," I announce to the aunts, who nod in unison.

I climb the stairs two at a time to reach the extra bedroom. Entering the small blue bedroom, Claire is an immaculate picture of a stunning being, looking as though she has just come from a beauty pageant. Sitting up in the bed, her hair is shiny and black with not a strand out of place, delicately surrounding the sharp edges of her face. Her skin is like porcelain while her lips are red, her eyes are bright golden green, and her fangs make her look all the more beautiful when she smiles.

My dubious look to Ollie must have spoken volumes because he says, "It's okay. She's hungry, but she has endured the change remarkably well."

"Hey," Claire says to me, and there's no anger within the inflections of her voice.

"Hi, pretty," I say gently as I take a seat on the edge of the bed. "How are you feeling?"

"I feel okay. Ollie told me what happened. I'm really just worried about what this means for my daughter."

"Everything will be okay," Ollie assures her, gently stroking her face. "Bash and I will help you figure this out. You will never not have us, okay?"

"Okay," she replies.

"Here, drink this," Ollie says, handing her a bag of blood.

Hesitantly, she takes it, her hand steady. When she puts the bag to her lips, she starts off by drinking slowly, but as the first drops of the crimson liquid hit her throat, her color lightens and she starts gulping.

She returns the bag to Ollie when the contents are empty.

"Better?" he asks.

"A little."

"Well, we have more when you need it, okay? Just let us know."

She nods. Ollie bends down and kisses her.

"We have to travel to New York," Bash interjects. "And soon."

"Why?" Claire asks with a blink.

"More of what we didn't have time to tell you," I answer, nervously cracking my knuckles. "There are things about us that are happening right now that we couldn't burden you with while you were still digesting that your boyfriend is a vampire."

"Like what?" she presses, a tinted concern infecting her voice.

As Ollie, Bash, and I tell her all about everything–the mark, the warlocks, the grimspawns, Laureya being a formweaver and now a vampire, me becoming the phoenix, and now the Luminara Queen and the Riftstorm Conflict, even though it's more information than a normal person could handle–Claire's face rearranges from curiosity to concern but never from shock to utter confusion, like a mortal person's face would.

What comes next is something that not even Ollie was expecting.

"We also need Mom to help get the wolf curse off Sayah," Bash says.

The look in Ollie's eyes tells me that Bash has not confessed that I'd fallen in love with him and turned into the wolf.

"Come again?" Ollie says, more to Bash than to me.

I look back to Bash, who is shifting against the door jamb, crossing his arms over his chest and shrugging. "Yeah, she formweaved for the first time a week ago. Guess she's in love with me or some shit," he answers sheepishly.

"I'm confused," Claire states.

"When we discovered that Laureya was part formweaver, part demon, I discovered that made me part formweaver, too. And to formweave for the first time, you have to fall in love with a demon."

"I'm part demon," Bash tells the group almost sarcastically, as if we didn't already know.

Well, Claire didn't know.

"Say?"

"I'll tell you more about that when you and I are alone."

"Girl talk," Bash quips. "But if we want to get that curse off you before we have to go to Feylight Grove, I suggest we get moving. You coming, Claire?"

"I think you should," Ollie says before she can respond. "Until you get the hang of this, I recommend you stay by us."

"Yeah, I think I will. Sarah can stay with my parents for a few weeks."

"What about you, Sayah?" Ollie asks. "What will you do about Gauge?"

"Oh, more family drama. Derek will be okay with it; Gauge will not."

"You'll make it up to him," Bash reassures me.

I hate the thought of leaving Gauge again, but I've been spending as much time with him as I can since summer began.

"Great," Bash says. "When you feel well enough, Claire, we should go."

There's a flash of color, and a lamp is knocked over as Claire tries to get out of bed, unaccustomed to her new power of movement.

"Whoa, are you okay?" Ollie asks, righting the lamp on the desk she knocked over.

Claire touches her hand to her temple to steady the dizziness. "I think so."

"Another thing we need to go over"— Ollie pulls her into him—"is speed. It's one of our…"

"Gifts," Bash finishes.

"Yeah, that," Ollie agrees. "You'll get used to it and learn how to control it. You have to just force yourself to move at normal speeds. When you want to move with that speed, you just . . . take your foot off the brake and fly."

"Sounds exhilarating," Claire responds.

"Oh, it is," Bash smirks.

"Can we go try?" Claire asks, gazing at Ollie like a little girl who just got a new tricycle and wants to go try it out.

"Soon, my love. Very soon." He kisses her on her nose.

"Why don't you just take her out now?" I ask. "It's late, and I have to wrap up some things with my aunts. I also need to make her a sun necklace."

"You should probably get some rest, Say," Bash adds.

"Don't you guys need rest, too?" I ask, but I already know the answer.

"We never need rest," Ollie argues. "We could go on for days without it. We just choose to go to sleep because it gets boring staying up all night every night."

"We don't ever need rest?" Claire asks, intrigued.

Ollie gives her a seductive look. "Never."

"All right, love birds, all right," Bash interjects. "Ollie, let's go out and give her a lesson. Sayah, you do your thing. We'll see you when you wake up."

I walk past Bash in the doorway, and on my way, he pinches my side. "Dream of me," he says with a wink.

I smile and descend the stairs.

I awake to the sound of talking from the floor below. I'd forgotten to shut my bedroom door, and sound travels well in my house.

Pulling myself out of bed, I go downstairs, grabbing the necklace I'd made for Claire on my way.

The aunts, Bash, Claire, and Ollie are having coffee in the dining room.

"Good morning, beautiful," Bash says as I enter.

"Morning," I greet, making my way to the coffee pot. I hand the necklace to Claire before I do.

"Put that on soon," Ollie instructs her.

"Why?" she asks, fingering the chain of the necklace. "What does it do?"

"It prevents you from bursting into flames in the sun," Bash answers, his hands wrapped around a cup of, no doubt, black coffee.

Claire hands it to Ollie and lifts her hair so he can clasp it for her. Luckily, the sun isn't quite up yet, so the light in the dining room isn't enough to hurt her.

"What are you guys talking about so loudly?" I ask.

"The aunts were just telling us everything they know about the fae," Bash supplies. He's sitting at the counter-height dining room table with the others.

"And how is that?" I ask, putting my cup underneath the spout and pressing the button.

"Good," Bash answers after sipping his coffee. "I was just curious why the fae weren't included in the tales about all the world's dark things. They play quite the role."

"We didn't know that you would get mixed up with them," Maggie answers cynically.

"When Dom was first marked, you didn't think it would be important to summon Freya then to find out about the fae king being the one who makes the warlocks?" Bash snipes back.

"It really didn't even cross our minds that it was connected," Hilda defends.

"Either way," I chime in, pouring creamer into my coffee. "We have a dangerous mission now. Is there anything you two can supply to help us prepare for whatever the hell we're getting into?"

"Nothing other than the obvious," Hilda answers, shifting in her chair. "It sounds as though she wants Bash. So, for him, he needs to just be prepared for anything."

"Well, if it's a war she's fighting against her brother–and one she seems to be losing–I want to help however I can. I'm going to offer myself to her services."

"Sayah, no!" Hilda gasps.

"That's suicide," Maggie seconds.

"Sayah, I don't think that's wise," Ollie adds.

"Yeah, babe, I'm with them," Claire chimes in. "I mean, I don't know much about anything in this realm, but none of it sounds like something you should get involved in."

"I'm doing it," I confirm. I've thought a lot about this and have made the decision. No one is going to sway me. "Tallyn seems like she's this evil fairy who has nothing but mischief planned, but I think it goes deeper than that. I feel she's losing her realm to her mean older brother, and I want to help her. I think we all should. In the end, we will gain something out of this. It may be dangerous, but I think it'll be worth it. We can help save the Luminara Domain."

"She does have a valid point," Bash agrees.

"Bash, you can't be serious," Ollie argues. "This is suicide."

"I don't see how," Bash adds. "She wants my blood to help make a demon army; she can use Sayah for her powers—we all have gifts and powers. We can only offer it to her and see what she says. If she feels that she can use us, then we can help. If she doesn't, I will go. You guys take Dom and be done with it. I'll be out of there as soon as she gets what she needs from me, anyway."

"I just don't think this is wise," Hilda says again. "No good can come of this."

"That may be true, Aunt Hilda," I say, "but I've decided. I am, of course, going with the boys, but I will offer to help. I want to help her save the Luminara Domain. No good can come of Trystan winning the last piece of it. If he's opening portals to other realms to gain an army to take down the good part of that realm, I feel we are all doomed. Earth as we know it could be destroyed."

"Yeah, you guys should have seen the place she met me last," Bash chimes as I lean on the counter, cupping my mug. "It was the ruins of one of her regions. It was devastating. While I don't care for the broad much, I still feel we are all better off if her brother does not win this one."

"Just be careful with whatever you choose," Hilda warns. "Dealing with the Luminara and Neverdusk alike is never straightforward. Even if you help her and even win the war, which I think is impossible, you will still owe her something. They are never in debt to anyone, nor are they ever grateful or feel they need to repay someone. It won't end up in your favor, and you may just lose your lives for it."

"Then so be it," I answer. I really don't feel like I'm going to die for this choice. Either way, my mind is made and I want to go.

"Then should we get going to New York and get the Full Moon Curse taken off you?" Bash asks, stroking my hand. "I'm sure my family will want to come to Feylight Grove, too, so we can all travel together."

"We can go, but I think I want to leave the wolf curse. I think I'll be able to master it. Something in my bones is telling me it wants me to leave it be. I don't want to change."

"Oh, so you have fallen in love with a demon?" Hilda asks suspiciously.

I had forgotten that part of the tale while explaining all that had happened since we left Washington to the aunts.

"She couldn't resist my charms any longer," Bash says snidely, batting his eyelashes.

"Poor Dominic," Maggie replies, laying her chin in her hand. "What do you think he's going to say about that?"

"I don't know," I mutter. My heart sinks. "I couldn't help it. Bash was the one who has been by my side since he disappeared. And, like he said, I fell for him. We can't help who we fall in love with."

"Do you love Dom still?" Ollie asks innocently.

Something inside me catches on something jagged within myself at his question.

Did I ever really even love him?

"Truthfully, Ollie, I have love for Dom. But something in my heart never loved him the way I do Bash. I began loving Bash in my dreams. This powerful, all-consuming love I wished I would feel for Dom. But I don't. I will not string him along, and I will not lie to him. There is someone in this world for him; I just don't think that someone is me."

Bash's blue eyes are locked on mine and the flutter in my heart for him sears me, bends me like softened metal, splintering the steel in my resolve. There's no explaining what I feel for Bash—as there are no words in existence that can explain it. I just know it's something I can no longer ignore or fight.

"Well, like I told you before," Ollie continues, interlacing his fingers with Claire's. "I will not judge you for who your heart chooses. Just know that you both will probably lose Dom forever."

This drives some sort of wedge through my ribs. Losing Dom forever isn't what I ever wanted. I never meant to hurt him.

I have to see him—have to talk to him and tell him myself.

"Just promise me one thing?" I ask.

"What's that?" Ollie answers.

"Please let me be the one to tell him. I don't want it to come from anyone else."

Ollie's face softens. "You have my word, Sayah. I will not tell him a thing until you do."

I give him one of my nervous smiles. "Thank you."

THE STOLEN CHILD

-SAYAH-

When we land in New York, Claire seems tense at the thought of entering a house full of vampires. I remember how I feared the same when Dom had brought me here for the very first time.

Opting not to have Adaline pick us up this time, Ollie had Hattie and Scarlet leave his car so we wouldn't have to rent one or pay for a taxi or rideshare.

On the way to the cabin, Bash and Ollie try to debrief Claire on what to expect of the family as soon as we arrive.

According to Ollie, Claire's transformation into a vampire had been the smoothest and least painful transition they had ever seen. Bash thinks this has something to do with her Dark Gift, as he likes to call it.

Claire, so far, has yet to have any inkling as to what it may be.

As Ollie pulls up to the mansion, I observe Claire looking up at the house in wonder, more so than with trepidation.

It's fitting that my best friend is a vampire now and seemingly a good one. All my life, Claire has been this being to be reckoned with, a force of nature all her own. It makes sense that she took the transition better than anyone the Sangravelli boys had ever seen.

As the Suburban halts at the end of the drive and Ollie kills the engine, he looks over to Claire, who's sitting in the passenger seat and puts his hand on her leg.

"Ready?"

"As ready as I'll ever be," she answers, her voice unwavering.

Ollie and Bash exit the vehicle, and I put my hand on Claire's shoulder from the backseat. "They really aren't that bad. They're scarier looking than anything. Just be yourself. It'll all be okay."

Claire nods before stepping out when Ollie opens the door for her.

I let Bash hold my hand as we climb up the steps to the cabin.

Inside, no vampires are present in the main rooms, so we make our way to the spell room, where voices are coming from.

Upon entering the spell room, Adaline, Jasantha, Hattie, and Scarlet sit among the couches, not surprised to see us.

"Took you long enough," Jasantha snipes at us.

"Sorry, we couldn't help how fast the plane flies," Bash shoots back.

I look behind me to see Claire's eyes fixated on Jasantha. All the Sangravelli women are enchantingly beautiful, but there's always something about Jasantha that has everyone drooling over her. Maybe the siren in her lures people to her like vampires do.

"And who might this be?" Jasantha asks, her eyes flashing purple when they land on Claire.

"Family, this is Claire," Ollie answers for her. "She's my girlfriend."

"Making new flings into vampires, are we?" Hattie snaps, her tone full of venom.

"C'mon, Hattie, really?" Ollie pulls Claire into the room and sits with her by the fire.

"There was an incident," Bash tells them, leading me to the same table by putting his hand on the small of my back.

"What kind of incident?" Adaline questions, her face hard and expressionless. "A different one than the wolf incident?"

Judging by the looks on the sisters' faces and their harsh glances toward me, I figure Adaline had mentioned the formweaving to them.

"Crazy neighbor massacre. No time to get into that now," Bash gripes with a shrug. "We need to talk about Tallyn and what she wants from me."

"What did you do now, Bash?" Adaline demands, turning to face those at the table.

"Nothing more than last time," Bash retorts. He's already reaching for the bourbon and pouring some into a glass on the table.

"Only offered himself to save your other son," I find myself saying and regretting it the minute the words leave my lips.

Standing up to the matriarch of the family is not something I had in mind for the day, but I can't help the annoyance that spills forth in my tone.

"What?" Adaline asks, her eyes cutting to Bash rather than me.

"Tell her the story, Bash," Ollie cuts in.

Bash inhales a deep breath and recounts his experience with Tallyn in the ruins of the Luminara Domain.

"What have you done?" Adaline asks when he's done speaking.

"I didn't do anything," Bash snaps back.

"You made a deal with the devil and started a war!" Scarlet shouts, shooting to her feet.

Bash stands, too, and knocks over the stool he'd been sitting on. "To save your beloved brother, you harlot!"

Within a blink of an eye, Scarlet is in front of Bash, staring him down. Her eyes go into their cat-eye shape and the whites take over, so only very little green remains around the rims.

I'm so close to them hovering over me that I slip out of the chair and go around to stand by Claire, who's anxiously frozen.

"And dooming us all in the process!" Scarlet hisses.

Bash's blue eyes also go white, and Ollie moves over to stand between them with the same quickness that Scarlet had used.

"You both need to stop," Ollie demands. "This is not a war between us!"

"Yeah, how does me giving myself over to her to save him doom us all?" Bash spits at Scarlet over Ollie's shoulder.

"Oh, you self-centered piece of shit. How can you be so daft?" Scarlet screams.

Hattie and Adaline move toward the commotion while Jasantha remains on the couches.

"Daft? What the hell do you mean, you twit? I'm saving your precious Dominic!"

With a wave of Scarlet's hand, an explosion leaves it and hits Ollie, making him tumble backward into Bash. They fall with a force so hard that they slam into the shelves and knock some of Adaline's jars down, which sends glass shattering across the floor.

In that instant, Claire stands. As I watch, her hazel eyes go silver; the table lifts from the ground and slams into Scarlet, pinning her on the ground and knocking the breath out of her.

Jasantha stands, and her eyes go purple as she begins her sunder, that ear-piercing song that's supposed to subdue.

Bash arises from where he fell and cautiously watches the scene unfold.

Claire seems to hear nothing; she only looks at Scarlet, who is pinned under the table. Even as Scarlet struggles to get the table off her, Claire doesn't move.

Ollie rushes to Claire to snap her out of her trance while

Bash heads for Jasantha to stop her screeching. Adaline merely watches the commotion from where she is.

When Ollie shakes Claire out of her trance, and Scarlet can get the table off her, she speeds toward Claire to kill her, but Ollie shoves her back and she launches across the room.

"*Stop!*" Adaline shouts.

Jasantha ceases her wailing, and Scarlet rises from where she had fallen, the look in her eyes telling the tale of Claire's death.

"What the hell was that?" Bash asks from the broken shelves.

Her eyes returning to normal, Claire surveys the room, seemingly unbothered by what she has just done.

Ollie cautiously leads her over to stand out of the way.

Scarlet flies at Claire, seething with anger, and Adaline knocks her down, this time with only a movement of her arm. "Stop! All of you. Now!"

The dark and dangerous Everett storms into the room, his eyes blazing like broken glass in fire, his features hardening the corners of his mouth into a ragged and worried frown.

"What the hell is going on in here?" he demands, eyes scanning the disheveled room, the overturned table and chairs, Scarlet on the floor, looking furious.

"It would appear as though this new girlfriend of Ollie's has quite the little gift they didn't warn us of," Adaline answers, still holding her palm toward Scarlet to keep her down.

"We didn't know, Mom," Ollie snaps, standing protectively near Claire, who still hasn't spoken a word since we arrived. "We are just now finding out about this as you are."

"Behave," Adaline says to Scarlet as she lets her palm fall and moves closer to Claire. "That is an extraordinary Dark Gift, Claire. Quite extraordinary indeed."

"She transitioned better than anyone I have ever seen, too," Ollie offers.

"Really?" Adaline asks.

Carefully, Adaline picks up Claire's chin with her long,

skinny pointer finger, eyeing her closely, trying to see deep inside her eyes. Claire neither moves nor speaks; she just holds Adaline's eyes with her own.

Bash picks up the table and puts it upright, snagging the unbroken bottle from the unscathed shelf. "She was shot and died. Ollie saved her by turning her. She took the transition better than anyone we've both ever seen. And now she can move shit with her mind. Lucky us."

"Interesting," Adaline coos, still eyeing Claire so close she could kiss her.

"What do you think it means?" Claire finally asks. Her eyes speak of a yearning to know the things locked inside Adaline's mind.

"I'm not sure," Adaline admits, finally letting Claire's face go.

"She's even immune to my siren song," Jasantha says, still hovering near the couches.

"If you can even call that a song," Bash retorts, taking a long pull from the bourbon bottle.

Jasantha's eyes give that purple glimmer, and Adaline holds up her hand. "Not now."

"Either way," Bash continues undisturbed, "we all will be of real help to Tallyn."

At this, Adaline's eyes go cold, dark, and angry. "What?" she asks, and the ice in her voice fractures the inflections, shattering the tension in the room.

"I'm going to offer myself to her to help," I answer when no one speaks for a few minutes. "We figured we all have something that could help her thwart her brother."

Adaline's breathing becomes stressed. "We *all*?" she asks, looking from Ollie to Bash. "Have something that could help Tallyn? Are you all mad?"

"Mom, listen," Bash pleads, coming around the disheveled table to face her, "we learned things about her and the realms. She has Dom; she wants me. And—"

"She's an evil fairy that wants nothing but her own means, Bash!" Adaline speaks calmly, yet her tone is seething.

"Trystan has stolen most of the realm from her, turning it into the Neverdusk Dominion, and is now using the Arcane Nexus and Eclipse wars to steal the remaining bit from her—Feylight Grove," Bash deadpans. Although Adaline listens, her eyes say she's not really hearing it.

"That can't be good for any of us," Ollie adds when Adaline doesn't speak.

"How does that have anything to do with us?" Adaline asks, turning to face Ollie.

"Trystan's using his warlocks to open other realms to create a Dark Army to take Tallyn down. That is why there is an influx of grims in the mortal world. If the Neverdusk Dominion wipes out the Luminara, there is no telling what that will do for Earth, Mom. We could all be in danger. We have all talked and feel that it would be in our best interest to offer to help in taking down Trystan."

Adaline doesn't speak again; she merely walks to the bar, leans on it, and puts her head in her hands. "This does not involve us, boys. We have no part in her war."

"Mom, she has Dom," Bash repeats. "She will not give him up without something in return. If I give her what she wants, she'll release him, set me free of my addiction, and use my blood to defeat Trystan. If we help her, we can help her take down Trystan."

"And you speak of this as if that will free you from her, Bash! You do not know her like I do, Sebastian; you have no idea what she's capable of!"

"How else do you propose we get Dom back?" Bash shoots back, his voice rising an octave. "I have already promised her. She marked me." At this, he rolls his sleeve, and shows her the golden rune tattooed on his arm.

Moving swiftly, Adaline grabs his arm and looks closely. "Bash, what the hell have you done?"

"I only meant to get Dom back for you. For her," he says, turning his head to look at me.

Adaline's eyes meet mine, and the torment of something rests gently on her irises.

"She, who is in love with you, so much so that she turned into a wolf, yet yearns for the return of the first brother who still loves her?"

"What?" Scarlet breathes, still angry-looking, and bedraggled.

Guilt gnaws at me at that moment, knowing how my heart has made me unintentionally switch brothers.

"None of that matters right now," Bash protests, trying to keep the tension in the room from boiling over. "Sayah has decided to offer herself to Tallyn as well. With her powers, there's no telling what defenses can be used against the Eclipse Wars. Freya told us this new war will be called the Riftstorm Conflict. And with us—"

"I will not be involved in helping her with anything!" Adaline stresses again. "That woman is a monster and the reason you all are vampires!"

The room goes cold with fragrant knowledge that Adaline, again, has something she has kept secret from them all for a long time.

Bash's lips fall open and he gazes at her intently, waiting for her to divulge what she meant by those words.

"Great," Bash utters, moving back over to the table with the bourbon. "More secrets from the queen of lies. Go ahead, Mom, spill it. We're all waiting. We've learned more about you in the last few weeks than in two hundred and eighty-two years."

"Sebastian, enough," Everett grumbles, tension in his shoulders making his posture rigid.

"What, Dad?" Bash snipes at him. "Do you have knowledge of this as well? If so, please indulge us."

Everett storms toward Bash, who squares his shoulders to brace himself for impact when Adaline shatters a glass on the floor.

"I had no choice!" she screams. Her eyes seep into white with green rims, the horizontal pupils on full display. Her skin is bright white, and her fangs protrude from her mouth like icicles dangling from a dark cave on a winter night. "Enough! All of you! If you don't all shut the *fuck* up, sit the *fuck* down, and listen to what I have to say right now, so help me Freya, I will burn this house to the ground with every one of you in it!"

The room goes quiet with terror.

I look at Claire to ensure she's doing okay, and she sits frozen, watching.

I can only imagine what's going on in Claire's mind. This is her first time meeting her boyfriend's parents, yet this is the world they belong in.

The terrible, terrifying, midnight madness that seems to encompass the family always.

"I first met Tallyn when I was at my mother's grave," Adaline begins, grabbing herself the bottle of Grey Goose and sitting at the table. Bash hovers in the background with his bourbon. "I had just lost my fifth baby. I was crying to my mother, who had lost her life during childbirth with my youngest sibling. I was distraught, kneeling at her grave in the rain, crying to her about why I couldn't have a child. Tallyn showed up out of nowhere. I didn't trust her, even at first, but I was so lost and heartbroken I would have let anyone hold me. Everett did what he could, but it is a woman's job to home the babes, to grow them in their bellies; and when one can't, only another woman knows that grief. She came up and knelt with me. Her dress was long and made of leaves and berries; I noticed her ears were pointed, and her eyes were like a cat's. I knew there was something off about her but I didn't care. When she spoke of the shaman, she made me promise that if I were to seek out this shaman, she would get something in return from me. I made her that promise, not knowing what it was I was actually promising. She told me where to find this shaman and promised they would help me birth the children I so desperately wanted. What she didn't specify, and what fae are so wonderfully well versed in, is hiding the meaning behind what they really want."

Adaline pauses and pours herself a glass of vodka. She takes a drink and holds the glass, gazing down into the clear liquid. She suddenly stands and walks over to her shelves, where she picks up a small crystal ball. Walking back to the table, she sets down the ball and lays her hands on it.

The ball gathers light, and the room fades away as it does.

We're in a cabin in the woods, and it's night. There's a small bassinet by the window. There are women in brown dresses with white aprons and white bonnets. They are nurses. Adaline's in labor on the bed, Everett in the corner. One nurse is between the woman's legs at the foot of the bed.

"Push!" she shouts.

Adaline is sweaty and mad, clutching onto the other woman's hand as she screams and pushes. The baby from the bassinet is crying, and Everett goes over to it, picking the child up out of the bassinet. He looks to be about nine or ten months old, with black hair and blue eyes.

Bash.

Adaline screams again.

The nurse grabs the infant that slithers out of her and holds the baby upside down, patting it on its tiny, bloody back.

The baby cries.

"It's a girl!" the nurse cries.

Adaline falls back onto the pillows, exhausted.

The nurse takes a tool and cuts the umbilical cord. The other nurse approaches her with a blanket and lies the crying baby into it. With a quick wrap, the other nurse walks back to Adaline and hands her the baby.

Adaline looks at her newborn baby girl and kisses her on her head.

"Sariana," she says, and looks happily over to Everett.

The strong man has a tear in his eyes as he bounces Bash up and down to calm him. Laying Bash back in his bassinet, he pads over to Adaline and wraps his arms around her shoulder, kissing the top of her head and then the baby's.

There's a sudden shift of air. A circular opening hued in green appears, and Tallyn steps down through it as though stepping down from a doorway. She's dressed in red silk, her long black hair falling down her body in curls, a crown of thorns and berries resting atop her head.

Both Adaline's and Everett's eyes blow wide with shock.

"Ah, I see my payment has arrived now," she speaks, her red lips shining in the moonlight spilling in through the only window.

"What?" Everett asks, glancing from Adaline to Tallyn.

Adaline's expression morphs from shock to sorrow, as though now realizing something she hadn't before. She holds Sariana closer to her chest. "No!"

Everett takes a step closer to Tallyn.

The candlelight flickers in the room even though there is no wind.

Tallyn's eyes light up. She waves her hand, and Everett falls to the floor, unconscious.

"No!" Adaline screams again, her arms grasping the baby, who's now crying louder.

"A promise is a promise, my pet," Tallyn says, sweeping closer to the bed.

The two nurses stand stock-still; one tries to come between Tallyn and the bed, and her neck swiftly spins to the side with a twist of Tallyn's wrist, cracking and popping, signifying the broken neck.

"I never promised you my child!" Adaline laments, trying to squirm out of bed but still bleeding and in pain from having just given birth.

"*Think about that now, Adaline,*" *Tallyn says, still moving ever closer to Adaline and the baby.*

Adaline winces while trying to escape the side of the bed Tallyn isn't on. "*You said that if I sought out your shaman, I would have my babies. You never said I would owe you one!*"

"*I told you the gifts that be lay within your first newborn girl.*"

"*I didn't think that meant giving you my child!*" *Adaline shouts, falling out of bed with the baby, blood spilling down her legs.*

Too weak to run, Adaline falls to the floor and hunches over the child, the baby screeching in her arms.

Tallyn's upon her, laying her hand on Adaline's tense and protective shoulder, cradling the wailing infant in her arms with a hold that might have crushed her.

At the touch, her skin lights up and she relaxes. Her gaze looks forward to settle on the wall, and the vacant look in her eyes says that she's giving up the fight, although not willingly.

"*Give me the child,*" *Tallyn commands.*

Adaline, still resisting, shakes her head, tears spilling down her tired face.

"*Now!*"

When Adaline doesn't move, Tallyn kneels and shoves her hands through Adaline's hold on Sariana to grab the crying infant. Adaline musters all her strength and shifts away from the prying hands, falling against the side of the bed. "*No!*"

Tallyn's dark eyes turn angry. She snaps, and the rumble that shoots forth shakes the house. Something inside Adaline shakes as well. She shudders as light from within her flashes like lightning; that same light evoking something inside the baby over by the window in the bassinet.

He begins to scream.

Adaline goes limp after that light escapes her, and Tallyn moves over to her, grabbing the baby wrapped in a white sheet from her arms. Adaline holds on to the sheet as Tallyn walks away, pulling one loose that fell to the floor.

"Will I never see my baby again?" Adaline asks as Tallyn approaches the door.

"I will tell her about you one day," Tallyn says, her cold, green eyes scanning the babe in her arms in a shivering evil yet nurturing way. "I will send a Whispering Leaf for you, and maybe I will let you see her. But she belongs to the Luminara Domain now. She will be my Lumen Maid. My daughter. She will not want to return to your world, no matter how hard you try to convince her that she does."

Adaline stares at Tallyn with a subdued hatred. An energy of pure and solid loathing emanates around her in her spellbound and frozen state. The angle of her lips and the gesture of her eyes say that she would have killed Tallyn in that moment if she hadn't been under her spell.

Tallyn sneers and walks back through the portal, disappearing as soon as she does.

Adaline falls to the floor, suddenly unfrozen, and lets out a harrowing and agonized breath that comes with a bout of sobs so loud and full of pain that the crying babe in the corner stops his own.

Adaline crawls to the other side of the bed and falls onto Everett's heaving chest, waking him from his sleep.

Silence resounds as the spell room comes back into view. I can hear everyone breathing, not speaking, no words coming to anyone's mind. Bash stands frozen behind her, not moving an inch. Ollie has his hand on Claire's shoulder, and in Claire's eyes a small tear glistens. Scarlet rises from the ground and follows Jasantha to comfort their mother.

"Mom, we had no idea," Scarlet says as Hattie joins them.

I feel like a fly on the wall in a room I don't belong in, listening to a conversation I have no right to hear.

This is Adaline's pain.

Her firstborn daughter had been ripped from her arms, stolen by a fae that, up until now, I had wanted to help.

The hatred I had felt for Adaline shatters at my feet. Even

though I should loathe her for taking my family from me, I can see why she did it.

How can I go and offer to help a being who stole a baby from the arms of a mother who had been desperate to have children?

"It was a long time ago," Adaline almost whispers, laying her head on the hand Scarlet rests on her shoulder.

"Why didn't you ever say anything about this?" Hattie asks. A look of sorrow and guilt colors her face in an intimate way that softens her features, and for once, she doesn't look like the terrifying creature that she is.

"There was nothing to say about it," Adaline utters. "It was my fault. My misunderstanding led to the loss of my first daughter. I just had to spend the rest of my life making sure that every other child of mine didn't fall prey to her ever again." At this, she turns to look at Bash.

His eyes meet hers, and he quickly looks away, taking a drink of the brown liquid.

"Did you ever get to see her? Does she know that you exist?" Scarlet asks.

"Tallyn let me see her once. She sent me a Whispering Leaf when you all were teens or so—before you turned into vampires. I went to a park overlooking the water. I picked a bench and sat there for a long time, waiting, and anticipating them showing up. When they did, Tallyn sat next to me. She told me that Sariana wanted nothing to do with me, but Tallyn made her come to see where she came from. Sariana just stood behind me, not saying anything. She had long black hair, black like Tallyn's. I turned to look at her over my shoulder. Her eyes caught mine momentarily, and then she looked away and out into the water. I knew that her mind was gone, belonging to Tallyn, just like I fear that Dom's is."

"Which is why we have to go save him," Bash cuts in. "Look,

Mom, I'm sorry that this happened to you. But maybe when we go there and offer to help, to get Dom back and help her thwart her brother, she'll give us Sariana back."

"Really, Bash?" Adaline snaps, looking at him with her mother's glare. "You really think she'll just give my daughter back to me after this long of a time? You are out of your fucking skull."

"What we have learned so far," Bash continues, "is that the portals to the Luminara Domain are all connected. She has had her hooks in Dom probably since Mederio got him. When he was sending us messages and wrote Sayah that note, he was able to get to Colorado by using the portals in the Luminara Domain, which meant he was hers all along. But not enough to stop him from going to Sayah and writing her that note. That must mean there are flaws in her mind control. We can get to him; we can get to *her*. We can use our strengths. We will have something to level her with if we help her defeat her brother and save the Luminara Domain. We can use Jasantha's power to subdue Sariana to see if she is still in there. This can be a good thing, Mom, if you just—"

"*Enough!*" Everett shouts at his son. "Can't you see my wife has suffered enough? All she ever wanted was children. That was all this was ever about. She wanted children, and when she saw a way to make that happen, she suffered for it. The fact you all are vampires is only because she wanted to protect you! This —all this is because she is a mother who only wanted to love and raise her children! She will not help you help Tallyn, Sebastian; just let it go!"

A tear slides out of Adaline's eye, and Bash looks away from Everett, ashamed.

"I know you have to go, Bash. You have that thing on your arm. But I will not go with you. I cannot help you with this."

Bash nods quietly and slides away.

The sand of the lake's banks is squishy and wet from the receding water as I walk along it, searching for arrowheads, or anything shiny, while letting my mind wander.

Hatred.

Loss.

Empty.

Those are the words I felt before Adaline's story.

She took my family from me.

Looking into her eyes at times—there are times I want to rip her heart out and hand it to her so that she may understand the pain she's caused me.

But now I realize she knows my pain.

I've lost babies before. It's a loss no mother should ever endure.

I would dismantle the world and bring everything to ruin to keep Gauge safe. Nothing would keep me from that, not even taking someone else's mother from them.

This is what Adaline did to me for her own children.

To try and save them from the grimspawn.

I still need to have a chat with her about it; but for now, we have a bigger dilemma.

If I decide to help Tallyn defeat her brother, I'd be aiding an evil fairy who stole a baby from an innocent woman. Regardless of how long ago it was, it's still relevant and real; the pain of it is like rocks on Adeline's soul, weighing it down, carrying it with her wherever she goes.

It's not until I feel his presence behind me that I stop walking.

"I hate when you do that," I breathe, stopping to look at the lake.

"Sorry. Vampire," he states, standing beside me, his tone dipped in honeyed sarcasm.

I turn to face Bash, and he looks sad and broken. "You okay?"

"Not really. Are you?" he rasps as we fall back into footfalls along the lake.

"Not really. I don't know what to do."

He grabs my hand, and I let him hold it. "What are your options?"

"Well...to go with you and help you help her. Or to stay, go back home, and let it all go."

His grip on my hand tenses at this comment.

"Not let you go. Just this war. How can I help a woman who stole a baby from another woman? As a mom, I still can't imagine what that was like. We only saw a snippet of what she went through. I can't imagine what she experienced after."

"Well, she had the rest of my siblings, so she got through it somehow." His dark brows draw together in tight concern. "What is your heart telling you to do?"

"Part of me still wants to help Tallyn. Even though I know she's a terrible being, I feel that if we don't help her, Trystan will defeat her, and who knows what that will be like here on Earth. I don't think it could be good."

"That's what I fear the most. If we don't, Trystan will run the realms. Before, Earth and the realms never coalesced. They co-existed. But now, I fear he will let all the guards down and let the fae roam free, including whatever other beings he's collected from other realms. I just see it going very badly."

"Hey, how do you think Sariana is still alive?" I ask, suddenly stricken with the notion. "I mean, she's not a vampire. Or is she?"

"She'd almost have to be," Bash says, looking curious. "Fae are immortal, but she isn't fae. Since she's part of my mother and was in her after she had that other shaman perform a protection spell that turned into our curse, she would have had to have died at some point and come back as a vampire."

"If she is, wouldn't the mind control that Tallyn has on her have worn off the moment her heart stopped?"

"You would think. I am still trying to figure out how it works. What are you getting at?"

"That there's something your mother isn't telling us. Unless Tallyn has just made her so happy where she is, she hasn't wanted to come home. But if it were me, I would want to know my real mother, my siblings, and the world I came from. But again, that's just me."

Bash stops walking. "That's an interesting point. I wonder what it is she's not telling us."

"She's your mother. She seems to have a vault of secrets."

Bash's sapphire eyes scan the lake. "Shit, not even a vault; she has like a whole fucking catacomb of secrets."

"What should I do, Bash? If I choose to help Tallyn, I'll lose any chance of your mom and I ever burying the hatchet. She'll hate me forever, and I'll continue to hate her. And if I don't, I could have a hand in undoing the world as we know it. I'm completely torn."

His gaze collides with mine. "Who is my mom but one woman? And even if you do go and help Tallyn, who's to say you two won't hash it out and be friends? If you volunteer to go help and your powers end up saving the world as we know it, how could she ever hate you? If she did, she'd be stupid. And I would always choose you. Over any of them."

"You would?"

He grabs both of my hands and strokes their backs with his thumbs. "Of course. You are the reason I want to be a better man, the reason I exist. I want no tomorrows that you're not in.

Your soul speaks to mine in the only language it has ever understood. You are the parts of my book that I underline. I will love you long after my breath stops."

Before I can answer, he bends down and takes my lips in his.

A LETHAL BITE

-SAYAH-

As the Dread Harvest Eclipse approaches, tensions are high in the household. Adaline is still adamant that she will not help Tallyn. She is upset and marred by the fact her children are going. Hattie, Scarlet, and Jasantha agreed to come along for their own reasons. Everett will not betray his wife, so he's staying behind with her.

Scarlet has convinced herself that she'll bring their sister back; Bash and Ollie are ever the pessimists about this.

While the Shadow Hunt Moon looms on the horizon, I know I'm going to have to succumb to the weave. The dread of it taunts me daily, and it isn't that I'm afraid of the pain. I'm afraid of weaving here at Adaline's house and possibly threatening those who dwell here.

As I'm coming down the stairs for coffee, Adaline is cleaning the kitchen sink.

"Good morning," I say, heading straight for the coffee maker.

"Morning," Adaline sputters, not looking up from her cleaning.

I quietly grab a cup from the cabinet.

"It's a full moon tonight," Adaline mentions, as though plucking the dread right from the sinews of my being.

The tone of her voice makes me straighten up inside, as though the thought of what she's speaking of strikes a chord deep within me. "The Dread Harvest Eclipse," I confirm, pressing the button to roar the coffee pot to life, surprised at how rough-hewn my voice sounds.

Her hardened warrior eyes scrape mine and scratch something along my bones. "You haven't mentioned anything about wanting me to get the curse off you like we did with your sister," she inquires, turning the water off to regard me.

Though I can never really read her, our dislike for each other is now matched by class and rank.

"I'm not sure I want it off," I answer honestly, spooning sugar into the cup.

"Why on Earth would you not?" Adaline responds, drying her hands on a dishtowel.

"I don't know," I tell her, reaching into the fridge for the creamer. "It was given to me for a reason. It would be bad to remove a part of myself, at least not before understanding why I have it first. My mom and my aunt told me I was being conditioned for this, the phoenix role I have. What if this is part of it, you know?"

"No, I don't," Adaline says shortly. "But then again, I'm a vampire, and we are natural enemies. I can't pretend I like it or that I understand it. But I will help you if you want it off you, not that you will ever change your mind about it."

"I understand," I say, still minding my coffee.

As I pull it off the counter to walk in the opposite direction, Adaline sighs and asks, "What is it about him that you fell for?"

I turn, feeling a rush of feelings for Bash simmer to a boil on the surface of me.

I wasn't prepared to talk of my love for her other son, knowing I'm betraying Dom somehow.

I lean my hip on the counter, holding my coffee cup close to my chest. "He just kind of snuck up on me. I mean, with the dreams, something was always drawing him to me. But the more time I spent with him and saw his humanity peeking through, the more I knew it was for me that the human in him came forth. I really don't know how to explain it, but I guess the fact that the demon in him had all but conquered him, and then the light in me battled it, made me fall for him against my will. You saying the things you had about him and then hearing the same sort of thing from Ollie's lips. I tried resisting him; I really did. But part of me knew all along that I didn't belong with Dom. And when Bash told me all about my different smiles...oh, my. Yeah, that's when I fell. All bets were off."

The look on Adaline's face is almost serene. Kind of like how I would imagine a Viking's face after a battle. Fierce and full of blood but peaceful they're still standing. That's how Adaline looks now, without the blood.

"He said something about your smiles?"

At this, my heart almost skips a beat. I feel nervous and flushed, how I felt once talking to a manager of mine when I wanted to impress her but knew she didn't like me. This is that same feeling, almost as though a nervous giggle is about to burst forth from my mouth at any moment. Adaline is interested in something I'm saying. Something her firstborn, cold-blooded killer had said to me that was nice and humanly.

"Oh, Adaline, it was the sweetest thing. He was drunk, but he told me I have five different kinds of smiles, and then he proceeded to tell me about each one and why he loves them. I can't even tell you what that meant to me, but I fell for him fully that night. But me falling for him was unintentional and caught me completely off guard."

"Well. Good for Bash. I just hope you let Dom down easy when the time comes."

This pulls at the string that has been loosening in me for a while now.

As the late afternoon sun settles in the sky, highlighting the blue of it, I find Claire on the patio, Ollie not at her side for once.

I push open the doors and join her on the deck.

"This is beautiful," Claire murmurs, her green eyes lost on the lake and the trees.

"How are you doing?" I ask her, sitting beside her on the turned patio chairs to see the scenery.

"I really don't know, Say. My whole life flipped upside down, and the funny thing is, I don't feel any different."

I contemplate this for a time, but simultaneously, I know that this was always meant for her. She was always meant to be a vampire. I knew it in the way that she was never book smart but could run the streets with a gangster's grit. How she never took to books but could command a group of people with the inflections of her voice. She never was good at anything, never had passions or dreams or aspirations; yet Claire had an air about her that she would conquer worlds with a flick of her hair. She had no accomplishments that decorated her walls, no degrees from high school or college, but people bowed down to her, would follow her to the depths of hell. People envied her, men wanted her, and women wanted to be her. She was always a vampire, she just never knew it.

"And what of your gift that you have? What did that feel like?"

Claire looks over at me and regards me with a clarity I've

never seen in her. Our whole life, I felt as though Claire was a bit foggy. There was a haze that surrounded her, and she was always trying to find herself in the mist. Now it seems she found something that has always been right in front of her, that's been with her all along.

"All this pent-up energy just surged through me, and I felt I had to let it out or I might explode. I wasn't angry with Scarlet—I don't even know the bitch. But all this buzzing engulfed me, and I released it. I didn't even know what I was doing; I just wanted her to stop hurting her brothers, and the table just listened to me. I didn't command it to do anything at all. It just . . . moved."

"It's wild, isn't it?"

"You've done something like that before?"

I think about all the witchy shit that I've ever done and know it's of the same material that Claire's gift is. A manipulation of energy. "Not to that extent, but yes. It's all just a motion of energy. You connect to it and find your link with it. It's called entanglement. The notion that everything is connected by energy, and we all have the ability to sync to it—most of us just don't know how. You becoming a vampire opened the door to it. Now, you just have to learn how to bend it to your will. It will take practice, but you will master it. It was always a part of you; you just didn't know it."

"Will you help me?"

I take Claire's hand in mine. "Of course I will help you."

The sound of the door opening interrupts our moment of solitude and camaraderie. We both turn toward the sound and see Bash and Ollie coming out to join us.

"What are you girls up to?" Ollie asks as he sits on the arm of Claire's chair. He strokes her face, bending to kiss her on the lips.

"Just talking of her newly found gift," I answer. "What about you guys?"

"Well, plot twist," Bash says, leaning on the railing, and eyeing us with his dazzling blue eyes. "Laureya's here."

"What?" I gasp, my heartbeat quickening. I don't need any of whatever my sister is here to dish out. "What the fuck does she want?"

"She texted about an hour ago," Bash says, his nose crinkling at the bridge as it does when he's about to share information he doesn't particularly like. "Said she's with an entourage and felt I needed her help. She flew here with them to aid us in our quest to defeat the crazy fairy."

"And they're here?" I turn in my chair to see if I can glimpse Laureya through the windows.

"Well, not at this house at this moment, but they're in New York. At the airport. Getting a rideshare here."

"She got a feeling?" I repeat, not liking how the jealousy crawls up and bites me in the back of the throat. "So she gets feelings now?"

"I don't know, Say. Why? You jealous?" Bash sniggers, coming over and kneeling before me. "What I think is that she still has a touch of that bloodlink bond and is connected to me. What I feel, though—hey—" He pulls my chin toward him when I try to look away. "What I feel is that the more people we have to bring to help Tallyn, the more likely our chances are of getting her on our side and getting her the fuck out of our lives for good."

"Cool," I say, fighting the urge to scream. "Well, hope this all works out."

*A*n hour passes before the rideshare arrives. Bash, Ollie, Claire, and I are now arranged around the firepit in the back by the lake. When I see Laureya, I feel the familiar pang of anger set in and shove it down.

"Hello, beautiful people!" Laureya calls, her heels digging into the ground, making her gait awkward. Her winged red sunglasses adorn her face and make her red hair and lipstick more prominent. She got all the singed hair cut off, and now her hair falls in a perfect bob, outlining her angular face.

"Just sit down and shut up, La La," Bash snaps. He's sitting next to me with a bottle of bourbon in his lap, his black pants and black boots setting off the ominous tone of his attitude toward her.

That makes me feel a little better.

Laureya and her entourage intermingle around the lit fire pit. However, the sun is still sparkling in the blue sky, so it's not quite dark enough for the fire to be poignant.

"Who're your friends?" Bash asks, his own blue eyes covered by the dark aviators he's wearing.

"This is Ryan," Laureya introduces the tall, gangly fellow sitting beside her. He has a disheveled mop of brown hair and facial hair that's of the sort where it doesn't grow in right and shouldn't be on one's face, but he's either too lazy or too proud to shave it. "And then this is Laith." She gestures to the handsome man with deep chocolate skin, a puff of hair, and broad shoulders hovering in the background. I wonder why Laureya chose to hook up with Ryan and not Laith.. "Then this is Drealle, and that is Kaston." Drealle and Kaston appear to be a thing; they walk with arms around one another. Drealle's a short, curvy little thing with thick thighs and a round middle. She also has dark skin, and her long hair hangs down her back in bejeweled locs. Kaston's a little taller than she is but still kind of impish, with dark, curly brown hair on his head and sunglasses to block his eyes.

"Charmed," Bash says cynically. "Now tell me why you're here."

Laureya pulls down the red glasses for a better look at Bash.

"I told you, I got a vision. I know you're heading to Feylight Grove, and I need to help you. That is all."

"That's why you flew you and four of your cronies all the way here to New York when we could have just portaled you in?"

"Portaled me in?" Laureya asks, looking at me as if I'll divulge the answer.

"Never mind," Bash sighs, backing out of the storytelling before it's too late. "What did you see in this vision?"

Laureya grabs the bottle of bourbon from between his legs and pulls a long drink from it. I fracture a bit at the gesture, my sister's hands too dangerously close to his—my—cock. "I saw fire. Mayhem. Madness. Fairies being ripped apart. Fae being devoured. And you, her, him, and some others at the heart of it all." After taking another drink, she gets closer to Bash, leaning in close to whisper for him to hear. But, you know, everyone around is a vampire. "And that little bloodlink bond you have over me won't let me allow you to go to war without me."

There's a rumbling inside me that I'm not too familiar with just yet but remember it from the first night I formweaved. I feel the fault lines within me begin to crack, and I push at it as hard as possible. It isn't nighttime yet. The moon isn't up—the sun's still out—and there's no rhyme or reason why the form threatens to come so soon.

I clear my throat, and Laureya leans back in her chair, still holding the bourbon. "How are these fucks out in the sunshine, sis?" I ask, my viciousness dripping.

She scoffs. "I had a witch friend make them the sun talismans like you, *sis*," she snipes back. "Seems like you're not as special as you think you are."

Bile rises but I swallow it back. "Does Ryan here know about that bloodlink bond to Bash?" I blurt out and watch as Ryan's face shatters.

"What?" he asks as Laureya's mouth falls open.

"You bitch!" she shouts and stands.

At that moment, I can't hold the weave in any longer. Before I know it, red-hot rage takes over my sight and I feel my bones rearrange. Bash jumps to his feet, knocking the chair back, and Claire and Ollie do the same. The agonizing tearing rips through me, and as I scream, I feel the howl emerge, see the skin melt away, watch as my peach color becomes blonde fur, and fire also emerges from the embers of the weave.

Laureya begins to weave as well, her image folding in on herself. A big, red wolf emerges from the folds, the same fire playing at the ends of her fur.

There's commotion. I can hear Bash's voice trying to coax me into forming back, but all I can think about is my rage. The pent-up aggression toward Laureya and wanting to rip her apart. I lunge at my sister and try to bite her, but Laureya ducks and runs for the beach.

I chase her and dive, landing on her back and slashing at her, feeling the tearing of fur and skin beneath my claws. There's a whimpering followed by a sharp pain in my leg. Without looking to see what it is, I go to bite my sister on the neck but am clotheslined from the side, smashing into a tree. Flipping myself upright and shaking off the dirt, I see that it's Bash in full vamp mode.

"Sayah, control yourself," he seethes, but I only see Laureya and her fiery fur lingering beyond Bash's shoulder.

Sprinting toward my sister, Laureya meets me with the same rage and we collide, slashing at each other with our razor-sharp claws. I'm growling and trying to bite Laureya on her neck again. Just as I'm about to bite down, another person is knocking me away.

This time, it's Ryan.

He has me pinned to the ground, his white eyes boring down into me, and as much as I try to wriggle my way out of his grasp, I can't. Before I know it, his neck is spinning to the side, accompanied by the crack of a broken neck.

Lifeless, but not dead.

Vampires are more challenging to kill than that.

Laureya, not knowing he isn't actually dead, lunges at Bash and bites his arm, causing a sizzling sound followed by a deep-throated scream.

I see red again. But instead of lunging at Laureya, I will myself back together and run to Bash, who's clutching his bite and falling to the ground.

"Bash!" I shout. "Fuck!"

"It's all right, love," Bash groans out, looking at me while his white irises bleed back to blue. "I've lived a good life. This is how it ends for me. I'm okay with that. Because I met you."

"No! Stop it right now!" I shout. "Ollie, what do we do?"

Ollie's running up to us, Claire a skitter behind him.

Laureya forms back to herself and is upon Ryan, stroking the side of his face.

"Bash," Ollie says, falling to his brother's side. "Shit."

"It's all right, brother. It's just my time, that's all."

"Stop saying that!" I yell. "Fuck! This never would have happened if you hadn't shown up!" I scream in Laureya's general direction.

"He killed my boyfriend!" she shouts back, tears running the mascara down her face.

"He's not dead, you twit," Ollie shouts over to her. "He's just unconscious. Takes more to kill a vampire than to just break their necks."

"Let's get him inside," I say, helping Bash to his feet. "How long does it take for the venom to . . ."

"To kill me?" Bash answers, leaning on me. "Not sure. Never been bitten by a formweaver before."

"Maybe your mom will know." I pull him up to the house.

When we get to the spell room, Bash stumbles to the couch and falls upon it, kicking his feet up. His black boots leave dirt marks on the brown leather.

"I'll go find my mom," Ollie says, flashing off.

"Where's the Christmas decorations?" Bash asks, beads of sweat appearing on his forehead.

"Honey, it's July. Christmas isn't for months." I find a cloth to wipe his forehead with it.

He's burning up.

"That's a shame. I love the lights. Twinkly little lights."

"Bash!" Adaline cries as she enters the room, falling to his side. "Oh, no," she says, examining the wolf bite on his arm. The puncture wounds have turned purple, swelling his arm while bits of yellow sizzling in the middle. Red lines are crawling up his arm under his white skin.

"He was just asking where the Christmas decorations were," I tell her.

"The venom is in his system. See this line here? It's beginning to travel toward his heart. Once it reaches there, he will be taken over with madness, lost in hallucinations until his heart stops."

"Is there anything that we can do?" I ask, tears welling in my eyes.

"No, no cure has ever surfaced for us for formweaver venom," Adaline says.

This can't be it.

This can't be the way that Bash dies.

There must be something I can do to save him.

"Ollie? There has to be something . . ." I plead, feeling the world's weight begin to crush me; those fault lines always threatening to break apart and fracture me are wavering. This can't be the end of our story.

This can't be the end.

"Olllllieeeeee," Bash stammers drunkenly, "Come here, Ollie. Come."

Ollie moves to sit on the floor beside the couch Bash lies on.

"Yes?" he asks, tears in his eyes.

"You were always my favorite brother," Bash tells him, taking Ollie's hand and putting it on his chest. "Always so loyal. Even being my younger brother, I still always looked up to you."

"Bash," Ollie says, wiping the tear from his eye with his other hand. "I always looked up to you, too."

"I don't know why. I'm an evil fucker."

Ollie laughs.

"Say. My beautiful Sayah." Bash holds Ollie's hand and reaches out to me for mine. "I will miss you the mostest. You reminded me of everything I could never have—everything that could never want me, and yet . . . you do. You despised me when you knew you wanted me, and my world turned upside down. By you," he says as though the words are being dragged out of him, "I am forever undone."

I can't help the tears falling from my eyes. While that darkness threatens to engulf me, I still cling to hope that he's going to be okay. There has to be something I can do.

"You're not leaving me, Bash. I won't allow it."

"Ah, ever the optimistic. That's what I love about you."

"I can't let you leave like this, Bash. There will be something. There has to be. I feel it."

His dark blue eyes scan mine, and he smiles crookedly. "I believe you." He then looks beyond me and gasps. "What the fuck are you doing here?"

I glance over my shoulder and see nothing where he's looking. "Who Bash?"

Bash sits up and looks over to the corner with terror. "Her! She's not supposed to be here. I killed her!"

Ollie looks, too.

"He's beginning to hallucinate," Adaline says. "Seeing people he's killed before. It's not uncommon for the formweaver venom to bring back past violence. I saw it once. It isn't pretty. We may have to lock him in the cell downstairs."

"No, no, no, I killed you! Don't come near me!" he shouts, climbing over the couch, and falling over the side.

Adaline runs to him and pulls him up, looking at his arm. The red line is almost to his armpit now.

The house trembles under an unexpected seismic force, sending vibrations that ripple through the walls. All the shelves and jars within them rattle, pictures dancing in their frames, their once steady positions now disrupted by the intense quaking. Every delicate ornament in the room hums in protest against the sudden disturbance, adding discord to the otherwise serene ambiance.

As if scripted by some cosmic force, an otherworldly spectacle unfolds in a symphony of crackling energy. At the room's heart, a green luminous circle materializes. It shimmers with an ethereal luminescence, a gateway to realms unknown, commanding attention like a beacon in the darkness.

Emerging from the celestial rift is Tallyn, the revered Luminara Queen. Her majestic presence defies the laws of conventional entry. Her gaze, a blend of wisdom and mischief, surveys the chamber with grace that bespeaks centuries of regal heritage.

The lingering reverberations of her arrival hum in the air, leaving an ineffable impression transcending the chaotic setting. In her wake, the mortal fabric of the house seems to hold echoes of the celestial, as if the very walls whisper secrets of the realms touched by the Luminara Queen's presence.

"No!" Adaline shouts at her. "You get the fuck out of my house!"

"Relax, ice queen, I'm here to save your child for you," she states calmly. Her black hair is up in a perfect bun adorned with two golden combs in the shape of skulls; her pointy ears are embellished with jewels, and her black leather dress is tight at the top like a corset that billows down at the skirts, a slit up one leg showing her thigh-high black boots.

"You can save him?" Adaline asks, pulling Bash up. He staggers and winces, trying to focus on the fairy before him.

"I can, but we have to go now. Bring him to me."

"I am going with you!" I announce. "He will not be leaving without me."

"Nor me," Ollie states.

"I am going, too," Claire adds.

"Yes, I know what you were all planning to do, and I appreciate it. I am not going to deny the help you were going to offer. But if we are going, we need to go before that venom hits his heart."

"I will go, too, then," Adaline says.

"What?" Ollie asks.

"He is my son, and he is dying. If this crazy fairy is saying she can save him, then I will go, too. Go grab your sisters and father, Ollie."

"There is no time," Tallyn states. "We all go now. I'll send a portal for the rest when we settle him. C'mon."

Tallyn moves aside and lets the Sangravellis enter the portal first. Adaline stumbles through with Bash, Ollie, and Claire, and I go to the portal.

Tallyn grabs my arm before I do.

The features of her face are stoic, breakable, looking like perfect porcelain. She regards me with calm interest. "*He* is there, you know. He knows everything. I have shown him."

My heart falls. "Why would you do something like that?" I ask her, her hauntingly orange eyes piercing into mine.

Her angular brows arch further. "Because I need his mind to be free of you. To be mine."

I yank my arm away. "I wanted to be the one to tell him."

"It's too late for that," she states, shifting her weight toward the buzzing portal. "But in all honesty, I don't think he cares much."

That bites me in a way I didn't know it would. Whatever sorrow I'd felt for the fae with her brother stealing her realm from her is momentarily halted. After all, she is still fae, and would only ever care about her own gains.

Tallyn grins as though some of my inner thoughts have come to her, and then she pushes me through the portal.

FEYLIGHT GROVE

-SAYAH-

The sound of whooshing air rushes at my head, enough to cause all other sounds to be muted against them. Light and every other element are voided; it's just dark and unfathomable. It feels as though I've toppled off a large skyscraper; my insides shoot up to the top of my skull, and the rush of air hitting my face in the dark nearly derails me. The feeling of free-falling into nothing makes terror grip me in a way that I've not known before, tumbling into complete and utter pitch blackness.

As soon as I hit the hard, cold ground, I can't help the vomit that spews from me. I'm relieved to be on solid ground, but the contents of my stomach are also here.

When it feels as though nothing else will come out of me, I fall onto my back, looking up at the sky.

It's nighttime where we landed. All around me is a vast open field of green. The sky is a different color—a pale purple with cotton candy clouds. There are two moons and a planet with rings that are very close to the surface of this Earth.

It must be an illusion.

Everything feels distorted, like I'm looking at my life through fractured, sea-worn glass.

As my stomach settles and my breathing returns to normal, I look to see where the others have landed.

From what I can see, there are mountains, lakes, and water-falls, all of which are similar to what I'm used to in Colorado. What makes Feylight Grove different, though—or at least the realm we landed in—is that the mountains are floating.

Tallyn's a short distance ahead, with an even more sickly looking Bash.

On the fringes of the fields, unicorns, and pegasus are grazing on the purple plants. Tallyn outstretches her wings and sings an enchanting melody, and three giant pegasus bound up into the air. The largest one lands in front of Tallyn, another lands right in front of me, and a third touches down in front of Claire and Ollie. Tallyn lifts Bash up on hers and climbs on, looking over at me and the others to do the same.

First, I'm trying to wrap my head around the fact that the most beautiful mythical creatures are real. They're giant and gorgeous, and I want to bring one home with me and name her Sparkles. I've loved unicorns since I was a little girl, and the fact that I'm twenty feet from one, I can barely remember how to breathe.

The pegasus in front of me whinnies, and I jump. Its beautiful white nose is inches from my face. I stroke the side of its mane, and the hair is like fine silk.

"You are just . . . beautiful."

The gorgeous horse nuzzles into my neck and I melt, not wanting this moment to end but knowing that time is of the essence. I struggle to get on to the large horse, not wanting to pull its mane to hoist myself up. Adaline appears suddenly, using her vampire talent to effortlessly bound up onto the horse, and then offers her hand to me to help pull me up.

I watch as Ollie and Claire do the same.

Tallyn clicks her tongue and her pegasus leaps into the air, barreling toward one of the floating mountains.

I hear Adaline do the same, and our horse lifts into the sky.

There are no reins to drive the flying horses, but ours is fine to follow the others into the valley of the floating mountains.

We linger in and out of the clouds, ducking under lower mountains and up through valleys. I try to watch the ground below to glimpse this magical place, but that feeling of queasiness still sits in my stomach. When we reach a clearing, one more large mountain comes into view, with a gleaming castle atop.

The pegasus glides to the top, and the castle gates open to what lies beyond: a large drawbridge leading up to a stone staircase, golden doors glistening in moonlight. Ivy and other plants twine up the sides of the castle, the many towers and spires all covered in the greenery.

Tallyn hops down from her winged horse, and Bash, now even more pale, falls forward a little into where she had just sat. She pulls his arm and he tumbles off the horse, slamming onto the ground with a groan.

"Bash!" I cry as the others land beside us, jumping off before the hooves even touch the ground.

"No time!" Tallyn shoves at me, pulling him up and rushing him toward the stairs.

"You know, we move much faster than you if you would just tell us where to go!" Adaline calls after her as she jumps down from the horse.

Bash stumbles after her while Adaline, Ollie, Claire, and myself follow.

Bash staggers to the side and vomits on the stairs. I fall to his side to rub his back to help him however I can.

Tallyn stands sentry over him, surveying us, impatience decorating her flawless fairy features.

When Bash looks up to me, beads of sweat are dripping

down his face, his black hair slimy from it. The sides of his mouth twist upward to form his crooked smile, and I feel it will be okay for a moment.

Then Bash's face crinkles, and he tilts his head. "Sadie? What are you doing here?"

Words do not form in my mind, and I don't know what to say.

He thinks I'm Sadie now.

"All right, c'mon now, little bird," Tallyn coaxes, pulling Bash up by the crook of the arm.

Once inside, the grand entryway is still covered in those vines, even inside. An enormous tree with twisted ivy curls up its trunk is in the center of the castle. There is a hole in the middle for an entryway to more floors and spaces, but the branches of the tree form staircases on either side of the massive entrance.

Tallyn goes up the right side while we follow closely behind. We twist and turn through long stone hallways that seemingly never end. Windows pierce through the stone, and in between the windows are old and new paintings of what look to be regal fae, princes and princesses, kings and queens, all dressed in foliage designed into royal regalia. Shadows dance in rhythm to the torches that line the stone walls. Finally, there is a large wooden door at the end of one of these halls that we come to.

Why couldn't we have just portaled here?

A massive half-tester bed rests in the center of the room, intricate green curtains tasseled into knots on each side. Thick blue and gold sheets embroidered with living vines are smoothed over the surface, and lilacs and other flowers perfume the air. The wood of the bed is thick walnut, engraved with designs of a coat of arms for a lineage on the headboard.

At the end of the room is a balcony with tower-length windows, green lacy curtains blowing in the breeze, and the night moons twinkling in the background.

Tallyn lays Bash down on the bed and then hurries to one of her cabinets, pulling down a big box made of delicate wood that looks like it should house ancient and expensive royal jewelry.

Placing it on the bed, she opens it and pulls out a glittering silver unicorn's horn–it looks like a thick white willow branch of twisted wood–a velvet pouch with a ribbon tied around the top, and a bag of blood.

"No! Leave me alone!" Bash screams at the corner of the room, seeing someone who isn't there. He closes his eyes and shakes his head wildly, his legs shaking, and knees bending up and then unbending. "Get out of here, you devil! Leave me be, demons! *Leave me be!*"

The sound of Bash's screams is almost unbearable, the sound echoing into the terse silence. The red line on his arm is now hidden beneath his shirt.

Tallyn takes the horn, grabs his arm with the bite, and shoves the unicorn horn through the wound. Bash screams and thrashes. Tallyn holds fast to his arm, pulling the velvet bag's ribbon open with her teeth. Once opened, she removes the horn from the puncture and upends the contents of the velvet bag on the bite.

Herbs of an unknown nature fall onto the opening, causing the skin to turn a bright yellow.

Tallyn twists the top of the blood bag open and puts it in his mouth.

He spits out the blood at first, covering her and the blankets on the bed. But she takes her other hand, soothes his forehead, speaks Elder into his ear, and his twitching ceases.

Tipping the blood into his mouth, he drinks this time, lifting his unwounded hand to help push the contents down.

"That's a good boy. Yes. Drink," she coos, sitting on the bed beside him and stroking his forehead.

We are standing at the foot of the bed, watching, not knowing how to help or what to say.

When the blood is gone, Tallyn rises from the bed, walking it over to the fireplace where she tosses the bag.

"What happens now?" Adaline asks her, eyeing her son, who is motionless on the bed.

"Now we wait," Tallyn answers dryly. She moves to a large table by the balcony and retrieves a bottle from one of the shelves. The bottle is wide and unmarked, filled with a thick, silver liquid.

"What did you give him?" Ollie asks, sitting at the table but still keeping a watchful eye on his brother.

"A mixture of sorts," Tallyn answers, taking down five glasses and setting them on the table. "The magick from the horn of a unicorn. A mixture of moonshadow drift derries, celestial ember fragrance, fae startups, crimson heart essence, and stardust ephemera. And some of the blood from a descendant of the creator of the formweavers." As she answers, she pours the bottle's contents into the glasses.

"The creator of formweavers?" Adaline asks.

Tallyn pours Adaline a drink of the silver liquid and spins it toward her. "Yes. Doubt me?"

Adaline shakes her head as she takes a seat at the table. "I'm not drinking that."

Tallyn gives Adaline a sidelong look. "It's not poison. I wouldn't waste my good poison on you."

Tallyn pours four more and slides one to each remaining person, even taking one herself. She eyes Adaline as she takes a drink.

"What is it?" Claire asks.

"Angel tears," Tallyn answers, as though it's a clear and logical answer. "A concoction of juice from the Jupiter Stranding trees, absinthe, and alcohol from the angel plants. It'll take the edge off."

"Sayah doesn't drink alcohol," Claire answers.

Tallyn's eyes graze me, and I feel unworthy of her in that glance.

"How long will it take for Bash to recover from the bite?" Adaline asks.

Tallyn sips on the silver liquid and walks toward the bed where Bash lies motionless, her heels clicking on the flagstone. "If he recovers," Tallyn says grimly.

"Excuse me?" Adaline asks, her voice rising twelve octaves. "You said that you could save my son."

"I can, and I did. I just don't know if he will fully recover from it. I have had vampires bitten by formweavers and got through my cure with minimal consequences. But I have never had a demon-hybrid bitten by a phoenix hybrid. There's no telling what will happen to him."

Adaline emits disconsolate noises from her lips, and she scales toward the balcony, the soft wind rippling the green curtains inwards.

"The magick from the unicorn horn will stop the spread of the formweaver venom. The herbs will combat the hallucinations. The blood will keep him from turning or dying. But there will still be some side effects. I just don't know how adverse they will be."

"But he will survive?" Adaline presses.

"He *should* survive," Tallyn responds blankly.

Adaline sighs heavily and returns her gaze to the night sky.

"The moon will be at its peak soon." Tallyn looks at Bash. As she turns, the look on her face does not falter. It's still as composed and firm as a stone statue. "Trystan will use the Dread Harvest Eclipse and the Wild Hunt to open up all the portals to every other realm he can find. And then he'll come to claim Feylight."

Adaline doesn't turn to face Tallyn; she merely leans against the balcony's wrought iron and looks down.

"What other realms are there?" Claire asks innocently, fishing some speck of something out of her glass.

Tallyn walks back over to the table. "Thousands. Maybe millions. I don't know. But I do know that I need your help now more than ever. If we don't keep Feylight from him, he'll let all the lines between Earth and the other world blur. Earth will forever change. And I will be able to do nothing to stop it."

"What is it that he wants from you?" Ollie asks. "I mean, what happened between you two?"

Tallyn takes a long drink from the glass and sits. "Trystan and I are twins. But because I was born first, when our mother fell ill, she left all the realms to me. Trystan hated that and began to feud with me early on. He learned at a young age how to master the warlocks and how to create them using demons. It is he who owns them. As we got older, the fights got bigger. He began to use the Eclipse Wars to create bigger armies. I thought giving him some of the realm would assuage him. But something in him had changed. Maybe it was from opening the portals. Maybe from turning fairies into dark fae. But whatever it was, that was when the Neverdusk and Luminara Courts divided, and he made the Neverdusk Dominion. Things had been okay for us for a time; that is why I could go into Neverdusk. It was always a very uneasy alliance, though. He wants Feylight. Feylight Grove is a nexus connecting various fae realms and other supernatural dimensions. It acts as a central hub, allowing swift and strategic access to different territories. Trystan's desire for expansion and dominance fuels his interest in the strategic position."

"What makes Feylight so special?" I ask and almost cower at the looks she gives me.

Tallyn slides her finger down the side of the glass, smearing the condensation. "The Grove can amplify magical energies and powers. Any spell or enchantment performed within its boundaries becomes exponentially more potent. For a fae king like

Trystan, hungry for increased magickal prowess, controlling Feylight offers an unparalleled advantage in strengthening his abilities and those of his followers. We also have portal manipulation here, which means the Grove is endowed with the rare ability to open portals not only into other realms, but anywhere. Trystan seeks to exploit this feature for conquest and to extend his influence beyond the fae realms. The strategic advantage of striking from unexpected locations makes Feylight Grove a coveted asset."

"If that were true, why didn't we just portal here instead of into that valley to ride on those horses?" Ollie asks the very question I'd had while coming here—not that I didn't mind riding on the most magickal being I've ever encountered.

"I have a magickal barrier around this mountain for the eclipse. I know not of what Trystan has planned."

"And what happens if he wins?" Adaline inquires.

Tallyn's expression immediately darkens. "If he acquires Feylight, he will conquer all that power, and I will lose all my magick. I will lose my hold, and the world will go to darkness. He will have the power of the nexus and Ephemeral Harmonics, which is what the Grove does, as it resonates with a unique harmonic frequency that enhances the connection between fae beings. This resonance allows for stronger alliances, coercion, or manipulation of other fae, making it a tool for political maneuvering and control. Trystan aims to consolidate power over the fae by manipulating these harmonics. It also has life infusion, which can infuse life force into its surroundings, making the flora and fauna within its borders exceptionally vibrant and resilient. Trystan seeks to tap into this life-infusing magick for personal rejuvenation and to create an army of enchanted beings loyal to him. With the right power, it can even raise the dead. He seeks the destruction of the rest of the realms, including Earth. Bash visited me once in a part of the realm that he had destroyed. It is how the entire world will look should

Trystan get a hold of it. The shadows of the Neverdusk Dominion are eating all the other realms. If he gets it to Earth, he and the Nightshades will eat the light—it will devour the sun. Earth will fall to eternal darkness."

Silence befalls the room as we all picture what this means for humanity and us.

"And what does he have to do with Mederio and Matrasia?" I ask after some time.

"Mederio and Matrasia were his warlocks. They made the grimspawns to feed their immortality, which would feed Trystan's. That is how he first found Dom and was using him to make dark fairies. He was using Dom to do his bidding, and stealing his blood, turning the fae into awful, evil things. When I learned he was creating an army and now had a vampire, I suddenly met the brother of the one working with mine; I knew I had to get Dom away from Trystan somehow. He was planning to steal Feylight out from under me. When Dom was on his murder spree, he came to murder a witch by the name of Celestina Belvedez. I was there that night and blew my fairy dust in his face, so he would also answer to me. Once I had him, I would bring him to my realm and take his blood, as I tried to take Bash's once.

"Then I infused him with fairy blood—with my blood. He was so dejected from murdering all those people that I had to do something. Once I did that, though, he was completely mine. I was able to control him without Mederio knowing. I'm the one who made him go to Colorado to break up with Sayah. He was still slightly Mederio's at the time, but once that bond was broken with Mederio's death, I was able to sweep in and take him away with me to Feylight. Not before I made some armies of my own using his blood, in Luminara portals in Colorado, New York, and California. I also have a stash of Bash's blood that I plan to use for the same purpose. I don't know what kind of fae Bash's blood will create. I still don't know what kind of creatures Trystan will pull out of the realms on the Wild Hunt, either. That is why when I saw you all plotting—as I am connected to Bash's mind from that rune I put on him—I thought I could use your help. There is a weapon that I can make out of Sayah's phoenix power. Ember Flare Orbs—a bomb that will literally obliterate anything in its path from here to a hundred miles from here."

"How did he get into my house?" I ask. Though I sink into myself for asking such a question.

"I portaled him in."

"And where is my other son?" Adaline asks, finally turning around.

"He's around here somewhere," Tallyn answers simply, as though he's making tea in the kitchen within the same house walls.

There's still hatred for this woman that swims from Adaline to me, and I can feel it thickening as the fae tells her story. Once, my heart went out to Tallyn for her losing the realm to her brother; but now that I have heard her story from her lips, that part of me is waning.

"When will all of this start?" Ollie asks, holding on to the glass but not drinking from it.

"He usually attacks after the new moon. Once the full moon's power has waned, he has replenished his armies. It should give Bash time to improve and aid us in our fight."

Adaline laughs an evil laugh, and all the room's eyes fall on her. "Our fight. I'm sorry, I just . . . it's funny how it turned into our fight now."

"I didn't force you to come," Tallyn spits at her.

Adaline's eyes go white and her skin flashes pale. "No, you forced my children to. You already have one; you had to take two more. What is it with my children that you crave as your own so badly? Barren yourself, are you?"

Tallyn stands so forcefully that the entire table shakes, and the candles in their sconces waiver from the wall. "You better watch your tone, or I will kill both your boys before you get to see their faces again."

The thundering in my heart is so loud I'm sure the others can hear it. I pray that with everything I have, Adaline will just shut up and let Tallyn win this argument. Two alpha females—supernatural beings at that—this is undoubtedly not going to end well. I don't want to lose one, if not both, of the men I have come to love.

A defeated look slides across Adaline's face, and her eyes return to their usual green.

Tallyn's cat eyes watch her as she turns and returns to the balcony.

My heart returns to its average pace. I know Tallyn needs both Sangravelli brothers to complete her task, but that still doesn't say what she's capable of.

"I'll send the portal for the others," Tallyn offers. "You all might want to get some rest. I'm sure Adaline will want to stay with Sebastian, but I can show you all the other rooms if you like. There is nothing further we can do tonight about Bash or the Dread Harvest Eclipse."

Ollie remains seated next to Claire, still holding his silver drink. Claire observes Tallyn carefully. I remain where I am, eyes moving from Bash to Tallyn. Adaline's looking out at the floating mountains.

"This way," Tallyn speaks again. Claire, Ollie, and I reluctantly stand to follow.

She opens the door and leads us to two more doors a short distance from her room.

"Either of these will do," she says, opening one and then the other. "I'll send someone up soon to bring you all some food. There are bells in any room; ring them for service anytime. These rooms have a shared bathroom. Help yourself to anything you need."

"Thank you," Ollie says.

Tallyn bows her head slightly and saunters off.

I follow Ollie and Claire into the room, as I don't want to be alone. Not tonight. Not in this strange place, this strange land. Especially with Dom on the loose somewhere.

I don't know if I'm ready to see him yet.

"You okay, girl?" Claire asks. We are both perched on the large bed in the cold room as Ollie starts a fire in the fireplace.

"I'm not sure. I'm worried about Bash. Worried about this war and helping. Worried about…"

"Dom?" Claire finishes for me.

"Yes. Worried about seeing him again and what he will say. Tallyn told me that she already told him about Bash and me. I just wanted to be the one to tell him." A mixture of guilt and resentment swims within my bones and storms me like an army storming a castle. I wanted to be the one to tell Dom of Bash and I, but then I remember the note and the way it felt to know he was there; *he was right fucking there!* And didn't say anything to me. It feels like he's a coward and hides behind the things he really doesn't have any control of. I am over him; I don't want to be with him, but I don't want to hurt him. I know I betrayed him, but who's betrayal is worse here?

"All of this has my head spinning," Claire mutters, taking the words right out of my mind.

"Yeah, me too," Ollie seconds. "I just can't believe her brother would war over this place with his twin. Making monsters out of fae—I don't know how this is going to end."

"Badly," I tell him. "Hey, Ollie, did your vision change about us coming here? When you decided to come?"

Ollie doesn't speak for a time; he just keeps adding kindling to the fire.

"Babe?" Claire presses.

"Nothing good," he answers finally.

"Please tell us," I beg, scooping a pillow into my lap. "What did you see?"

His green eyes are cold. "Death, Sayah, I saw death. And lots of it. There's fire, blood, murder, mayhem, and lots of people losing their lives. I didn't see anything good come out of this."

"You mean we lose the war?" Claire asks.

"I didn't see the vision end. I stopped it. It was too bloody. And people were getting hurt. You—" He stops abruptly.

"Do I die?"

"No. You don't die. But you might get hurt. We all might." Taking a match from the mantle, he tosses it in, and the fire roars to life.

I shift uncomfortably and exhale a ragged breath. "Your visions don't always come true to the exact way you see them, do they?" I ask this more for Claire, knowing she may not know the things Bash told me about Ollie's visions.

He sits next to Claire. "No, but they're damn close. We just need her to portal the others here, use our combined powers, and get you to make those Ember Flare Orbs. Those are our gauntlet."

"What are they?"

"They're little glowing blue orbs that are imbued with your power. When you throw them, they obliterate anything within a mile radius. They're powerful."

"How do I make them?"

"Tallyn helps you. With her magick and some from my mom and you. You guys will figure that out. Those will be our saving grace."

"And Bash? Did you see anything about him?" I ask, playing with a string coming out of the pillowcase.

"I just saw that he . . ."

The sounds of Adaline yelling Bash's name and a large crash cuts Ollie off.

We quickly run to the room and burst through the door to

find Bash standing over Adaline with a giant sword, her arm bleeding and Bash in full vamp mode.

"Bash!" Ollie runs up to him, shoving him away from Adaline. Bash turns on Ollie, his fangs bared, making an awful hissing sound.

"No! Don't hurt him; he's hallucinating," Adaline yells, rushing to her feet to stand between the brothers.

Bash, black hair wet with sweat and skin still as pale as before, flashes out the door.

"Fuck!" Ollie curses.

"Claire," I cry, "ring that bell; maybe Tallyn will come."

Claire flashes to the corner and pulls a rope that rings a bell somewhere beyond our room.

"What happened?" Ollie asks, pulling Adaline to the bed as she holds her bleeding arm, the large gash already sewing itself up.

"He just started thrashing around, yelling, calling for Sadie. I tried to comfort him, and when he opened his eyes, he saw someone he had murdered before. He flashed over to the sword on the mantel and began swinging it at me. When I tried to get him out of it, he cut me and then jumped on me. That's when I screamed. I was trying to get him to snap out of it."

"I thought Tallyn said her method was going to stop that from happening."

"Actually," Tallyn answers as she enters the room, "I never said it would stop the hallucinations. I said the herbs should combat them. It still means any venom left in his system can cause them."

"Well, where has he gone then?" Adaline shouts at Tallyn.

"Right here," comes a familiar voice that hollows out my stomach and makes my heart sink to my knees.

Dominic.

A BOND WITH THE WRATH OF DEMONS

To my dismay, but already knowing it's him, I turn my head to see Dom standing in the doorway, gripping his disheveled-looking brother by the collar, holding him at arm's length.

Once my heart returns to my chest from my knees, heat floods my blood, coursing through my veins at full speed, making me lightheaded and as though I'm going to faint. His eyes are not on me but Tallyn, awaiting her command.

"Wonderful, Dominic, bring him here," she orders.

Dom walks over to her, pushing his brother toward her as he thrashes, trying to swing his arms at whatever is in front of him. "We should really bring him to the dungeon, my love. At least until his hallucinations stop. I found him tormenting a poor servant. I don't know if he will recover from the bites."

She holds Bash easily, his face holding all the agony of a fallen planet; broken and beautiful, but blue eyes so bright and blue the rest of the world still appears dull. Even in his madness.

"Which maid was it?" she asks as Bash thrashes. "Was it bald, or was it tall?"

"Aberforth," Dom answers, his bemused tone belies the impudence in his words. He still has not made eye contact with me or with a single member of his family.

"Ah, the tall one. Good. That fucking mole needs a little thrashing. Always snooping about. Maybe it'll put his ass in line."

"Dom?" Ollie utters.

Dom turns his head slightly to look at Ollie, yet no recognition flashes in his eyes. "Yes?" he asks, as though acknowledging a stranger on the street.

Ollie's face crumbles into worry. "Dom, it's me, Ollie. Do you not recognize your own brother?"

Dom blinks once or twice before shifting his gaze to Adaline, to me, then back again at Ollie. "No, I recognize you. I just don't care."

His voice is calm and indifferent. He seems like himself, yet he is not at all the same.

"We have been worried sick about you," Adaline says, still holding the makeshift bandage on her arm, even though the wound is all but healed by now.

Bash flails and lunges at Ollie; Dom whips him back with a yank of the shirt.

Dom turns his attention back to Tallyn, ignoring his mother. "My love, the dungeon. He will not stop this nonsense for some time."

"Yes, that should be good. I'll take him. Give him to me."

Dom hands her the collar of Bash's shirt, and she pulls some dust out of her pocket and blows it into Bash's face.

He immediately calms down and lets his arms hang down at their sides.

"Where are you taking him?" Adaline demands when Tallyn makes for the door, anger making the lean edges of her face even harsher.

"To the dungeon. He'll be fine. He just needs to get the venom out of his system, and I don't want him killing any more of my servants while doing so."

"I'm going with him," Adaline states, following Tallyn out the door.

I feel the awkward rush of anticipation over what will happen next, being that Ollie, Claire, and Dom are the only ones left in the room.

Having been looking after Tallyn as she leaves, Dom also makes to exit the room.

Ollie grabs his arm before he can, holding him firm.

"Dom, what happened to you, brother? You're not being you."

Dom looks down at Ollie's hand on his arm, then up into his eyes. "I am being me. This is just who I am now."

"But you're not under Mederio's spell anymore. You can leave this place. Bash made a bargain with Tallyn that would leave him in your stead to come home with us. Things have changed a bit with the approaching war, but you're free to leave here, to come home."

"I will not be leaving. Even after the war has ended. I will stay in her service. She needs me."

Although I did not know what would come of me being here to save Dom, not knowing how he would take the news that I was not in love with him but his brother, I'd not anticipated him not wanting to leave. He wants to stay behind with her even after the war is over.

The information stings a bit, but I know I deserve it.

"That's just crazy, Dom," Ollie continues, letting go of his arm. "You're not making any sense. It has to be her spell. You would never abandon your family for the fae. Not the Dom I know."

"No?" Dom retorts, a slice of bitterness entering his tone. He inches so close to Ollie that he could have licked his nose. "Maybe that was me before the woman I loved turned on me and left me for my brother, whom I hate. Maybe once I learned of her betrayal, I stopped fighting Tallyn's spells and let her sink her teeth all the way into me. And maybe, just maybe, I fell in love with that fae, and I want to stay here with her where I belong now."

A defensive bubble rises in my throat that makes me want to scream out and confront him about his letter to me. Dom broke up with me first.

But nothing comes. I sit frozen, listening to the two brothers talk.

"You can't be serious," Ollie says, not backing down from Dom standing so close to his face. "How could you love someone like that? Do you not know of the sister she stole from our mother before any of us were born? Do you not know that Bash, the demon whom you so hate, offered himself to her in your stead so you could come home to Sayah, even though he's been in love with her since before you even knew she existed? And what about the fact that you were leaving a trail of bodies bound by a scarlet ribbon so that we could somehow find you and save you? What about all of that, Dominic, huh?"

"I know of Sariana, yes. She and I have become quite close while being here." Dom moves away from Ollie and walks toward the table with the bottle of silver liquid. "About Bash offering himself to her . . . he is like the fae. There had to be something he gained out of it all. Otherwise, he never would have agreed to it. To you, it seemed he was being selfless, but not to me. No, I know better. I know of his love for my girlfriend; it was the same with Sadie. He always wants what he can't have—what I have. That will never change. The trail of bodies was me. But it was not so that you would save me. No, that was just for show. I enjoyed ripping those women's heads off, and I will continue to do that when this is all over. Because that is who I have always been; I've just been fighting it my entire life. There is no use fighting it anymore. That's what Tallyn has shown me. That's why I love her. Because at least with her, I can be who I really am. Unlike with her." Dom inclines his head at me and takes a drink straight out of the bottle, not making eye contact with me. "She was trying to make me into something I wasn't. Killing people who deserved to die. Ha!" The maniacal laughter that emits from his throat gives me the chills. "Who is she to decide who has the right to live? Ridiculous."

"Dom, none of this is you," Ollie starts again, treading delicately, walking toward him with a caution that anticipates Dom will turn on him.

Claire and I stay far enough back, sitting on the bed Bash had been in not that long ago.

"You keep saying that," Dom spews, anger coloring his voice a little more than before. "You are naïve and childish, Oliver. For you to not notice that has always been in me makes you not as close of a brother as I once thought. I can't help who I am. And neither can Bash. Maybe he was the one who was supposed to be good, and I was the evil one all along. Maybe we've just been getting it wrong all these years. Time to let those old ways die and be who we really are."

"You keep spitting this bullshit at me like it is going to phase me," Ollie snarls, stepping into Dom's bubble. "I know this is whatever that bitch has been feeding you, and we need to find a way to get you to snap out of it. You haven't been the bad one, Dom. Odin's ghost. Don't you think I know my own brother better than that?"

Dom jumps up into Ollie's face so fast that it's a blur of movement and colors. The rattling and spinning table is the only proof the movement happened at all. "Call her that again, and you will meet your end, too, Oliver, just like your brother, Bash."

The air turns charged, as if an escaped live wire has taken the place of half the oxygen.

Ollie's eyes go white, and his fangs emerge. He shoves Dom, and he flies again at an inhuman pace, hitting a bookshelf against the wall and knocking the contents on top of him.

Dom, calm and composed, stands and brushes off his shirt. He then runs at Ollie and drives him into the opposite wall, rattling the stones that make up the castle.

"Stop it now!" I shout futilely, knowing it will not do any good.

Ollie takes his elbow and drives it into Dom's backside; a thundering blast of air comes forth from his lips at the blow. Dom pulls up and socks Ollie in the face, causing blood to spurt from his nose and mouth, where his fist makes contact.

I look at Claire and nod, and Claire, eyeing both brothers in combat, concentrates intently on the items surrounding them. With a thunderous crash, every item resting on the ground hovers, including the two men. Claire holds her hands out and separates the left from the right, leaving the right hand where it is. Dom floats away from Ollie.

"What the fuck is going on?" Dom shouts as he floats toward the wall he had crashed into.

"Atta girl, babe!" Ollie calls to Claire, still hovering in the air. "All right, let me down, love. I have a plan."

Claire guides her right hand downward, and with it, Ollie descends to the ground.

"You better have your bitch put me down right now, Oliver, or so help me Odin, you both will both regret it." Dom is pinned against the wall, slightly above the ground.

Ollie carefully lands and walks over to him.

"Lower him just a bit, love," Ollie says to Claire, who lowers her left hand in response.

Dom's body lowers just enough so his feet are a few inches above the ground.

"Binadamu ganzi," Ollie says to Dom, and with those words, Dom's eyes go blank.

"Ollie!" I cry, running over to them. "What did you just do?"

"I made him numb," Ollie answers, waving a hand in front of Dom's face. He does nothing in response to the gesture.

"But what will that do now?" I query, taking a step closer.

"Nothing at all," Dom answers, looking down at me. "Tell her to let me down."

"Don't let him down," Ollie says to Claire over his shoulder.

"Is he going to go berserk and murder us all when you let him down?" I ask.

"No," Dom answers. "Just you." His look is cold and hard. The soft, handsome face I once remembered is gone, and now all that remains is a blank and evil canvas, someone on the edge of violence.

The chills are back.

What did Ollie just do?

"Ollie?" I say, backing away from Dom.

"I suggest you say the other part of that saying, Ollie," Dom speaks smoothly, "otherwise I may do just that."

"I just wanted you to snap out of Tallyn's spell. I don't want you to kill anyone."

"You can't snap me out of the spell because there isn't one. I told you. This is me. And now it's me with even less empathy for her than before. It's in your best interest to say the other part. Who knows what will happen if you don't and your girlfriend over there wears out and drops me?"

Ollie's calm eyes are on mine, filled with worry.

"Do it, Ollie," I instruct, backing further away.

"Binadamu nakupenda," Ollie almost whispers, and there's virtually no change in Dom's demeanor.

"Now have her put me down before her arm gives out on her."

Claire's left arm is shaking, and the look on her face is plastered with anxiety. Ollie nods, and Claire lowers her left hand.

Dom floats back to the ground.

I find myself taking more steps backward, still frightened that Dom will lunge at me and kill me. I will and can still burn him if he bites me.

"Now," Dom says, stepping toward Ollie, "run along with your little girlfriend, and let me talk to Sayah."

Ollie gives Dom a questioning look, and my heart tries to escape my chest again.

His mouth quirks up at the sides. "Relax. I'm not going to kill her. Hell, I'd probably still burn up if I tried. I just have some things I want to say. In private."

Ollie looks at me, and I find myself nodding.

Even though Dom seems as though he's under some sort of spell, there's still something about him I trust.

Time will tell if it ends up being a fault of mine.

I give Claire a smile. Though I can almost smell the intensity of the situation—the mortality in my own veins as though it weighs in the balance.

Dom could kill me if he wants to.

He will just die himself in the process.

He walks over to the balcony, and my feet and head want me to stay put, but my heart betrays me and I follow him.

Out into the cool night air, the sky boundless with stars, the Dread Harvest Eclipse in full display in the lavender sky.

Any other night, and this would be romantic.

Had it not been for the deadly look in his eyes, it might have been.

"I know you love him," Dom says to me. His brown hair, which he once wore spiky, is now smooth and reflecting the moon's silvery glow.

Words are stuck in my throat.

Of all the times I played this moment over in my head—how I wanted to tell him and what I wanted to say—are now frozen on my tongue.

He leans on the wrought iron banister, his green eyes soft in a vacant and dejected way. "I saw you. Tallyn let me see in her crystal. You two walking on that lakeshore. Him kissing you. You liking it. That rune on his arm let her see everything and, in turn, let me see what she wanted me to see."

"Dom—"

"Save what you want to say until I say what I need to."

I nod and join him at the banister of the balcony.

"I always knew a part of you was hesitant to love me. I felt it from the very beginning. Knowing that Bash was in your mind, I know it was always because of him that you would never fully love me, and I hate him for that. That being said, I also know what it's like to have someone love you in a way you could never love them back. By writing you that note, even though I was under a spell, I set you free to love the person you will love in the same way. Knowing now it was me who ended your mom, regardless of whether it was intentional or not, you would never love me back. We are not meant to be together. We were never soulmates, and I knew that. I just wanted to love you a little longer. But life has other plans for me. Maybe it was always meant to be like this. Maybe I was the one to lead you to your heart and soul. To guide you to the person your soul was meant to be with. And not only that; as much as I hate Bash, I know you are good for him. I can see that. I could see that in the vision of you two on the lake. The way he spoke to you and held your hands. The way he told you that you made him want to be a better person. The way he said that your soul makes his soul lighter. But he, in turn, makes you understand your darkness. He helps you to see that not all dark things are all darkness, and not all light things are all light. The light needs the dark to truly shine. And with that, I can be okay with you two being together. You belong with him, not with me, and I will never hate you for that. I can only do what is best for me and know I have to let you go. That would be the best thing for both of us."

The things he's saying confuses me.

A moment ago, he was staring at me with hatred in his eyes. My heart sank at the realization he could kill me with one snap. And now he's pouring his heart out to me, telling me all these things that make my heart chase after him again.

Words are still vacant in my mind, and I cannot for the life of me figure out what to say to him.

"I love Tallyn now, Sayah. I wish to stay here with her and remain with her. And in doing that, you are free to return with Bash and live the rest of your days with him. I wish to never see either of you again."

The confusing merry-go-round I've just experienced with Dom in the last five to ten minutes feels like I'm having a conversation with someone I've never met, or someone I'm just getting to know. The Dom from last month who cradled my grief and helped me find magick and was there when I became the phoenix. . . the man who was devastated at finding out he was the reason my parents are dead; how he murdered innocent people at that hotel and was going to end himself for it. The Dom whose family means everything to him and the connection he has with his twin and his relationship with Ollie. That Dom is gone.

No... *This isn't Dom.*

This has to be some sort of formweaver who's taken Dom's face.

This is not right.

But I can't say that, in case I'm right.

I swallow the words down and settle on these new ones. "Are you sure that's what you want, Dom?"

At last, he looks at me, and the tear at the bottom of his eye glistens in the moonlight. "I am sure."

"But Dom, I don't want that. I do have love for you. I never meant for this to happen this way. I never meant for you to get marked and then for Bash to get addicted to my blood and leave you in that darkness. Then for Tallyn to come swoop you up and take you hostage. I never meant to formweave, to fall in love with Bash, to break your heart. I never asked for any of this!"

I feel the tears falling before I knew they had formed in my eyes.

He shrugs, as if this is a casual chat between exes. "None of us ever mean for this stuff to happen, Sayah. We can only acknowledge it when it does and let the pain change us how it will. This is our path. We must embrace it."

"Dom, I don't feel you are truly being you right now. You would never want to stay here, leave your family, and be part of the fae. You would never have said that you enjoyed killing all those people, and the ribbons were just for show! That isn't who you are."

"How would you know, Sayah? Honestly. You have never gotten to know the real me. We didn't have that sort of time together. How do you know I wasn't just putting on a show for you when I murdered those people at that hotel? You and I were just a blip in the breeze of time in my lifespan. Tallyn understands what it's like to be like me and live for centuries. She understands me more than you ever could. And when I had to endure you breaking my heart, she was there to pick up the pieces. I owe her my life and intend to make it up to her for the rest of it."

The angry bubbles are now back, teetering on an edge that's about to make me reckless.

"You broke up with me! In a note! You were in my bedroom and scared me half to death and left a fucking note for me to find! Bash was there for me to pick up the pieces of my broken heart that you caused! *You killed my mom!* Don't you dare play the victim in this, Dom. You ended things with me before anything ever happened between me and Bash!" The tone of my voice has risen, and I know Ollie and Claire will be able to hear from the next room.

"Yes, but I wasn't the one dreaming of your sibling and falling in love with them in my subconscious. Things between you and Bash began long ago, longer than before I ever went dark."

He has me there.

"Dom, look," I say as my voice becomes brittle, pulling his hand from the banister and holding it in mine. His skin is cold and clammy, unlike his soft, delicate touch had been before. "Regardless of where things are between us. Please don't betray your family because of it. Be with Tallyn if you must, but still be a part of your family. Don't abandon them because of my stupid heart."

His eyes are soft again. His thumb strokes the back of my hand. But there's still something sinister slithering beneath his soul. He isn't entirely him, that is for certain.

"Of angels and monsters in this world, Sayah, you have found your way in with the monsters. And all the beautiful dark things will come clashing together soon. Let us not figure this out now. Let's wait until after the war to decide. Who knows; maybe we'll not even be around to make any of the decisions when it's all said and done." The finality in his voice is haunting. "A Bond with the Wrath of Demons will decide our fate."

His eyes rest on mine briefly and then track to something behind me, blowing wide with horror. Glancing over my shoulder, nothing is there, save for the empty balcony and rolling hills of scenery and night behind us. When I return my gaze to Dom, a long spear is shoving through his middle, making the most grotesque sound as it pierces him all the way through the middle of his rib cage.

"Dom?" I cry as the spear covered in woven thorns rips a hole through him, and blood pours down the front of his shirt. His face twists with raw pain, letting go of my hands to hold on to whatever it is that's skewering him, trying to stanch the bleeding. All sounds are vacuumed out of the world, and he falls to his knees, screaming into the night, though he makes no sound.

What materializes behind him as he falls chills me to my marrow.

He is perhaps the most beautiful-looking man I've ever seen —aside from Bash. He has cerulean eyes, dark blond hair hangs in waves, and he is much taller than me, wearing no shirt, and tight leather pants. Some thorns grow out of his sternum, cascading up to wrap around his neck and then flowing down his muscular arms. His abs are defined, as well as his pecks, and he has the most beautiful set of blue wings that spread from him, coming to rest on his back.

Trystan.

Dom falls to his side, still clutching the spear of thorns, and when I try to scream, nothing comes out. Ollie sees this and runs to the door, but Trystan swipes his hand in an aggressive motion. The glass doors slam shut and seal with more with his thorns.

"You are quite the anomaly, phoenix," he notes as he draws closer to me. His voice reminds me of snow melting in the mountains. It's cold and draining; the runoff frigid to the touch but somehow refreshing and clean. I feel frozen in my tracks. Looking down, I see Dom still writhing without sound as he and my feet are being wrapped in thorns.

I still have no voice either. I cannot move, no matter how much I try.

He stalks toward me; the thorns that seal me to mine and

Dom's fate are building, binding, crawling, wrapping up the side of the tower we are on and spiraling around the balcony. "Not only are you the phoenix, but you are also The Celestial Phoenix. I've been waiting a long, long time for you to be born."

"I don't know what that means." He finally lets me talk, wincing as one of the thorns crawling up my calf bites me. I try to reach for the phoenix power resting in my bones, summon any magick within my skin and form into anything else, pulling at every morsel of myself, begging anything to come to the surface—but nothing happens. My power is halted, frozen, leaving me completely vulnerable.

Ollie is now banging on the glass, as is Claire—they are trying to get the doors to open, but not even their vamp strength can rend it.

"It means"—he reaches me, and he smells of peppermint, pinecones, and mountains—"you are an extraordinary entity. Born of a rare convergence of angelic, formweaving, demonic, witch blood, which—in the wrong hands—would only mean my death and the death of my people—the only being that can kill my warlocks. You alone possess the power to tilt the favor of the Riftstorm Conflict in my sister's favor and neutralize the Neverdusk Dominion. I just can't have that, don't you see?" His cold fingers graze my cheek, and I turn away in repulsion, the thorns now reaching my middle.

Dom is starting to lessen his writhing, and my heart breaks into a million pieces, knowing there's nothing I can do to save him. The giant spear is sticking out of him, and the pool of blood around him is thick, coating the entire side he lies on.

Dom is dying, I am frozen, and all Ollie can do is watch.

"I will never help you," I spit at Trystan. "I will die first."

"Oh, my pet," he hedges, but it is neither malice nor anger on his tongue, but . . . intrigue. His voice is one I would follow anywhere. "You will not be dying. Nor aiding me. No, you will become my queen. By the time I'm done with you, you will never even remember who these filthy bloodsuckers are."

Before I can do anything, Trystan's other hand lifts, and when he opens his palm, a glittering pile of what looks like pulverized black coal rests within it.

"I will never—"

He blows the dust into my face, and the world crumbles to darkness.

To Be Continued . . .

ACKNOWLEDGMENTS

This one is for the women in my life. Gosh I am so lucky to be surrounded by some of the fiercest females I've ever met. I will not be able to thank you all, but these ones are definitely worth mentioning.

To the fiercest woman warriors I have had the pleasure of knowing and loving and having as my friends.

Mama. My angel. You are the reason I am who I am. Your overpowering desire to be whoever the fuck you wanted to be nestled into me and rests easily in my bones. I know you are part of the thunderstorms now, but know that your legacy lives on through me. And I gave that fierceness to my son, who is so unapologetically himself, I am so proud I made him.

Nikki. You've been my ride or die since we were 14. There are no words to express my gratitude for you. Thank you for loving me fiercely and unconditionally. Thank you for being you. You are the one who inspired me to go back to school and forge my own path without a man. You are one of the strongest people I know. You are so important to me and the strongest female I've ever had the pleasure of knowing. I am honored to call you my friend.

Tillie. Girl. You know what you mean to me. You and I have been through more shit than we can count. You are also my ride or die. Gosh I am so lucky to be surrounded by women who are so fierce and such a force to be reckoned with. You move mountains. You also inspired me to go back to school and chase my dreams. Without you and your unconditional love and guidance

I wouldn't be who I am today. I adore you and I am honored to call you my friend.

Candice. Candi-pants. You are the most loyal person and friend I've ever met. You challenged me to find myself and be myself and to not be ashamed of who the fuck I am. You never fail to let me know I am worth more, I deserve more, I am capable of more. You, my friend, will change the world. The memories we've made throughout my life are some of the most precious things I'll ever own. You are one of the strongest females I've ever laid my eyes on and that is why you are a vampire in this story. You are a force to be reckoned with. I love you. I'll always love you. You will conquer the world one day.

To the teachers who said I'd never amount to anything, to those who ever doubted me, to those who thought this was all a pipe dream, I thank you. To the mean girls who bullied me, to the mean girls who write not only bad reviews but mean ones, it's because of people like you that we succeed. We hustle so hard til our haters ask if we're hiring.

BunnieXo, I know I've never met you and you have no idea who I am, but thank you. Thank you for paving the way for us underdogs, proving to the world that us delinquents can conquer the world. It's been so amazing to watch you and Jason climb the fucking mountain to the top, lifting others, encouraging each other. You two are proof that determination, hard work, and encouragement for each other can break stereotypes, build kingdoms, and break worlds. We rise by lifting others. You two are my inspiration and I hope to one day see the success you two have seen by being unapologetically yourselves and giving to the world what you both offer—hope. I adore you. Cheers to Jelly for having an album named the same as this series.

To the Beautifully Broken.

ABOUT THE AUTHOR

Inara Gage is an indie author based in Northern Colorado. She resides with her son Gauge, her mastador Khaleesi, kitty Nox, and bunny tWitch. After the first two failures of publishing her first book, A Witch's Aura, she went all the way through grad school to learn how to market herself in this crazy, incredibly hard, and immensely trying self publishing world. This is her third book baby and she learned so much from all the trials and tribulations with the first one, she has authored five more books since and hopes to continue putting stories out into the world that you all will love and enjoy.